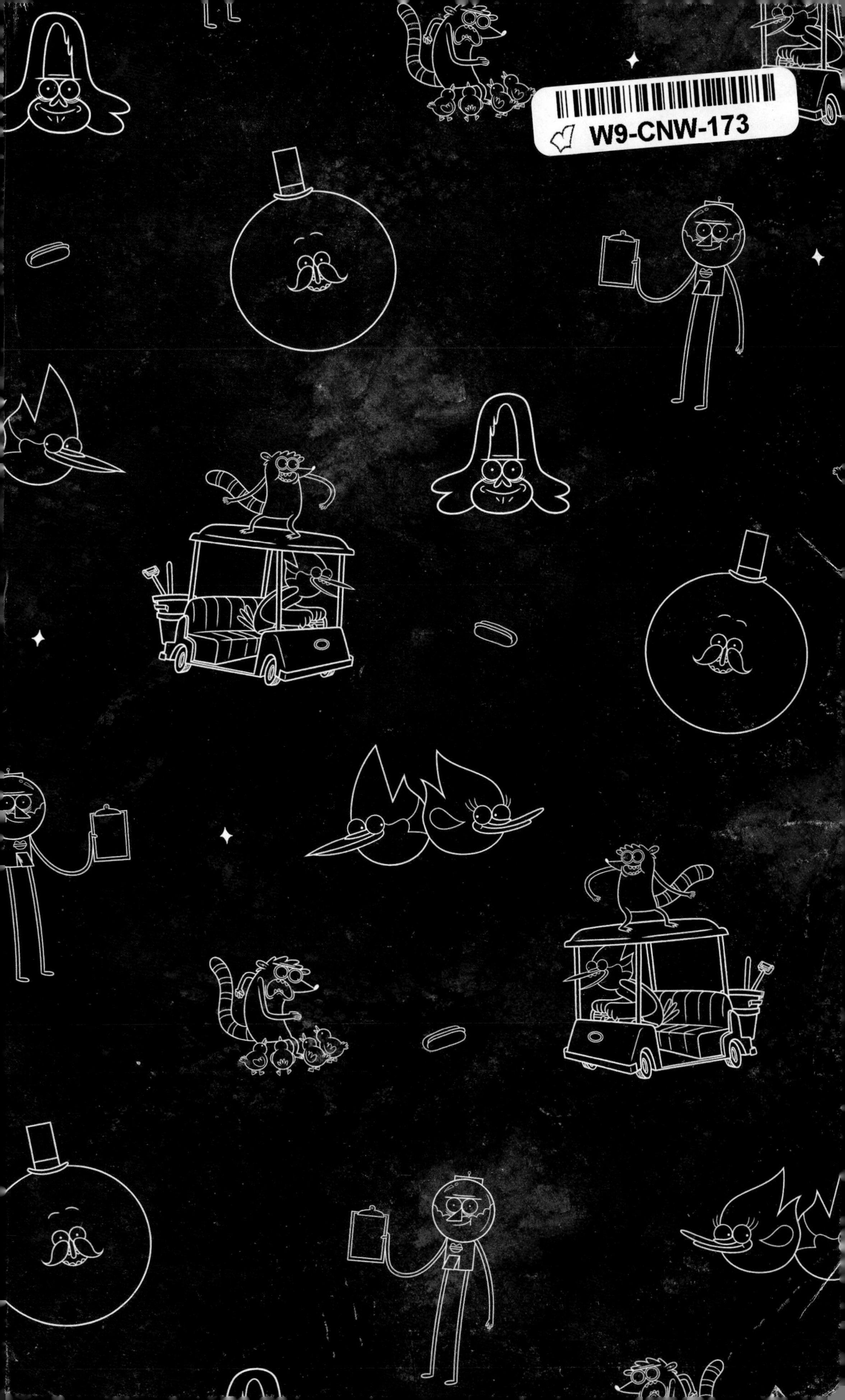

ROSS RICHIE CEO & Founder • MATT GAGNON Editor-in-Chief • FILIP SABLIK President of Publishing & Marketing • STEPHEN CHRISTY President of Development • LANCE KREITER VP of Licensing & Merchandising • PHIL BARBARO VP of Finance
ARUNE SINGH VP of Marketing • BRYCE CARLSON Managing Editor • MEL CAYLO Marketing Manager • SCOTT NEWMAN Production Design Manager • KATE HENNING Operations Manager • SIERRA HAHN Senior Editor • DAFNA PLEBAN Editor, Talent Development
SHANNON WATTERS Editor • ERIC HARBURN Editor • WHITNEY LEOPARD Editor • JASMINE AMIRI Editor • CHRIS ROSA Associate Editor • ALEX GALER Associate Editor • CAMERON CHITTOCK Associate Editor • MATTHEW LEVINE Assistant Editor
SOPHIE PHILIPS-ROBERTS Assistant Editor • AMANDA LaFRANCO Executive Assistant • KATALINA HOLLAND Editorial Administrative Assistant • JILLIAN CRAB Production Designer • MICHELLE ANKLEY Production Designer • KARA LEOPARD Production Designer
MARIE KRUPINA Production Designer • GRACE PARK Production Design Assistant • CHELSEA ROBERTS Production Design Assistant • ELIZABETH LOUGHRIDGE Accounting Coordinator • STEPHANIE HOCUTT Social Media Coordinator • JOSÉ MEZA Event Coordinator
HOLLY AITCHISON Operations Assistant • MEGAN CHRISTOPHER Operations Assistant • MORGAN PERRY Direct Market Representative • CAT O'GRADY Marketing Assistant • LIZ ALMENDAREZ Accounting Administrative Assistant • CORNELIA TZANA Administrative Assistant

REGULAR SHOW Volume Ten, January 2018. Published by KaBOOM!, a division of Boom Entertainment, Inc. REGULAR SHOW, CARTOON NETWORK, the logos, and all related characters and elements are trademarks of and © Cartoon Network. (S18) Originally published in single magazine form as REGULAR SHOW No. 37-40. © Cartoon Network. (S16) All rights reserved. KaBOOM!™ and the KaBOOM! logo are trademarks of Boom Entertainment, Inc., registered in various countries and categories. All characters, events, and institutions depicted herein are fictional. Any similarity between any of the names, characters, persons, events, and/or institutions in this publication to actual names, characters, and persons, whether living or dead, events, and/or institutions is unintended and purely coincidental. KaBOOM! does not read or accept unsolicited submissions of ideas, stories, or artwork.

BOOM! Studios, 5670 Wilshire Boulevard, Suite 450, Los Angeles, CA 90036-5679. Printed in China. First Printing.

ISBN: 978-1-68415-061-8, eISBN: 978-1-61398-738-4

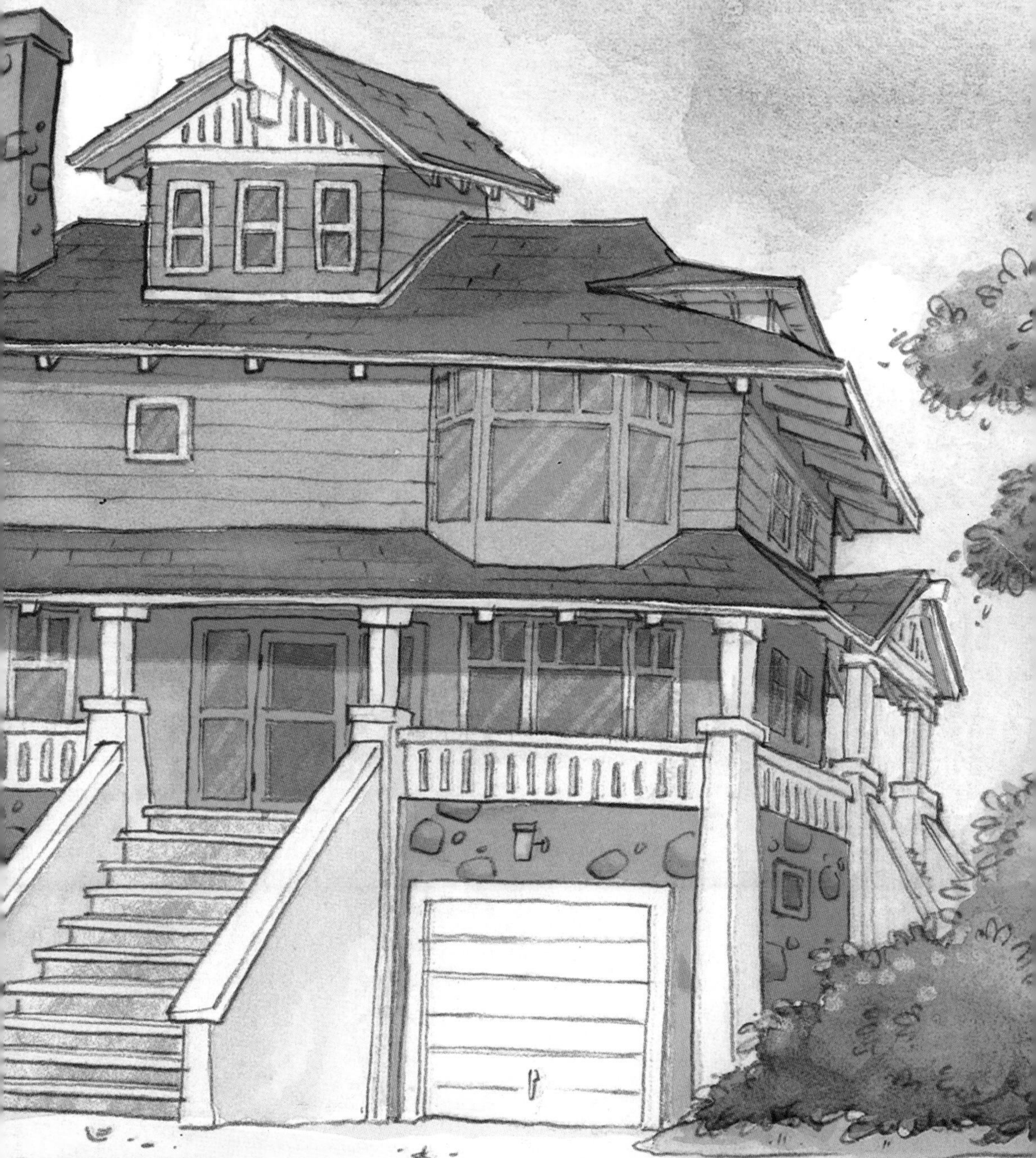

REGULAR SHOW™

A CARTOON NETWORK ORIGINAL

VOLUME TEN

REGULAR

CREATED BY JG QUINTEL

SCRIPT BY **MAD RUPERT**

ART BY **LAURA HOWELL**

COLORS BY **LISA MOORE**

LETTERS BY **STEVE WANDS**

COVER BY
JORGE CORONA
WITH COLORS BY JEN HICKMAN

DESIGNER
MICHELLE ANKLEY

ASSISTANT EDITORS
MARY GUMPORT &
SOPHIE PHILIPS-ROBERTS

EDITOR
SIERRA HAHN

SHOW ™
A CARTOON NETWORK ORIGINAL

"ICE CHALLENGE"

SCRIPT BY **ERICK FREITAS**
& ULISES FARINAS
ART BY **AUSTIN BREED**

"THE BOOK OF DEATH KWON DO"

BY **VICTOR SANTOS**

"NOTHING GOOD ON"

BY **PETER WARTMAN**

"ON THE HOOK"

BY **CHRISTINE LARSEN**

WITH SPECIAL THANKS TO
MARISA MARIONAKIS, JANET NO, CURTIS LELASH,
CONRAD MONTGOMERY, MEGHAN BRADLEY, KELLY
CREWS, RYAN SLATER AND THE WONDERFUL FOLKS AT
CARTOON NETWORK.

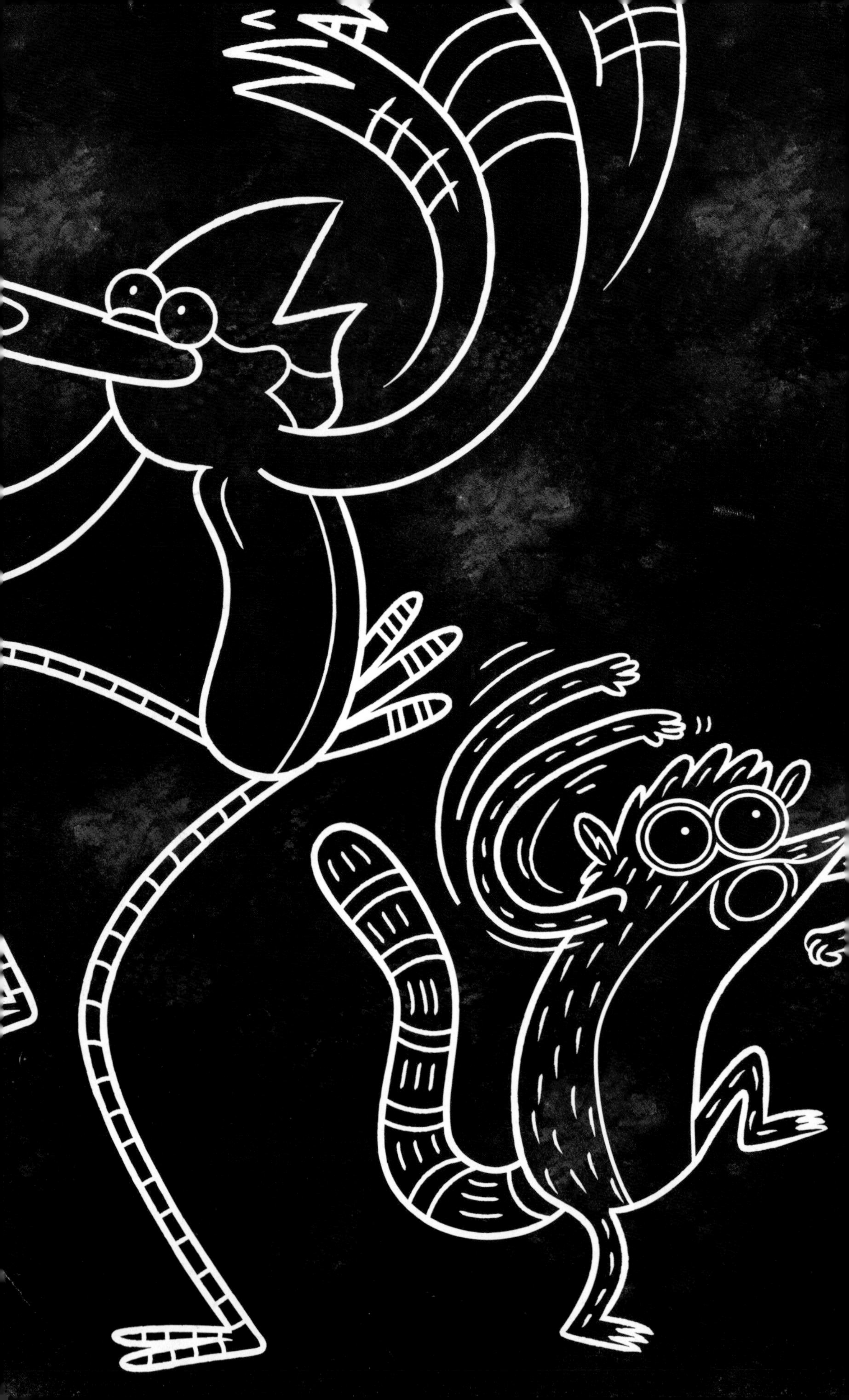

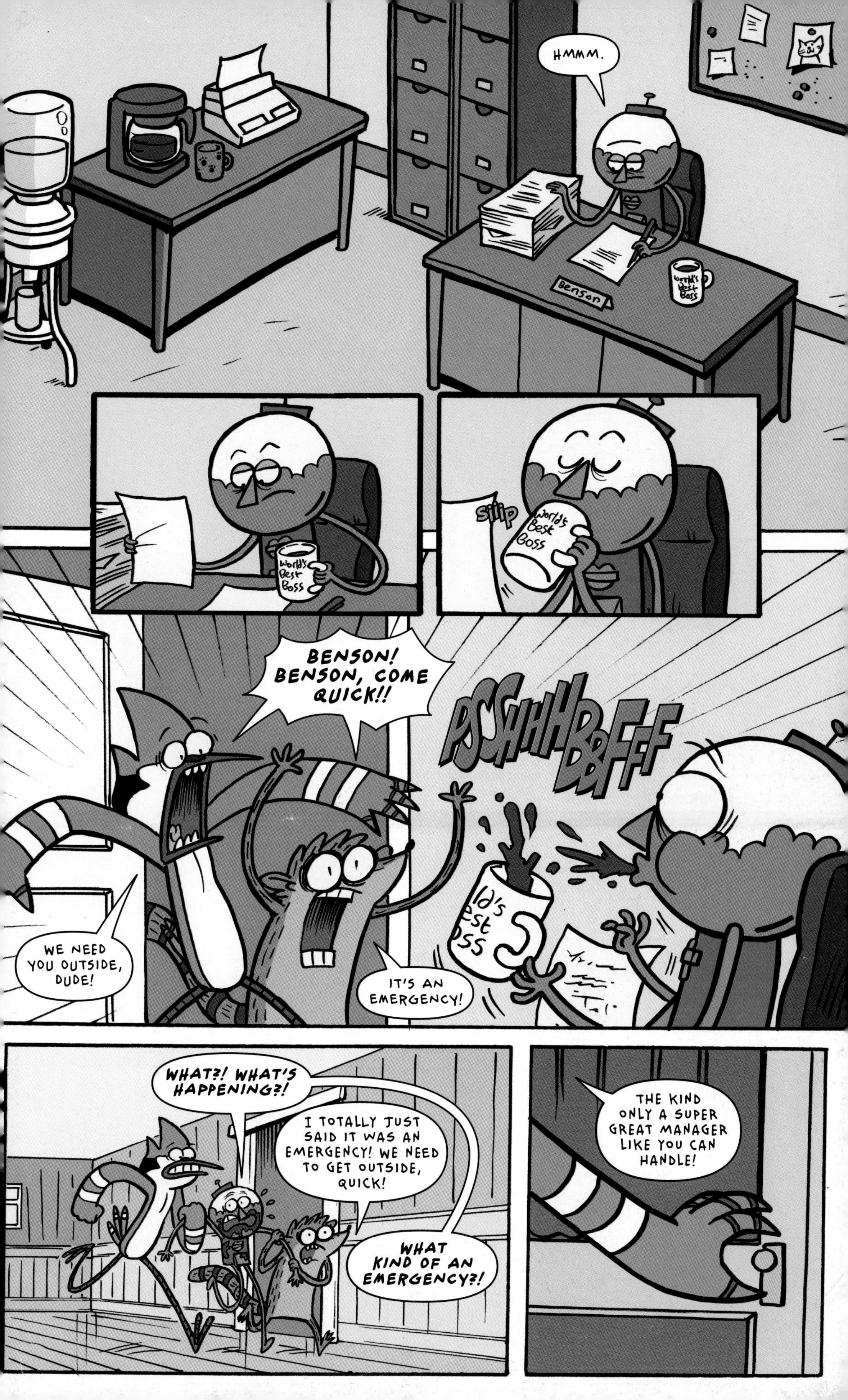
HMMM.
Benson
World's Best Boss
SIIIP
BENSON! BENSON, COME QUICK!!
WE NEED YOU OUTSIDE, DUDE!
IT'S AN EMERGENCY!
PSSHHHBBFFFF
WHAT?! WHAT'S HAPPENING?!
I TOTALLY JUST SAID IT WAS AN EMERGENCY! WE NEED TO GET OUTSIDE, QUICK!
WHAT KIND OF AN EMERGENCY?!
THE KIND ONLY A SUPER GREAT MANAGER LIKE YOU CAN HANDLE!

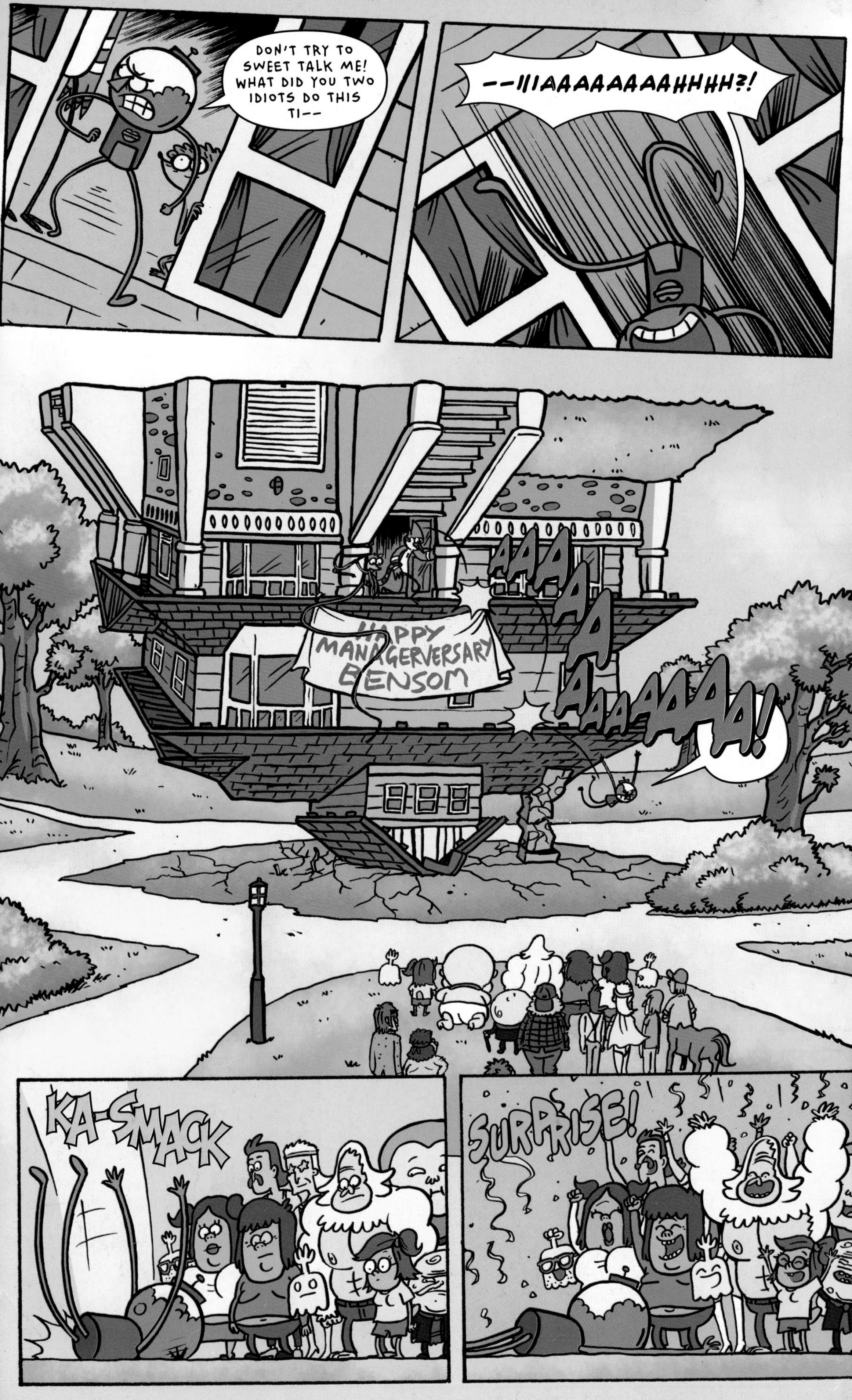
DON'T TRY TO SWEET TALK ME! WHAT DID YOU TWO IDIOTS DO THIS TI--
--!!!AAAAAAAAAHHHH?!
HAPPY MANAGERVERSARY BENSOM
AAAAAAAAAAAAA!
KA-SMACK
SURPRISE!

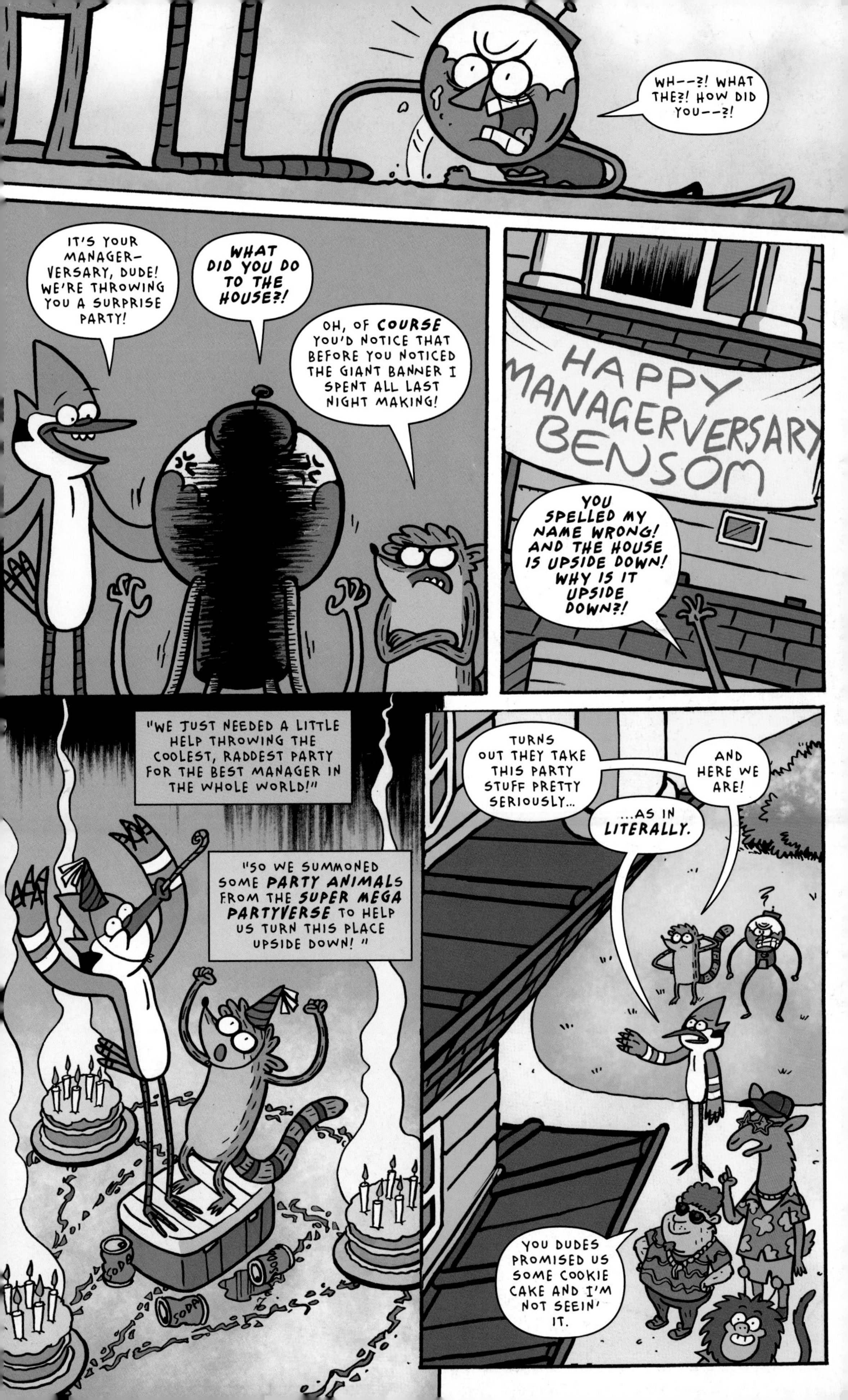
WH--?! WHAT THE?! HOW DID YOU--?!
IT'S YOUR MANAGER-VERSARY, DUDE! WE'RE THROWING YOU A SURPRISE PARTY!
WHAT DID YOU DO TO THE HOUSE?!
OH, OF COURSE YOU'D NOTICE THAT BEFORE YOU NOTICED THE GIANT BANNER I SPENT ALL LAST NIGHT MAKING!
HAPPY MANAGERVERSARY BENSOM
YOU SPELLED MY NAME WRONG! AND THE HOUSE IS UPSIDE DOWN! WHY IS IT UPSIDE DOWN?!
"WE JUST NEEDED A LITTLE HELP THROWING THE COOLEST, RADDEST PARTY FOR THE BEST MANAGER IN THE WHOLE WORLD!"
"SO WE SUMMONED SOME PARTY ANIMALS FROM THE SUPER MEGA PARTYVERSE TO HELP US TURN THIS PLACE UPSIDE DOWN!"
SODA
SODA
SODA
TURNS OUT THEY TAKE THIS PARTY STUFF PRETTY SERIOUSLY...
AND HERE WE ARE!
...AS IN LITERALLY.
YOU DUDES PROMISED US SOME COOKIE CAKE AND I'M NOT SEEIN' IT.

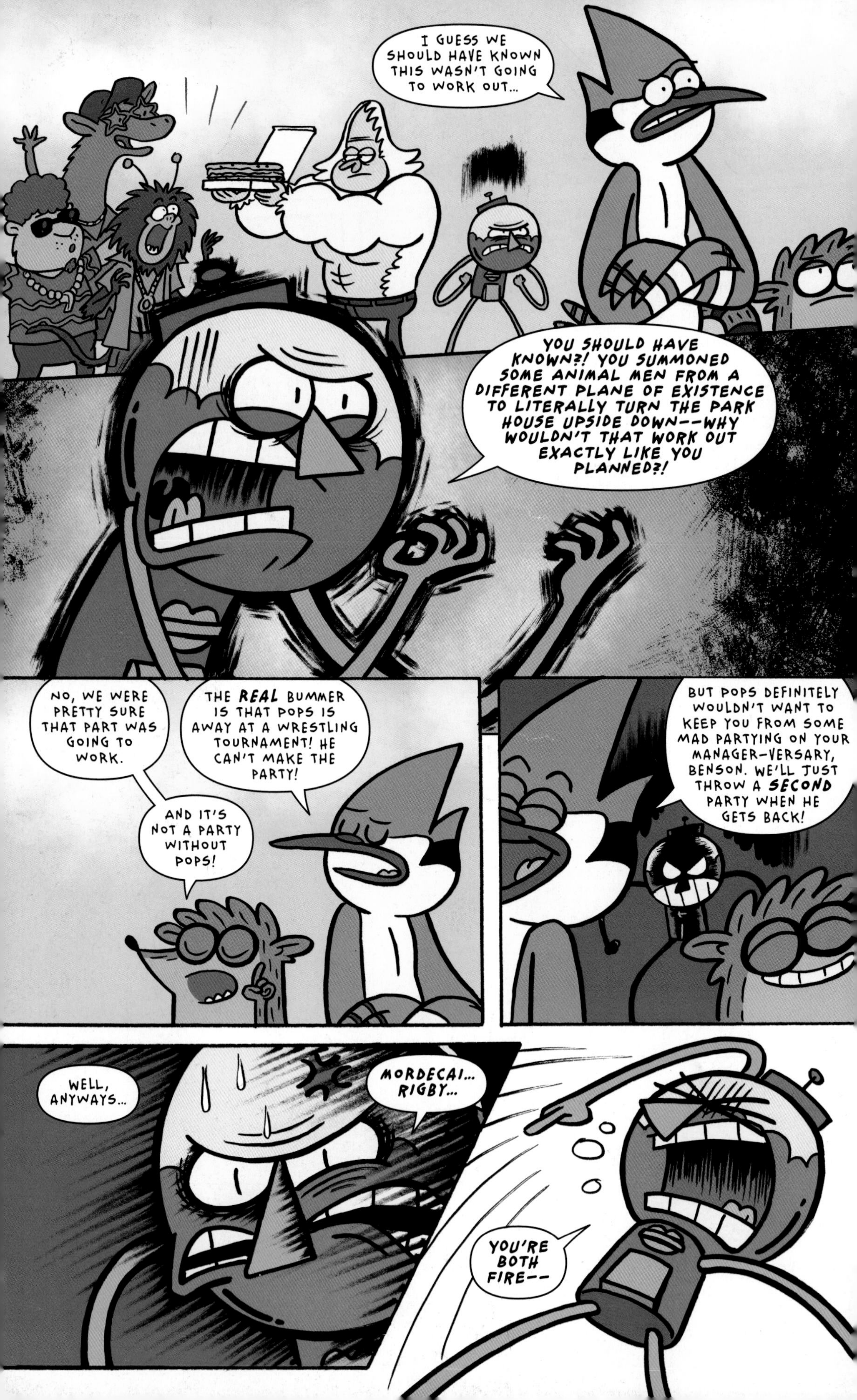

I GUESS WE SHOULD HAVE KNOWN THIS WASN'T GOING TO WORK OUT...
YOU SHOULD HAVE KNOWN?! YOU SUMMONED SOME ANIMAL MEN FROM A DIFFERENT PLANE OF EXISTENCE TO LITERALLY TURN THE PARK HOUSE UPSIDE DOWN--WHY WOULDN'T THAT WORK OUT EXACTLY LIKE YOU PLANNED?!
NO, WE WERE PRETTY SURE THAT PART WAS GOING TO WORK.
AND IT'S NOT A PARTY WITHOUT POPS!
THE REAL BUMMER IS THAT POPS IS AWAY AT A WRESTLING TOURNAMENT! HE CAN'T MAKE THE PARTY!
BUT POPS DEFINITELY WOULDN'T WANT TO KEEP YOU FROM SOME MAD PARTYING ON YOUR MANAGER-VERSARY, BENSON. WE'LL JUST THROW A SECOND PARTY WHEN HE GETS BACK!
WELL, ANYWAYS...
MORDECAI... RIGBY...
YOU'RE BOTH FIRE--

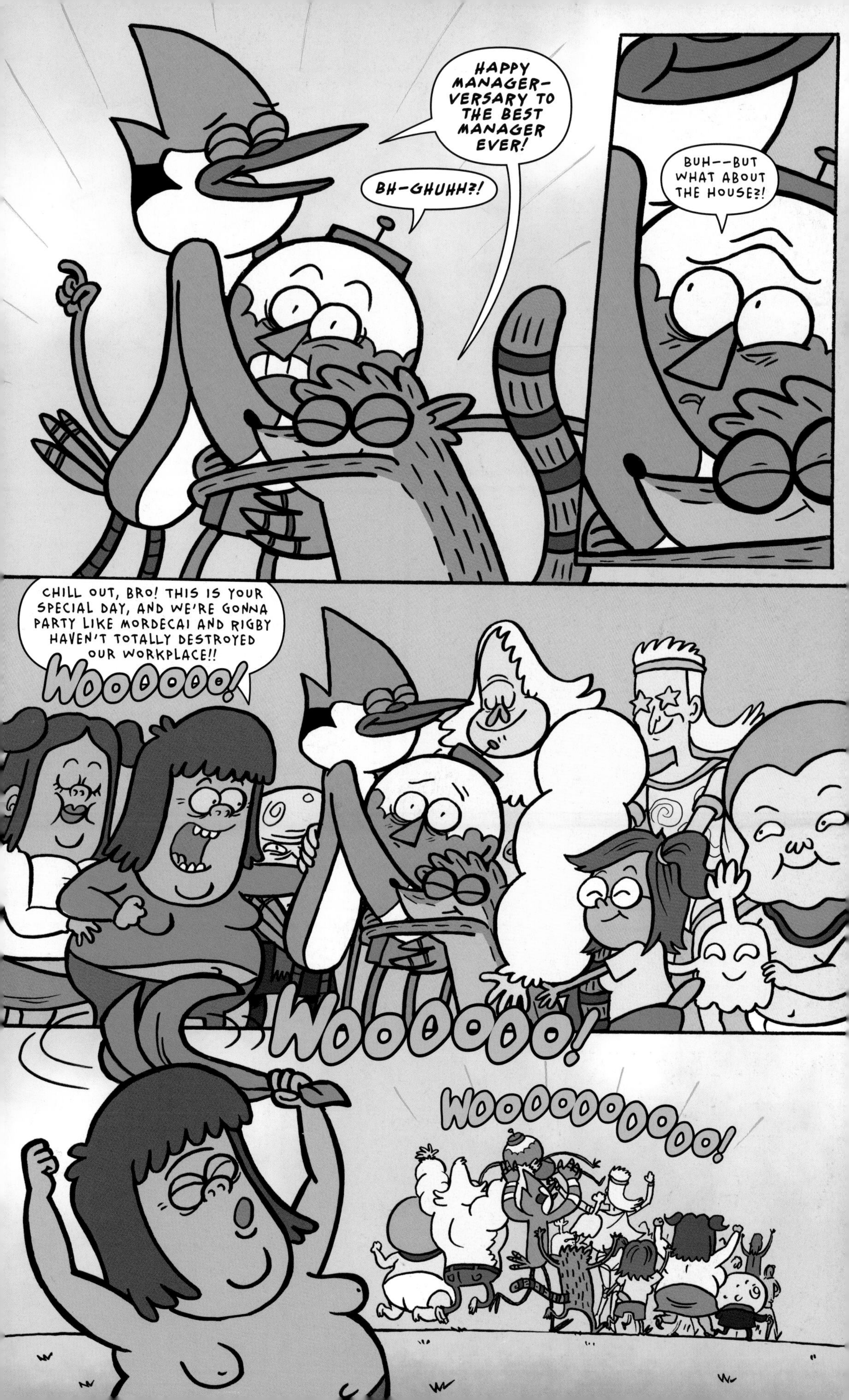
HAPPY MANAGER-VERSARY TO THE BEST MANAGER EVER!
BH-GHUHH?!
BUH--BUT WHAT ABOUT THE HOUSE?!
CHILL OUT, BRO! THIS IS YOUR SPECIAL DAY, AND WE'RE GONNA PARTY LIKE MORDECAI AND RIGBY HAVEN'T TOTALLY DESTROYED OUR WORKPLACE!!
WOOOOOO!
WOOOOOOO!
WOOOOOOOOOOOO!

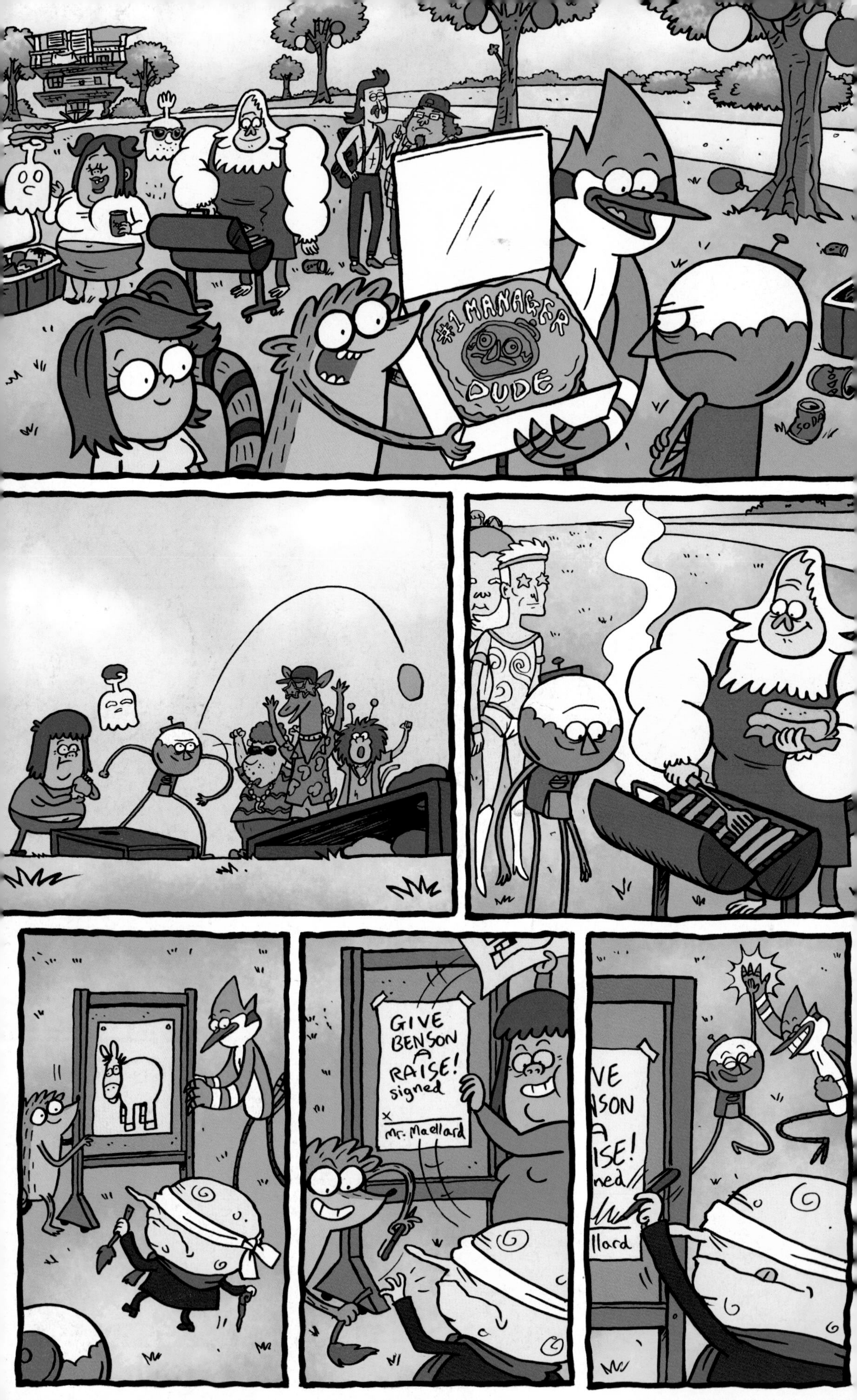
#1 MANAGER DUDE
SODA
GIVE BENSON A RAISE! signed
X
Mr. Maellard

DID YOU MANAGE TO HAVE A GOOD TIME?

YEAH! THESE HOT DOGS ARE INCREDIBLE!

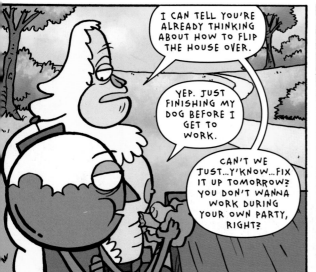

I CAN TELL YOU'RE ALREADY THINKING ABOUT HOW TO FLIP THE HOUSE OVER.

YEP. JUST FINISHING MY DOG BEFORE I GET TO WORK.

CAN'T WE JUST...Y'KNOW...FIX IT UP TOMORROW? YOU DON'T WANNA WORK DURING YOUR OWN PARTY, RIGHT?

DON'T GET ME WRONG, I APPRECIATE THE SENTIMENT. IT WAS REALLY NICE OF YOU GUYS TO THROW ME A PARTY. I JUST WISH MORDECAI AND RIGBY HADN'T BASICALLY DESTROYED THE WHOLE HOUSE TO DO IT.

THEIR HEARTS WERE IN THE RIGHT PLACE.

AND IF ANYBODY CAN GET THIS MESS FIGURED OUT, IT'S YOU, BENSON. I GUESS IT'S ONLY FITTING THAT THE BEST MANAGER IN THE WORLD WOULD MANAGE A PROJECT LIKE THIS ON HIS MANAGER-VERSARY.

ALSO, MY WORK ANNIVERSARY ISN'T FOR ANOTHER TWO MONTHS.

ALRIGHT, YOU SLACKERS! THIS IS MY PARTY, AND I WANNA SEE SOME REAL EFFORT! LET'S GET THIS HOUSE BACK IN ORDER!

SIGH... THOSE IDIOTS GOT THE DATE WRONG...

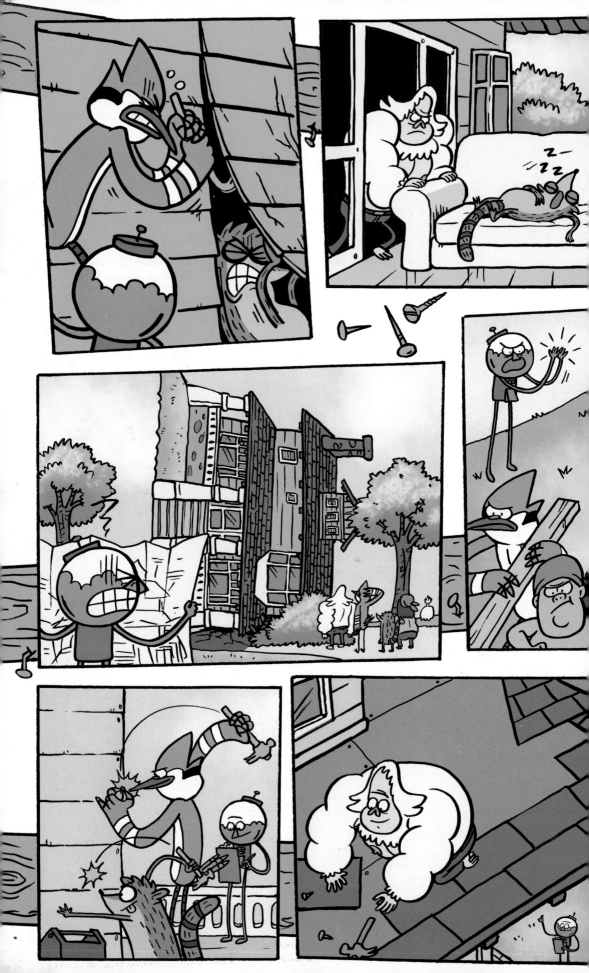

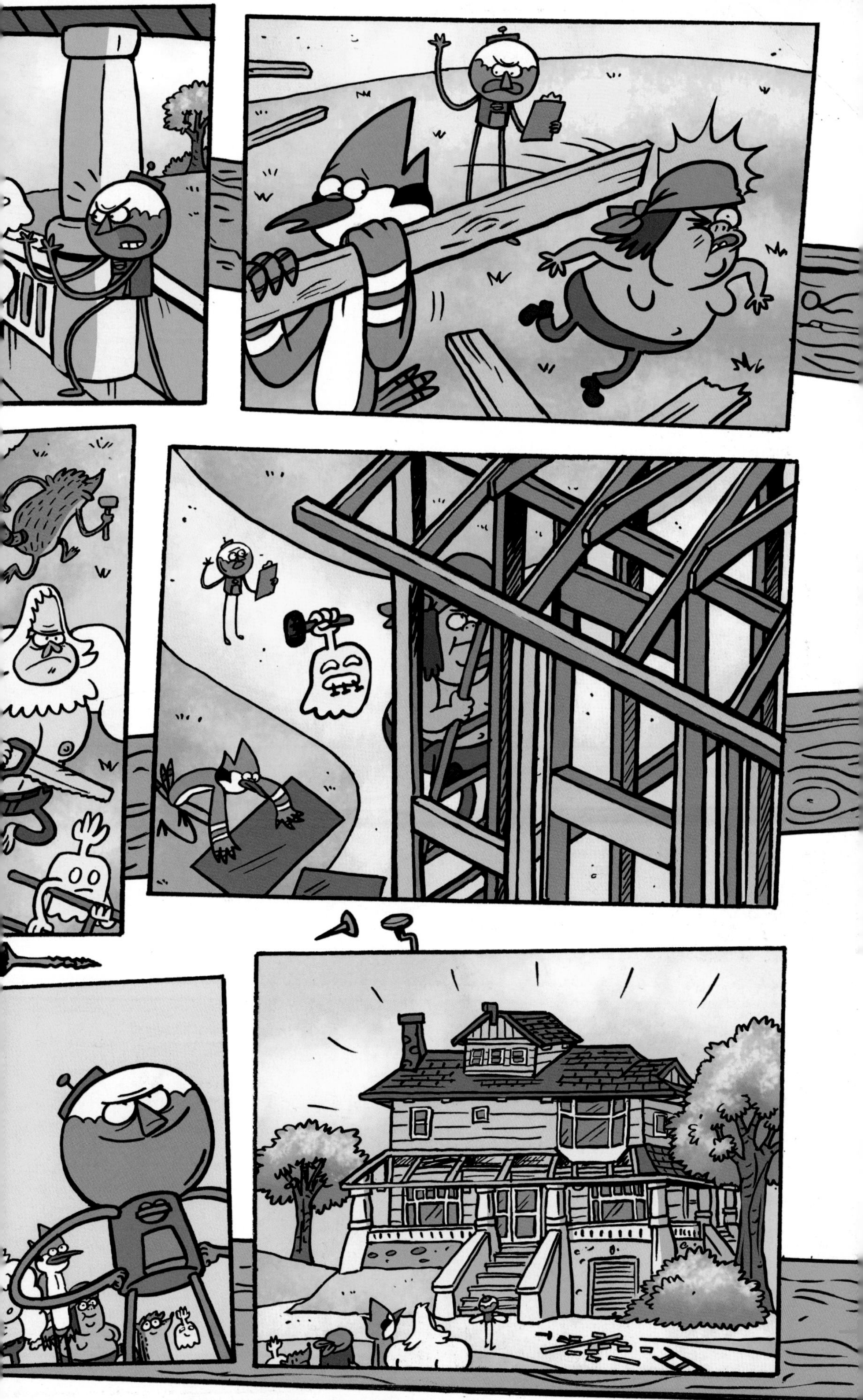

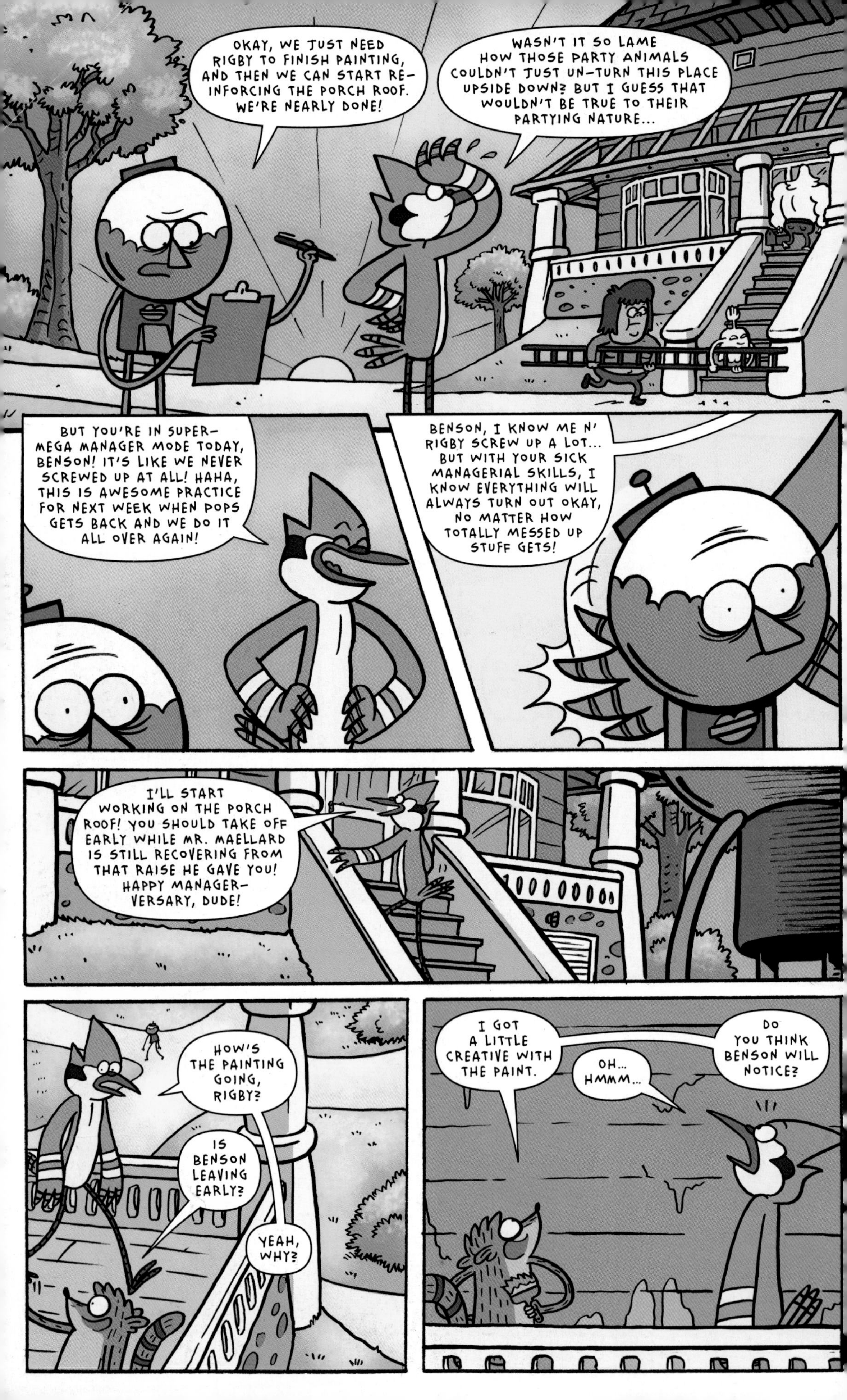
OKAY, WE JUST NEED RIGBY TO FINISH PAINTING, AND THEN WE CAN START RE-INFORCING THE PORCH ROOF. WE'RE NEARLY DONE!
WASN'T IT SO LAME HOW THOSE PARTY ANIMALS COULDN'T JUST UN-TURN THIS PLACE UPSIDE DOWN? BUT I GUESS THAT WOULDN'T BE TRUE TO THEIR PARTYING NATURE...
BUT YOU'RE IN SUPER-MEGA MANAGER MODE TODAY, BENSON! IT'S LIKE WE NEVER SCREWED UP AT ALL! HAHA, THIS IS AWESOME PRACTICE FOR NEXT WEEK WHEN POPS GETS BACK AND WE DO IT ALL OVER AGAIN!
BENSON, I KNOW ME N' RIGBY SCREW UP A LOT... BUT WITH YOUR SICK MANAGERIAL SKILLS, I KNOW EVERYTHING WILL ALWAYS TURN OUT OKAY, NO MATTER HOW TOTALLY MESSED UP STUFF GETS!
I'LL START WORKING ON THE PORCH ROOF! YOU SHOULD TAKE OFF EARLY WHILE MR. MAELLARD IS STILL RECOVERING FROM THAT RAISE HE GAVE YOU! HAPPY MANAGER-VERSARY, DUDE!
HOW'S THE PAINTING GOING, RIGBY?
IS BENSON LEAVING EARLY?
YEAH, WHY?
I GOT A LITTLE CREATIVE WITH THE PAINT.
DO YOU THINK BENSON WILL NOTICE?
OH... HMMM...

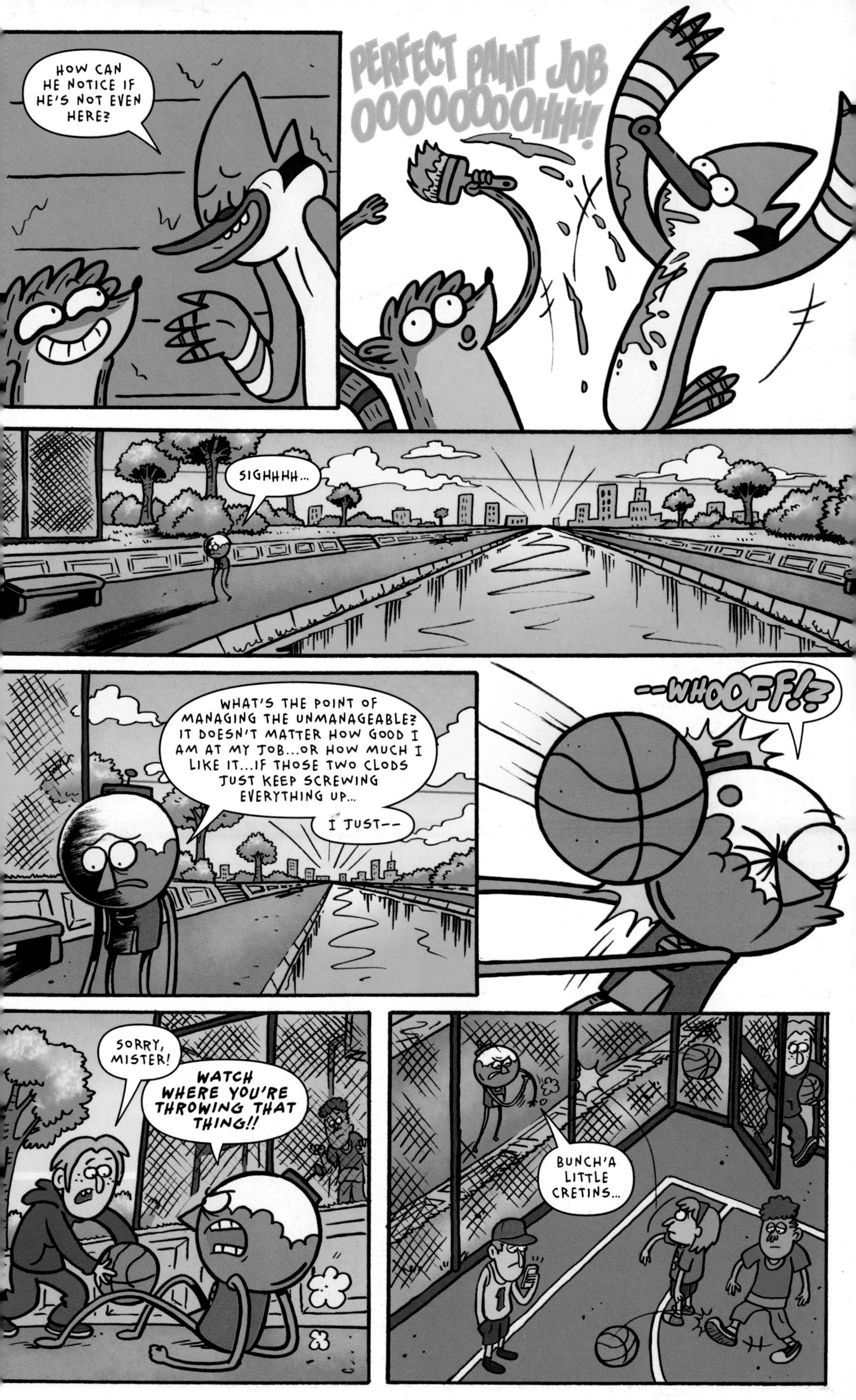
HOW CAN HE NOTICE IF HE'S NOT EVEN HERE?
PERFECT PAINT JOB OOOOOOOOOHHH!
SIGHHHH...
WHAT'S THE POINT OF MANAGING THE UNMANAGEABLE? IT DOESN'T MATTER HOW GOOD I AM AT MY JOB...OR HOW MUCH I LIKE IT...IF THOSE TWO CLODS JUST KEEP SCREWING EVERYTHING UP...
I JUST--
--WHOOFF!?
SORRY, MISTER!
WATCH WHERE YOU'RE THROWING THAT THING!!
BUNCH'A LITTLE CRETINS...

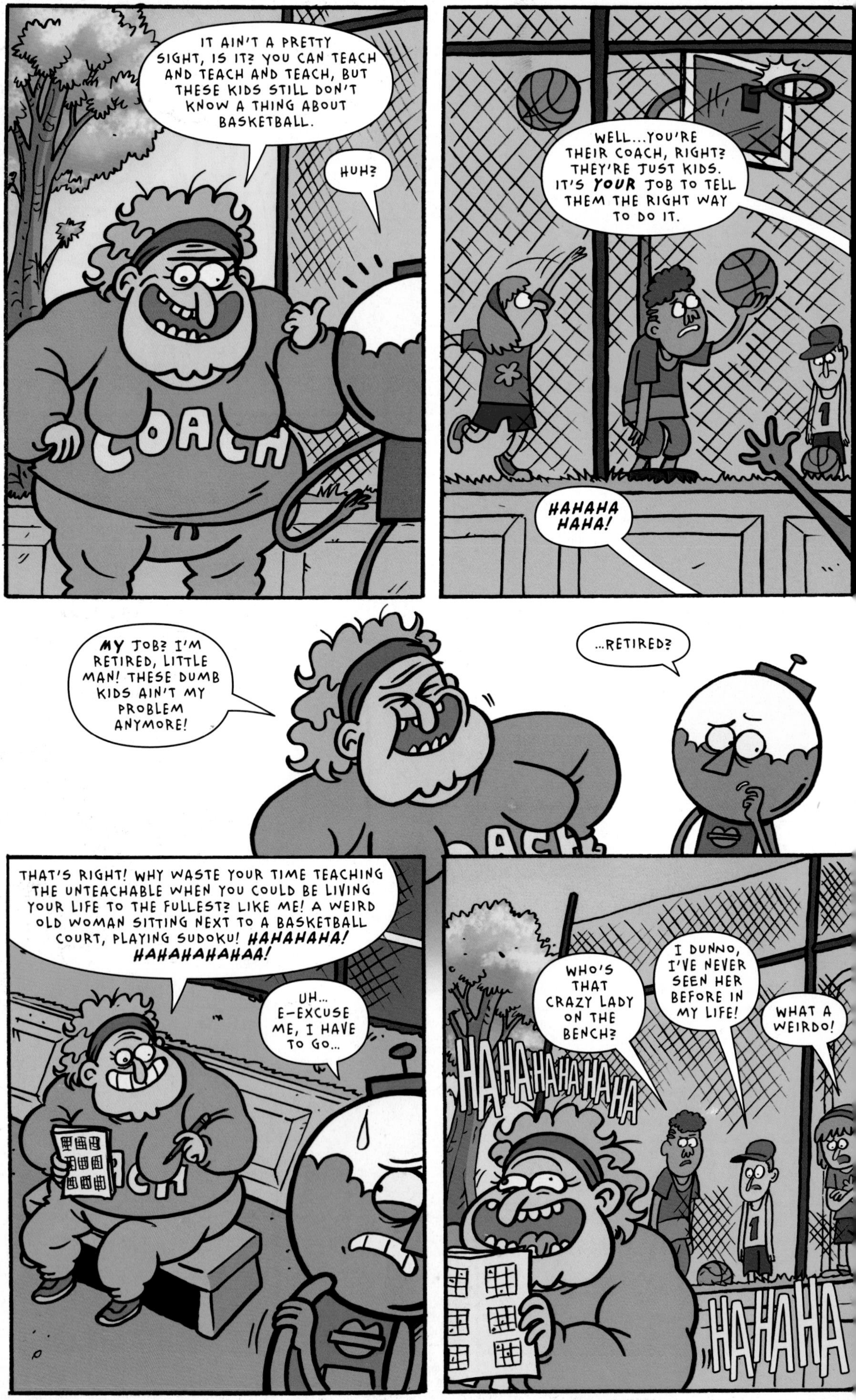
IT AIN'T A PRETTY SIGHT, IS IT? YOU CAN TEACH AND TEACH AND TEACH, BUT THESE KIDS STILL DON'T KNOW A THING ABOUT BASKETBALL.
HUH?
COACH
WELL...YOU'RE THEIR COACH, RIGHT? THEY'RE JUST KIDS. IT'S YOUR JOB TO TELL THEM THE RIGHT WAY TO DO IT.
HAHAHA HAHA!
MY JOB? I'M RETIRED, LITTLE MAN! THESE DUMB KIDS AIN'T MY PROBLEM ANYMORE!
...RETIRED?
THAT'S RIGHT! WHY WASTE YOUR TIME TEACHING THE UNTEACHABLE WHEN YOU COULD BE LIVING YOUR LIFE TO THE FULLEST? LIKE ME! A WEIRD OLD WOMAN SITTING NEXT TO A BASKETBALL COURT, PLAYING SUDOKU! HAHAHAHA! HAHAHAHAHAA!
UH... E-EXCUSE ME, I HAVE TO GO...
WHO'S THAT CRAZY LADY ON THE BENCH?
I DUNNO, I'VE NEVER SEEN HER BEFORE IN MY LIFE!
WHAT A WEIRDO!
HAHAHAHAHAHAHA
HAHAHA

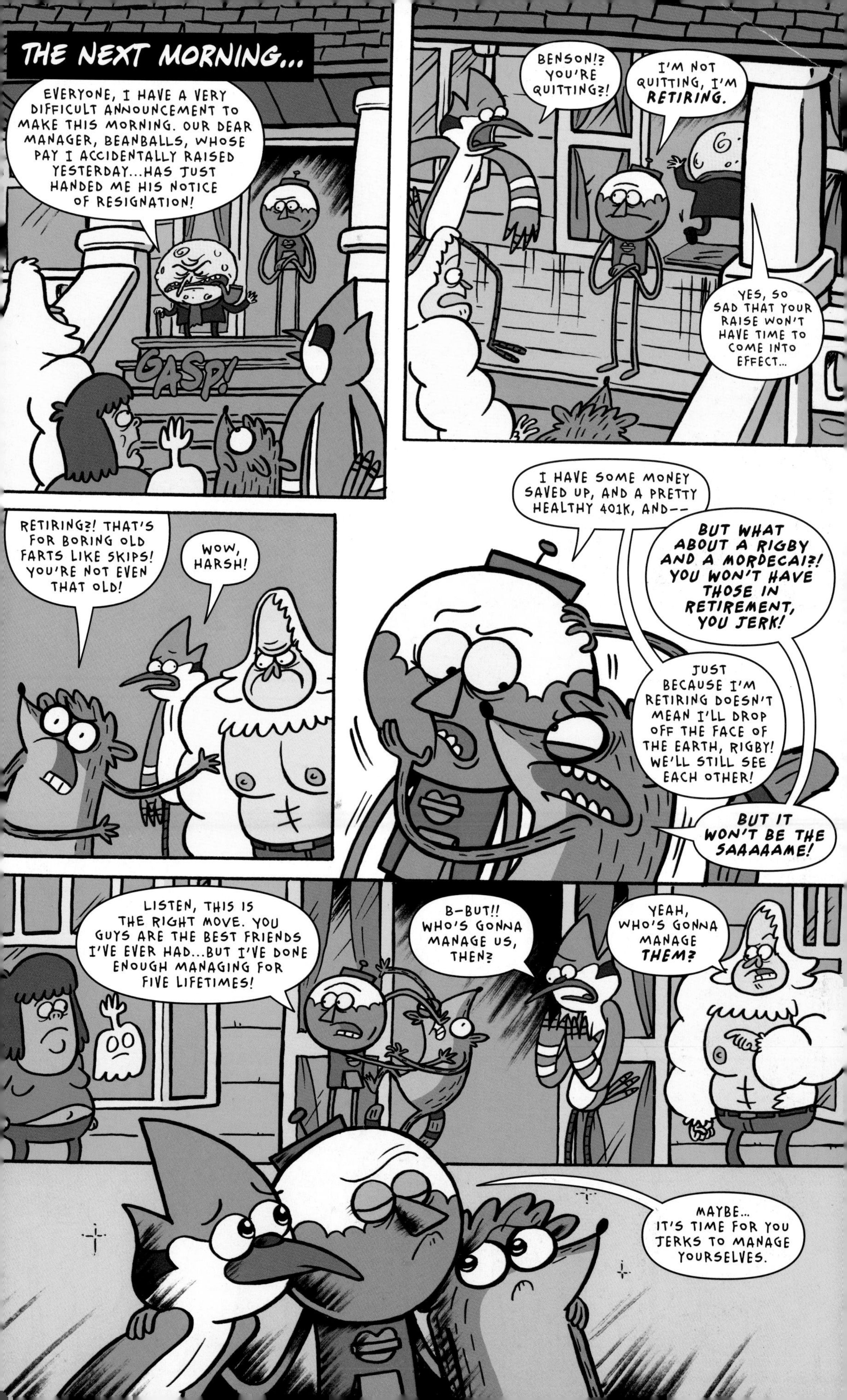
THE NEXT MORNING...
EVERYONE, I HAVE A VERY DIFFICULT ANNOUNCEMENT TO MAKE THIS MORNING. OUR DEAR MANAGER, BEANBALLS, WHOSE PAY I ACCIDENTALLY RAISED YESTERDAY...HAS JUST HANDED ME HIS NOTICE OF RESIGNATION!
GASP!
BENSON!? YOU'RE QUITTING?!
I'M NOT QUITTING, I'M RETIRING.
YES, SO SAD THAT YOUR RAISE WON'T HAVE TIME TO COME INTO EFFECT...
RETIRING?! THAT'S FOR BORING OLD FARTS LIKE SKIPS! YOU'RE NOT EVEN THAT OLD!
WOW, HARSH!
I HAVE SOME MONEY SAVED UP, AND A PRETTY HEALTHY 401K, AND--
BUT WHAT ABOUT A RIGBY AND A MORDECAI?! YOU WON'T HAVE THOSE IN RETIREMENT, YOU JERK!
JUST BECAUSE I'M RETIRING DOESN'T MEAN I'LL DROP OFF THE FACE OF THE EARTH, RIGBY! WE'LL STILL SEE EACH OTHER!
BUT IT WON'T BE THE SAAAAAME!
LISTEN, THIS IS THE RIGHT MOVE. YOU GUYS ARE THE BEST FRIENDS I'VE EVER HAD...BUT I'VE DONE ENOUGH MANAGING FOR FIVE LIFETIMES!
B-BUT!! WHO'S GONNA MANAGE US, THEN?
YEAH, WHO'S GONNA MANAGE THEM?
MAYBE... IT'S TIME FOR YOU JERKS TO MANAGE YOURSELVES.

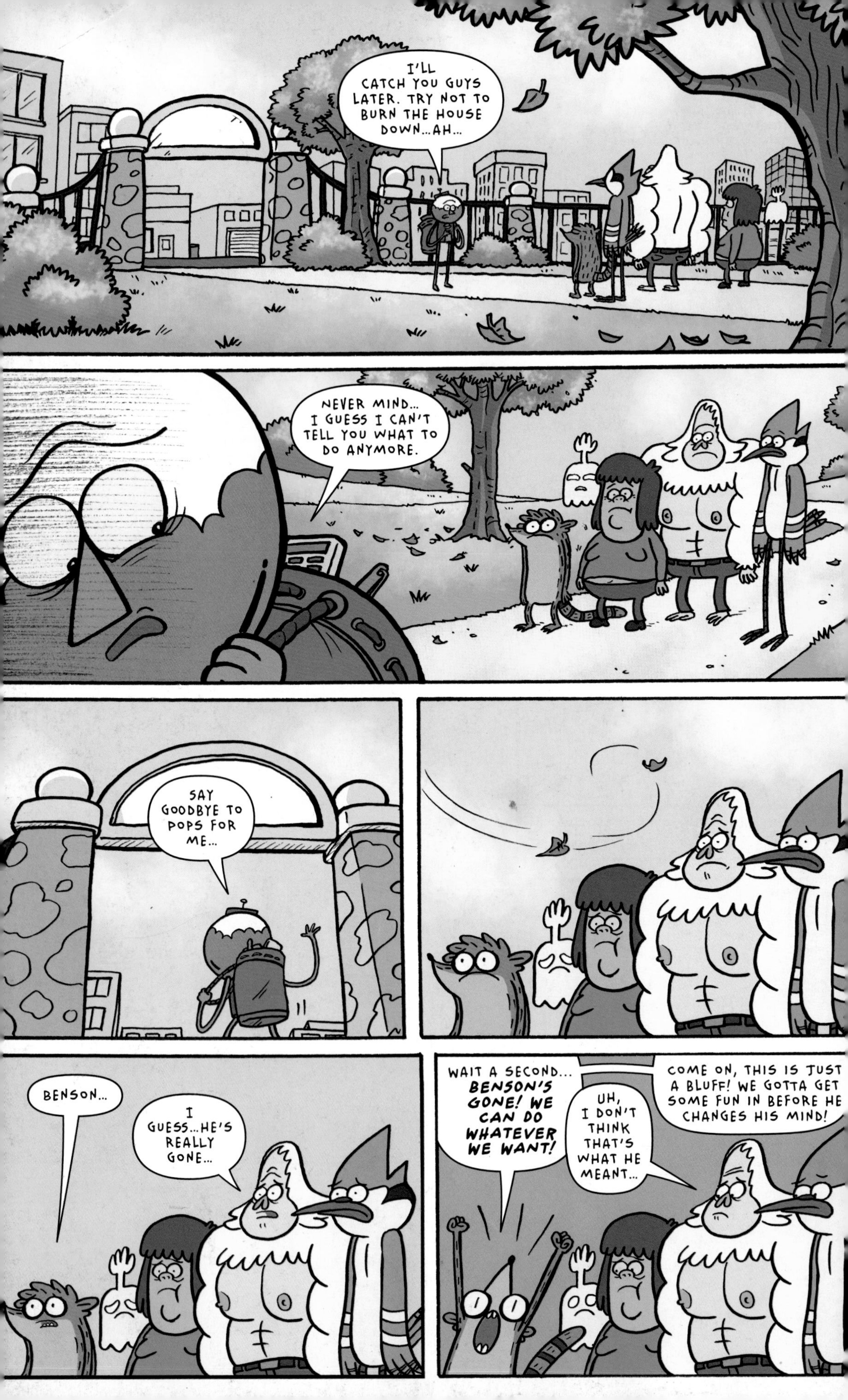
I'LL CATCH YOU GUYS LATER. TRY NOT TO BURN THE HOUSE DOWN...AH...
NEVER MIND... I GUESS I CAN'T TELL YOU WHAT TO DO ANYMORE.
SAY GOODBYE TO POPS FOR ME...
BENSON...
I GUESS...HE'S REALLY GONE...
WAIT A SECOND... BENSON'S GONE! WE CAN DO WHATEVER WE WANT!
UH, I DON'T THINK THAT'S WHAT HE MEANT...
COME ON, THIS IS JUST A BLUFF! WE GOTTA GET SOME FUN IN BEFORE HE CHANGES HIS MIND!

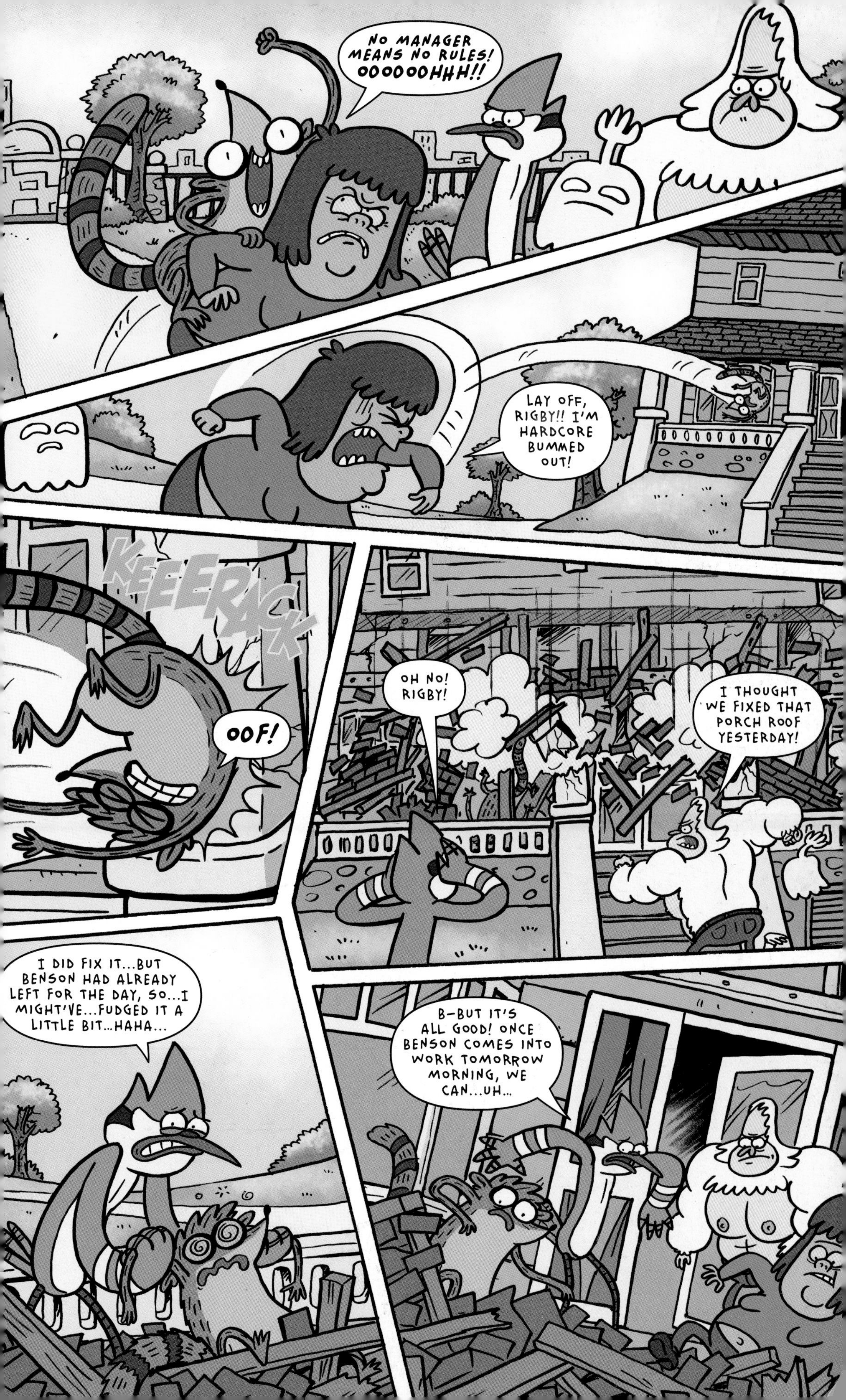
NO MANAGER MEANS NO RULES! OOOOOOHHH!!
LAY OFF, RIGBY!! I'M HARDCORE BUMMED OUT!
KEEERACK
OOF!
OH NO! RIGBY!
I THOUGHT WE FIXED THAT PORCH ROOF YESTERDAY!
I DID FIX IT...BUT BENSON HAD ALREADY LEFT FOR THE DAY, SO...I MIGHT'VE...FUDGED IT A LITTLE BIT...HAHA...
B-BUT IT'S ALL GOOD! ONCE BENSON COMES INTO WORK TOMORROW MORNING, WE CAN...UH...

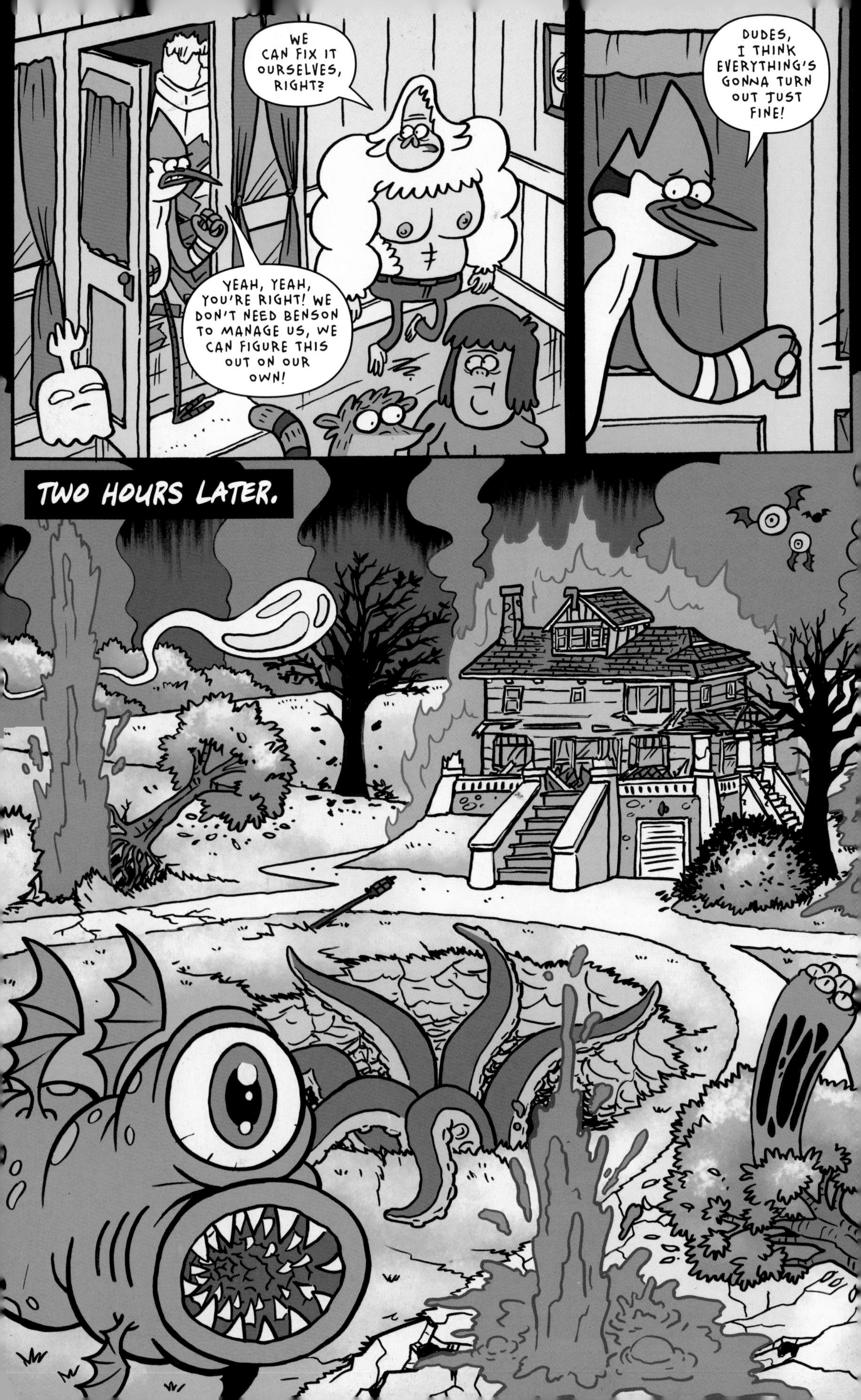
WE CAN FIX IT OURSELVES, RIGHT?
YEAH, YEAH, YOU'RE RIGHT! WE DON'T NEED BENSON TO MANAGE US, WE CAN FIGURE THIS OUT ON OUR OWN!
DUDES, I THINK EVERYTHING'S GONNA TURN OUT JUST FINE!
TWO HOURS LATER.

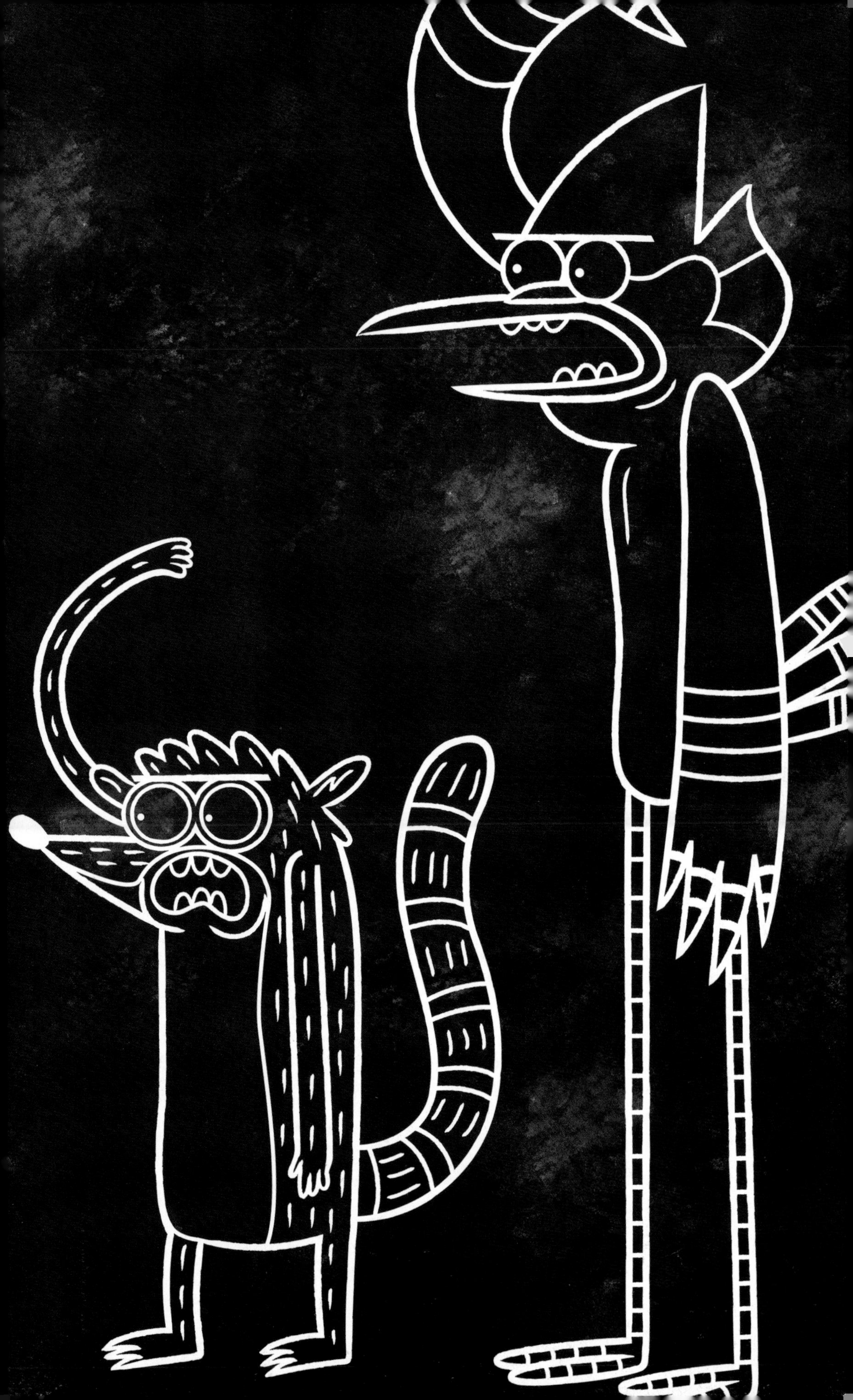

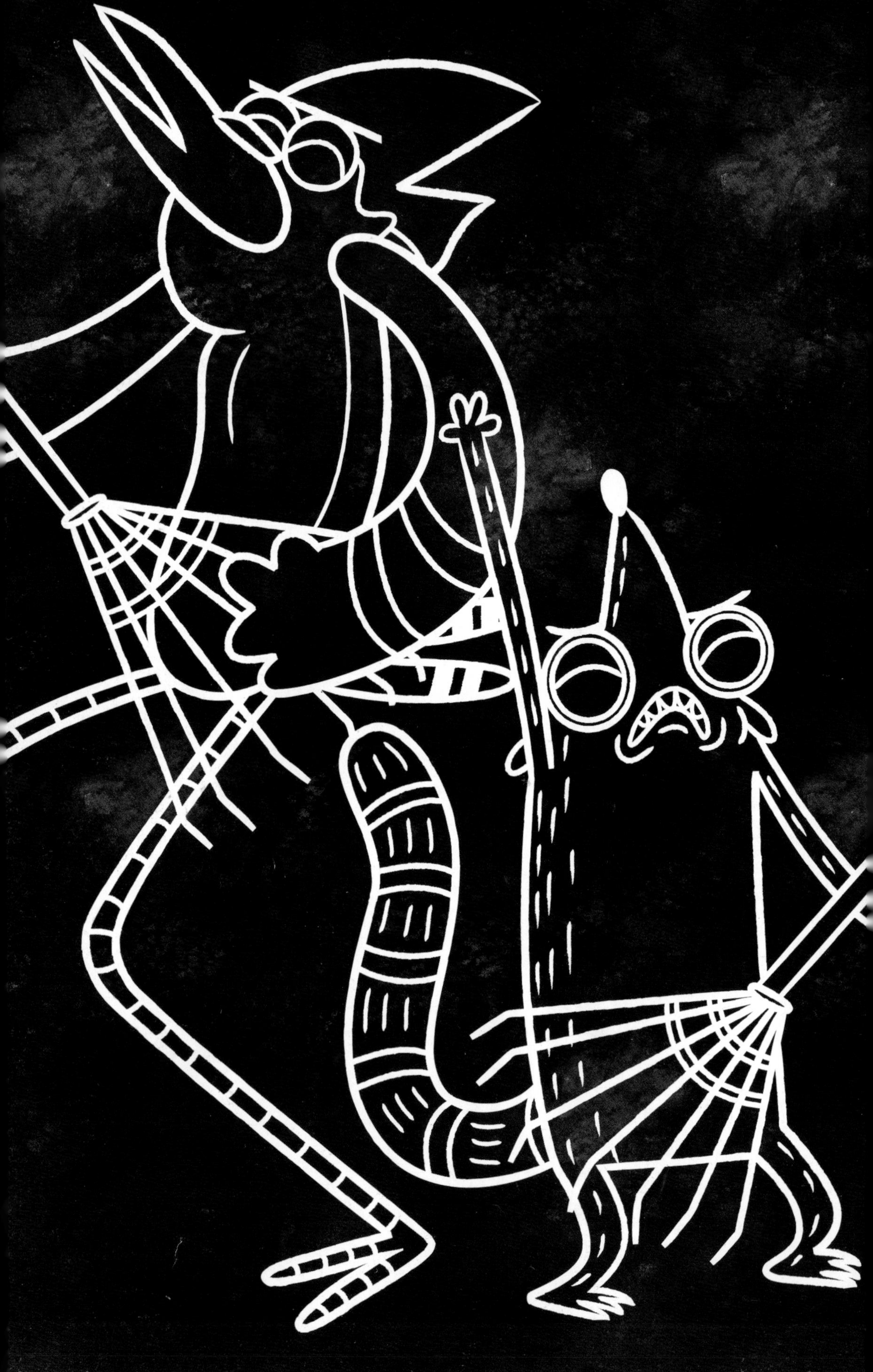

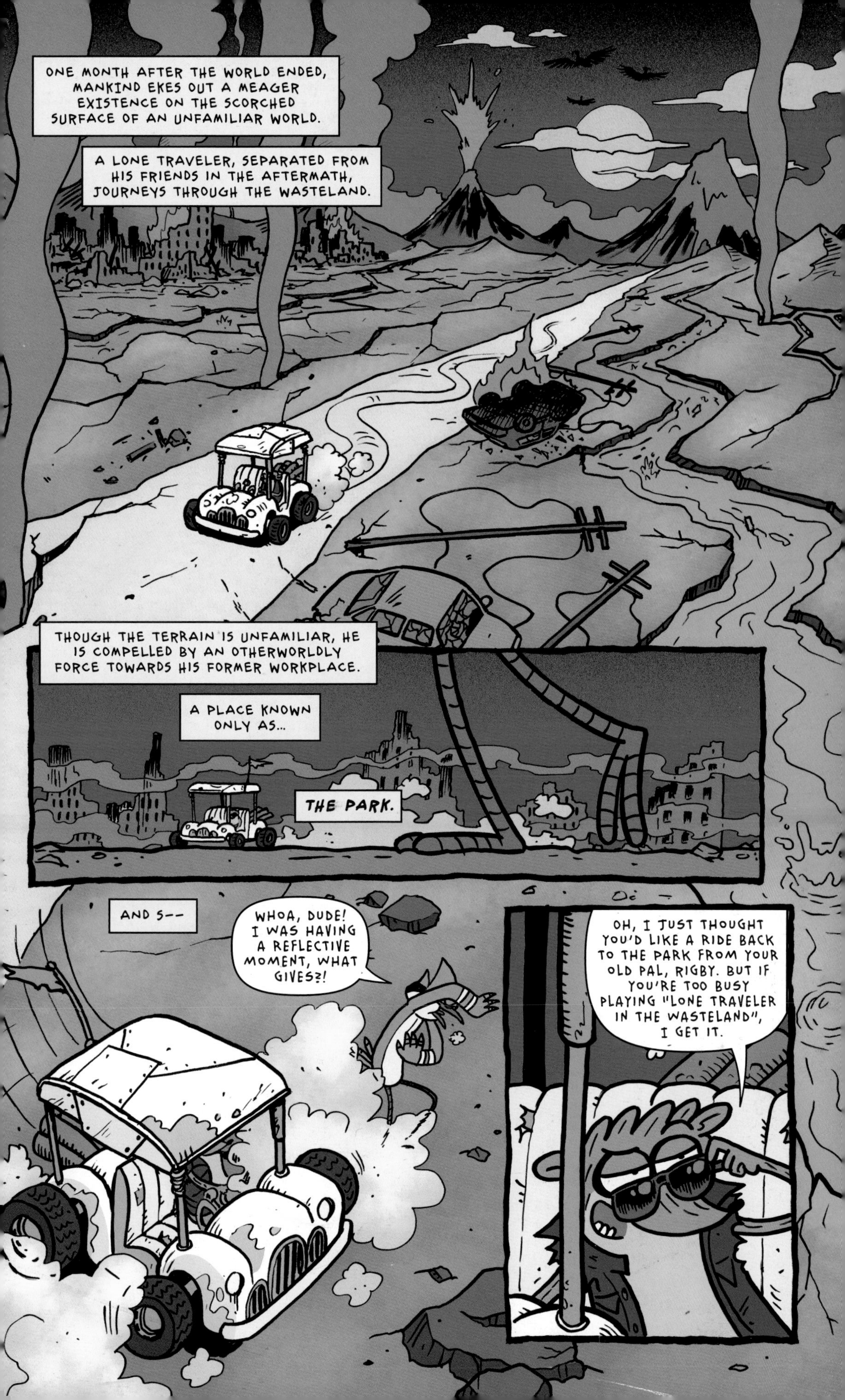
ONE MONTH AFTER THE WORLD ENDED, MANKIND EKES OUT A MEAGER EXISTENCE ON THE SCORCHED SURFACE OF AN UNFAMILIAR WORLD.
A LONE TRAVELER, SEPARATED FROM HIS FRIENDS IN THE AFTERMATH, JOURNEYS THROUGH THE WASTELAND.
THOUGH THE TERRAIN IS UNFAMILIAR, HE IS COMPELLED BY AN OTHERWORLDLY FORCE TOWARDS HIS FORMER WORKPLACE.
A PLACE KNOWN ONLY AS...
THE PARK.
AND S--
WHOA, DUDE! I WAS HAVING A REFLECTIVE MOMENT, WHAT GIVES?!
OH, I JUST THOUGHT YOU'D LIKE A RIDE BACK TO THE PARK FROM YOUR OLD PAL, RIGBY. BUT IF YOU'RE TOO BUSY PLAYING "LONE TRAVELER IN THE WASTELAND", I GET IT.

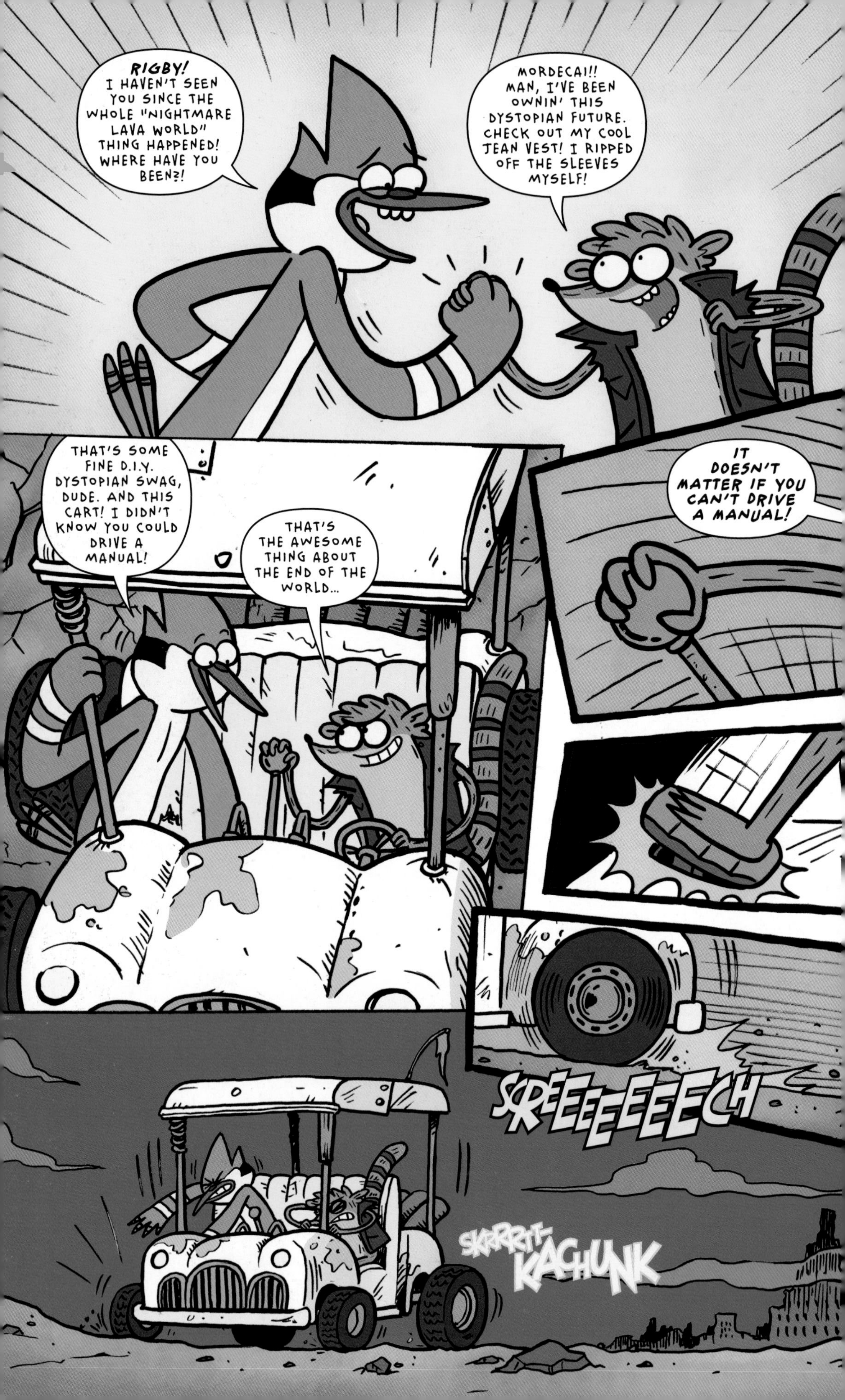
RIGBY! I HAVEN'T SEEN YOU SINCE THE WHOLE "NIGHTMARE LAVA WORLD" THING HAPPENED! WHERE HAVE YOU BEEN?!
MORDECAI!! MAN, I'VE BEEN OWNIN' THIS DYSTOPIAN FUTURE. CHECK OUT MY COOL JEAN VEST! I RIPPED OFF THE SLEEVES MYSELF!
THAT'S SOME FINE D.I.Y. DYSTOPIAN SWAG, DUDE. AND THIS CART! I DIDN'T KNOW YOU COULD DRIVE A MANUAL!
THAT'S THE AWESOME THING ABOUT THE END OF THE WORLD...
IT DOESN'T MATTER IF YOU CAN'T DRIVE A MANUAL!
SCREEEEEEEECH
SKRRRTT-KACHUNK

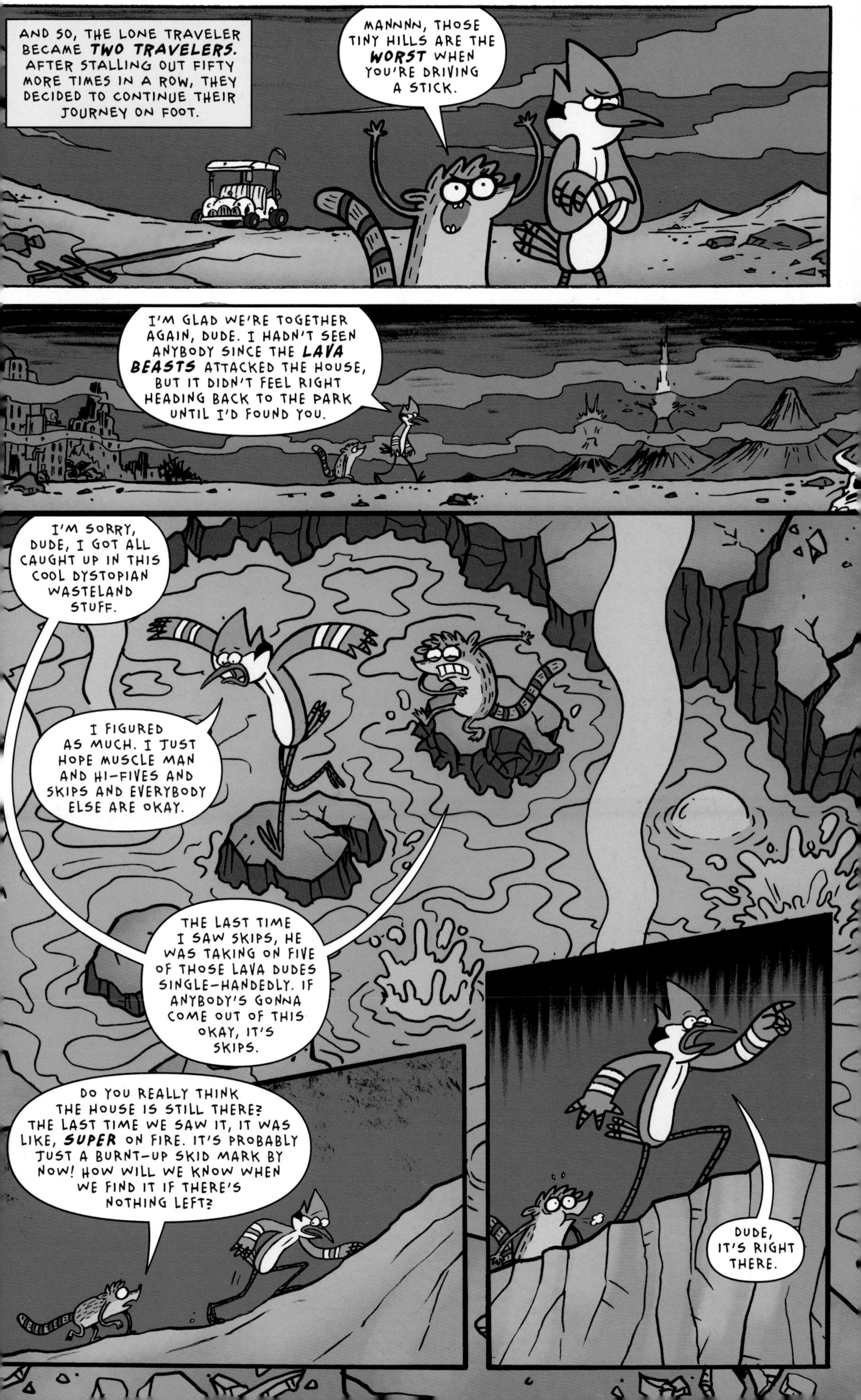
AND SO, THE LONE TRAVELER BECAME **TWO TRAVELERS.** AFTER STALLING OUT FIFTY MORE TIMES IN A ROW, THEY DECIDED TO CONTINUE THEIR JOURNEY ON FOOT.
MANNNN, THOSE TINY HILLS ARE THE **WORST** WHEN YOU'RE DRIVING A STICK.
I'M GLAD WE'RE TOGETHER AGAIN, DUDE. I HADN'T SEEN ANYBODY SINCE THE **LAVA BEASTS** ATTACKED THE HOUSE, BUT IT DIDN'T FEEL RIGHT HEADING BACK TO THE PARK UNTIL I'D FOUND YOU.
I'M SORRY, DUDE, I GOT ALL CAUGHT UP IN THIS COOL DYSTOPIAN WASTELAND STUFF.
I FIGURED AS MUCH. I JUST HOPE MUSCLE MAN AND HI-FIVES AND SKIPS AND EVERYBODY ELSE ARE OKAY.
THE LAST TIME I SAW SKIPS, HE WAS TAKING ON FIVE OF THOSE LAVA DUDES SINGLE-HANDEDLY. IF ANYBODY'S GONNA COME OUT OF THIS OKAY, IT'S SKIPS.
DO YOU REALLY THINK THE HOUSE IS STILL THERE? THE LAST TIME WE SAW IT, IT WAS LIKE, **SUPER** ON FIRE. IT'S PROBABLY JUST A BURNT-UP SKID MARK BY NOW! HOW WILL WE KNOW WHEN WE FIND IT IF THERE'S NOTHING LEFT?
DUDE, IT'S RIGHT THERE.

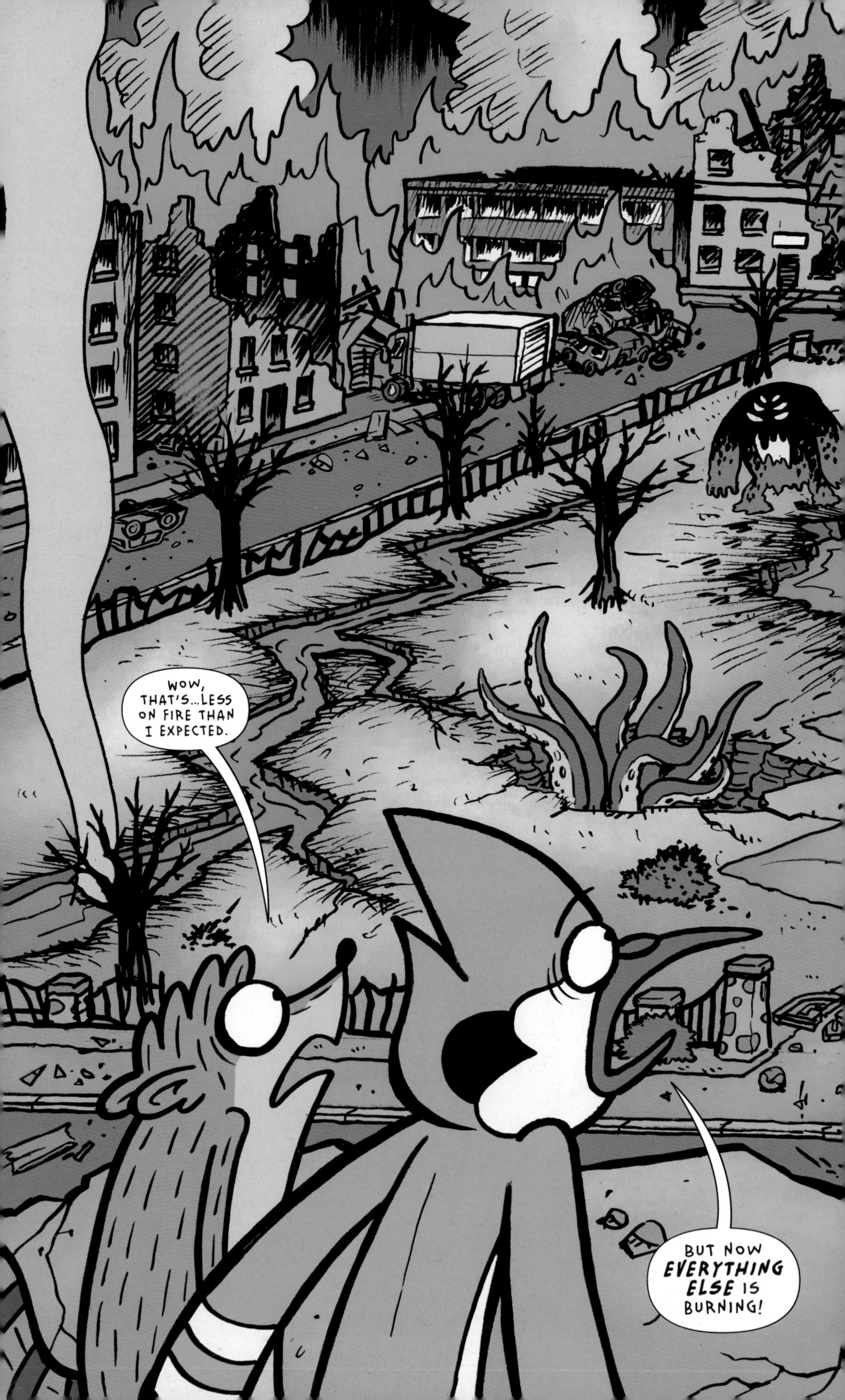
WOW, THAT'S...LESS ON FIRE THAN I EXPECTED.
BUT NOW EVERYTHING ELSE IS BURNING!

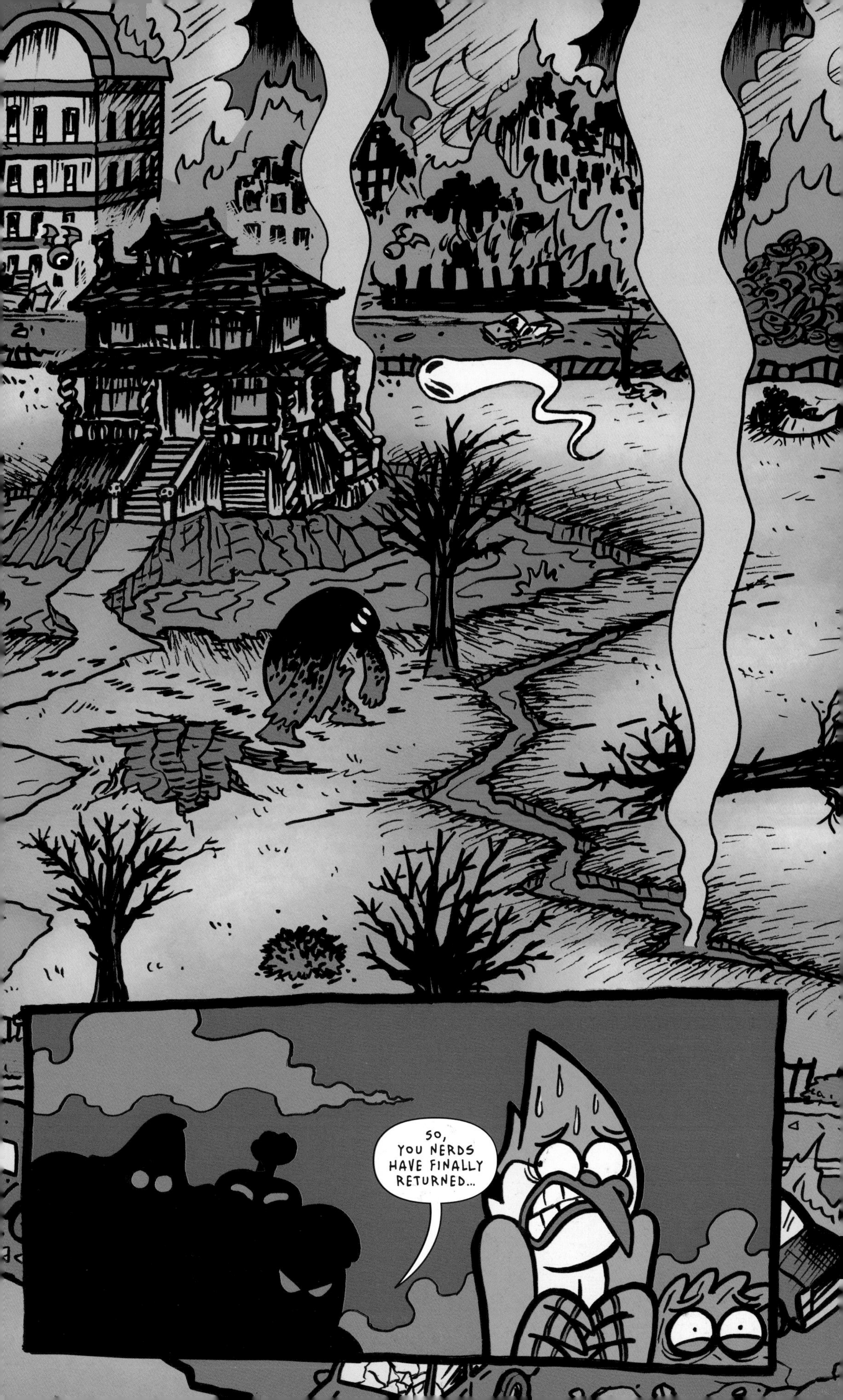
SO, YOU NERDS HAVE FINALLY RETURNED...

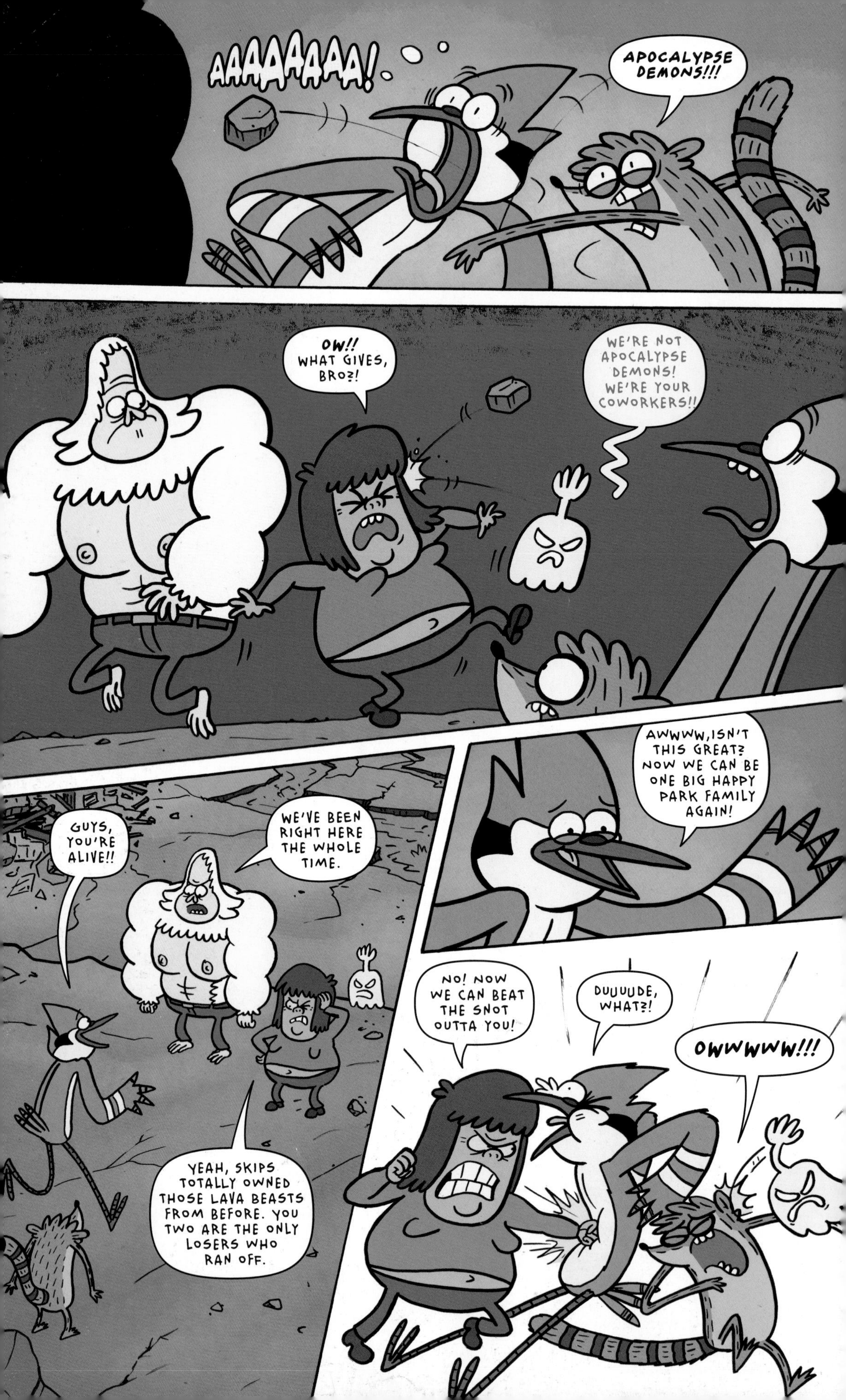
AAAAAAAA!
APOCALYPSE DEMONS!!!
OW!! WHAT GIVES, BRO?!
WE'RE NOT APOCALYPSE DEMONS! WE'RE YOUR COWORKERS!!
GUYS, YOU'RE ALIVE!!
WE'VE BEEN RIGHT HERE THE WHOLE TIME.
YEAH, SKIPS TOTALLY OWNED THOSE LAVA BEASTS FROM BEFORE. YOU TWO ARE THE ONLY LOSERS WHO RAN OFF.
AWWWW, ISN'T THIS GREAT? NOW WE CAN BE ONE BIG HAPPY PARK FAMILY AGAIN!
NO! NOW WE CAN BEAT THE SNOT OUTTA YOU!
DUUUUDE, WHAT?!
OWWWWW!!!

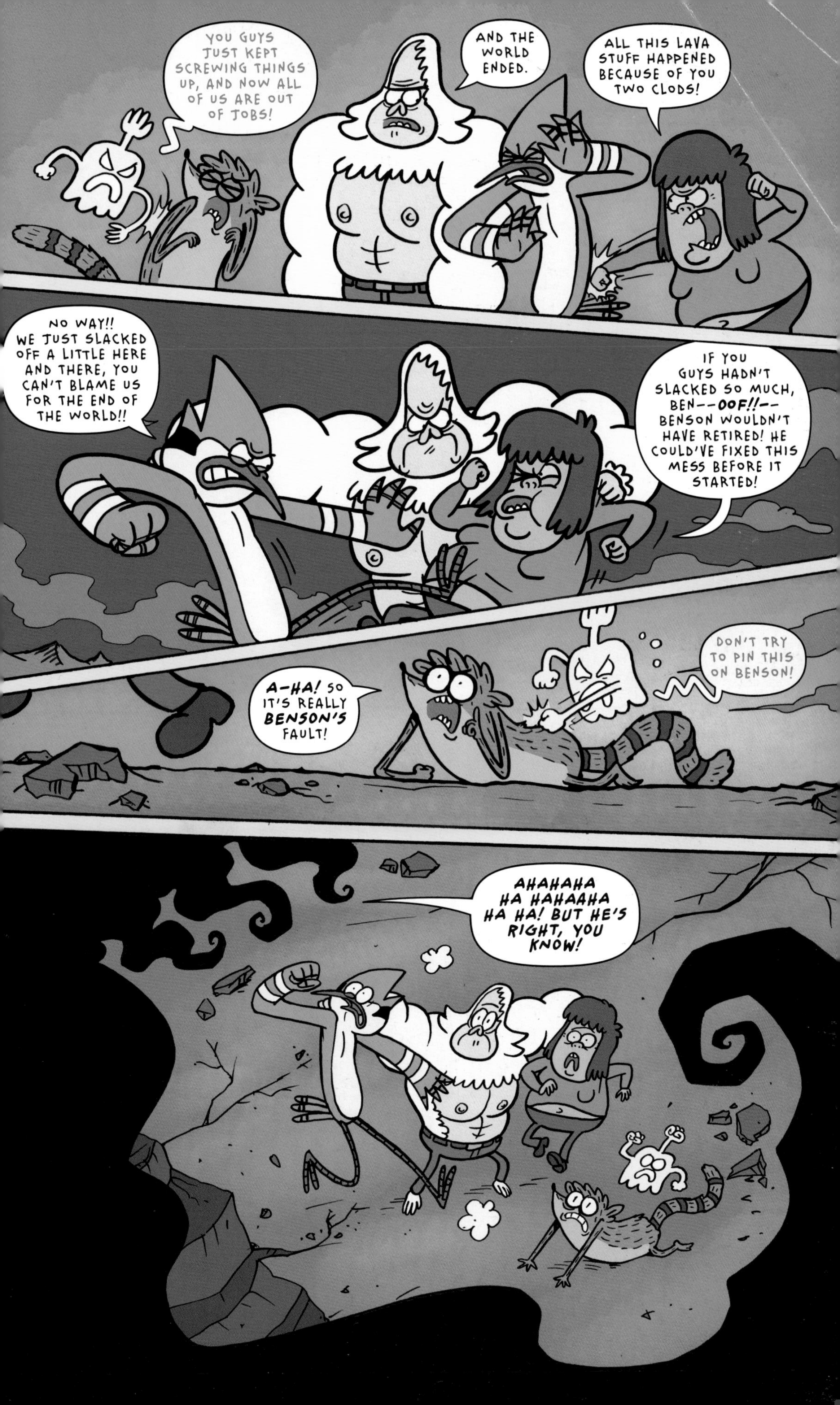
YOU GUYS JUST KEPT SCREWING THINGS UP, AND NOW ALL OF US ARE OUT OF JOBS!
AND THE WORLD ENDED.
ALL THIS LAVA STUFF HAPPENED BECAUSE OF YOU TWO CLODS!
NO WAY!! WE JUST SLACKED OFF A LITTLE HERE AND THERE, YOU CAN'T BLAME US FOR THE END OF THE WORLD!!
IF YOU GUYS HADN'T SLACKED SO MUCH, BEN--OOF!!-- BENSON WOULDN'T HAVE RETIRED! HE COULD'VE FIXED THIS MESS BEFORE IT STARTED!
A-HA! SO IT'S REALLY BENSON'S FAULT!
DON'T TRY TO PIN THIS ON BENSON!
AHAHAHA HA HAHAAHA HA HA! BUT HE'S RIGHT, YOU KNOW!

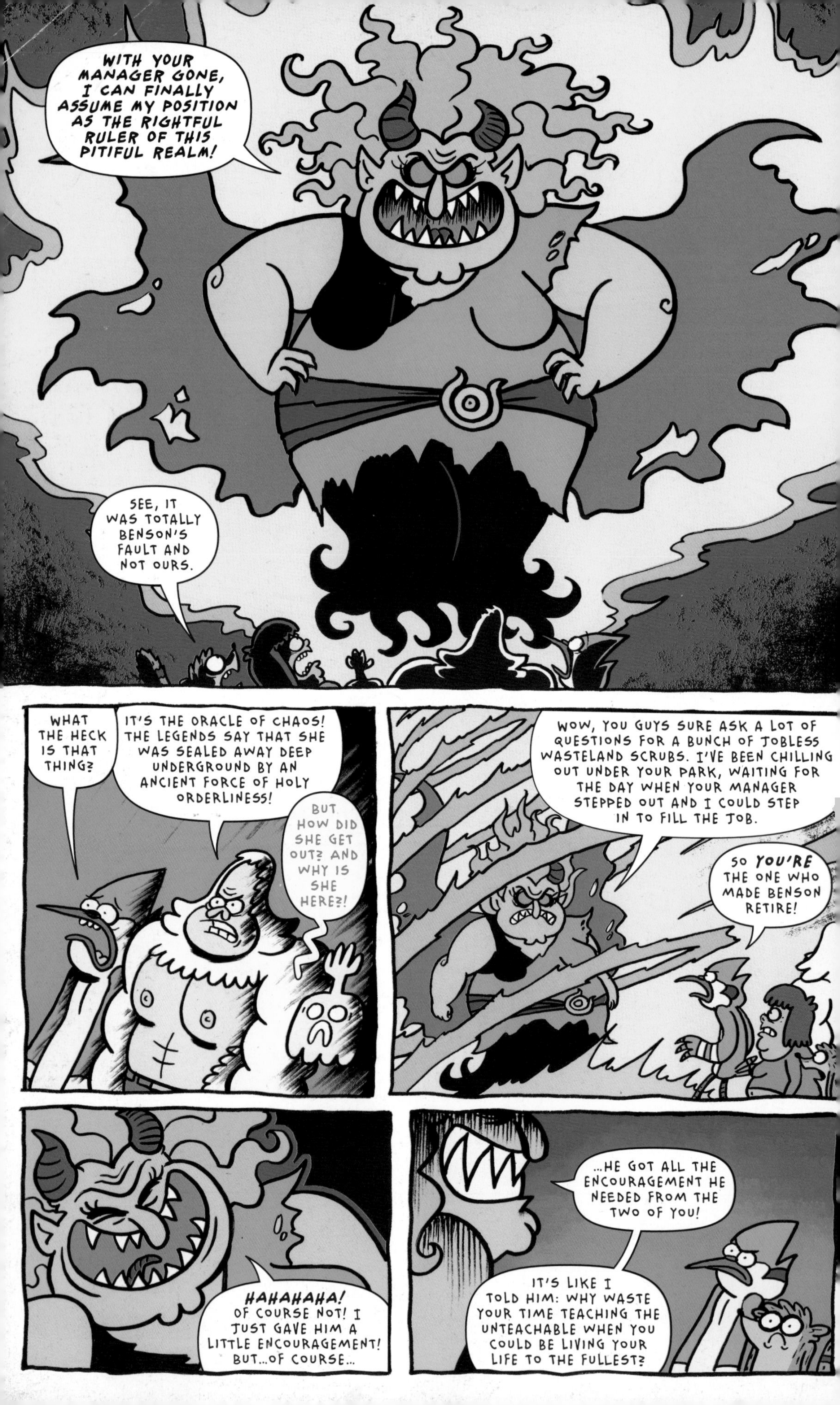
WITH YOUR MANAGER GONE, I CAN FINALLY ASSUME MY POSITION AS THE RIGHTFUL RULER OF THIS PITIFUL REALM!
SEE, IT WAS TOTALLY BENSON'S FAULT AND NOT OURS.
WHAT THE HECK IS THAT THING?
IT'S THE ORACLE OF CHAOS! THE LEGENDS SAY THAT SHE WAS SEALED AWAY DEEP UNDERGROUND BY AN ANCIENT FORCE OF HOLY ORDERLINESS!
BUT HOW DID SHE GET OUT? AND WHY IS SHE HERE?!
WOW, YOU GUYS SURE ASK A LOT OF QUESTIONS FOR A BUNCH OF JOBLESS WASTELAND SCRUBS. I'VE BEEN CHILLING OUT UNDER YOUR PARK, WAITING FOR THE DAY WHEN YOUR MANAGER STEPPED OUT AND I COULD STEP IN TO FILL THE JOB.
SO YOU'RE THE ONE WHO MADE BENSON RETIRE!
HAHAHAHA! OF COURSE NOT! I JUST GAVE HIM A LITTLE ENCOURAGEMENT! BUT...OF COURSE...
...HE GOT ALL THE ENCOURAGEMENT HE NEEDED FROM THE TWO OF YOU!
IT'S LIKE I TOLD HIM: WHY WASTE YOUR TIME TEACHING THE UNTEACHABLE WHEN YOU COULD BE LIVING YOUR LIFE TO THE FULLEST?

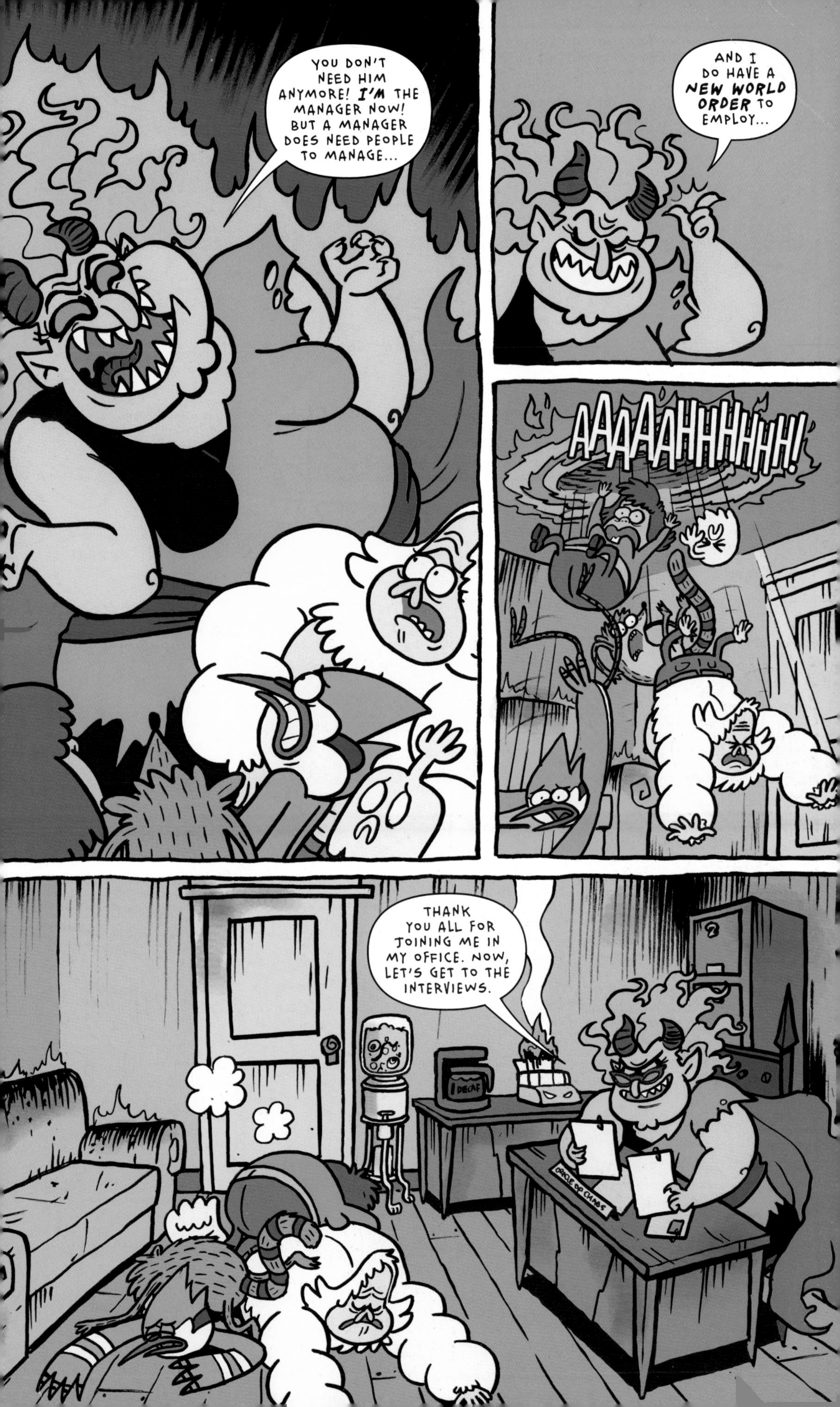

YOU DON'T NEED HIM ANYMORE! I'M THE MANAGER NOW! BUT A MANAGER DOES NEED PEOPLE TO MANAGE...
AND I DO HAVE A NEW WORLD ORDER TO EMPLOY...
AAAAAHHHHHH!
THANK YOU ALL FOR JOINING ME IN MY OFFICE. NOW, LET'S GET TO THE INTERVIEWS.
DECAF
ORACLE OF CHAOS

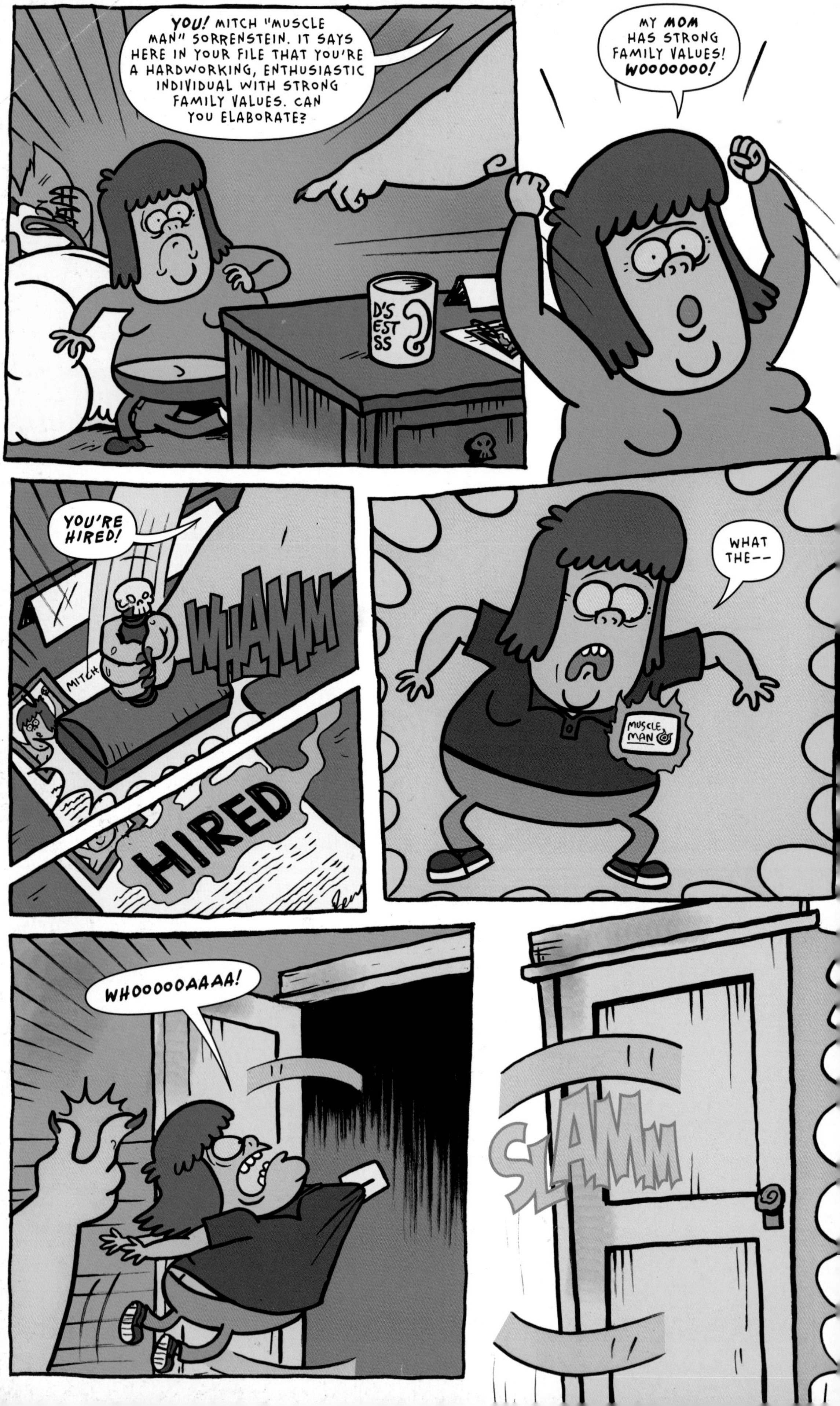
YOU! MITCH "MUSCLE MAN" SORRENSTEIN. IT SAYS HERE IN YOUR FILE THAT YOU'RE A HARDWORKING, ENTHUSIASTIC INDIVIDUAL WITH STRONG FAMILY VALUES. CAN YOU ELABORATE?
MY MOM HAS STRONG FAMILY VALUES! WOOOOOOO!
YOU'RE HIRED!
WHAMM
MITCH
HIRED
WHAT THE--
MUSCLE MAN
WHOOOOOAAAA!
SLAMM

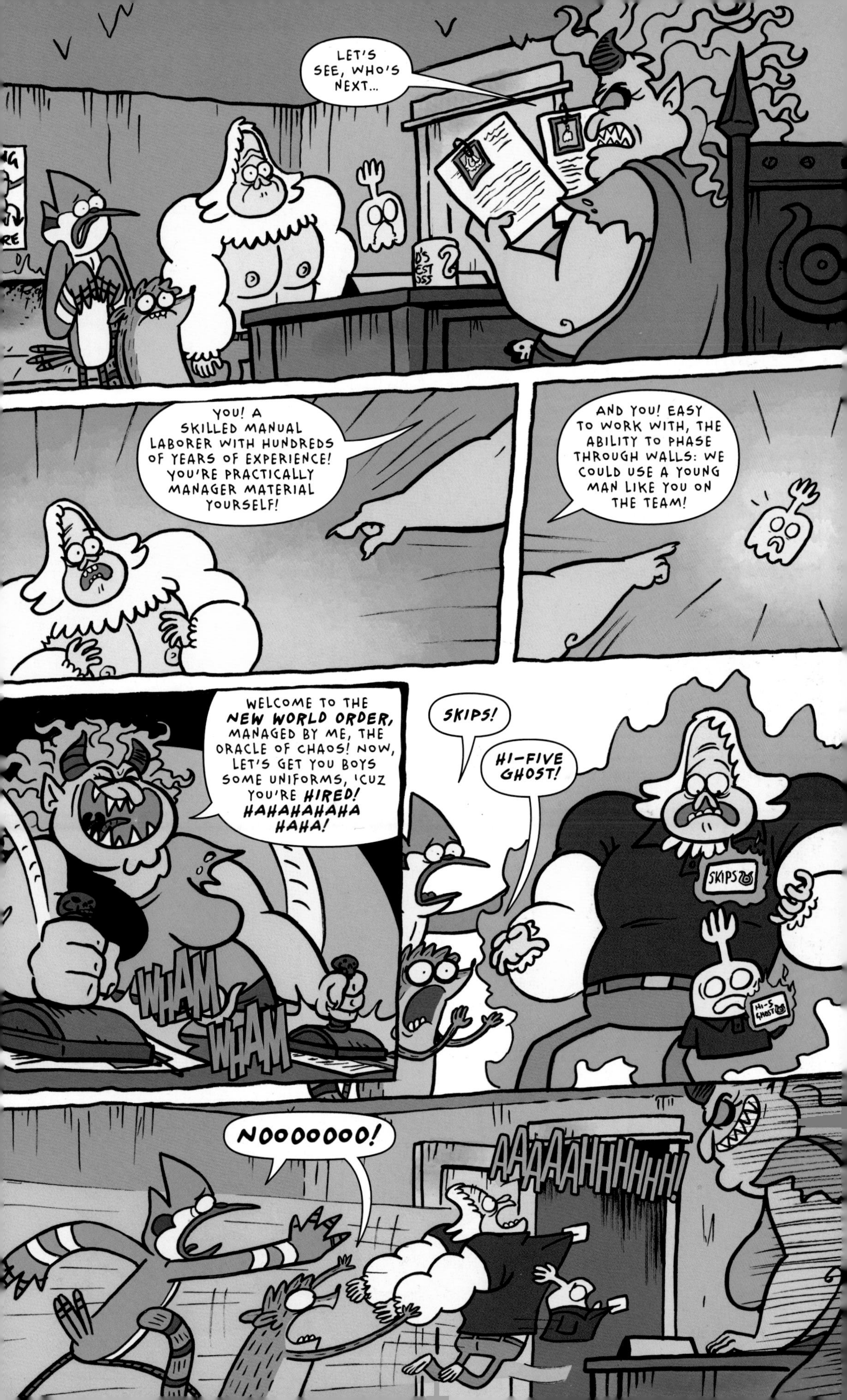
LET'S SEE, WHO'S NEXT...
YOU! A SKILLED MANUAL LABORER WITH HUNDREDS OF YEARS OF EXPERIENCE! YOU'RE PRACTICALLY MANAGER MATERIAL YOURSELF!
AND YOU! EASY TO WORK WITH, THE ABILITY TO PHASE THROUGH WALLS: WE COULD USE A YOUNG MAN LIKE YOU ON THE TEAM!
WELCOME TO THE NEW WORLD ORDER, MANAGED BY ME, THE ORACLE OF CHAOS! NOW, LET'S GET YOU BOYS SOME UNIFORMS, 'CUZ YOU'RE HIRED! HAHAHAHAHA HAHA!
WHAM
WHAM
SKIPS!
HI-FIVE GHOST!
SKIPS
HI-5 GHOST
NOOOOOOO!
AAAAAHHHHHH!

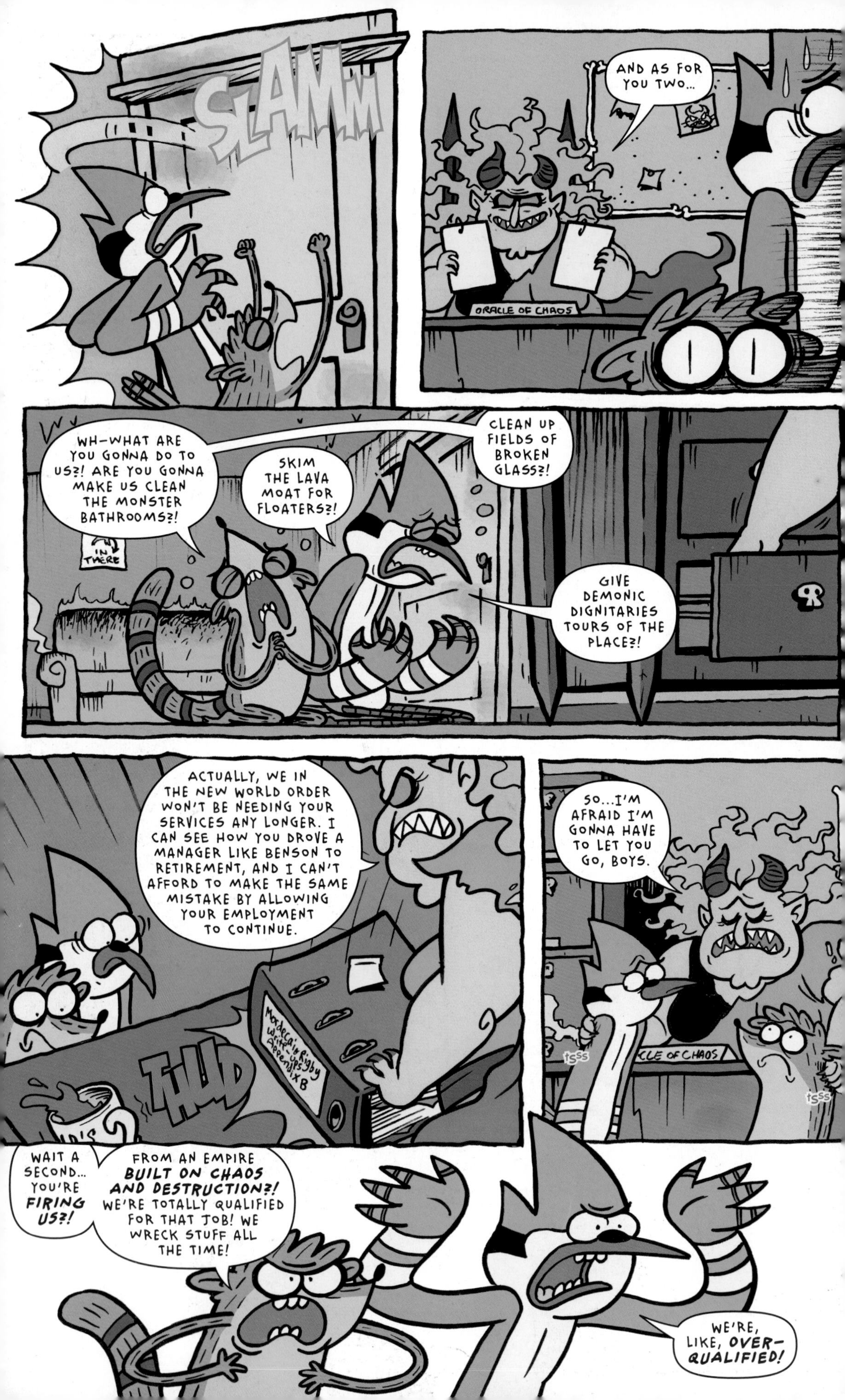
SLAMM
AND AS FOR YOU TWO...
ORACLE OF CHAOS
WH-WHAT ARE YOU GONNA DO TO US?! ARE YOU GONNA MAKE US CLEAN THE MONSTER BATHROOMS?!
IN THERE
SKIM THE LAVA MOAT FOR FLOATERS?!
CLEAN UP FIELDS OF BROKEN GLASS?!
GIVE DEMONIC DIGNITARIES TOURS OF THE PLACE?!
ACTUALLY, WE IN THE NEW WORLD ORDER WON'T BE NEEDING YOUR SERVICES ANY LONGER. I CAN SEE HOW YOU DROVE A MANAGER LIKE BENSON TO RETIREMENT, AND I CAN'T AFFORD TO MAKE THE SAME MISTAKE BY ALLOWING YOUR EMPLOYMENT TO CONTINUE.
THUD
Mordecai & Rigby Write-ups Appendix B
SO...I'M AFRAID I'M GONNA HAVE TO LET YOU GO, BOYS.
tsss
CLE OF CHAOS
tsss
WAIT A SECOND... YOU'RE FIRING US?!
FROM AN EMPIRE BUILT ON CHAOS AND DESTRUCTION?! WE'RE TOTALLY QUALIFIED FOR THAT JOB! WE WRECK STUFF ALL THE TIME!
WE'RE, LIKE, OVER-QUALIFIED!

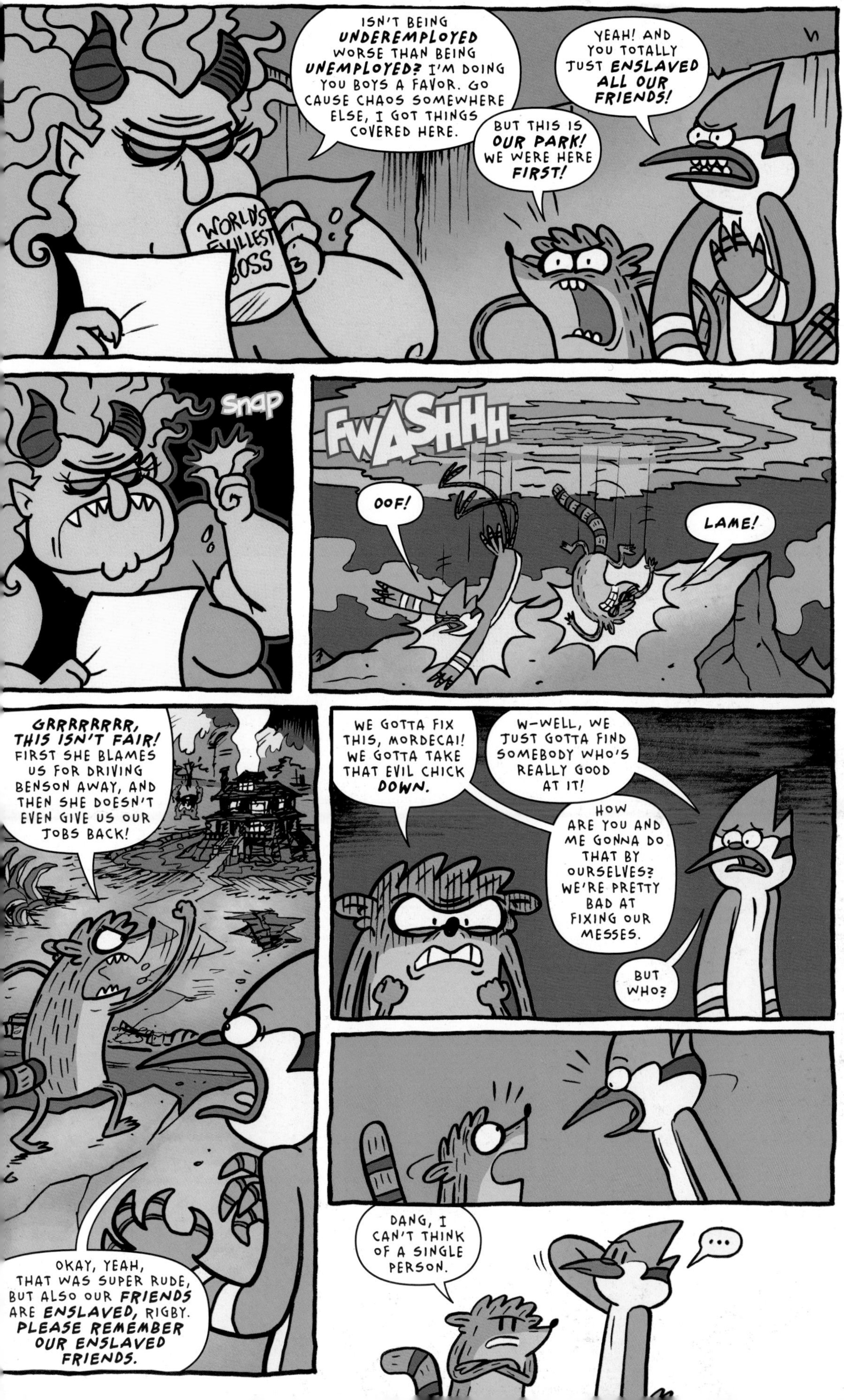
WORLD'S EVILLEST BOSS
ISN'T BEING UNDEREMPLOYED WORSE THAN BEING UNEMPLOYED? I'M DOING YOU BOYS A FAVOR. GO CAUSE CHAOS SOMEWHERE ELSE, I GOT THINGS COVERED HERE.
YEAH! AND YOU TOTALLY JUST ENSLAVED ALL OUR FRIENDS!
BUT THIS IS OUR PARK! WE WERE HERE FIRST!
SNAP
FWASHHH
OOF!
LAME!
GRRRRRRR, THIS ISN'T FAIR! FIRST SHE BLAMES US FOR DRIVING BENSON AWAY, AND THEN SHE DOESN'T EVEN GIVE US OUR JOBS BACK!
OKAY, YEAH, THAT WAS SUPER RUDE, BUT ALSO OUR FRIENDS ARE ENSLAVED, RIGBY. PLEASE REMEMBER OUR ENSLAVED FRIENDS.
WE GOTTA FIX THIS, MORDECAI! WE GOTTA TAKE THAT EVIL CHICK DOWN.
W-WELL, WE JUST GOTTA FIND SOMEBODY WHO'S REALLY GOOD AT IT!
HOW ARE YOU AND ME GONNA DO THAT BY OURSELVES? WE'RE PRETTY BAD AT FIXING OUR MESSES.
BUT WHO?
DANG, I CAN'T THINK OF A SINGLE PERSON.
...

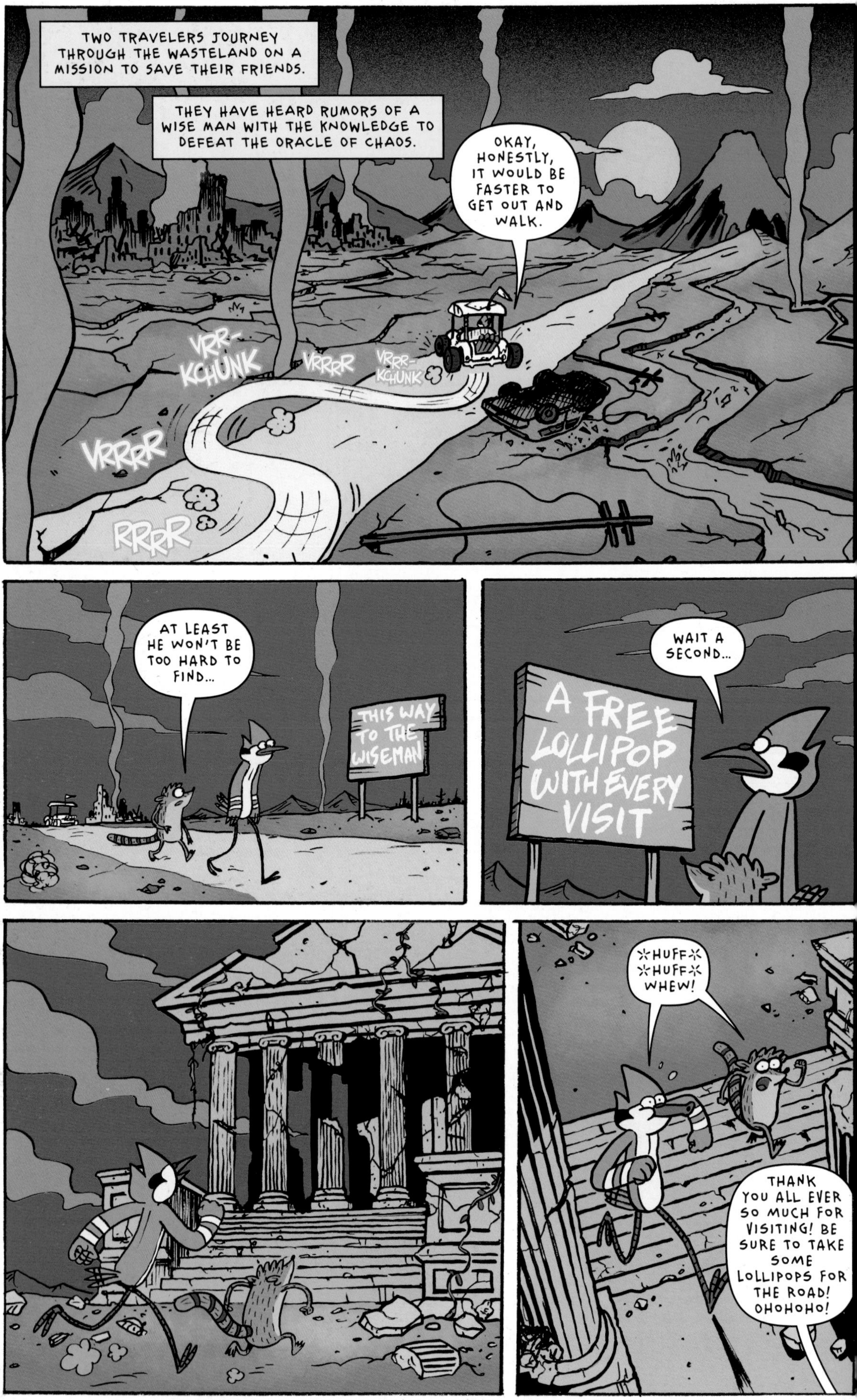
TWO TRAVELERS JOURNEY THROUGH THE WASTELAND ON A MISSION TO SAVE THEIR FRIENDS.
THEY HAVE HEARD RUMORS OF A WISE MAN WITH THE KNOWLEDGE TO DEFEAT THE ORACLE OF CHAOS.
OKAY, HONESTLY, IT WOULD BE FASTER TO GET OUT AND WALK.
VRR-KCHUNK
VRRRR
VRRR-KCHUNK
VRRRR
RRRR
AT LEAST HE WON'T BE TOO HARD TO FIND...
THIS WAY TO THE WISEMAN
WAIT A SECOND...
A FREE LOLLIPOP WITH EVERY VISIT
HUFF *HUFF* WHEW!
THANK YOU ALL EVER SO MUCH FOR VISITING! BE SURE TO TAKE SOME LOLLIPOPS FOR THE ROAD! OHOHOHO!

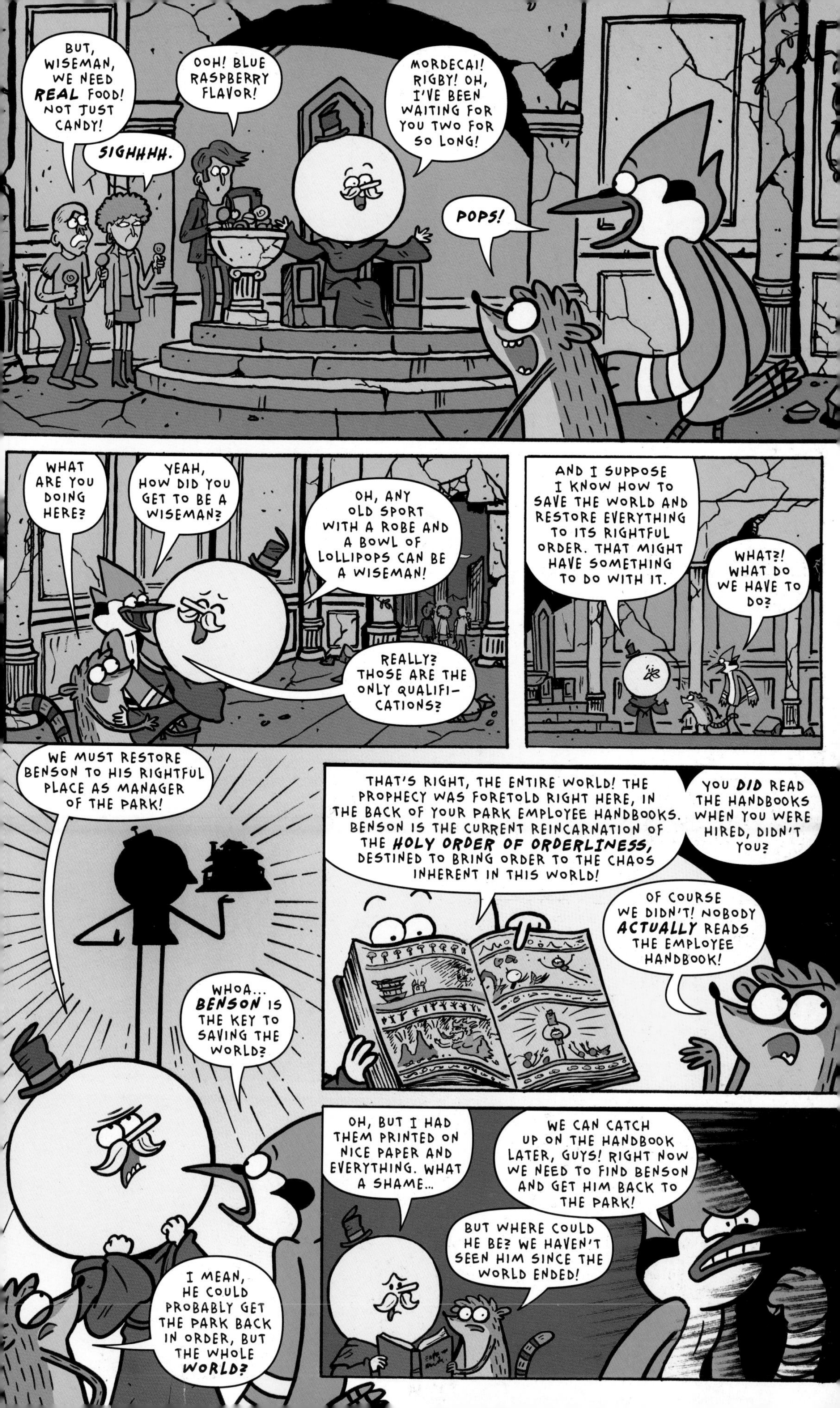
BUT, WISEMAN, WE NEED REAL FOOD! NOT JUST CANDY!
SIGHHHH.
OOH! BLUE RASPBERRY FLAVOR!
MORDECAI! RIGBY! OH, I'VE BEEN WAITING FOR YOU TWO FOR SO LONG!
POPS!
WHAT ARE YOU DOING HERE?
YEAH, HOW DID YOU GET TO BE A WISEMAN?
OH, ANY OLD SPORT WITH A ROBE AND A BOWL OF LOLLIPOPS CAN BE A WISEMAN!
REALLY? THOSE ARE THE ONLY QUALIFI-CATIONS?
AND I SUPPOSE I KNOW HOW TO SAVE THE WORLD AND RESTORE EVERYTHING TO ITS RIGHTFUL ORDER. THAT MIGHT HAVE SOMETHING TO DO WITH IT.
WHAT?! WHAT DO WE HAVE TO DO?
WE MUST RESTORE BENSON TO HIS RIGHTFUL PLACE AS MANAGER OF THE PARK!
WHOA... BENSON IS THE KEY TO SAVING THE WORLD?
I MEAN, HE COULD PROBABLY GET THE PARK BACK IN ORDER, BUT THE WHOLE WORLD?
THAT'S RIGHT, THE ENTIRE WORLD! THE PROPHECY WAS FORETOLD RIGHT HERE, IN THE BACK OF YOUR PARK EMPLOYEE HANDBOOKS. BENSON IS THE CURRENT REINCARNATION OF THE HOLY ORDER OF ORDERLINESS, DESTINED TO BRING ORDER TO THE CHAOS INHERENT IN THIS WORLD!
YOU DID READ THE HANDBOOKS WHEN YOU WERE HIRED, DIDN'T YOU?
OF COURSE WE DIDN'T! NOBODY ACTUALLY READS THE EMPLOYEE HANDBOOK!
OH, BUT I HAD THEM PRINTED ON NICE PAPER AND EVERYTHING. WHAT A SHAME...
WE CAN CATCH UP ON THE HANDBOOK LATER, GUYS! RIGHT NOW WE NEED TO FIND BENSON AND GET HIM BACK TO THE PARK!
BUT WHERE COULD HE BE? WE HAVEN'T SEEN HIM SINCE THE WORLD ENDED!

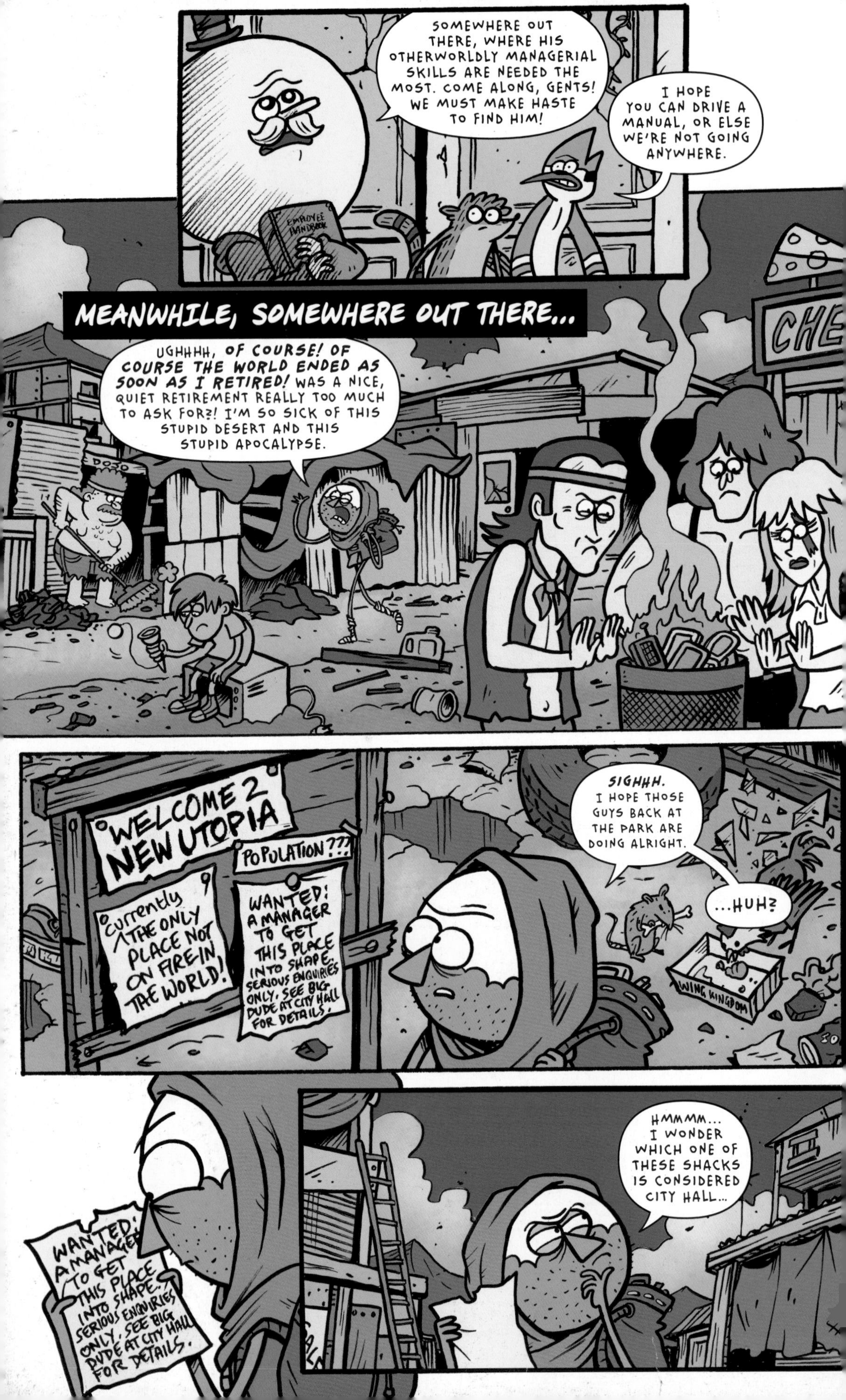

SOMEWHERE OUT THERE, WHERE HIS OTHERWORLDLY MANAGERIAL SKILLS ARE NEEDED THE MOST. COME ALONG, GENTS! WE MUST MAKE HASTE TO FIND HIM!
I HOPE YOU CAN DRIVE A MANUAL, OR ELSE WE'RE NOT GOING ANYWHERE.
EMPLOYEE HANDBOOK
MEANWHILE, SOMEWHERE OUT THERE...
UGHHHH, OF COURSE! OF COURSE THE WORLD ENDED AS SOON AS I RETIRED! WAS A NICE, QUIET RETIREMENT REALLY TOO MUCH TO ASK FOR?! I'M SO SICK OF THIS STUPID DESERT AND THIS STUPID APOCALYPSE.
DOJO
WELCOME 2 NEW UTOPIA
POPULATION ???
Currently THE ONLY PLACE NOT ON FIRE IN THE WORLD!
WANTED: A MANAGER TO GET THIS PLACE INTO SHAPE. SERIOUS ENQUIRIES ONLY. SEE BIG DUDE AT CITY HALL FOR DETAILS.
SIGHHH. I HOPE THOSE GUYS BACK AT THE PARK ARE DOING ALRIGHT.
...HUH?
WING KINGDOM
WANTED: A MANAGER TO GET THIS PLACE INTO SHAPE. SERIOUS ENQUIRIES ONLY. SEE BIG DUDE AT CITY HALL FOR DETAILS.
HMMMM... I WONDER WHICH ONE OF THESE SHACKS IS CONSIDERED CITY HALL...

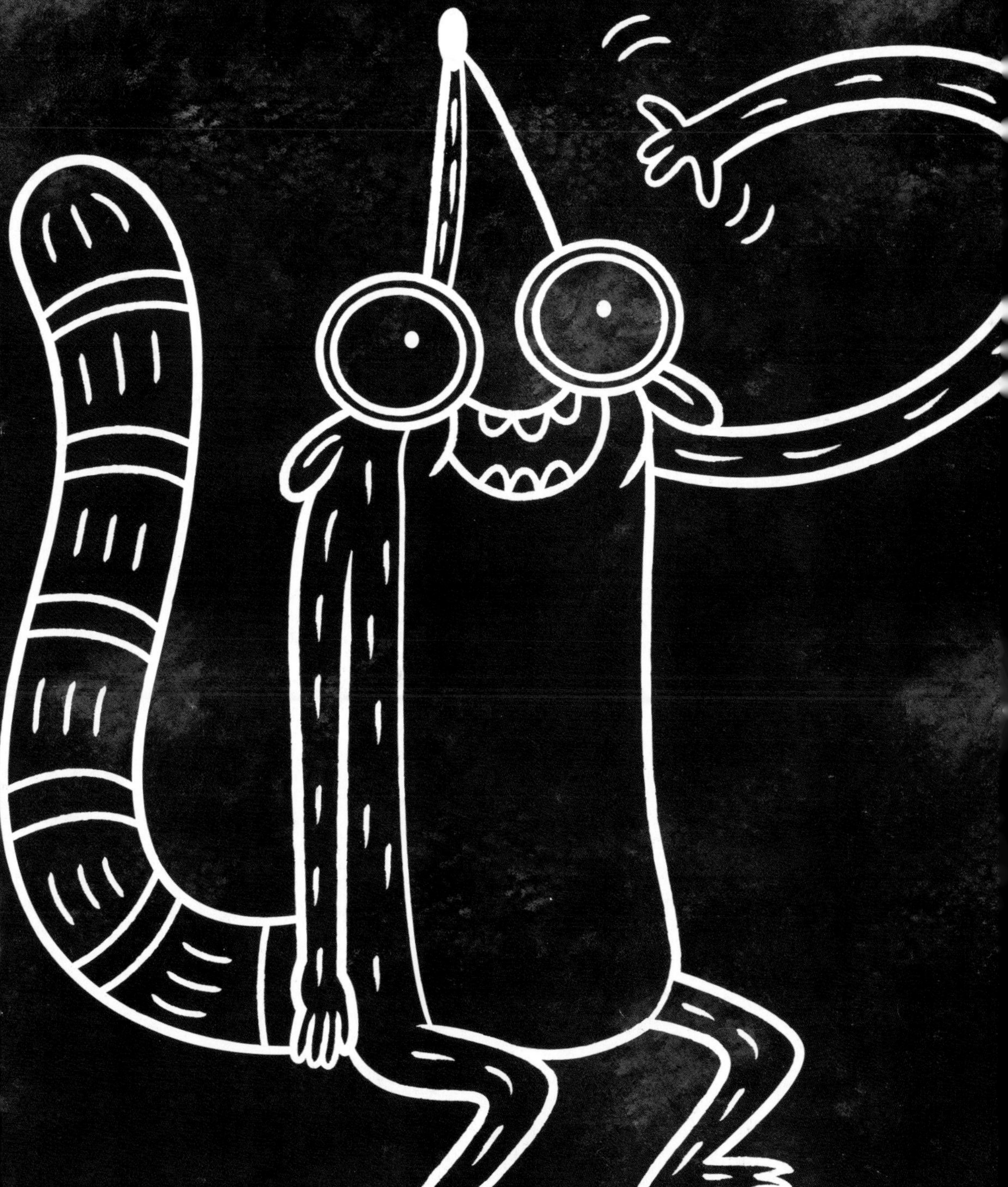

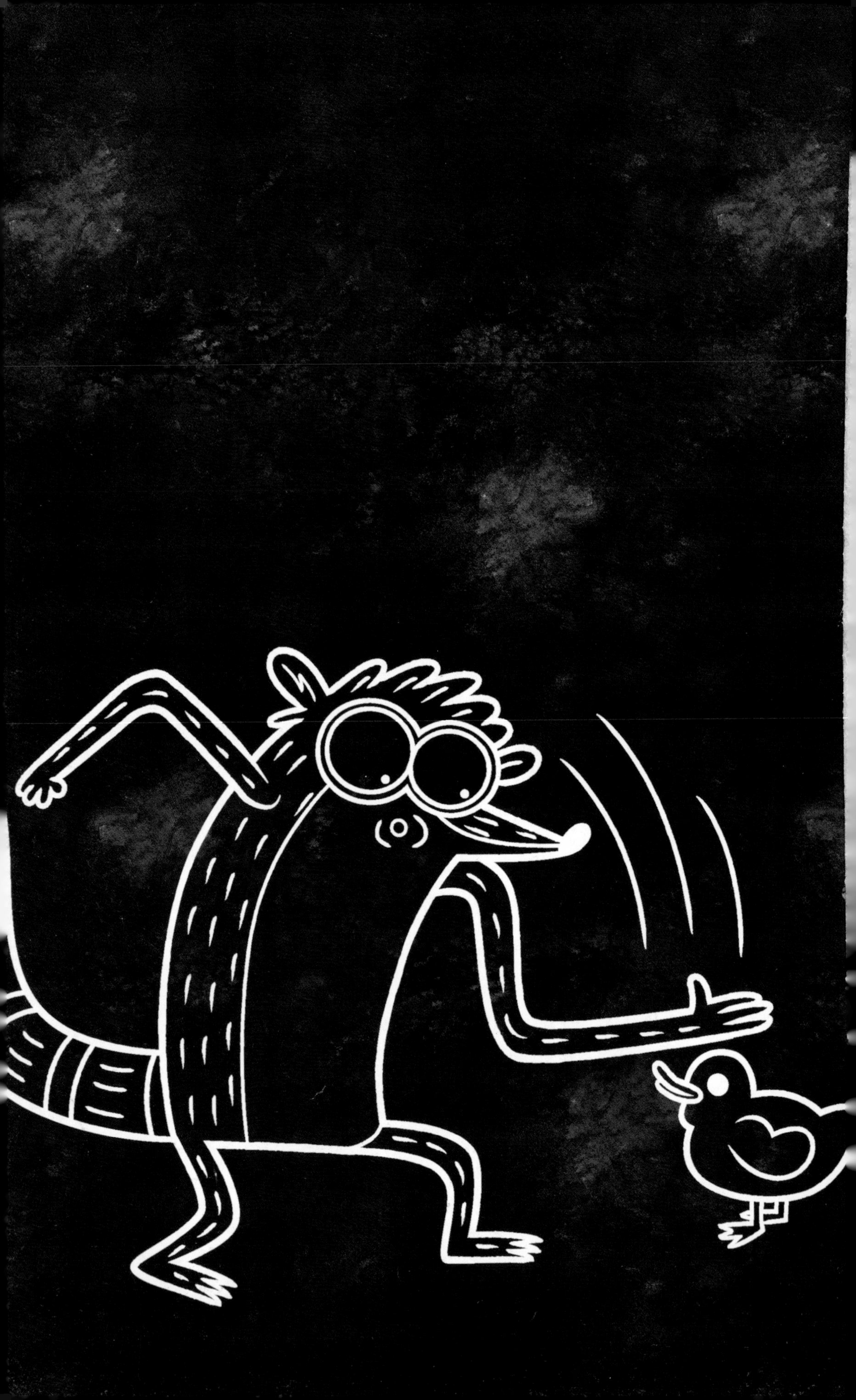

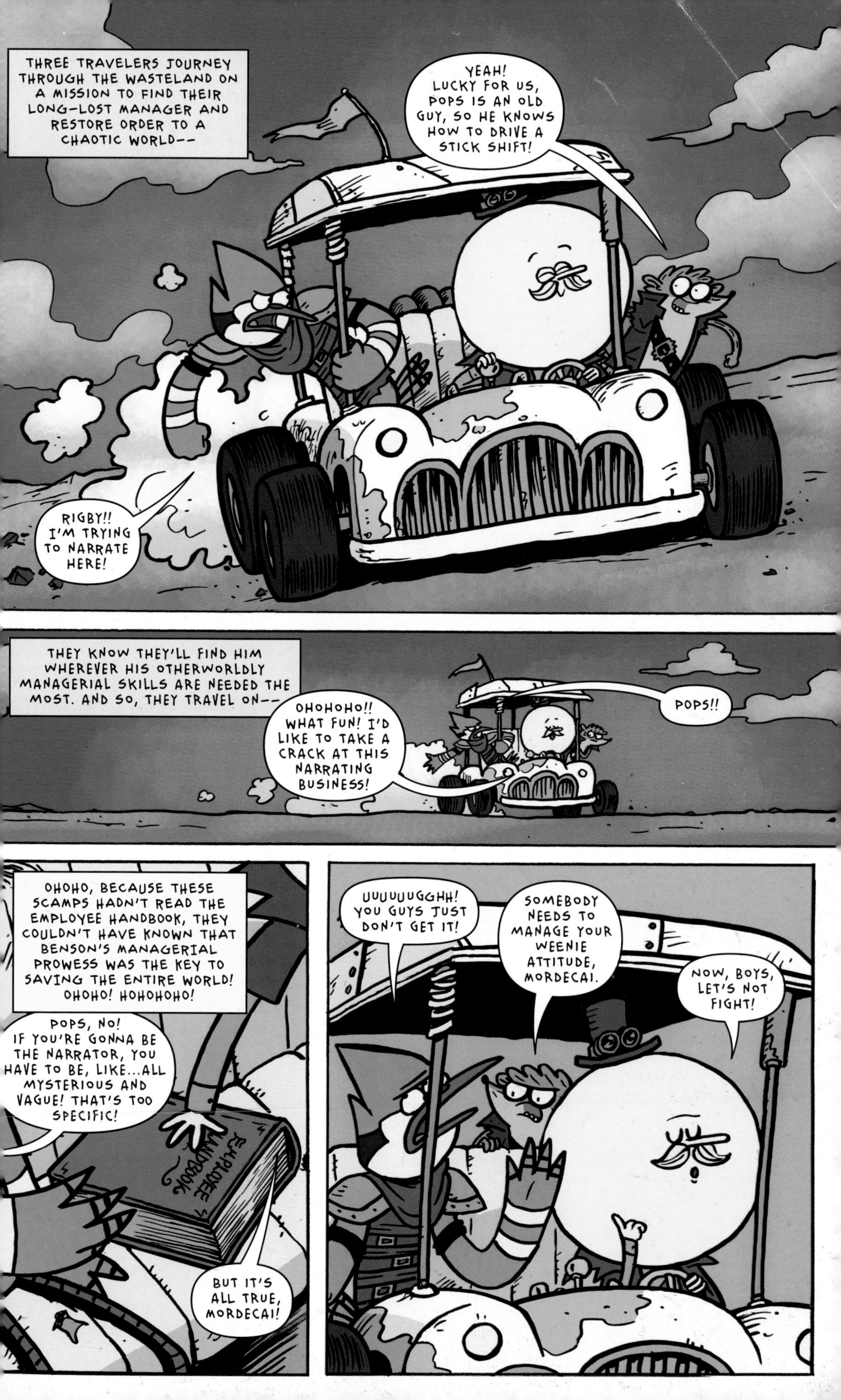

THREE TRAVELERS JOURNEY THROUGH THE WASTELAND ON A MISSION TO FIND THEIR LONG-LOST MANAGER AND RESTORE ORDER TO A CHAOTIC WORLD--
YEAH! LUCKY FOR US, POPS IS AN OLD GUY, SO HE KNOWS HOW TO DRIVE A STICK SHIFT!
RIGBY!! I'M TRYING TO NARRATE HERE!
THEY KNOW THEY'LL FIND HIM WHEREVER HIS OTHERWORLDLY MANAGERIAL SKILLS ARE NEEDED THE MOST. AND SO, THEY TRAVEL ON--
POPS!!
OHOHOHO!! WHAT FUN! I'D LIKE TO TAKE A CRACK AT THIS NARRATING BUSINESS!
OHOHO, BECAUSE THESE SCAMPS HADN'T READ THE EMPLOYEE HANDBOOK, THEY COULDN'T HAVE KNOWN THAT BENSON'S MANAGERIAL PROWESS WAS THE KEY TO SAVING THE ENTIRE WORLD! OHOHO! HOHOHOHO!
POPS, NO! IF YOU'RE GONNA BE THE NARRATOR, YOU HAVE TO BE, LIKE...ALL MYSTERIOUS AND VAGUE! THAT'S TOO SPECIFIC!
EMPLOYEE HANDBOOK
BUT IT'S ALL TRUE, MORDECAI!
UUUUUUGGHH! YOU GUYS JUST DON'T GET IT!
SOMEBODY NEEDS TO MANAGE YOUR WEENIE ATTITUDE, MORDECAI.
NOW, BOYS, LET'S NOT FIGHT!

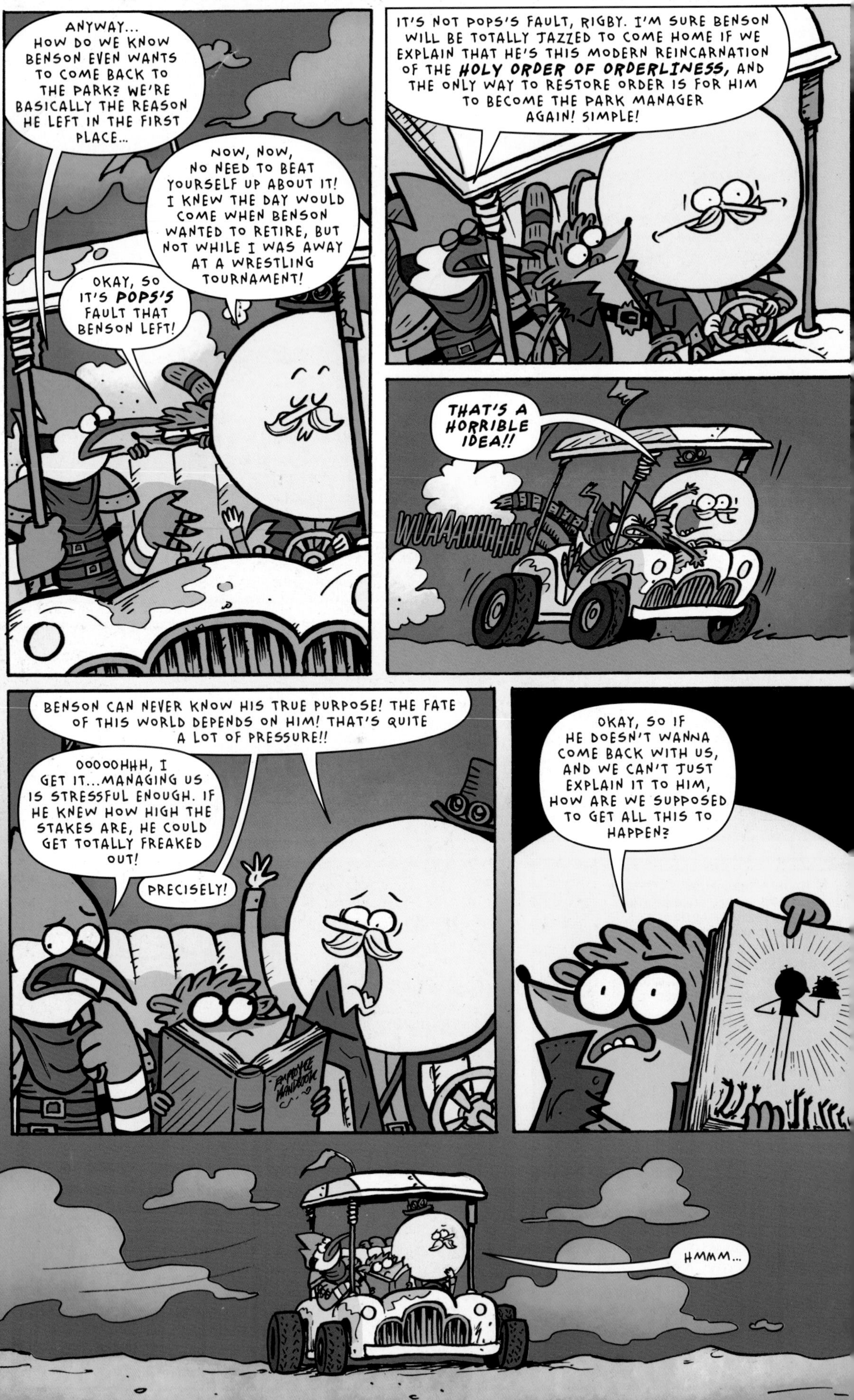
ANYWAY... HOW DO WE KNOW BENSON EVEN WANTS TO COME BACK TO THE PARK? WE'RE BASICALLY THE REASON HE LEFT IN THE FIRST PLACE...
NOW, NOW, NO NEED TO BEAT YOURSELF UP ABOUT IT! I KNEW THE DAY WOULD COME WHEN BENSON WANTED TO RETIRE, BUT NOT WHILE I WAS AWAY AT A WRESTLING TOURNAMENT!
OKAY, SO IT'S POPS'S FAULT THAT BENSON LEFT!
IT'S NOT POPS'S FAULT, RIGBY. I'M SURE BENSON WILL BE TOTALLY JAZZED TO COME HOME IF WE EXPLAIN THAT HE'S THIS MODERN REINCARNATION OF THE HOLY ORDER OF ORDERLINESS, AND THE ONLY WAY TO RESTORE ORDER IS FOR HIM TO BECOME THE PARK MANAGER AGAIN! SIMPLE!
THAT'S A HORRIBLE IDEA!!
WUAAAHHHH!
BENSON CAN NEVER KNOW HIS TRUE PURPOSE! THE FATE OF THIS WORLD DEPENDS ON HIM! THAT'S QUITE A LOT OF PRESSURE!!
OOOOOHHH, I GET IT...MANAGING US IS STRESSFUL ENOUGH. IF HE KNEW HOW HIGH THE STAKES ARE, HE COULD GET TOTALLY FREAKED OUT!
PRECISELY!
EMPLOYEE HANDBOOK
OKAY, SO IF HE DOESN'T WANNA COME BACK WITH US, AND WE CAN'T JUST EXPLAIN IT TO HIM, HOW ARE WE SUPPOSED TO GET ALL THIS TO HAPPEN?
HMMM...

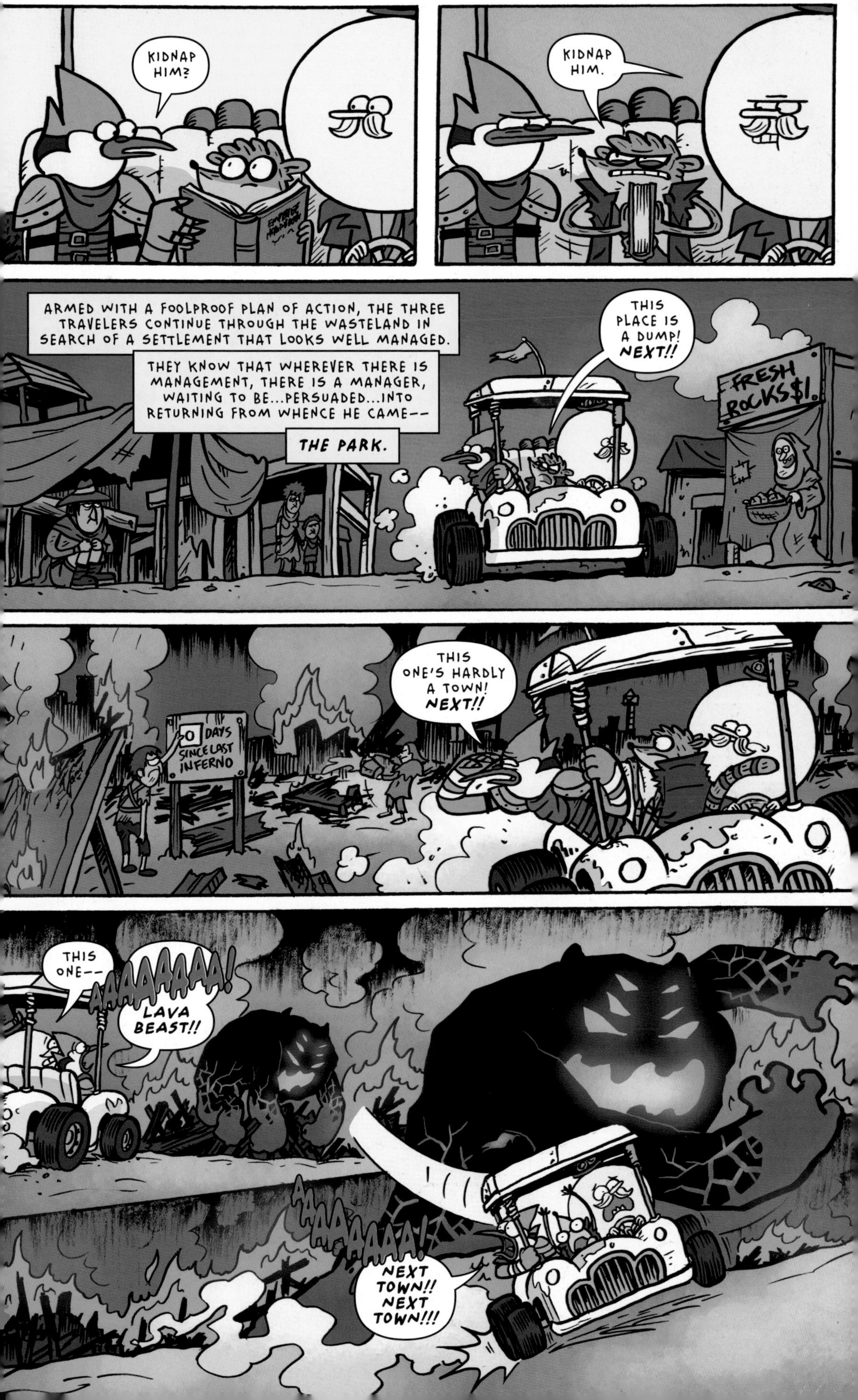
KIDNAP HIM?
KIDNAP HIM.
ARMED WITH A FOOLPROOF PLAN OF ACTION, THE THREE TRAVELERS CONTINUE THROUGH THE WASTELAND IN SEARCH OF A SETTLEMENT THAT LOOKS WELL MANAGED.
THEY KNOW THAT WHEREVER THERE IS MANAGEMENT, THERE IS A MANAGER, WAITING TO BE...PERSUADED...INTO RETURNING FROM WHENCE HE CAME--
THE PARK.
THIS PLACE IS A DUMP! NEXT!!
FRESH ROCKS $1.
THIS ONE'S HARDLY A TOWN! NEXT!!
0 DAYS SINCE LAST INFERNO
THIS ONE--
AAAAAAAA!
LAVA BEAST!!
AAAAAAAA!
NEXT TOWN!! NEXT TOWN!!!

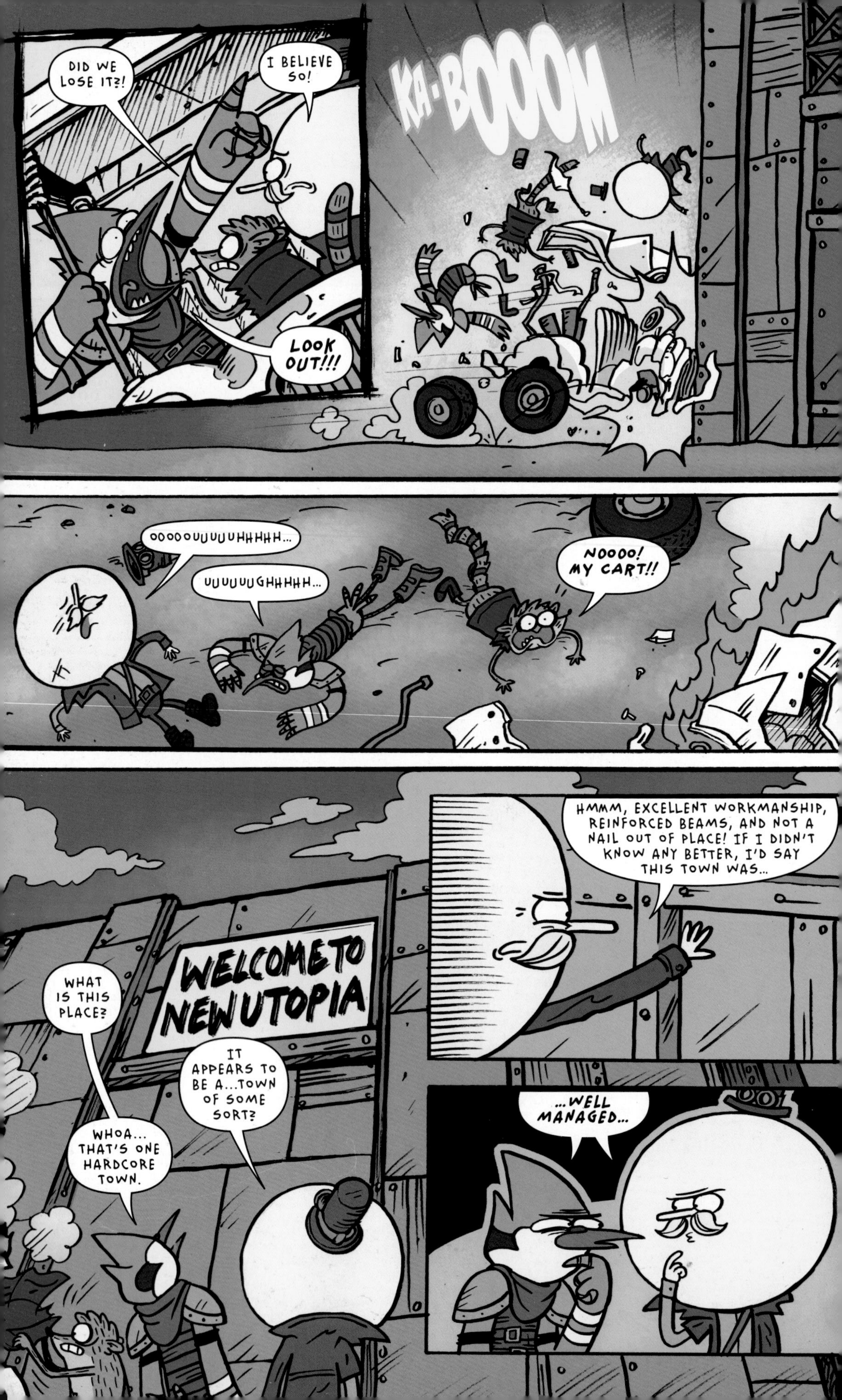
DID WE LOSE IT?!
I BELIEVE SO!
LOOK OUT!!!
KA-BOOOOM
OOOOOUUUUUHHHHH...
UUUUUGHHHHH...
NOOOO! MY CART!!
HMMM, EXCELLENT WORKMANSHIP, REINFORCED BEAMS, AND NOT A NAIL OUT OF PLACE! IF I DIDN'T KNOW ANY BETTER, I'D SAY THIS TOWN WAS...
WELCOME TO NEW UTOPIA
WHAT IS THIS PLACE?
IT APPEARS TO BE A...TOWN OF SOME SORT?
WHOA... THAT'S ONE HARDCORE TOWN.
...WELL MANAGED...

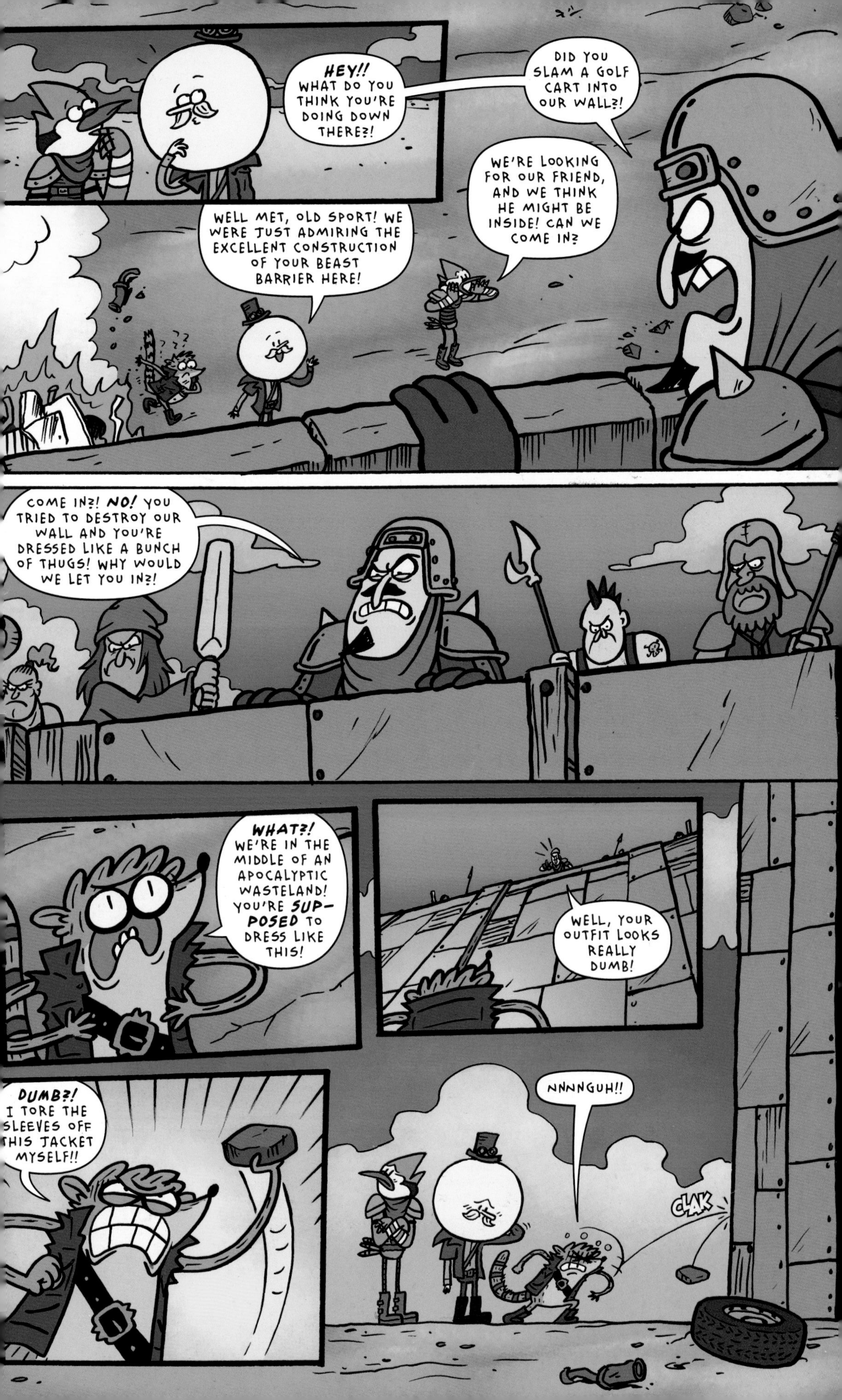
HEY!! WHAT DO YOU THINK YOU'RE DOING DOWN THERE?!
DID YOU SLAM A GOLF CART INTO OUR WALL?!
WELL MET, OLD SPORT! WE WERE JUST ADMIRING THE EXCELLENT CONSTRUCTION OF YOUR BEAST BARRIER HERE!
WE'RE LOOKING FOR OUR FRIEND, AND WE THINK HE MIGHT BE INSIDE! CAN WE COME IN?
COME IN?! NO! YOU TRIED TO DESTROY OUR WALL AND YOU'RE DRESSED LIKE A BUNCH OF THUGS! WHY WOULD WE LET YOU IN?!
WHAT?! WE'RE IN THE MIDDLE OF AN APOCALYPTIC WASTELAND! YOU'RE SUPPOSED TO DRESS LIKE THIS!
WELL, YOUR OUTFIT LOOKS REALLY DUMB!
DUMB?! I TORE THE SLEEVES OFF THIS JACKET MYSELF!!
NNNNGUH!!
CLAK

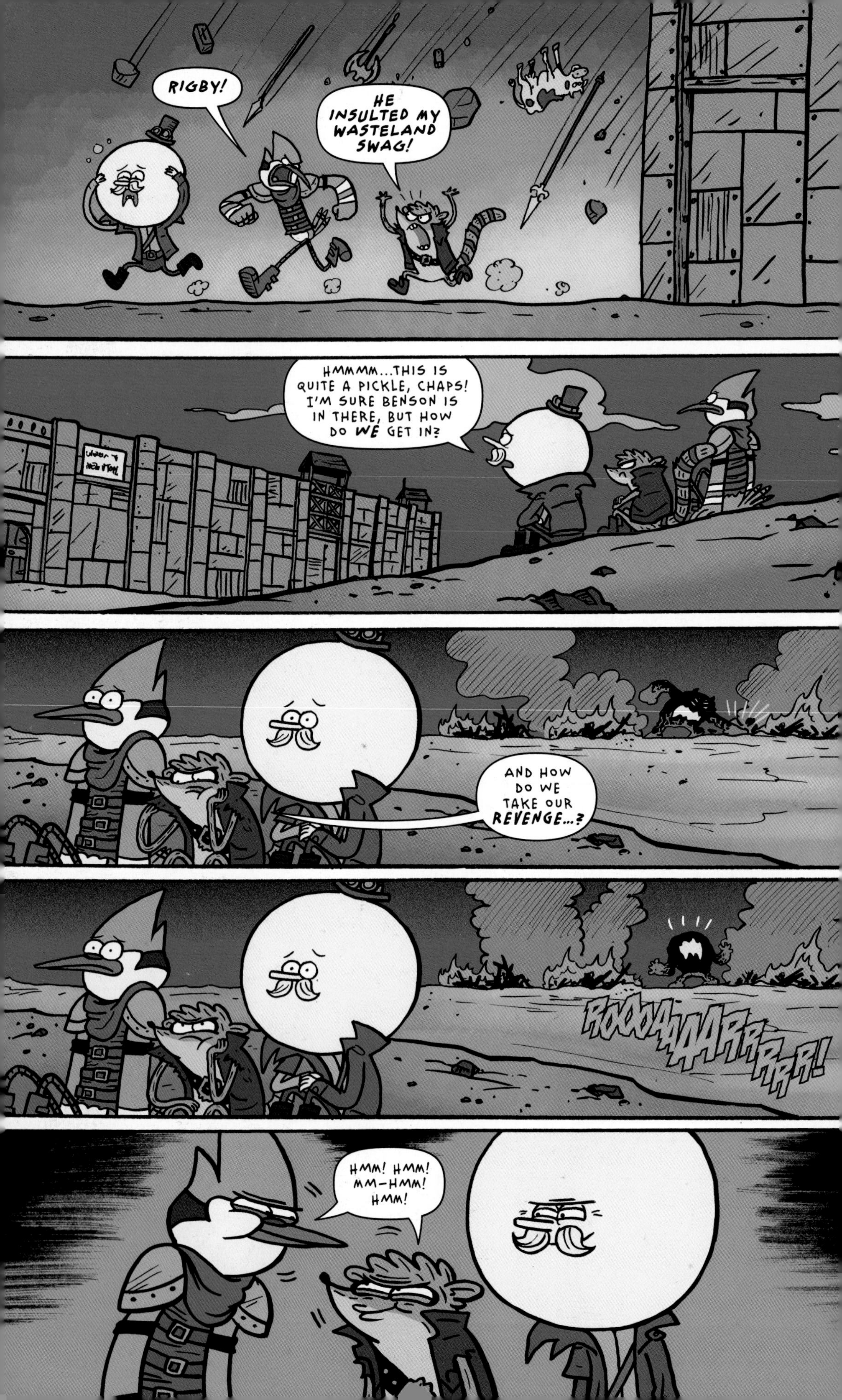
RIGBY!
HE INSULTED MY WASTELAND SWAG!
HMMMM...THIS IS QUITE A PICKLE, CHAPS! I'M SURE BENSON IS IN THERE, BUT HOW DO WE GET IN?
AND HOW DO WE TAKE OUR REVENGE...?
ROOOAAAARRRRR!
HMM! HMM! MM-HMM! HMM!

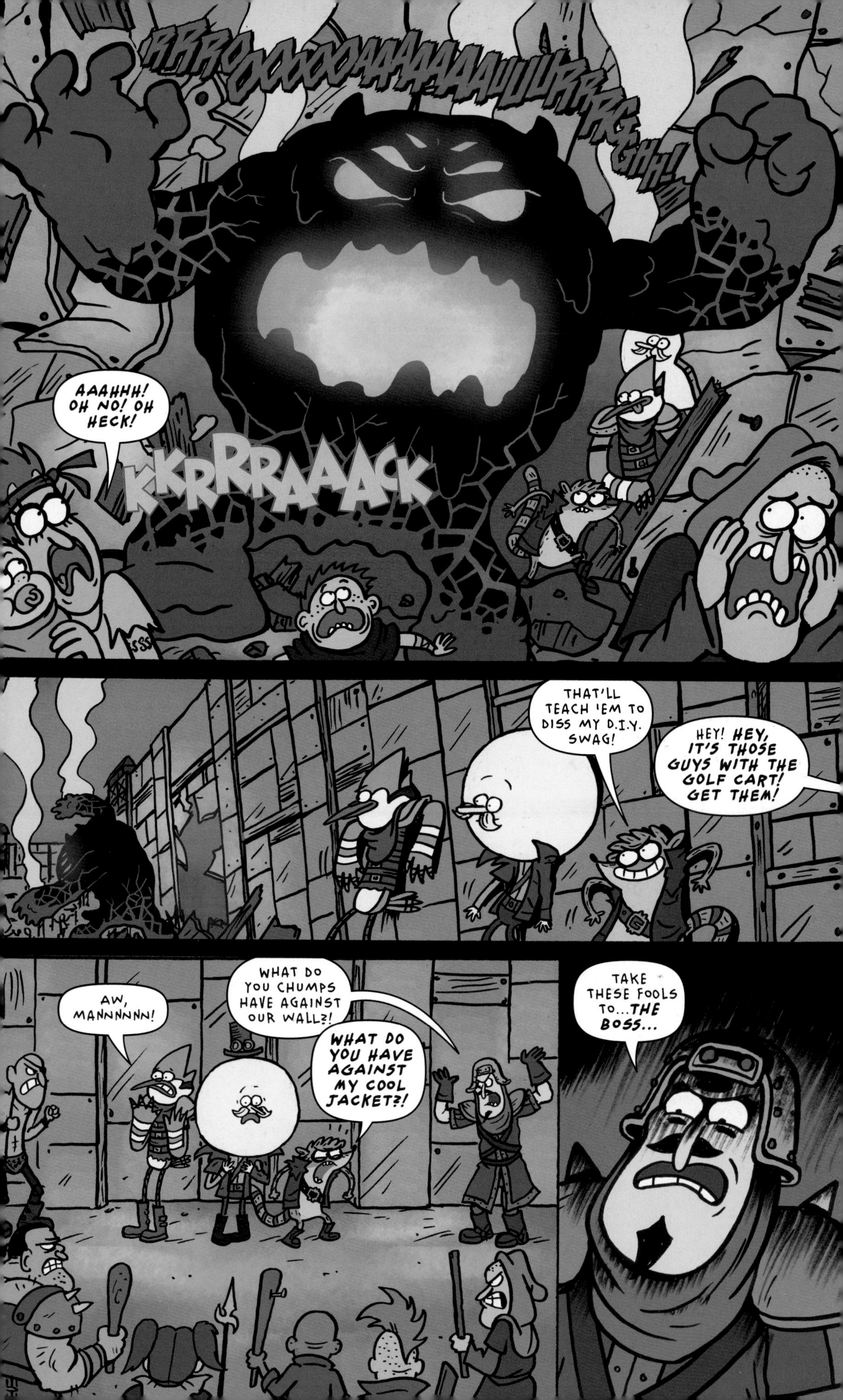
RRROOOOOOAAAAAAAAUUURRRGHH!
AAAHHH! OH NO! OH HECK!
KKRRRAAAACK
THAT'LL TEACH 'EM TO DISS MY D.I.Y. SWAG!
HEY! HEY, IT'S THOSE GUYS WITH THE GOLF CART! GET THEM!
AW, MANNNNNN!
WHAT DO YOU CHUMPS HAVE AGAINST OUR WALL?!
WHAT DO YOU HAVE AGAINST MY COOL JACKET?!
TAKE THESE FOOLS TO...THE BOSS...

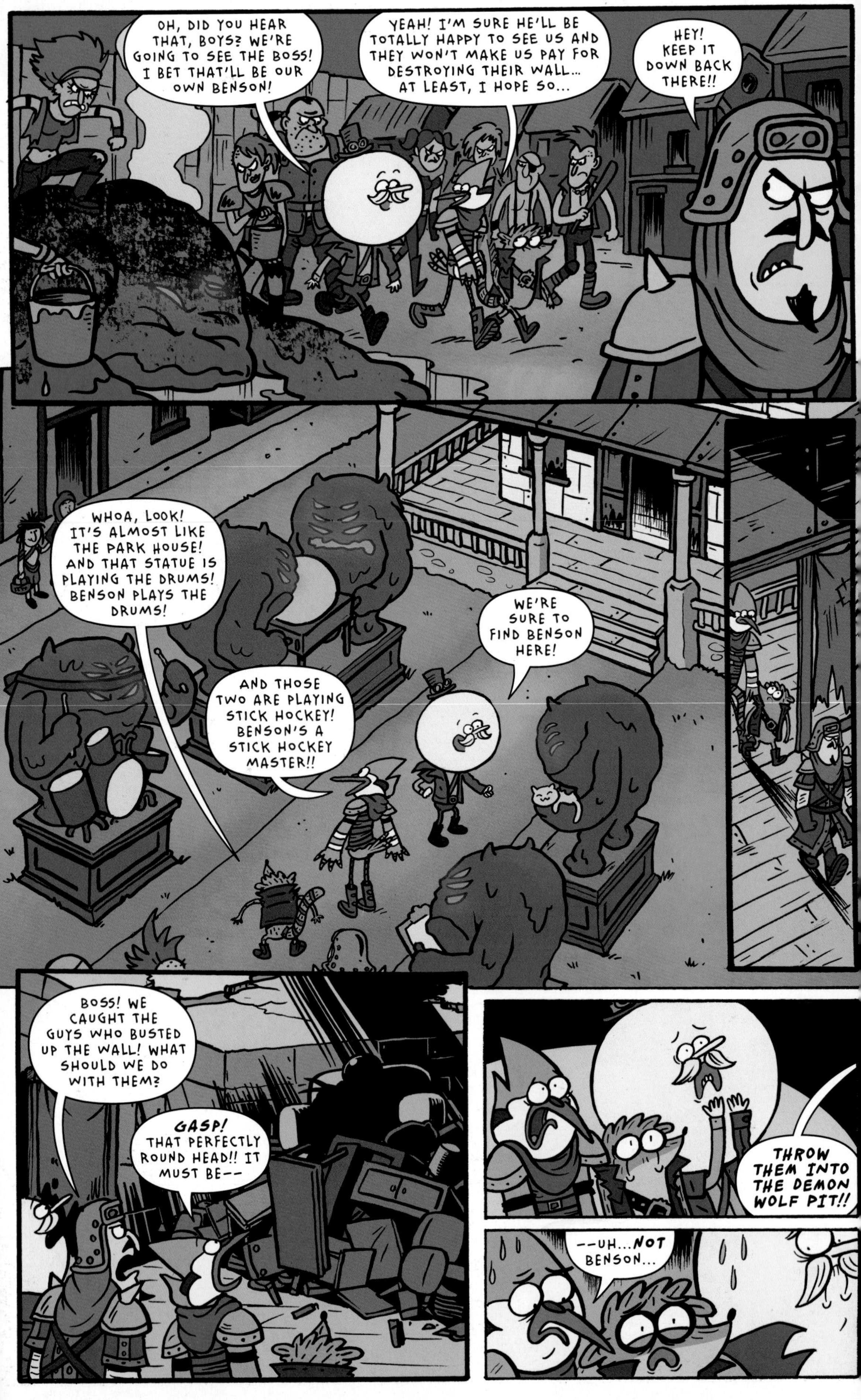
OH, DID YOU HEAR THAT, BOYS? WE'RE GOING TO SEE THE BOSS! I BET THAT'LL BE OUR OWN BENSON!
YEAH! I'M SURE HE'LL BE TOTALLY HAPPY TO SEE US AND THEY WON'T MAKE US PAY FOR DESTROYING THEIR WALL... AT LEAST, I HOPE SO...
HEY! KEEP IT DOWN BACK THERE!!
WHOA, LOOK! IT'S ALMOST LIKE THE PARK HOUSE! AND THAT STATUE IS PLAYING THE DRUMS! BENSON PLAYS THE DRUMS!
AND THOSE TWO ARE PLAYING STICK HOCKEY! BENSON'S A STICK HOCKEY MASTER!!
WE'RE SURE TO FIND BENSON HERE!
BOSS! WE CAUGHT THE GUYS WHO BUSTED UP THE WALL! WHAT SHOULD WE DO WITH THEM?
GASP! THAT PERFECTLY ROUND HEAD!! IT MUST BE--
THROW THEM INTO THE DEMON WOLF PIT!!
--UH...NOT BENSON...

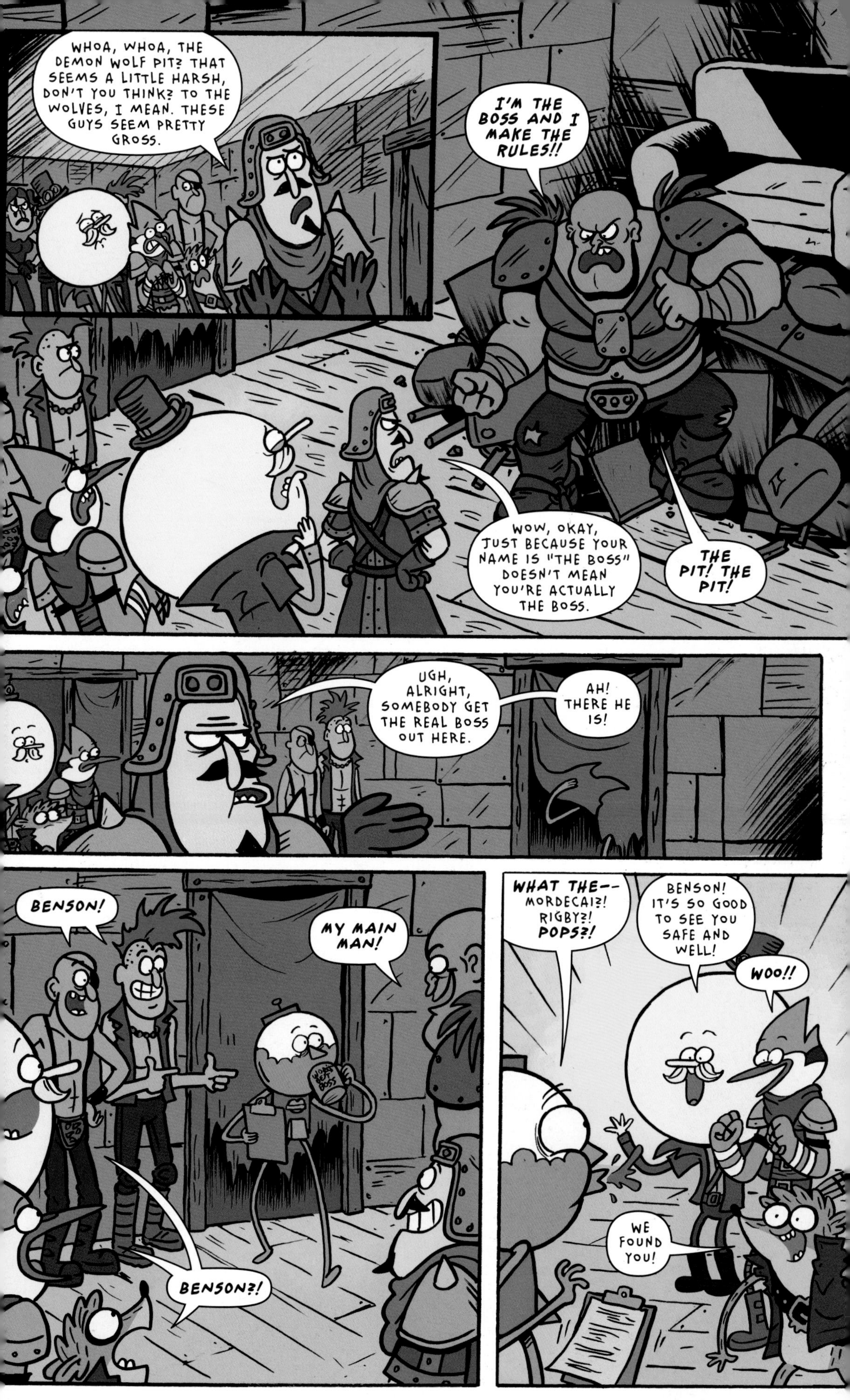

WHOA, WHOA, THE DEMON WOLF PIT? THAT SEEMS A LITTLE HARSH, DON'T YOU THINK? TO THE WOLVES, I MEAN. THESE GUYS SEEM PRETTY GROSS.
I'M THE BOSS AND I MAKE THE RULES!!
WOW, OKAY, JUST BECAUSE YOUR NAME IS "THE BOSS" DOESN'T MEAN YOU'RE ACTUALLY THE BOSS.
THE PIT! THE PIT!
UGH, ALRIGHT, SOMEBODY GET THE REAL BOSS OUT HERE.
AH! THERE HE IS!
BENSON!
MY MAIN MAN!
BENSON?!
WHAT THE-- MORDECAI?! RIGBY?! POPS?!
BENSON! IT'S SO GOOD TO SEE YOU SAFE AND WELL!
WOO!!
WE FOUND YOU!

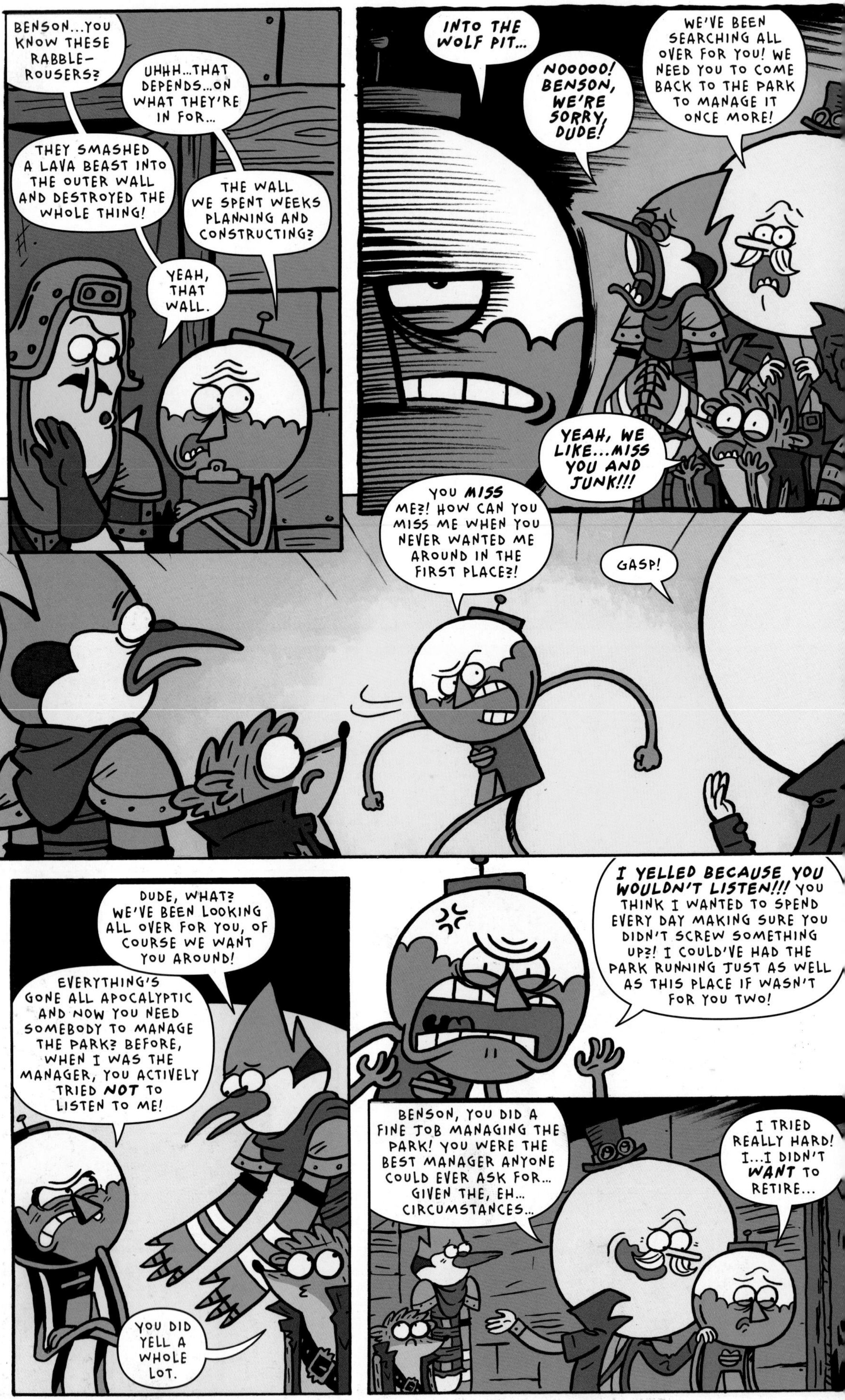
BENSON...YOU KNOW THESE RABBLE-ROUSERS?
UHHH...THAT DEPENDS...ON WHAT THEY'RE IN FOR...
THEY SMASHED A LAVA BEAST INTO THE OUTER WALL AND DESTROYED THE WHOLE THING!
THE WALL WE SPENT WEEKS PLANNING AND CONSTRUCTING?
YEAH, THAT WALL.
INTO THE WOLF PIT...
NOOOOO! BENSON, WE'RE SORRY, DUDE!
WE'VE BEEN SEARCHING ALL OVER FOR YOU! WE NEED YOU TO COME BACK TO THE PARK TO MANAGE IT ONCE MORE!
YEAH, WE LIKE...MISS YOU AND JUNK!!!
YOU MISS ME?! HOW CAN YOU MISS ME WHEN YOU NEVER WANTED ME AROUND IN THE FIRST PLACE?!
GASP!
DUDE, WHAT? WE'VE BEEN LOOKING ALL OVER FOR YOU, OF COURSE WE WANT YOU AROUND!
EVERYTHING'S GONE ALL APOCALYPTIC AND NOW YOU NEED SOMEBODY TO MANAGE THE PARK? BEFORE, WHEN I WAS THE MANAGER, YOU ACTIVELY TRIED NOT TO LISTEN TO ME!
YOU DID YELL A WHOLE LOT.
I YELLED BECAUSE YOU WOULDN'T LISTEN!!! YOU THINK I WANTED TO SPEND EVERY DAY MAKING SURE YOU DIDN'T SCREW SOMETHING UP?! I COULD'VE HAD THE PARK RUNNING JUST AS WELL AS THIS PLACE IF WASN'T FOR YOU TWO!
BENSON, YOU DID A FINE JOB MANAGING THE PARK! YOU WERE THE BEST MANAGER ANYONE COULD EVER ASK FOR... GIVEN THE, EH... CIRCUMSTANCES...
I TRIED REALLY HARD! I...I DIDN'T WANT TO RETIRE...

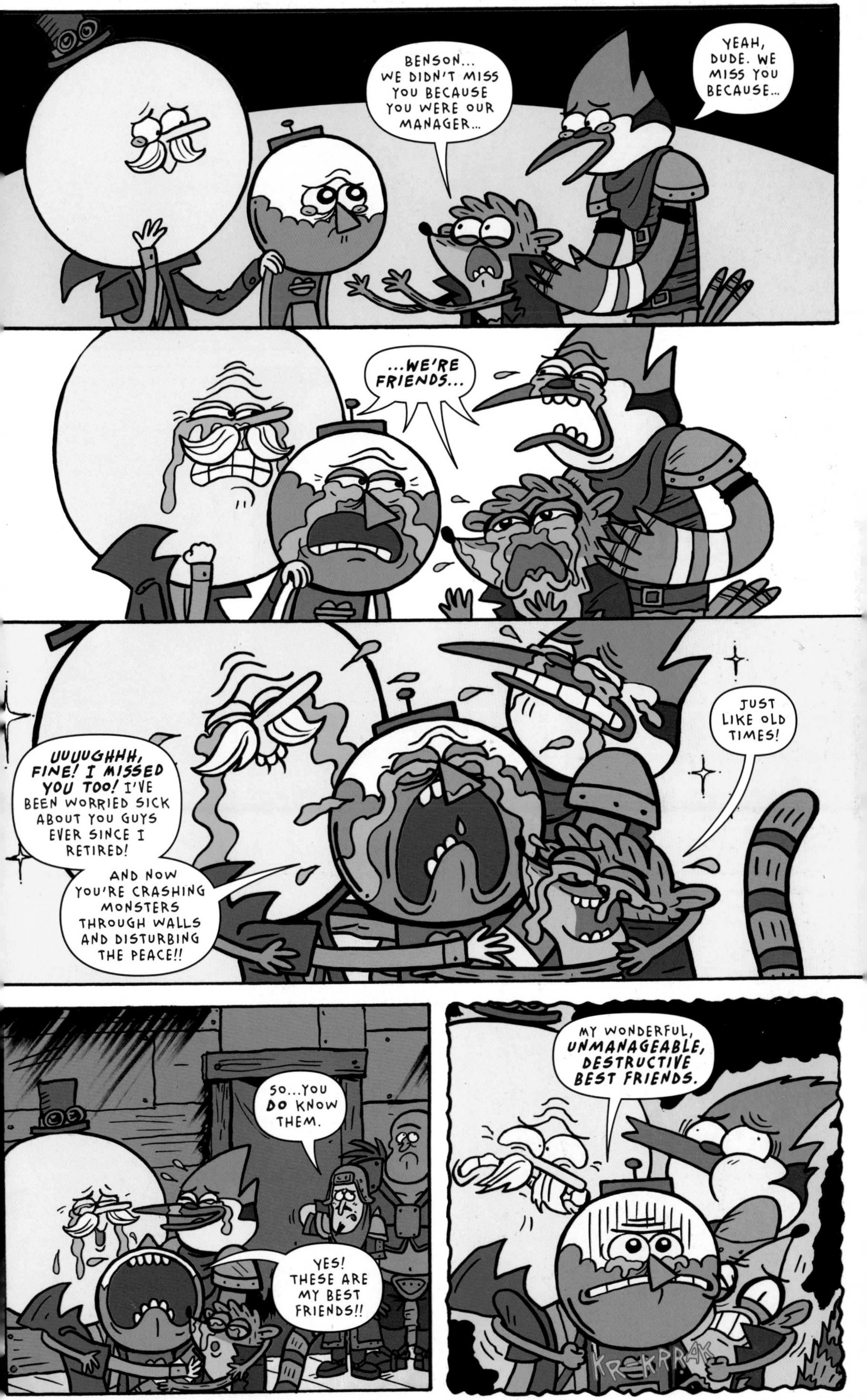
BENSON... WE DIDN'T MISS YOU BECAUSE YOU WERE OUR MANAGER...
YEAH, DUDE. WE MISS YOU BECAUSE...
...WE'RE FRIENDS...
UUUUGHHH, FINE! I MISSED YOU TOO! I'VE BEEN WORRIED SICK ABOUT YOU GUYS EVER SINCE I RETIRED!
AND NOW YOU'RE CRASHING MONSTERS THROUGH WALLS AND DISTURBING THE PEACE!!
JUST LIKE OLD TIMES!
SO...YOU DO KNOW THEM.
YES! THESE ARE MY BEST FRIENDS!!
MY WONDERFUL, UNMANAGEABLE, DESTRUCTIVE BEST FRIENDS.
KREKKRAK

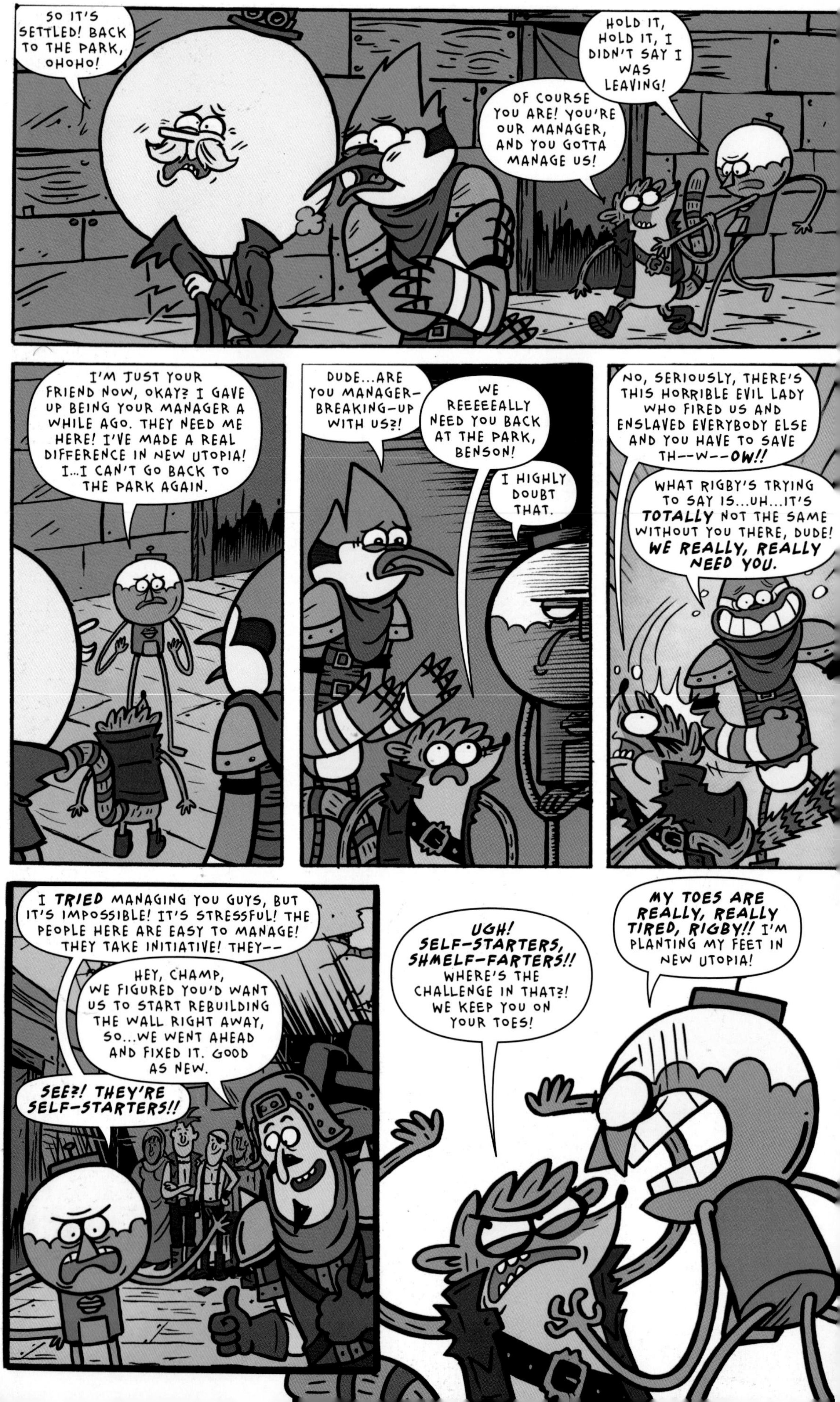
SO IT'S SETTLED! BACK TO THE PARK, OHOHO!
HOLD IT, HOLD IT, I DIDN'T SAY I WAS LEAVING!
OF COURSE YOU ARE! YOU'RE OUR MANAGER, AND YOU GOTTA MANAGE US!
I'M JUST YOUR FRIEND NOW, OKAY? I GAVE UP BEING YOUR MANAGER A WHILE AGO. THEY NEED ME HERE! I'VE MADE A REAL DIFFERENCE IN NEW UTOPIA! I...I CAN'T GO BACK TO THE PARK AGAIN.
DUDE...ARE YOU MANAGER-BREAKING-UP WITH US?!
WE REEEEEALLY NEED YOU BACK AT THE PARK, BENSON!
I HIGHLY DOUBT THAT.
NO, SERIOUSLY, THERE'S THIS HORRIBLE EVIL LADY WHO FIRED US AND ENSLAVED EVERYBODY ELSE AND YOU HAVE TO SAVE TH--W--OW!!
WHAT RIGBY'S TRYING TO SAY IS...UH...IT'S TOTALLY NOT THE SAME WITHOUT YOU THERE, DUDE! WE REALLY, REALLY NEED YOU.
I TRIED MANAGING YOU GUYS, BUT IT'S IMPOSSIBLE! IT'S STRESSFUL! THE PEOPLE HERE ARE EASY TO MANAGE! THEY TAKE INITIATIVE! THEY--
HEY, CHAMP, WE FIGURED YOU'D WANT US TO START REBUILDING THE WALL RIGHT AWAY, SO...WE WENT AHEAD AND FIXED IT. GOOD AS NEW.
SEE?! THEY'RE SELF-STARTERS!!
UGH! SELF-STARTERS, SHMELF-FARTERS!! WHERE'S THE CHALLENGE IN THAT?! WE KEEP YOU ON YOUR TOES!
MY TOES ARE REALLY, REALLY TIRED, RIGBY!! I'M PLANTING MY FEET IN NEW UTOPIA!

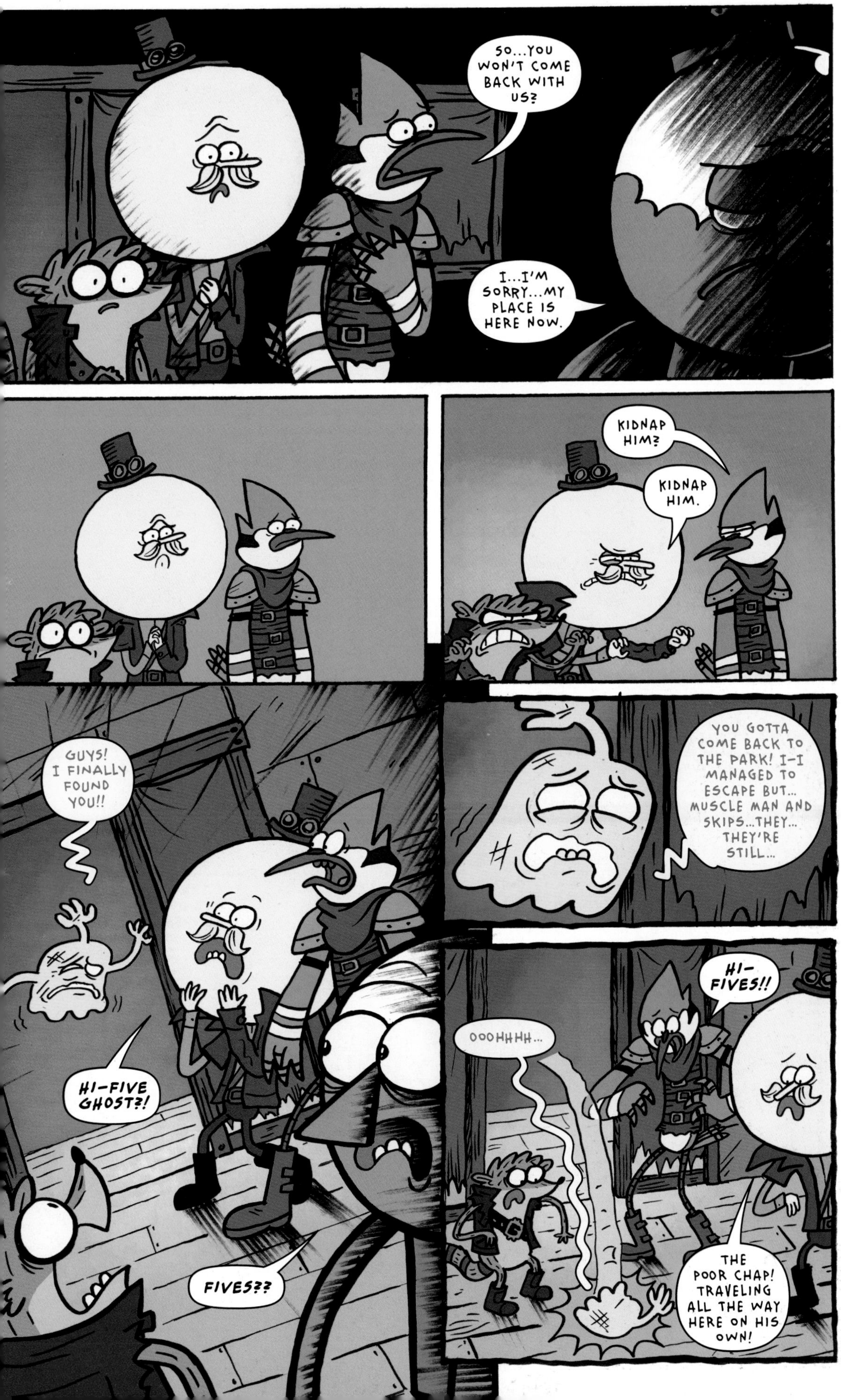
SO...YOU WON'T COME BACK WITH US?
I...I'M SORRY...MY PLACE IS HERE NOW.
KIDNAP HIM?
KIDNAP HIM.
GUYS! I FINALLY FOUND YOU!!
HI-FIVE GHOST?!
FIVES??
YOU GOTTA COME BACK TO THE PARK! I-I MANAGED TO ESCAPE BUT... MUSCLE MAN AND SKIPS...THEY... THEY'RE STILL...
OOOHHHH...
HI-FIVES!!
THE POOR CHAP! TRAVELING ALL THE WAY HERE ON HIS OWN!

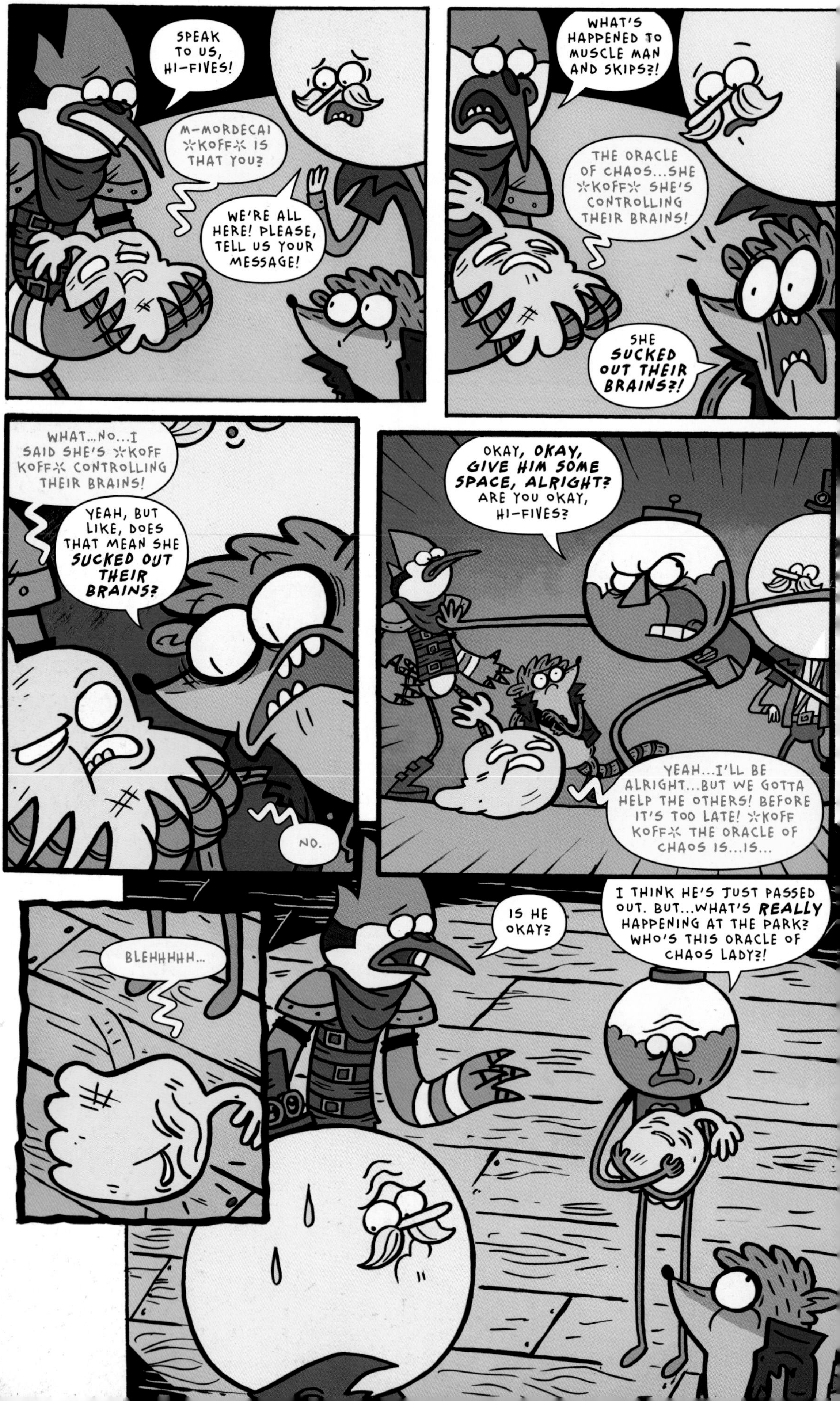

SPEAK TO US, HI-FIVES!
M-MORDECAI *KOFF* IS THAT YOU?
WE'RE ALL HERE! PLEASE, TELL US YOUR MESSAGE!
WHAT'S HAPPENED TO MUSCLE MAN AND SKIPS?!
THE ORACLE OF CHAOS...SHE *KOFF* SHE'S CONTROLLING THEIR BRAINS!
SHE SUCKED OUT THEIR BRAINS?!
WHAT...NO...I SAID SHE'S *KOFF KOFF* CONTROLLING THEIR BRAINS!
YEAH, BUT LIKE, DOES THAT MEAN SHE SUCKED OUT THEIR BRAINS?
NO.
OKAY, OKAY, GIVE HIM SOME SPACE, ALRIGHT? ARE YOU OKAY, HI-FIVES?
YEAH...I'LL BE ALRIGHT...BUT WE GOTTA HELP THE OTHERS! BEFORE IT'S TOO LATE! *KOFF KOFF* THE ORACLE OF CHAOS IS...IS...
BLEHHHHH...
IS HE OKAY?
I THINK HE'S JUST PASSED OUT. BUT...WHAT'S REALLY HAPPENING AT THE PARK? WHO'S THIS ORACLE OF CHAOS LADY?!

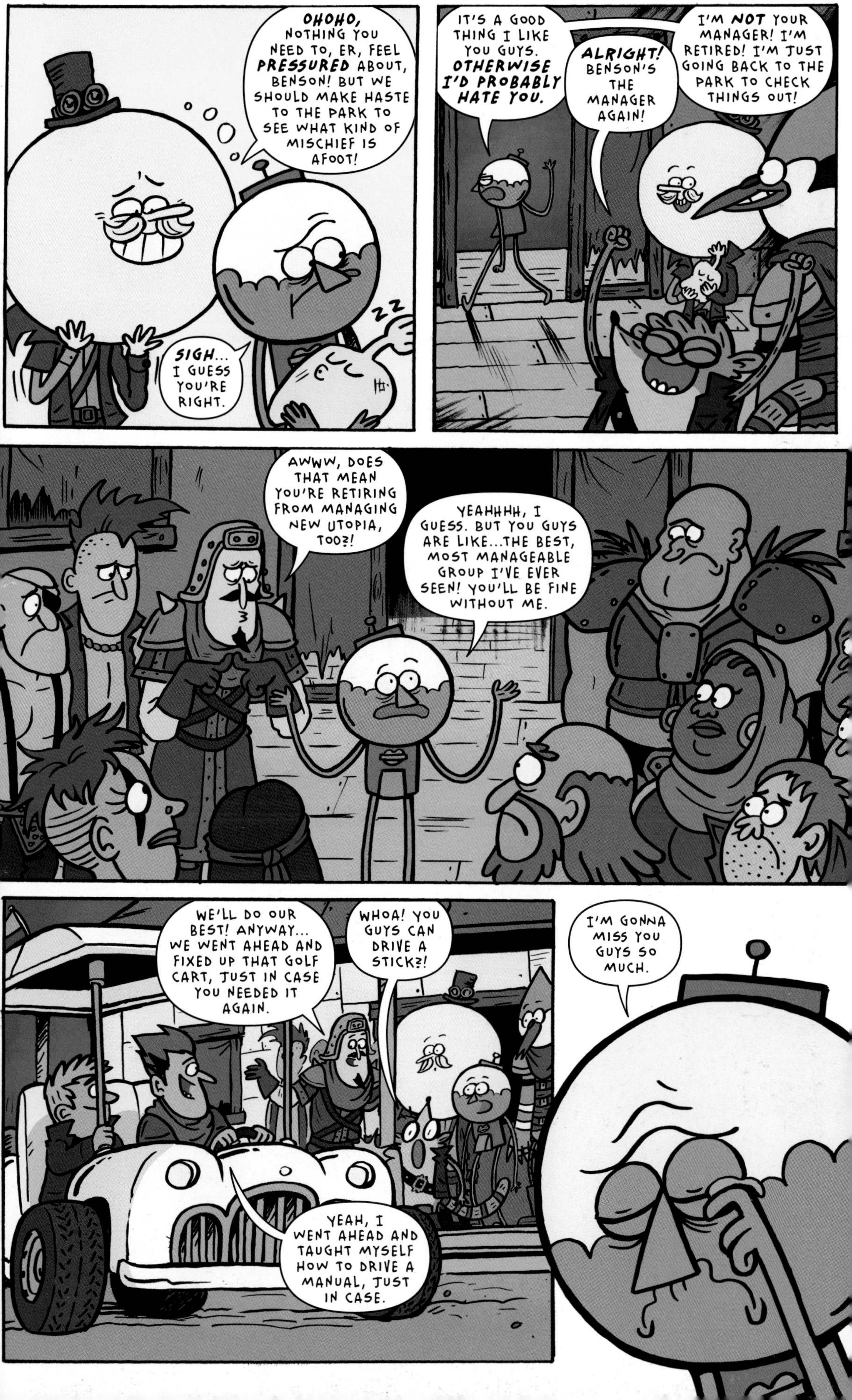
OHOHO, NOTHING YOU NEED TO, ER, FEEL PRESSURED ABOUT, BENSON! BUT WE SHOULD MAKE HASTE TO THE PARK TO SEE WHAT KIND OF MISCHIEF IS AFOOT!
ZZ
SIGH... I GUESS YOU'RE RIGHT.
IT'S A GOOD THING I LIKE YOU GUYS. OTHERWISE I'D PROBABLY HATE YOU.
ALRIGHT! BENSON'S THE MANAGER AGAIN!
I'M NOT YOUR MANAGER! I'M RETIRED! I'M JUST GOING BACK TO THE PARK TO CHECK THINGS OUT!
AWWW, DOES THAT MEAN YOU'RE RETIRING FROM MANAGING NEW UTOPIA, TOO?!
YEAHHHH, I GUESS. BUT YOU GUYS ARE LIKE...THE BEST, MOST MANAGEABLE GROUP I'VE EVER SEEN! YOU'LL BE FINE WITHOUT ME.
WE'LL DO OUR BEST! ANYWAY... WE WENT AHEAD AND FIXED UP THAT GOLF CART, JUST IN CASE YOU NEEDED IT AGAIN.
WHOA! YOU GUYS CAN DRIVE A STICK?!
YEAH, I WENT AHEAD AND TAUGHT MYSELF HOW TO DRIVE A MANUAL, JUST IN CASE.
I'M GONNA MISS YOU GUYS SO MUCH.

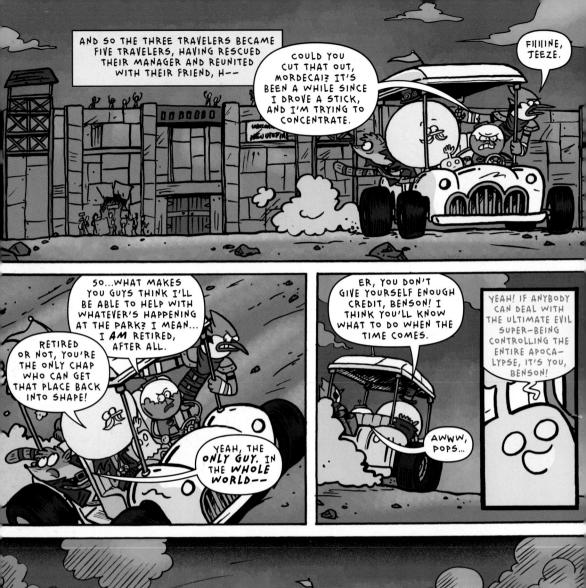

AND SO THE THREE TRAVELERS BECAME FIVE TRAVELERS, HAVING RESCUED THEIR MANAGER AND REUNITED WITH THEIR FRIEND, H--

COULD YOU CUT THAT OUT, MORDECAI? IT'S BEEN A WHILE SINCE I DROVE A STICK, AND I'M TRYING TO CONCENTRATE.

FIIIINE, JEEZE.

SO...WHAT MAKES YOU GUYS THINK I'LL BE ABLE TO HELP WITH WHATEVER'S HAPPENING AT THE PARK? I MEAN... I AM RETIRED, AFTER ALL.

RETIRED OR NOT, YOU'RE THE ONLY CHAP WHO CAN GET THAT PLACE BACK INTO SHAPE!

YEAH, THE ONLY GUY. IN THE WHOLE WORLD--

ER, YOU DON'T GIVE YOURSELF ENOUGH CREDIT, BENSON! I THINK YOU'LL KNOW WHAT TO DO WHEN THE TIME COMES.

YEAH! IF ANYBODY CAN DEAL WITH THE ULTIMATE EVIL SUPER-BEING CONTROLLING THE ENTIRE APOCA-LYPSE, IT'S YOU, BENSON!

AWWW, POPS...

WAIT, WHAT?

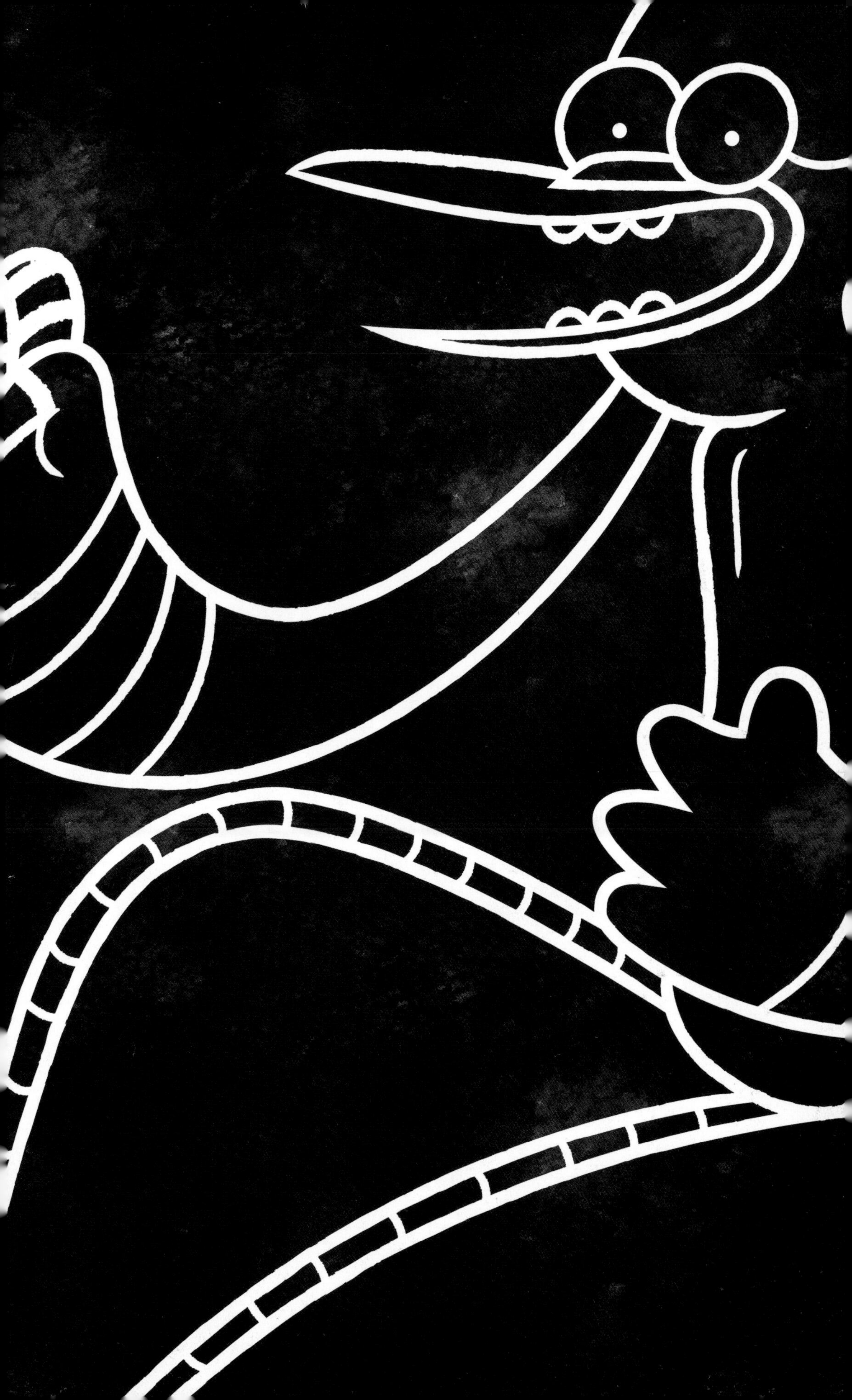

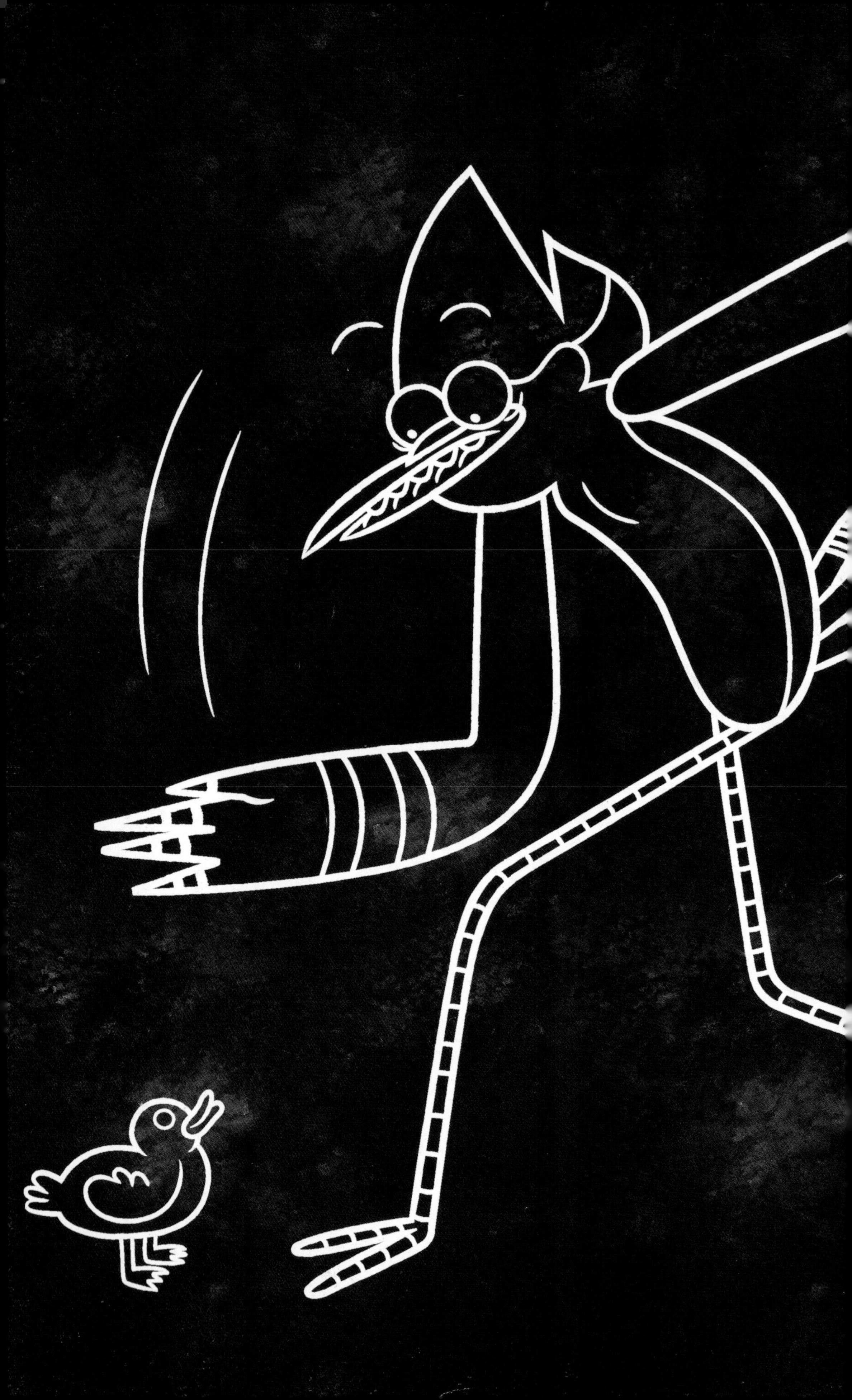

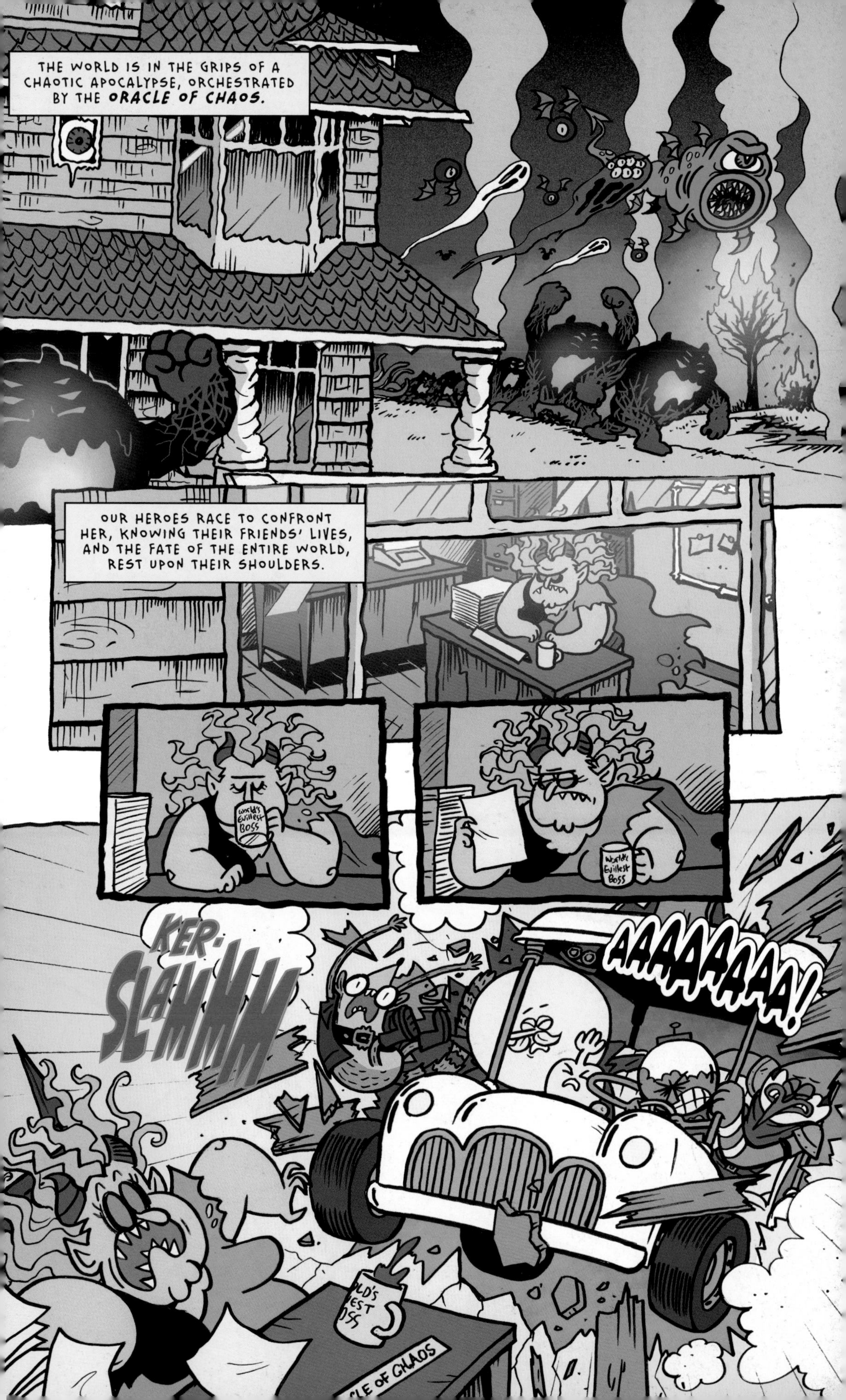
THE WORLD IS IN THE GRIPS OF A CHAOTIC APOCALYPSE, ORCHESTRATED BY THE ORACLE OF CHAOS.
OUR HEROES RACE TO CONFRONT HER, KNOWING THEIR FRIENDS' LIVES, AND THE FATE OF THE ENTIRE WORLD, REST UPON THEIR SHOULDERS.
World's Evillest Boss
World's Evillest Boss
KER-SLAMMM
AAAAAAAA!
CLE OF CHAOS

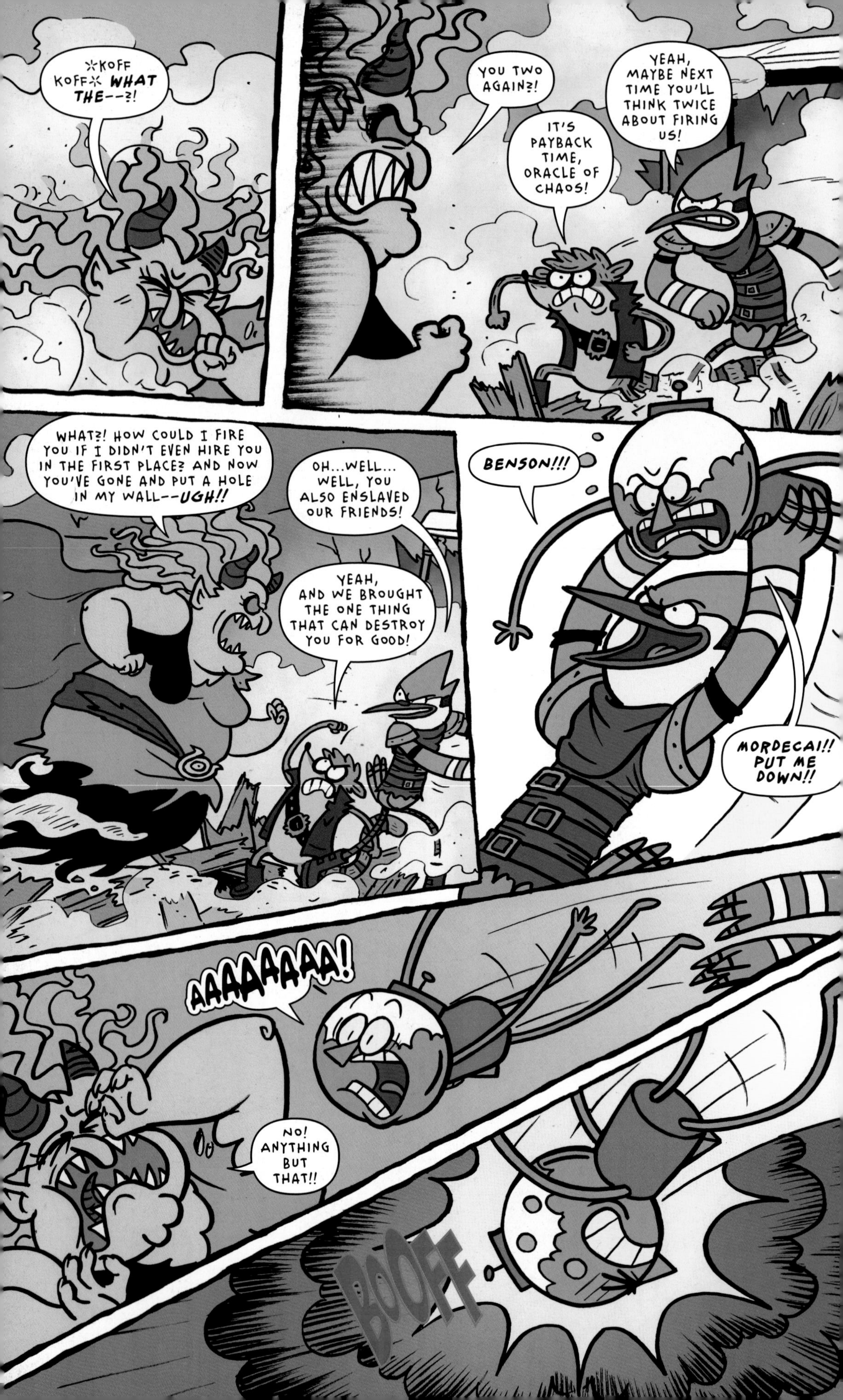
KOFF KOFF WHAT THE--?!
YOU TWO AGAIN?!
YEAH, MAYBE NEXT TIME YOU'LL THINK TWICE ABOUT FIRING US!
IT'S PAYBACK TIME, ORACLE OF CHAOS!
WHAT?! HOW COULD I FIRE YOU IF I DIDN'T EVEN HIRE YOU IN THE FIRST PLACE? AND NOW YOU'VE GONE AND PUT A HOLE IN MY WALL--UGH!!
OH...WELL... WELL, YOU ALSO ENSLAVED OUR FRIENDS!
YEAH, AND WE BROUGHT THE ONE THING THAT CAN DESTROY YOU FOR GOOD!
BENSON!!!
MORDECAI!! PUT ME DOWN!!
AAAAAAAA!
NO! ANYTHING BUT THAT!!
BOOFF

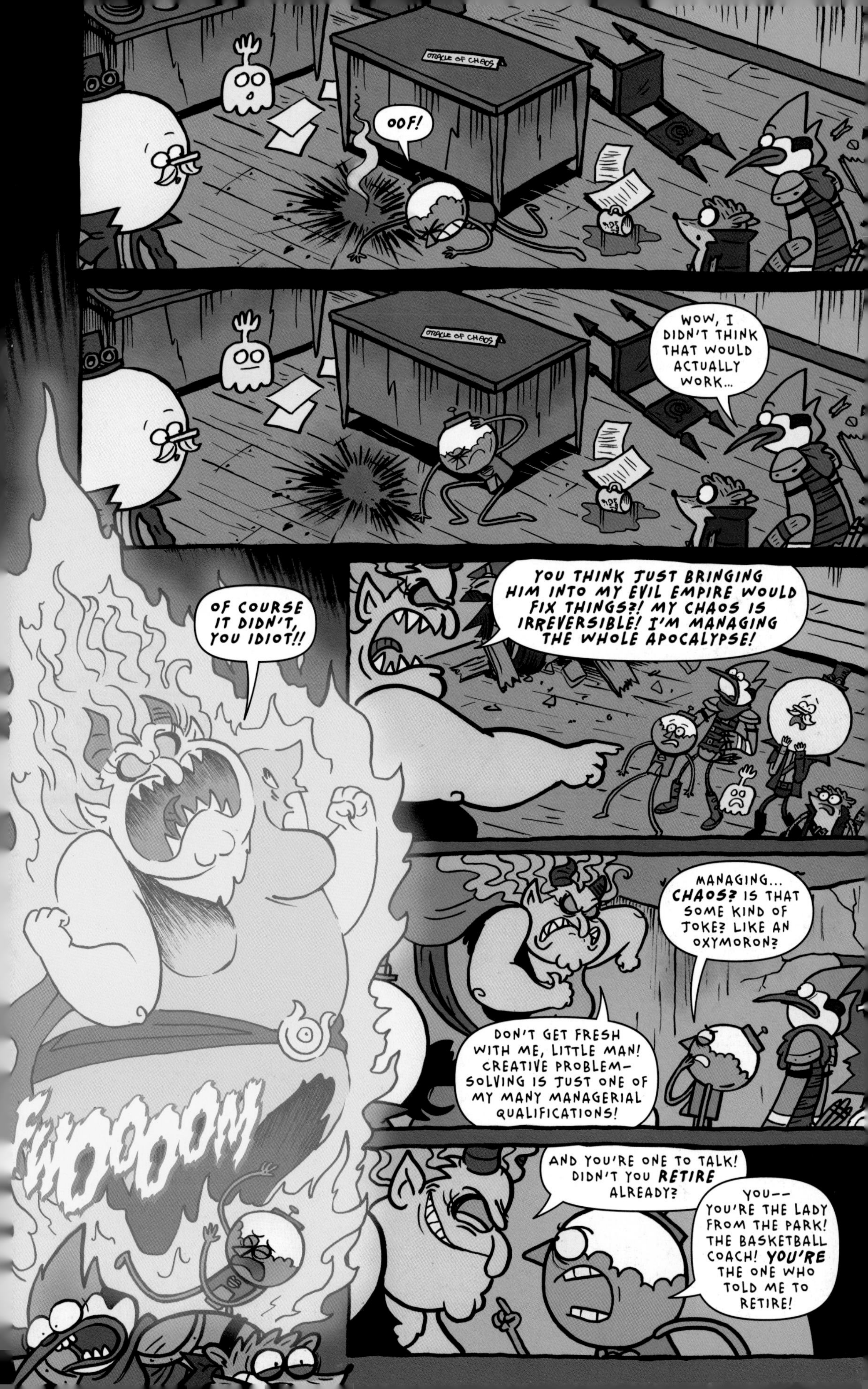
ORACLE OF CHAOS
OOF!
ORACLE OF CHAOS
WOW, I DIDN'T THINK THAT WOULD ACTUALLY WORK...
OF COURSE IT DIDN'T, YOU IDIOT!!
FWOOOM
YOU THINK JUST BRINGING HIM INTO MY EVIL EMPIRE WOULD FIX THINGS?! MY CHAOS IS IRREVERSIBLE! I'M MANAGING THE WHOLE APOCALYPSE!
MANAGING... CHAOS? IS THAT SOME KIND OF JOKE? LIKE AN OXYMORON?
DON'T GET FRESH WITH ME, LITTLE MAN! CREATIVE PROBLEM-SOLVING IS JUST ONE OF MY MANY MANAGERIAL QUALIFICATIONS!
AND YOU'RE ONE TO TALK! DIDN'T YOU RETIRE ALREADY?
YOU-- YOU'RE THE LADY FROM THE PARK! THE BASKETBALL COACH! YOU'RE THE ONE WHO TOLD ME TO RETIRE!

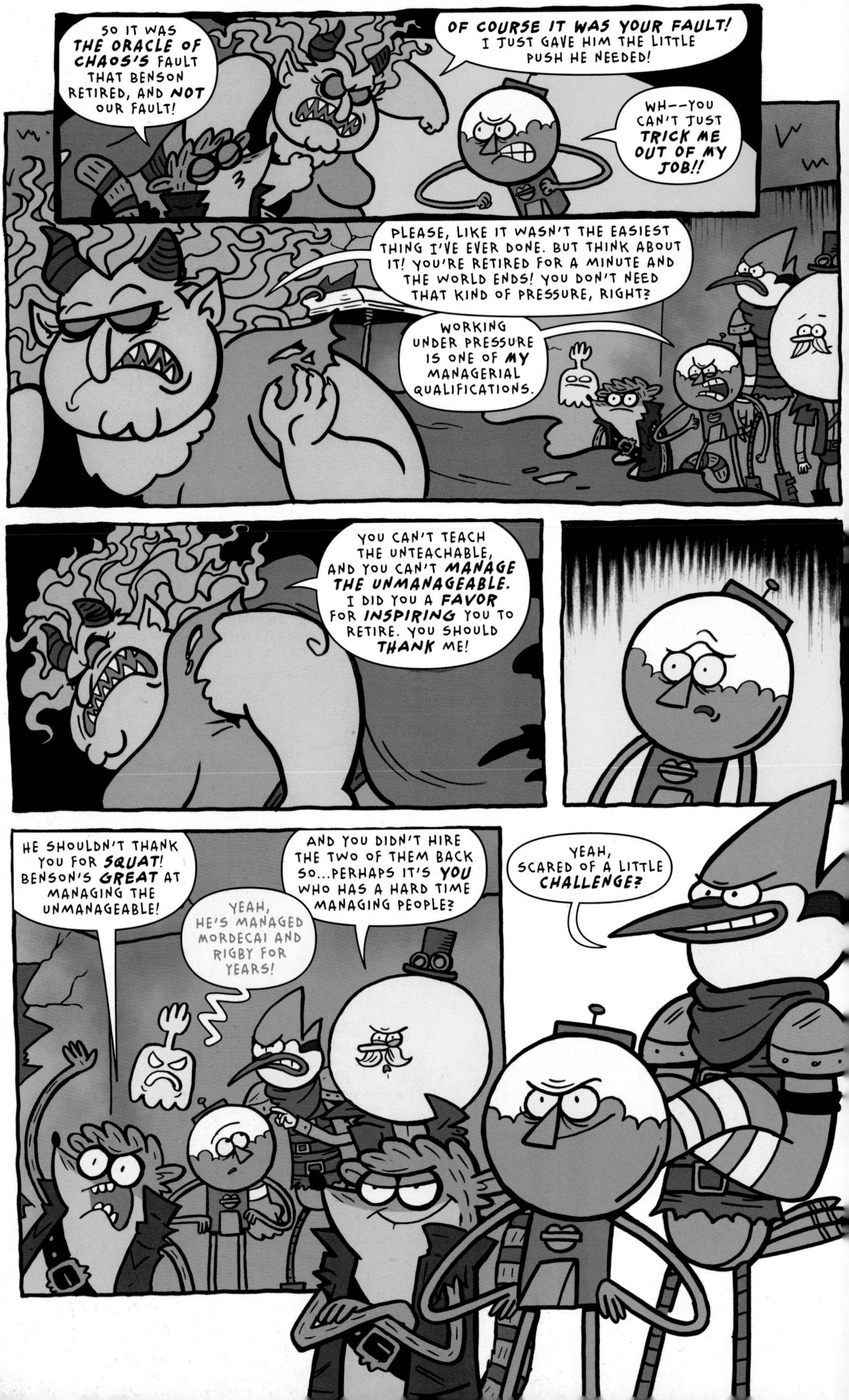
SO IT WAS THE ORACLE OF CHAOS'S FAULT THAT BENSON RETIRED, AND NOT OUR FAULT!
OF COURSE IT WAS YOUR FAULT! I JUST GAVE HIM THE LITTLE PUSH HE NEEDED!
WH--YOU CAN'T JUST TRICK ME OUT OF MY JOB!!
PLEASE, LIKE IT WASN'T THE EASIEST THING I'VE EVER DONE. BUT THINK ABOUT IT! YOU'RE RETIRED FOR A MINUTE AND THE WORLD ENDS! YOU DON'T NEED THAT KIND OF PRESSURE, RIGHT?
WORKING UNDER PRESSURE IS ONE OF MY MANAGERIAL QUALIFICATIONS.
YOU CAN'T TEACH THE UNTEACHABLE, AND YOU CAN'T MANAGE THE UNMANAGEABLE. I DID YOU A FAVOR FOR INSPIRING YOU TO RETIRE. YOU SHOULD THANK ME!
HE SHOULDN'T THANK YOU FOR SQUAT! BENSON'S GREAT AT MANAGING THE UNMANAGEABLE!
YEAH, HE'S MANAGED MORDECAI AND RIGBY FOR YEARS!
AND YOU DIDN'T HIRE THE TWO OF THEM BACK SO...PERHAPS IT'S YOU WHO HAS A HARD TIME MANAGING PEOPLE?
YEAH, SCARED OF A LITTLE CHALLENGE?

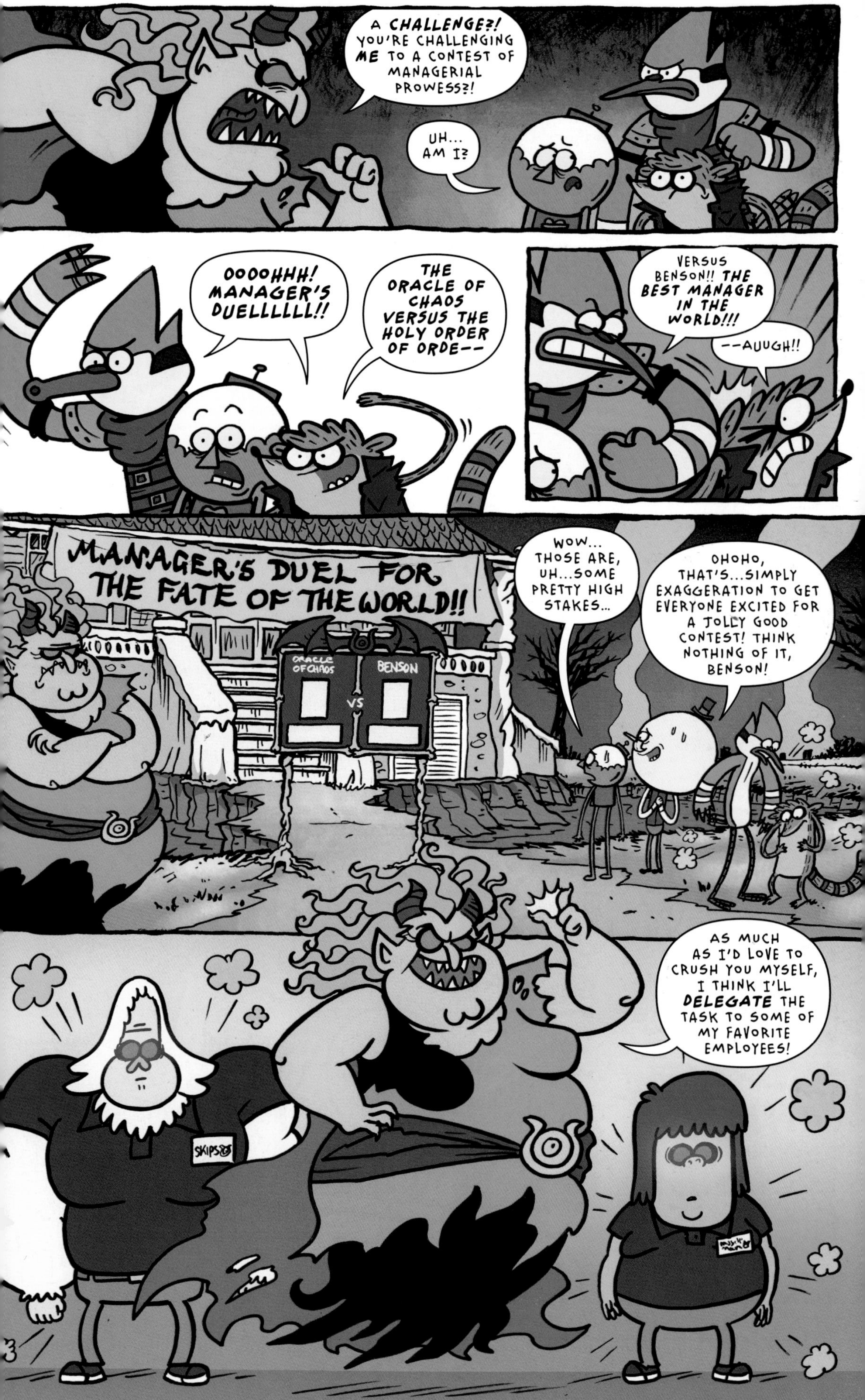
A CHALLENGE?! YOU'RE CHALLENGING ME TO A CONTEST OF MANAGERIAL PROWESS?!
UH... AM I?
OOOOHHH! MANAGER'S DUELLLLLL!!
THE ORACLE OF CHAOS VERSUS THE HOLY ORDER OF ORDE--
VERSUS BENSON!! THE BEST MANAGER IN THE WORLD!!!
--AUUGH!!
MANAGER'S DUEL FOR THE FATE OF THE WORLD!!
ORACLE OF CHAOS
VS
BENSON
WOW... THOSE ARE, UH...SOME PRETTY HIGH STAKES...
OHOHO, THAT'S...SIMPLY EXAGGERATION TO GET EVERYONE EXCITED FOR A JOLLY GOOD CONTEST! THINK NOTHING OF IT, BENSON!
AS MUCH AS I'D LOVE TO CRUSH YOU MYSELF, I THINK I'LL DELEGATE THE TASK TO SOME OF MY FAVORITE EMPLOYEES!
SKIPS

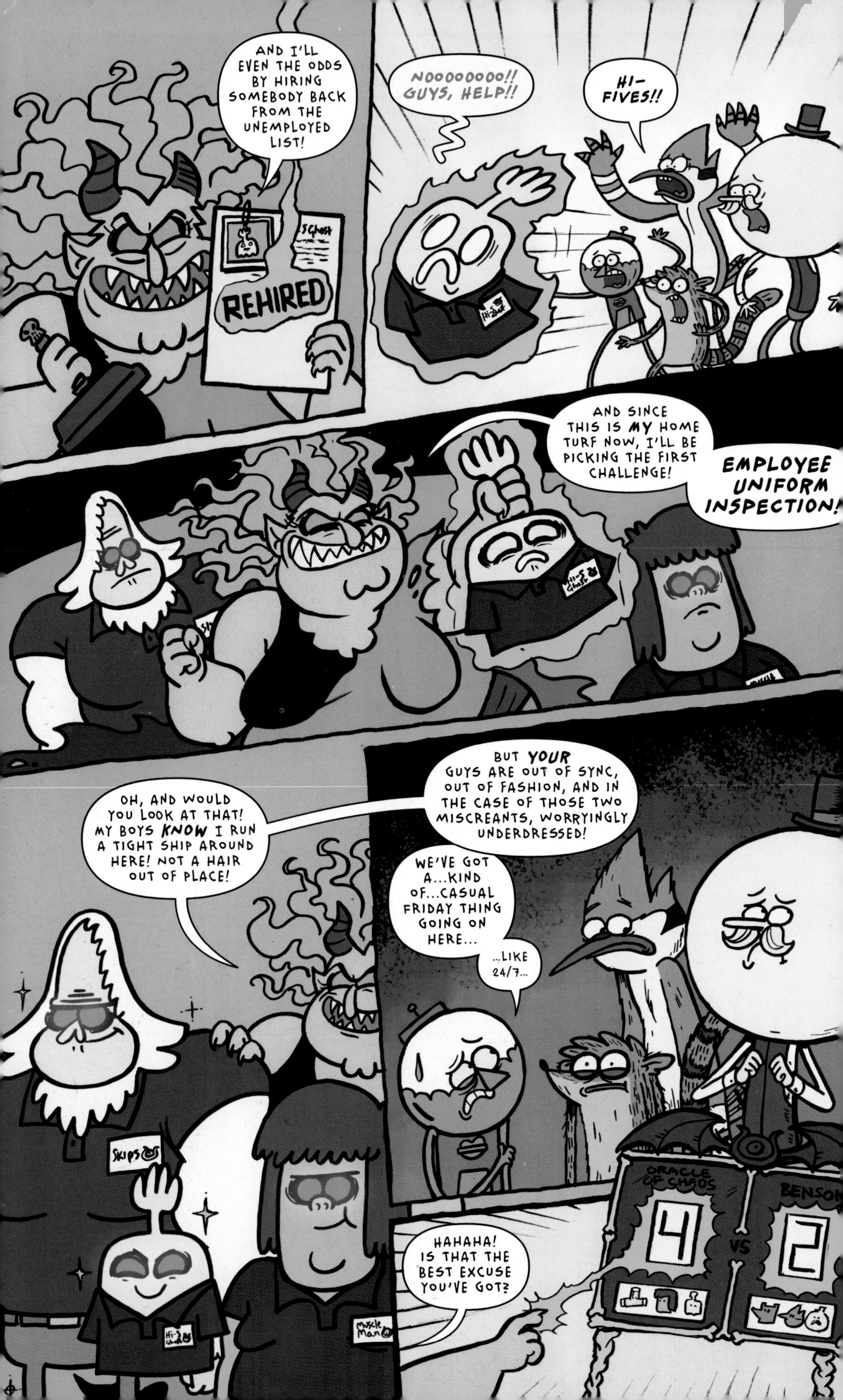

AND I'LL EVEN THE ODDS BY HIRING SOMEBODY BACK FROM THE UNEMPLOYED LIST!
REHIRED
NOOOOOOOO!! GUYS, HELP!!
HI-FIVES!!
AND SINCE THIS IS MY HOME TURF NOW, I'LL BE PICKING THE FIRST CHALLENGE!
EMPLOYEE UNIFORM INSPECTION!
OH, AND WOULD YOU LOOK AT THAT! MY BOYS KNOW I RUN A TIGHT SHIP AROUND HERE! NOT A HAIR OUT OF PLACE!
BUT YOUR GUYS ARE OUT OF SYNC, OUT OF FASHION, AND IN THE CASE OF THOSE TWO MISCREANTS, WORRYINGLY UNDERDRESSED!
WE'VE GOT A...KIND OF...CASUAL FRIDAY THING GOING ON HERE...
...LIKE 24/7...
HAHAHA! IS THAT THE BEST EXCUSE YOU'VE GOT?
SKIPS
MUSCLE MAN
ORACLE OF CHAOS
BENSON
4
VS
2

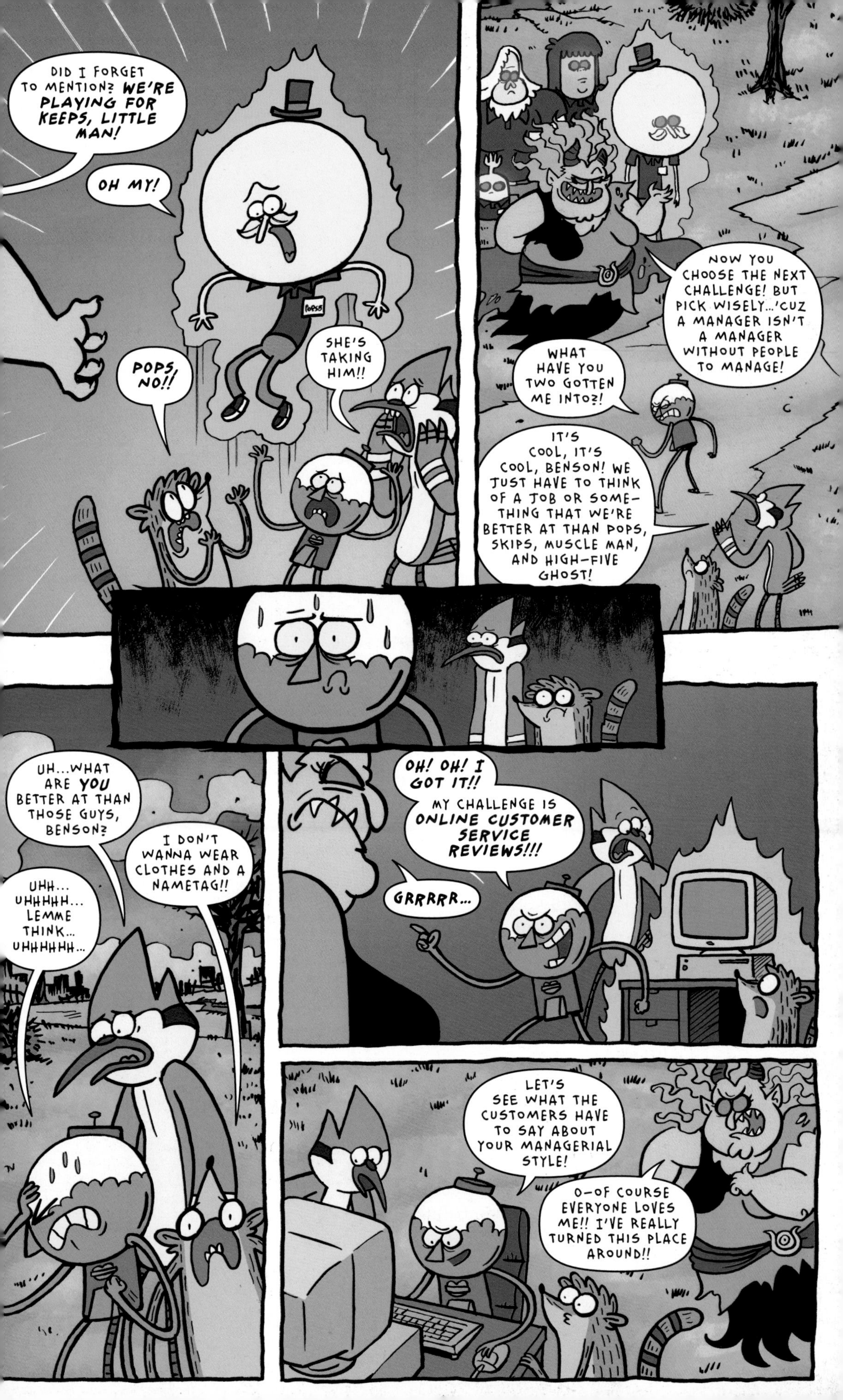
DID I FORGET TO MENTION? WE'RE PLAYING FOR KEEPS, LITTLE MAN!
OH MY!
POPS, NO!!
SHE'S TAKING HIM!!
NOW YOU CHOOSE THE NEXT CHALLENGE! BUT PICK WISELY...'CUZ A MANAGER ISN'T A MANAGER WITHOUT PEOPLE TO MANAGE!
WHAT HAVE YOU TWO GOTTEN ME INTO?!
IT'S COOL, IT'S COOL, BENSON! WE JUST HAVE TO THINK OF A JOB OR SOME-THING THAT WE'RE BETTER AT THAN POPS, SKIPS, MUSCLE MAN, AND HIGH-FIVE GHOST!
UH...WHAT ARE YOU BETTER AT THAN THOSE GUYS, BENSON?
I DON'T WANNA WEAR CLOTHES AND A NAMETAG!!
UHH... UHHHHH... LEMME THINK... UHHHHHH...
OH! OH! I GOT IT!!
MY CHALLENGE IS ONLINE CUSTOMER SERVICE REVIEWS!!!
GRRRRR...
LET'S SEE WHAT THE CUSTOMERS HAVE TO SAY ABOUT YOUR MANAGERIAL STYLE!
O-OF COURSE EVERYONE LOVES ME!! I'VE REALLY TURNED THIS PLACE AROUND!!

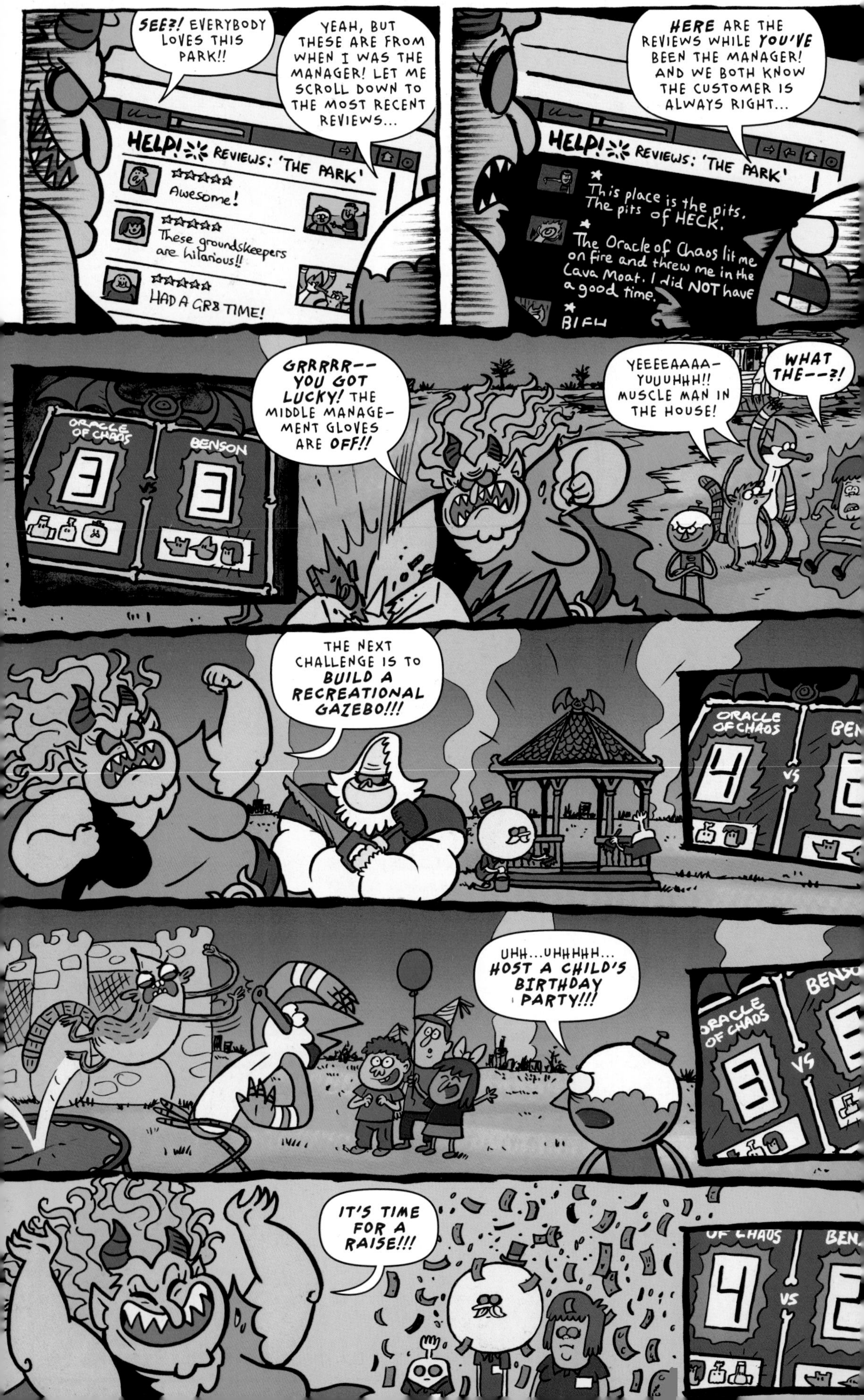
SEE?! EVERYBODY LOVES THIS PARK!!
YEAH, BUT THESE ARE FROM WHEN I WAS THE MANAGER! LET ME SCROLL DOWN TO THE MOST RECENT REVIEWS...
HELP! REVIEWS: 'THE PARK'
Awesome!
These groundskeepers are hilarious!!
HAD A GR8 TIME!
HERE ARE THE REVIEWS WHILE YOU'VE BEEN THE MANAGER! AND WE BOTH KNOW THE CUSTOMER IS ALWAYS RIGHT...
HELP! REVIEWS: 'THE PARK'
This place is the pits. The pits of HECK.
The Oracle of Chaos lit me on fire and threw me in the Lava Moat. I did NOT have a good time.
ORACLE OF CHAOS 3
BENSON 3
VS
GRRRRR-- YOU GOT LUCKY! THE MIDDLE MANAGEMENT GLOVES ARE OFF!!
YEEEEAAAA-YUUUHHH!! MUSCLE MAN IN THE HOUSE!
WHAT THE--?!
THE NEXT CHALLENGE IS TO BUILD A RECREATIONAL GAZEBO!!!
ORACLE OF CHAOS 4
VS
UHH...UHHHHH... HOST A CHILD'S BIRTHDAY PARTY!!!
ORACLE OF CHAOS 3
VS
IT'S TIME FOR A RAISE!!!
4
VS

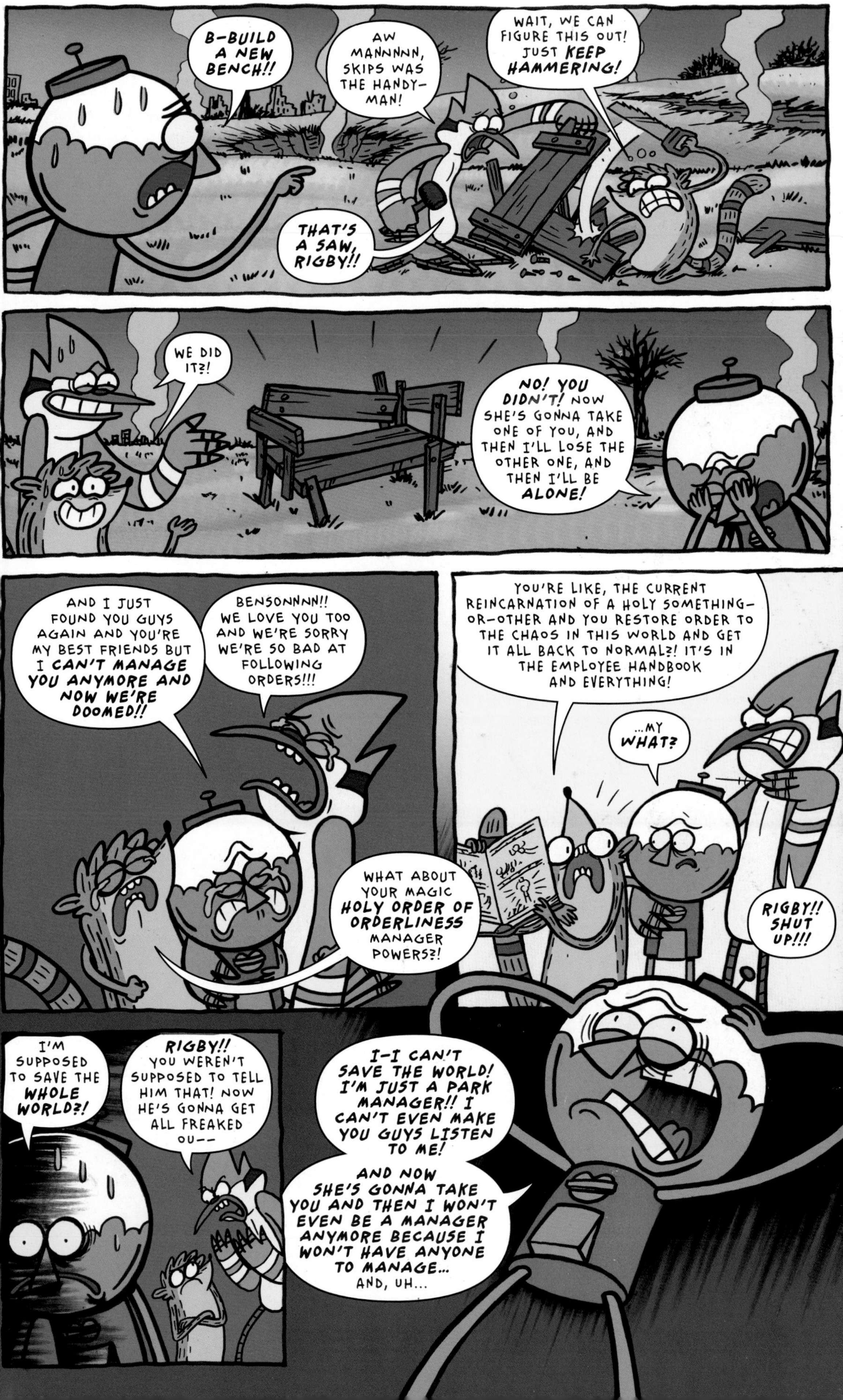

B-BUILD A NEW BENCH!!
AW MANNNNN, SKIPS WAS THE HANDY-MAN!
WAIT, WE CAN FIGURE THIS OUT! JUST KEEP HAMMERING!
THAT'S A SAW, RIGBY!!
WE DID IT?!
NO! YOU DIDN'T! NOW SHE'S GONNA TAKE ONE OF YOU, AND THEN I'LL LOSE THE OTHER ONE, AND THEN I'LL BE ALONE!
AND I JUST FOUND YOU GUYS AGAIN AND YOU'RE MY BEST FRIENDS BUT I CAN'T MANAGE YOU ANYMORE AND NOW WE'RE DOOMED!!
BENSONNNN!! WE LOVE YOU TOO AND WE'RE SORRY WE'RE SO BAD AT FOLLOWING ORDERS!!!
WHAT ABOUT YOUR MAGIC HOLY ORDER OF ORDERLINESS MANAGER POWERS?!
YOU'RE LIKE, THE CURRENT REINCARNATION OF A HOLY SOMETHING-OR-OTHER AND YOU RESTORE ORDER TO THE CHAOS IN THIS WORLD AND GET IT ALL BACK TO NORMAL?! IT'S IN THE EMPLOYEE HANDBOOK AND EVERYTHING!
...MY WHAT?
RIGBY!! SHUT UP!!!
I'M SUPPOSED TO SAVE THE WHOLE WORLD?!
RIGBY!! YOU WEREN'T SUPPOSED TO TELL HIM THAT! NOW HE'S GONNA GET ALL FREAKED OU--
I-I CAN'T SAVE THE WORLD! I'M JUST A PARK MANAGER!! I CAN'T EVEN MAKE YOU GUYS LISTEN TO ME!
AND NOW SHE'S GONNA TAKE YOU AND THEN I WON'T EVEN BE A MANAGER ANYMORE BECAUSE I WON'T HAVE ANYONE TO MANAGE... AND, UH...

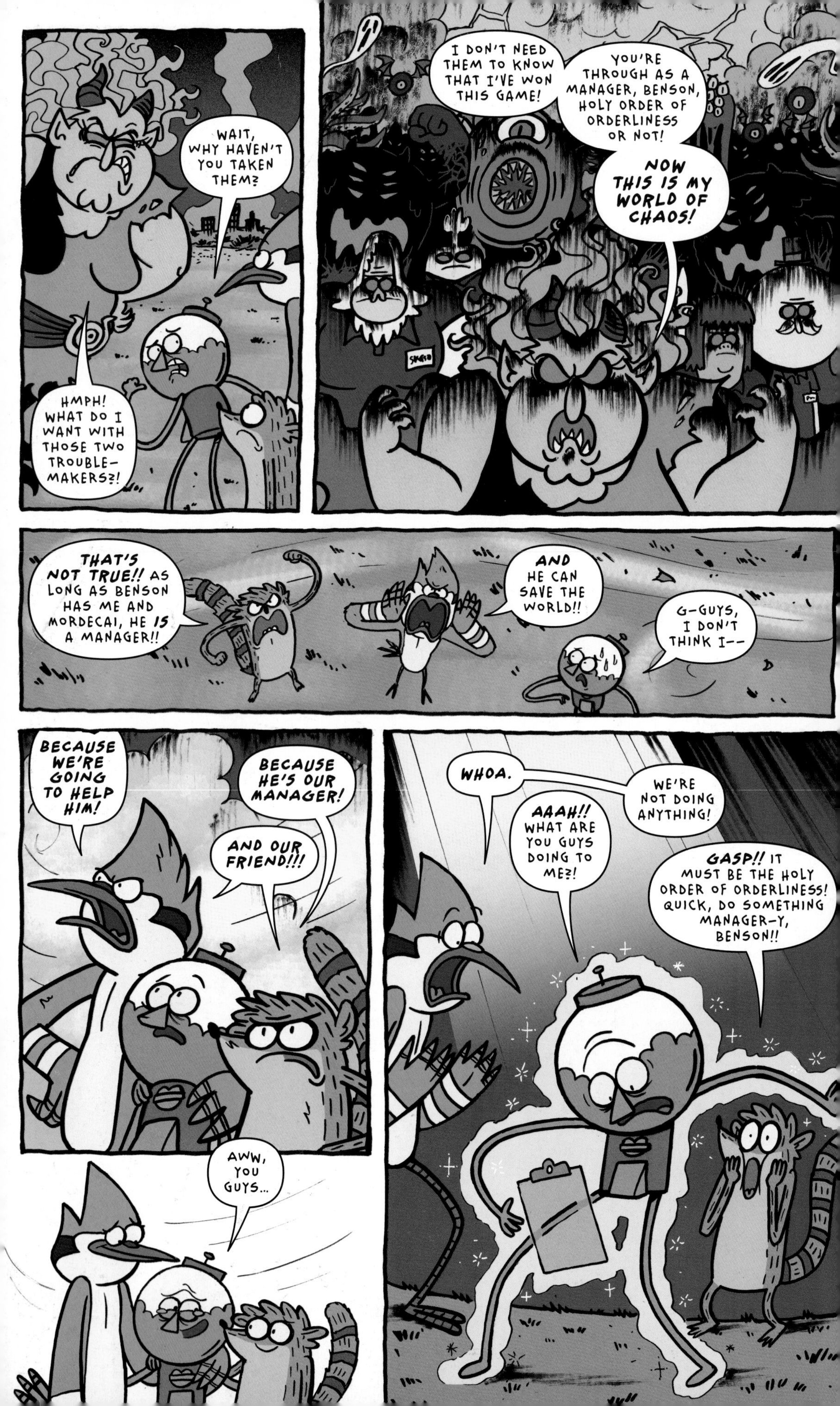

WAIT, WHY HAVEN'T YOU TAKEN THEM?
HMPH! WHAT DO I WANT WITH THOSE TWO TROUBLE-MAKERS?!
I DON'T NEED THEM TO KNOW THAT I'VE WON THIS GAME!
YOU'RE THROUGH AS A MANAGER, BENSON, HOLY ORDER OF ORDERLINESS OR NOT!
NOW THIS IS MY WORLD OF CHAOS!
THAT'S NOT TRUE!! AS LONG AS BENSON HAS ME AND MORDECAI, HE IS A MANAGER!!
AND HE CAN SAVE THE WORLD!!
G-GUYS, I DON'T THINK I--
BECAUSE WE'RE GOING TO HELP HIM!
BECAUSE HE'S OUR MANAGER!
AND OUR FRIEND!!!
AWW, YOU GUYS...
WHOA.
WE'RE NOT DOING ANYTHING!
AAAH!! WHAT ARE YOU GUYS DOING TO ME?!
GASP!! IT MUST BE THE HOLY ORDER OF ORDERLINESS! QUICK, DO SOMETHING MANAGER-Y, BENSON!!

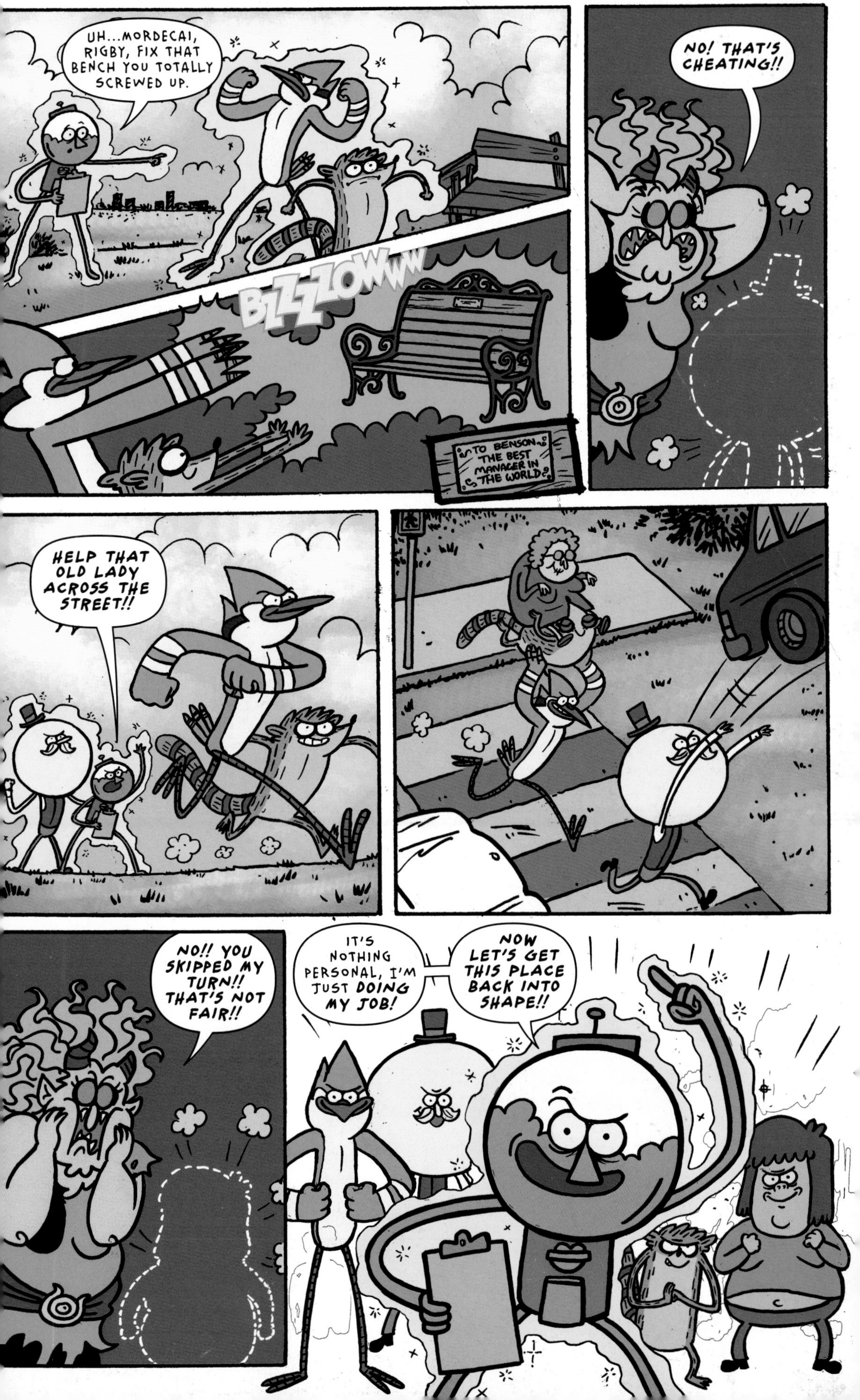
UH...MORDECAI, RIGBY, FIX THAT BENCH YOU TOTALLY SCREWED UP.
BZZZZOWWW
TO BENSON THE BEST MANAGER IN THE WORLD
NO! THAT'S CHEATING!!
HELP THAT OLD LADY ACROSS THE STREET!!
NO!! YOU SKIPPED MY TURN!! THAT'S NOT FAIR!!
IT'S NOTHING PERSONAL, I'M JUST DOING MY JOB!
NOW LET'S GET THIS PLACE BACK INTO SHAPE!!

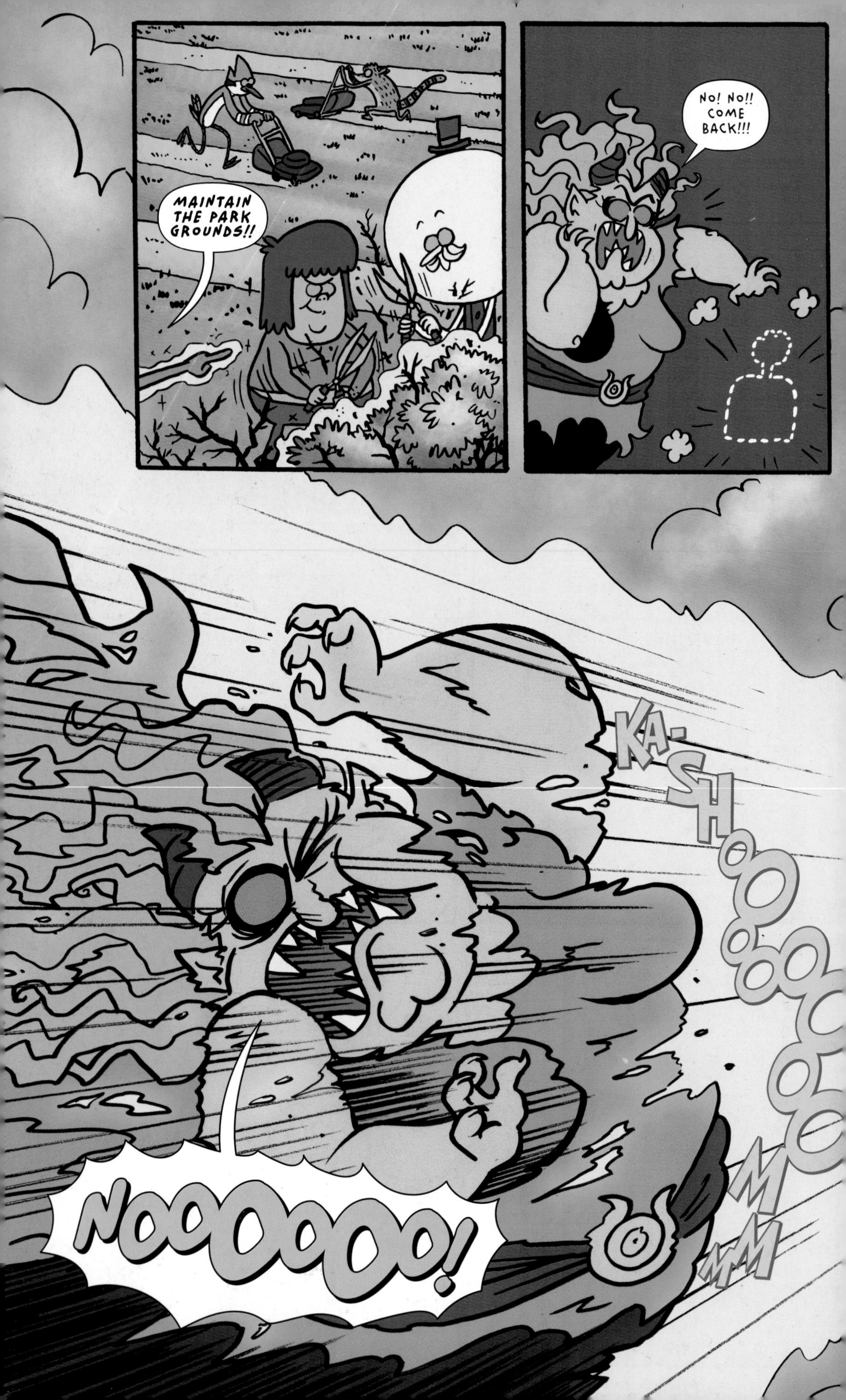
MAINTAIN THE PARK GROUNDS!!
NO! NO!! COME BACK!!!
KA-SHOOOOOOOOOMMM
NOOOOOOO!

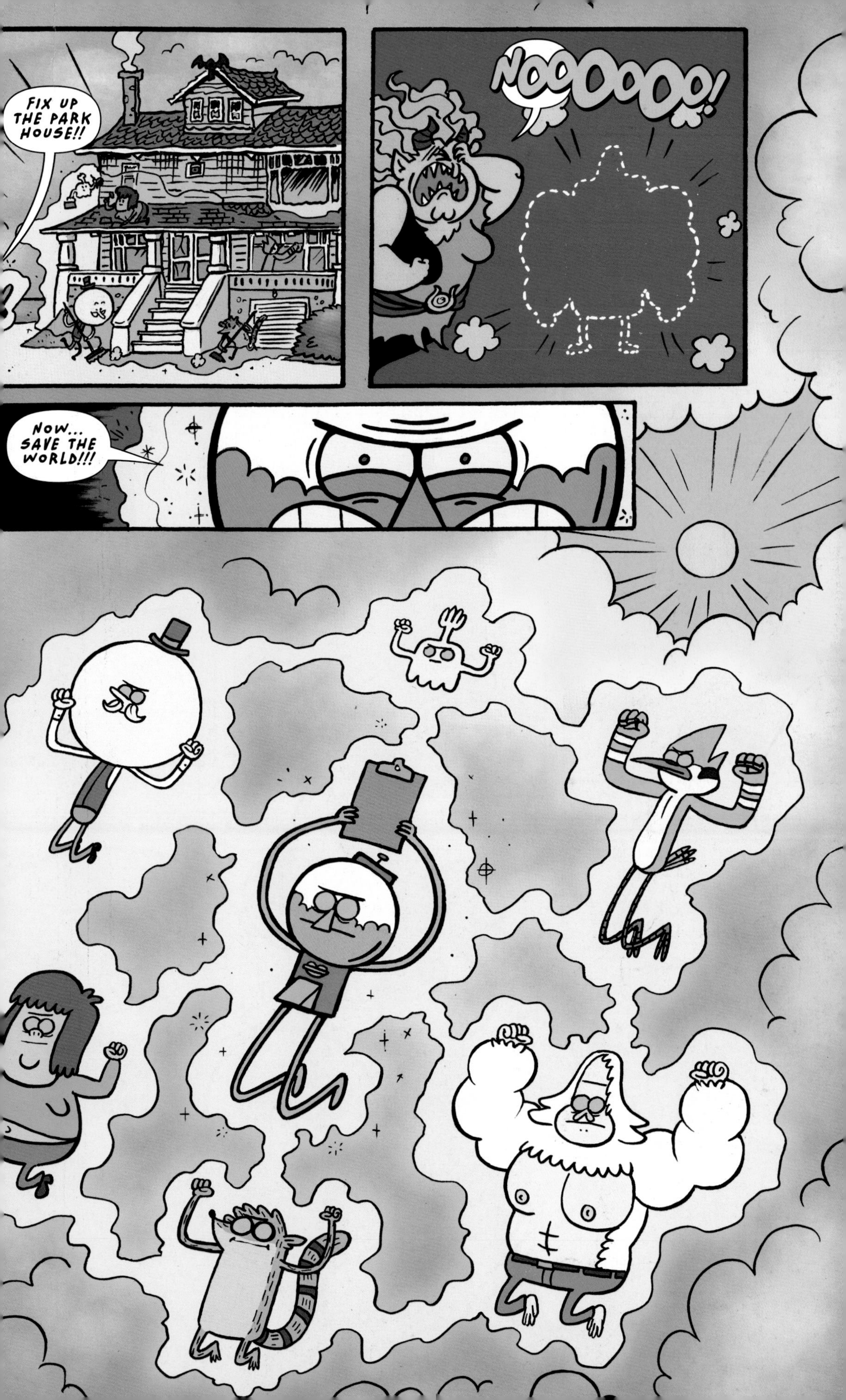
FIX UP THE PARK HOUSE!!
NOOOOOOO!
NOW... SAVE THE WORLD!!!

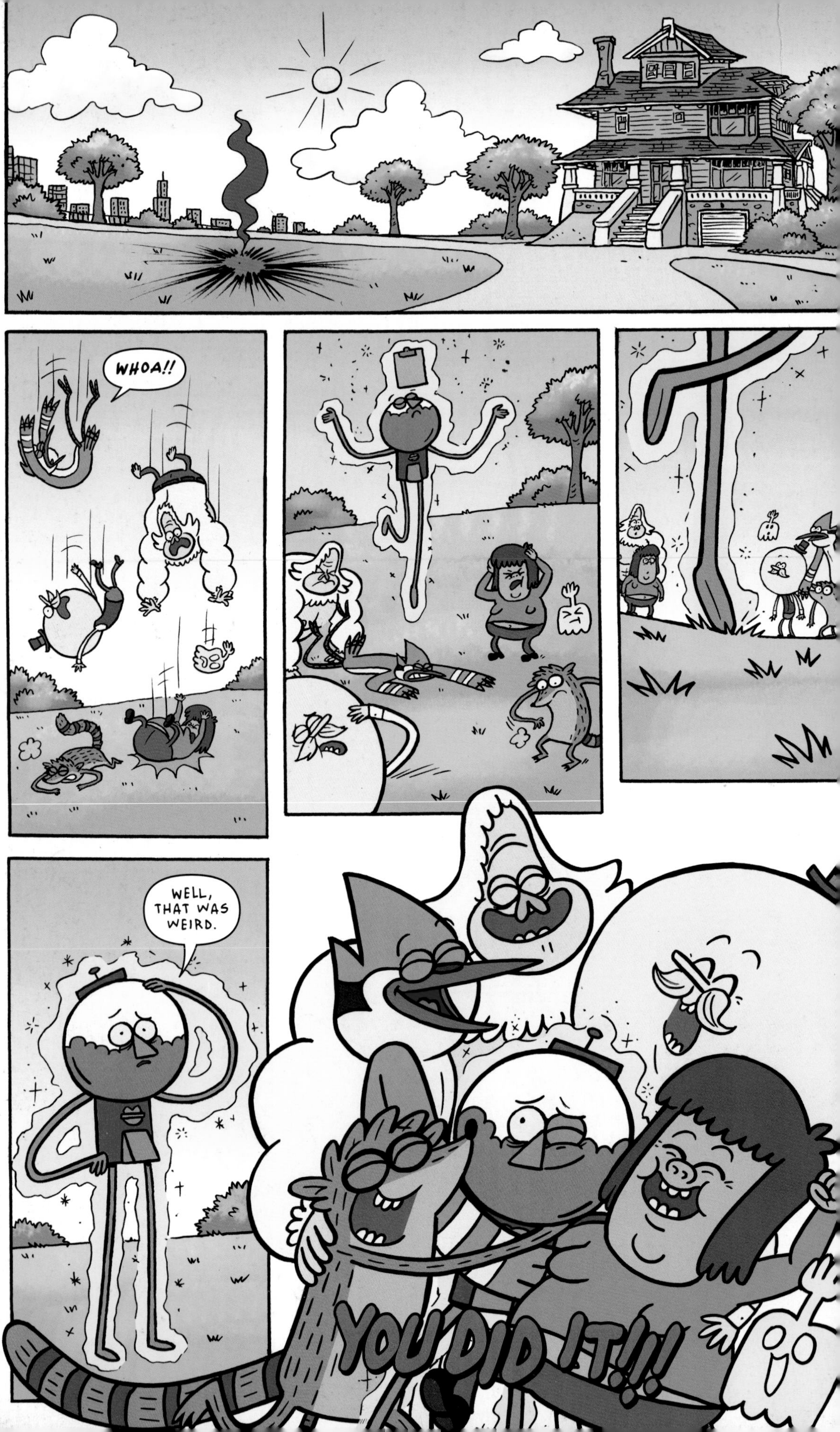

WHOA!!
WELL, THAT WAS WEIRD.
YOU DID IT!!!

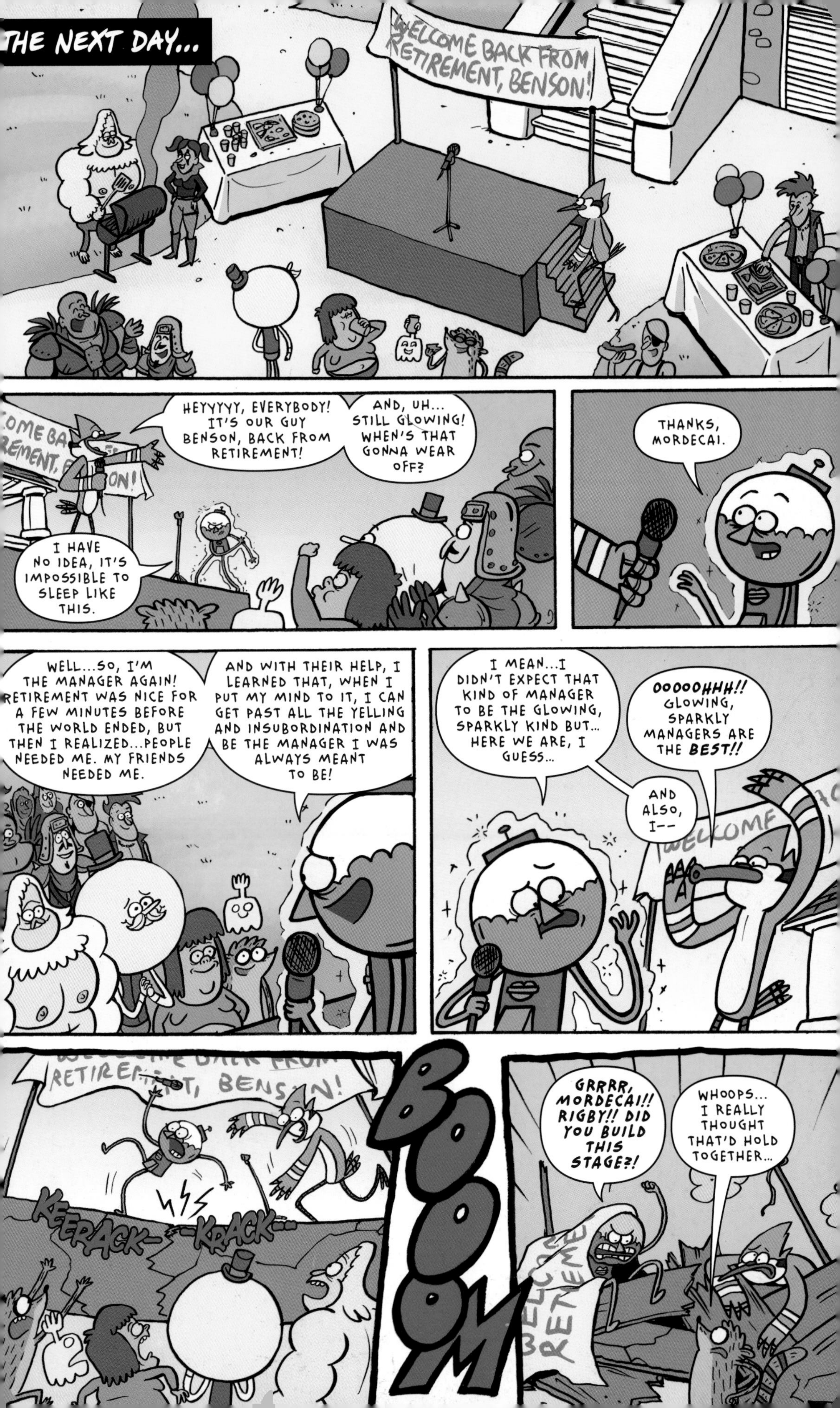
THE NEXT DAY...
WELCOME BACK FROM RETIREMENT, BENSON!
HEYYYYY, EVERYBODY! IT'S OUR GUY BENSON, BACK FROM RETIREMENT!
AND, UH... STILL GLOWING! WHEN'S THAT GONNA WEAR OFF?
I HAVE NO IDEA, IT'S IMPOSSIBLE TO SLEEP LIKE THIS.
THANKS, MORDECAI.
WELL...SO, I'M THE MANAGER AGAIN! RETIREMENT WAS NICE FOR A FEW MINUTES BEFORE THE WORLD ENDED, BUT THEN I REALIZED...PEOPLE NEEDED ME. MY FRIENDS NEEDED ME.
AND WITH THEIR HELP, I LEARNED THAT, WHEN I PUT MY MIND TO IT, I CAN GET PAST ALL THE YELLING AND INSUBORDINATION AND BE THE MANAGER I WAS ALWAYS MEANT TO BE!
I MEAN...I DIDN'T EXPECT THAT KIND OF MANAGER TO BE THE GLOWING, SPARKLY KIND BUT... HERE WE ARE, I GUESS...
AND ALSO, I--
OOOOOHHH!! GLOWING, SPARKLY MANAGERS ARE THE BEST!!
RETIREMENT, BENSON!
KEERACK--KRACK--
BOOOOM
GRRRR, MORDECAI!! RIGBY!! DID YOU BUILD THIS STAGE?!
WHOOPS... I REALLY THOUGHT THAT'D HOLD TOGETHER...

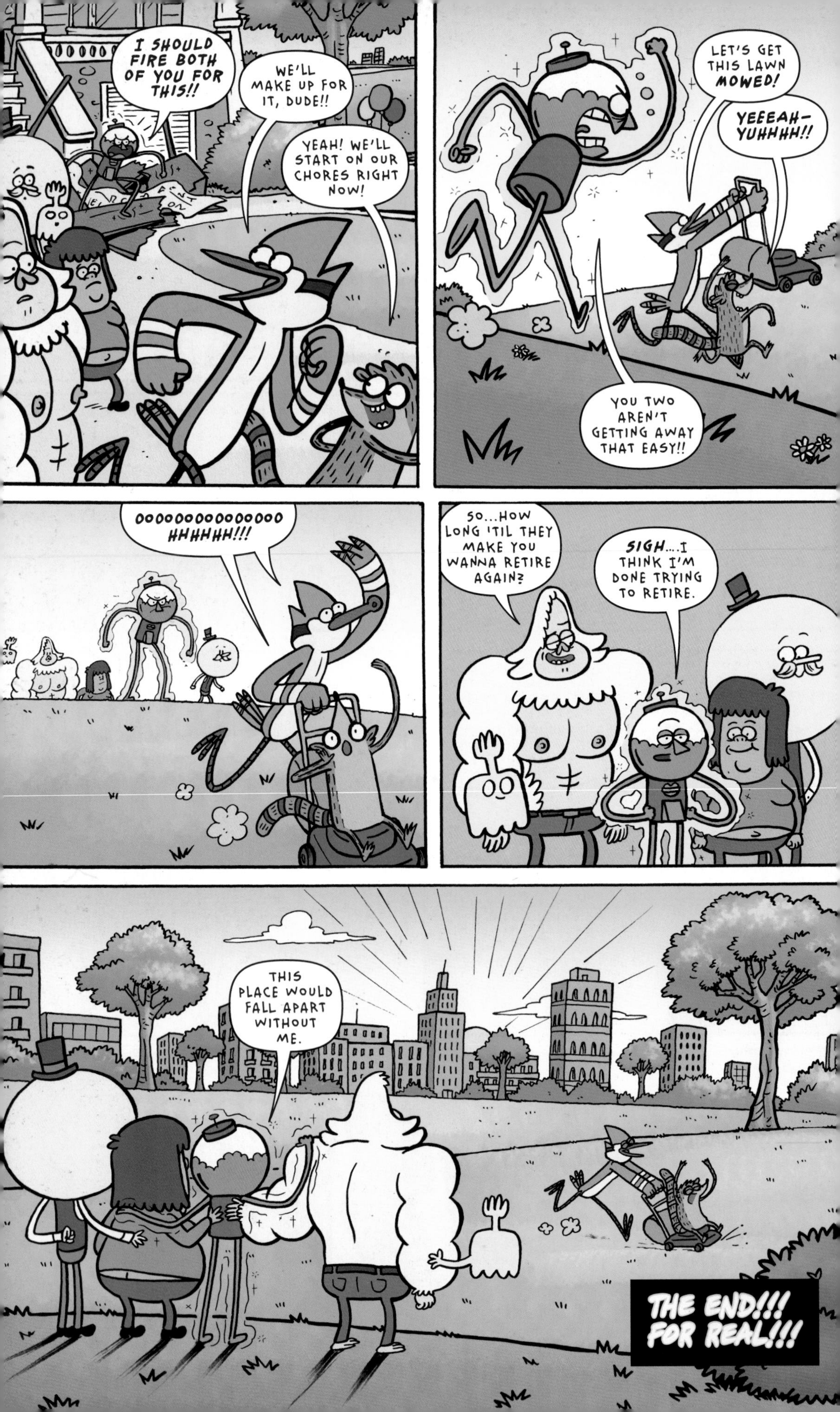
I SHOULD FIRE BOTH OF YOU FOR THIS!!
WE'LL MAKE UP FOR IT, DUDE!!
YEAH! WE'LL START ON OUR CHORES RIGHT NOW!
LET'S GET THIS LAWN MOWED!
YEEEAH-YUHHHH!!
YOU TWO AREN'T GETTING AWAY THAT EASY!!
OOOOOOOOOOOOOO HHHHHH!!!
SO...HOW LONG 'TIL THEY MAKE YOU WANNA RETIRE AGAIN?
SIGH....I THINK I'M DONE TRYING TO RETIRE.
THIS PLACE WOULD FALL APART WITHOUT ME.
THE END!!! FOR REAL!!!

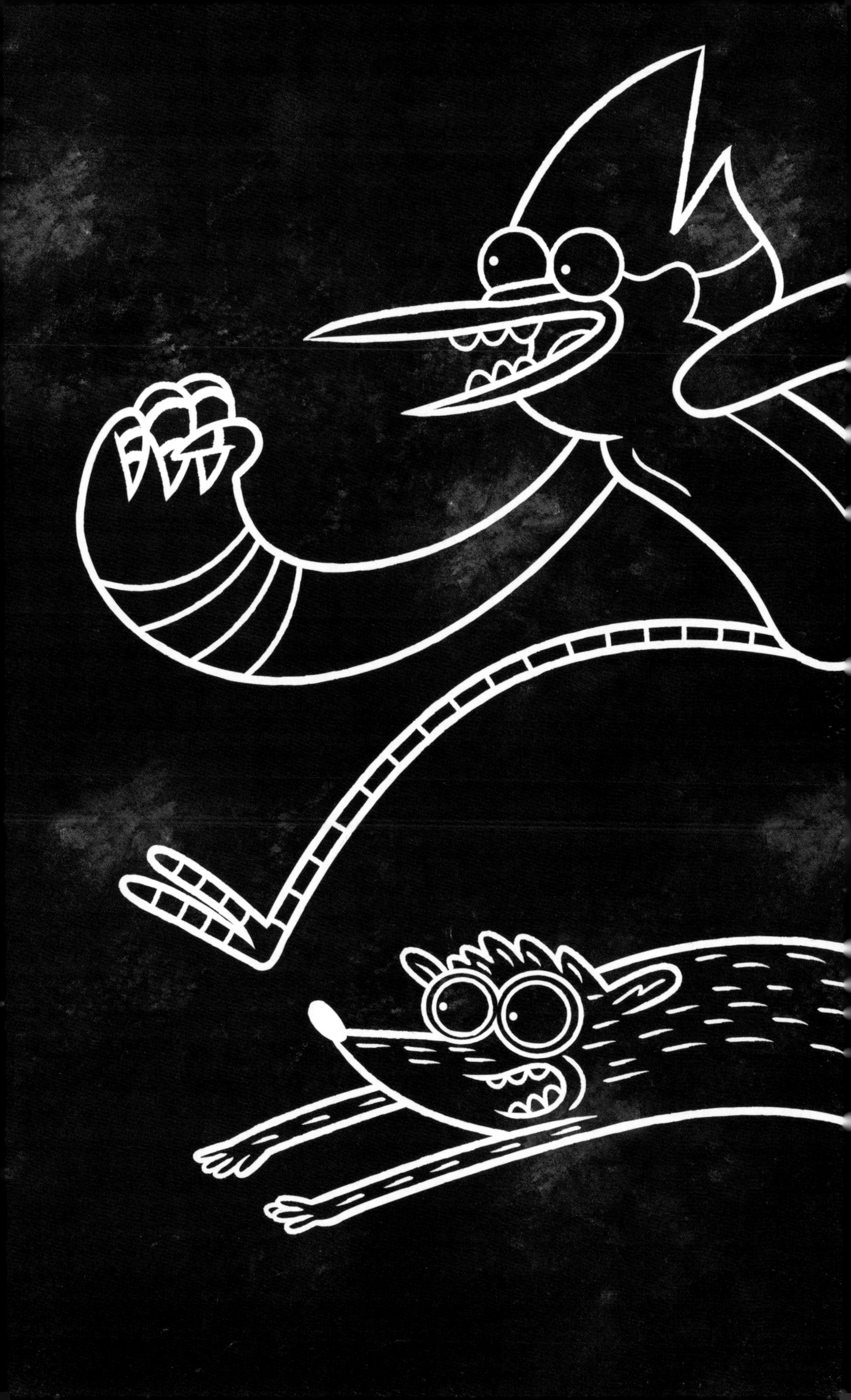

SHORT STORIES, BRO

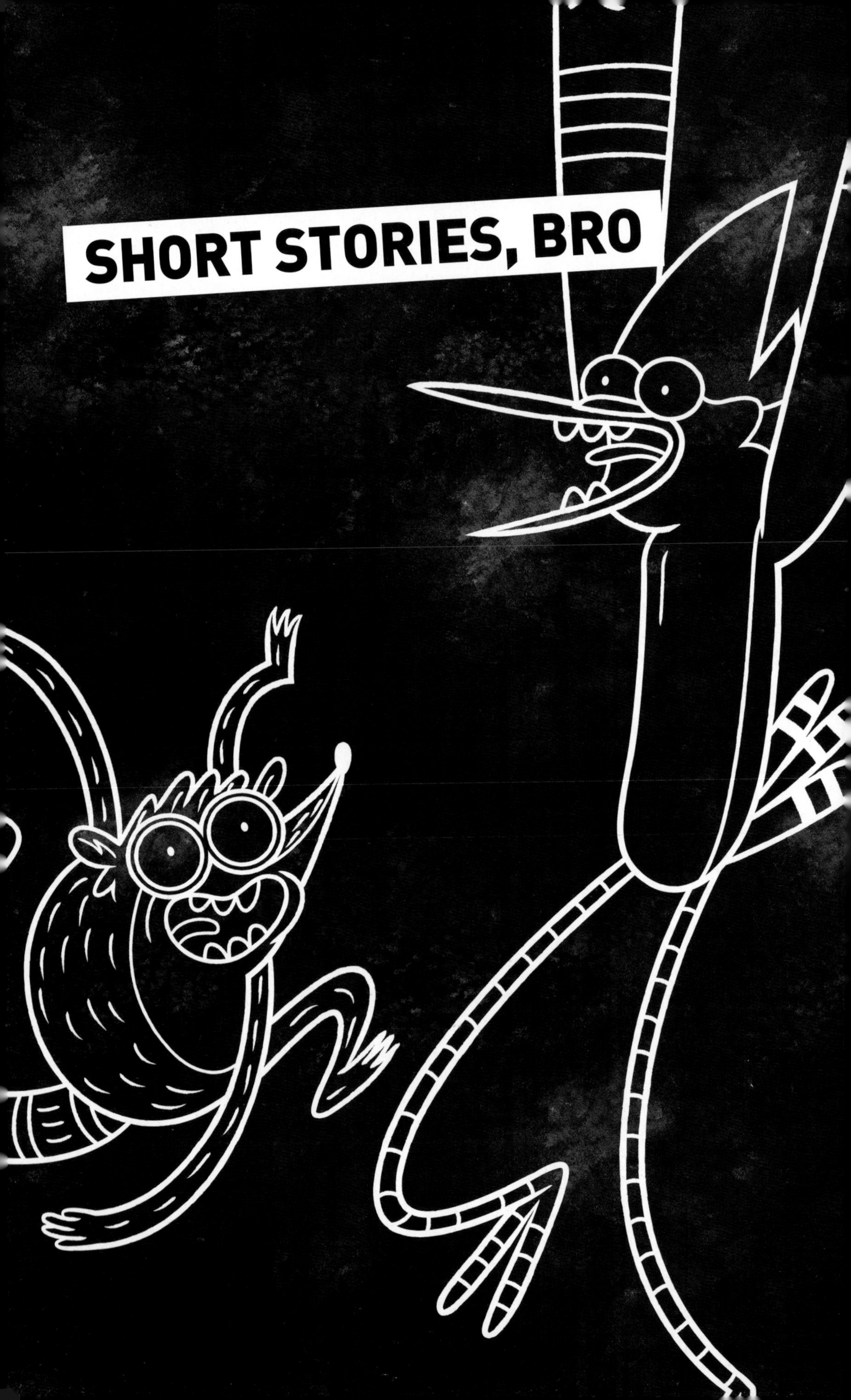

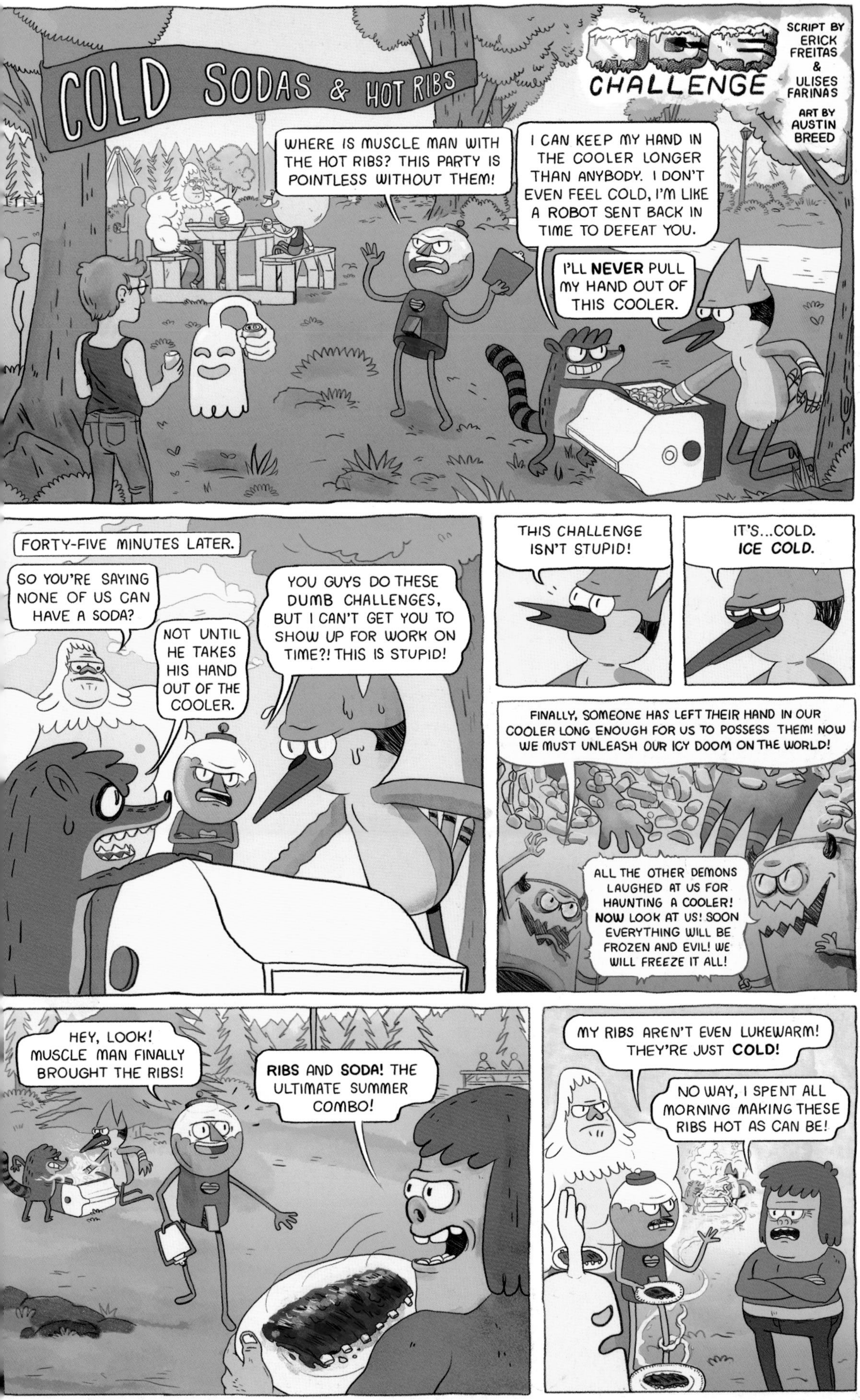
COLD SODAS & HOT RIBS
ICE CHALLENGE
SCRIPT BY ERICK FREITAS & ULISES FARINAS
ART BY AUSTIN BREED
WHERE IS MUSCLE MAN WITH THE HOT RIBS? THIS PARTY IS POINTLESS WITHOUT THEM!
I CAN KEEP MY HAND IN THE COOLER LONGER THAN ANYBODY. I DON'T EVEN FEEL COLD, I'M LIKE A ROBOT SENT BACK IN TIME TO DEFEAT YOU.
I'LL **NEVER** PULL MY HAND OUT OF THIS COOLER.
FORTY-FIVE MINUTES LATER.
SO YOU'RE SAYING NONE OF US CAN HAVE A SODA?
NOT UNTIL HE TAKES HIS HAND OUT OF THE COOLER.
YOU GUYS DO THESE DUMB CHALLENGES, BUT I CAN'T GET YOU TO SHOW UP FOR WORK ON TIME?! THIS IS STUPID!
THIS CHALLENGE ISN'T STUPID!
IT'S...COLD. **ICE COLD.**
FINALLY, SOMEONE HAS LEFT THEIR HAND IN OUR COOLER LONG ENOUGH FOR US TO POSSESS THEM! NOW WE MUST UNLEASH OUR ICY DOOM ON THE WORLD!
ALL THE OTHER DEMONS LAUGHED AT US FOR HAUNTING A COOLER! **NOW** LOOK AT US! SOON EVERYTHING WILL BE FROZEN AND EVIL! WE WILL FREEZE IT ALL!
HEY, LOOK! MUSCLE MAN FINALLY BROUGHT THE RIBS!
RIBS AND **SODA!** THE ULTIMATE SUMMER COMBO!
MY RIBS AREN'T EVEN LUKEWARM! THEY'RE JUST **COLD!**
NO WAY, I SPENT ALL MORNING MAKING THESE RIBS HOT AS CAN BE!

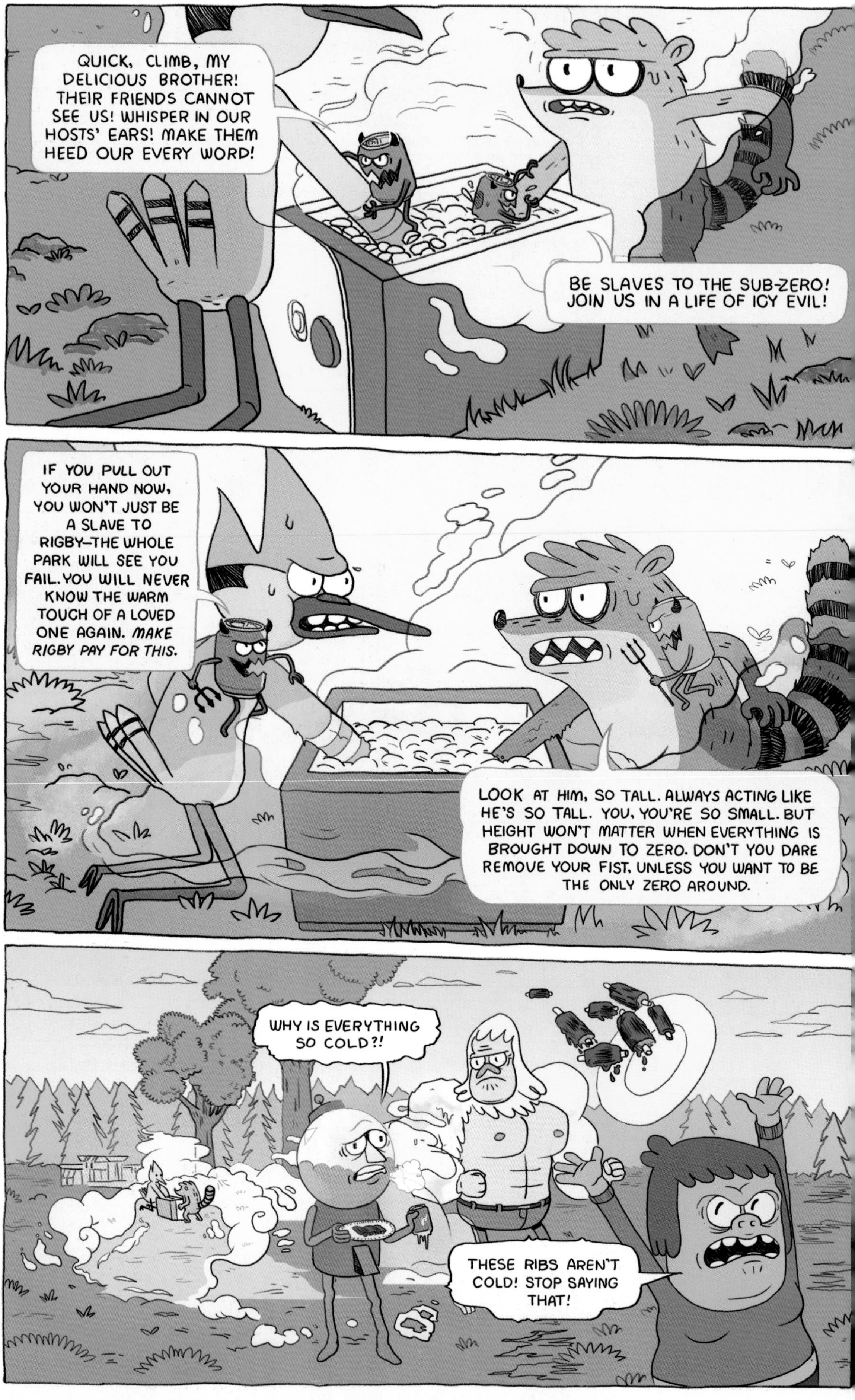
QUICK, CLIMB, MY DELICIOUS BROTHER! THEIR FRIENDS CANNOT SEE US! WHISPER IN OUR HOSTS' EARS! MAKE THEM HEED OUR EVERY WORD!
BE SLAVES TO THE SUB-ZERO! JOIN US IN A LIFE OF ICY EVIL!
IF YOU PULL OUT YOUR HAND NOW, YOU WON'T JUST BE A SLAVE TO RIGBY—THE WHOLE PARK WILL SEE YOU FAIL. YOU WILL NEVER KNOW THE WARM TOUCH OF A LOVED ONE AGAIN. *MAKE RIGBY PAY FOR THIS.*
LOOK AT HIM, SO TALL. ALWAYS ACTING LIKE HE'S SO TALL. YOU, YOU'RE SO SMALL. BUT HEIGHT WON'T MATTER WHEN EVERYTHING IS BROUGHT DOWN TO ZERO. DON'T YOU DARE REMOVE YOUR FIST, UNLESS YOU WANT TO BE THE ONLY ZERO AROUND.
WHY IS EVERYTHING SO COLD?!
THESE RIBS AREN'T COLD! STOP SAYING THAT!

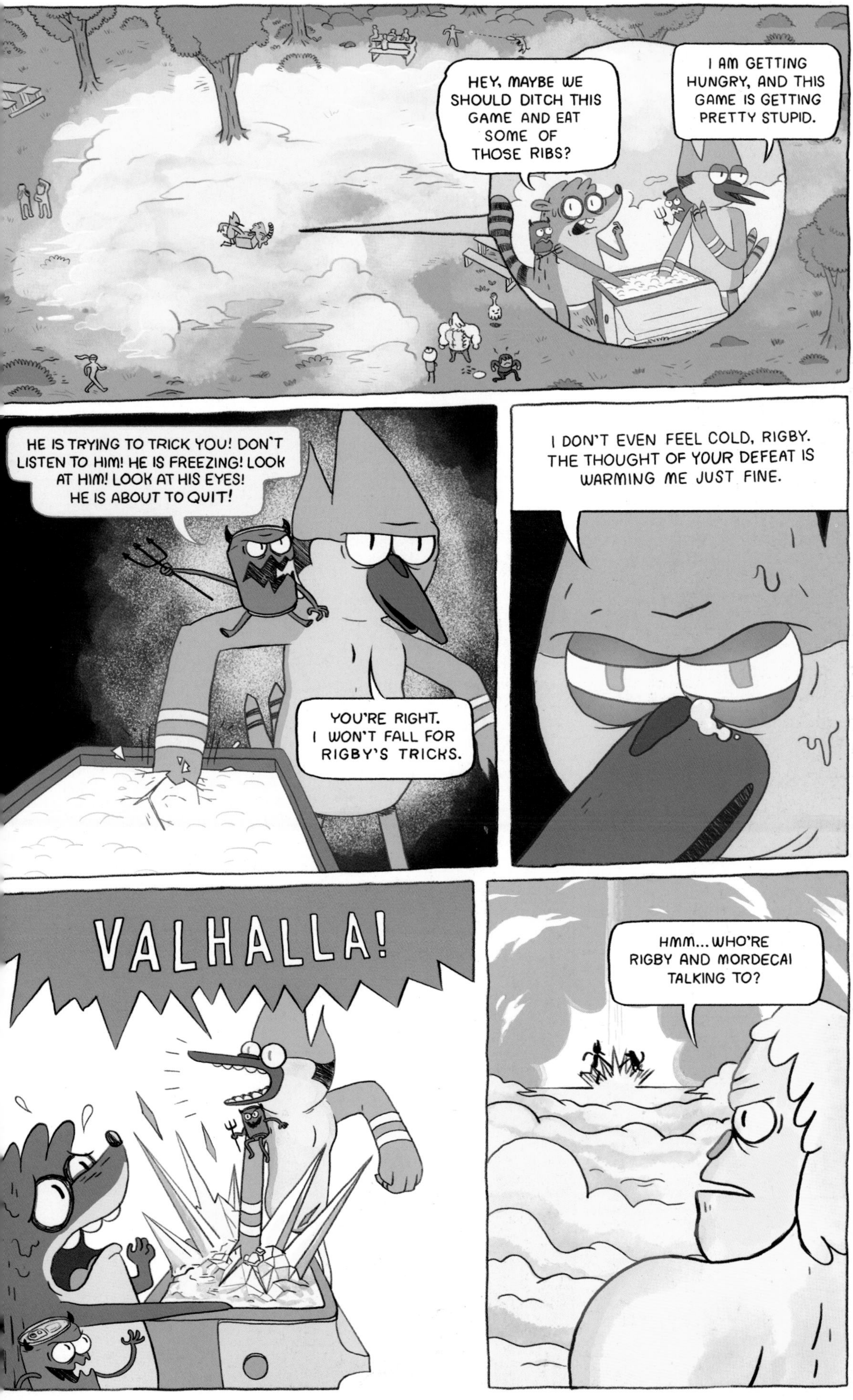

HEY, MAYBE WE SHOULD DITCH THIS GAME AND EAT SOME OF THOSE RIBS?
I AM GETTING HUNGRY, AND THIS GAME IS GETTING PRETTY STUPID.
HE IS TRYING TO TRICK YOU! DON'T LISTEN TO HIM! HE IS FREEZING! LOOK AT HIM! LOOK AT HIS EYES! HE IS ABOUT TO QUIT!
YOU'RE RIGHT. I WON'T FALL FOR RIGBY'S TRICKS.
I DON'T EVEN FEEL COLD, RIGBY. THE THOUGHT OF YOUR DEFEAT IS WARMING ME JUST FINE.
VALHALLA!
HMM... WHO'RE RIGBY AND MORDECAI TALKING TO?

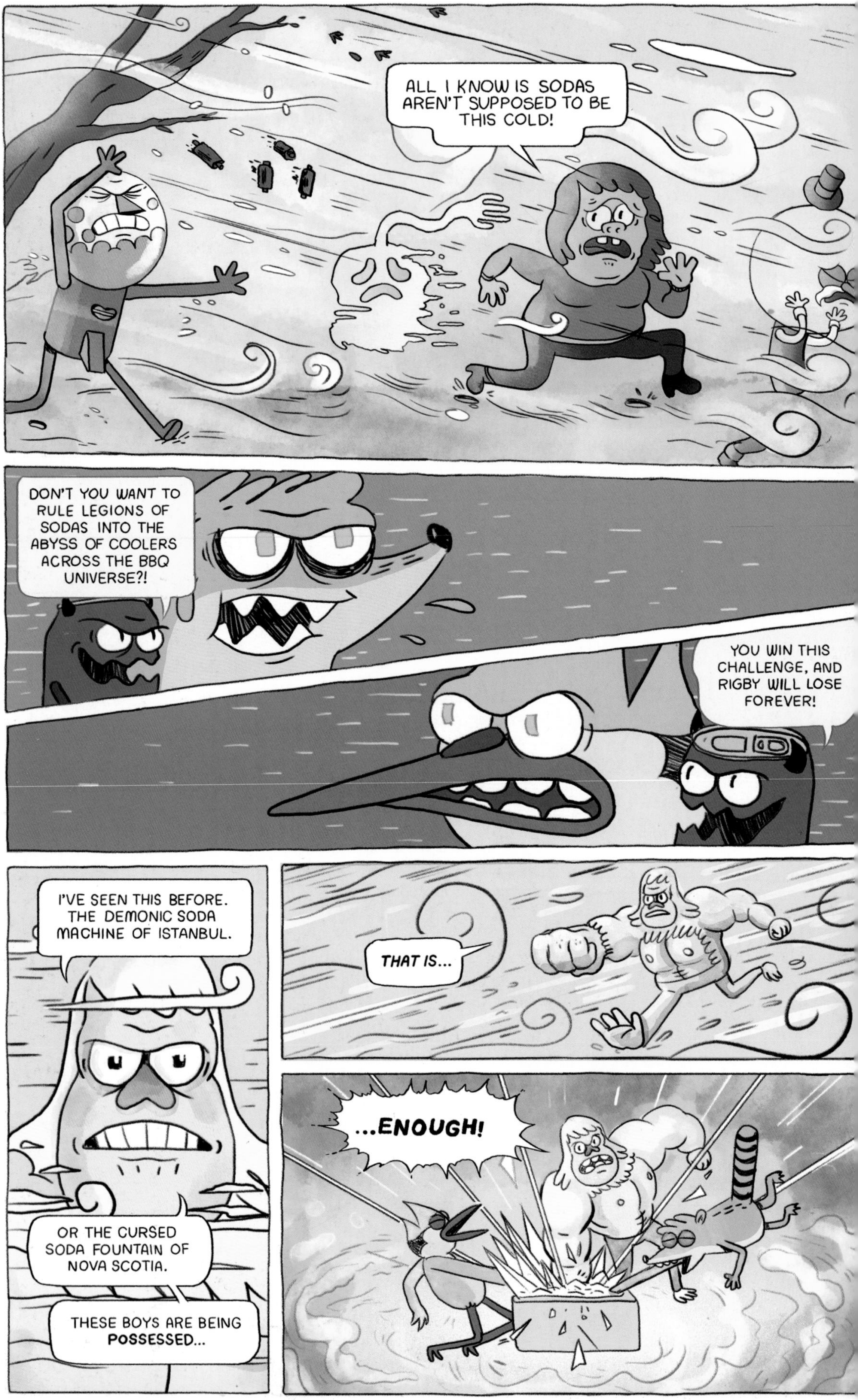
ALL I KNOW IS SODAS AREN'T SUPPOSED TO BE THIS COLD!
DON'T YOU WANT TO RULE LEGIONS OF SODAS INTO THE ABYSS OF COOLERS ACROSS THE BBQ UNIVERSE?!
YOU WIN THIS CHALLENGE, AND RIGBY WILL LOSE FOREVER!
I'VE SEEN THIS BEFORE. THE DEMONIC SODA MACHINE OF ISTANBUL.
OR THE CURSED SODA FOUNTAIN OF NOVA SCOTIA.
THESE BOYS ARE BEING POSSESSED...
THAT IS...
...ENOUGH!

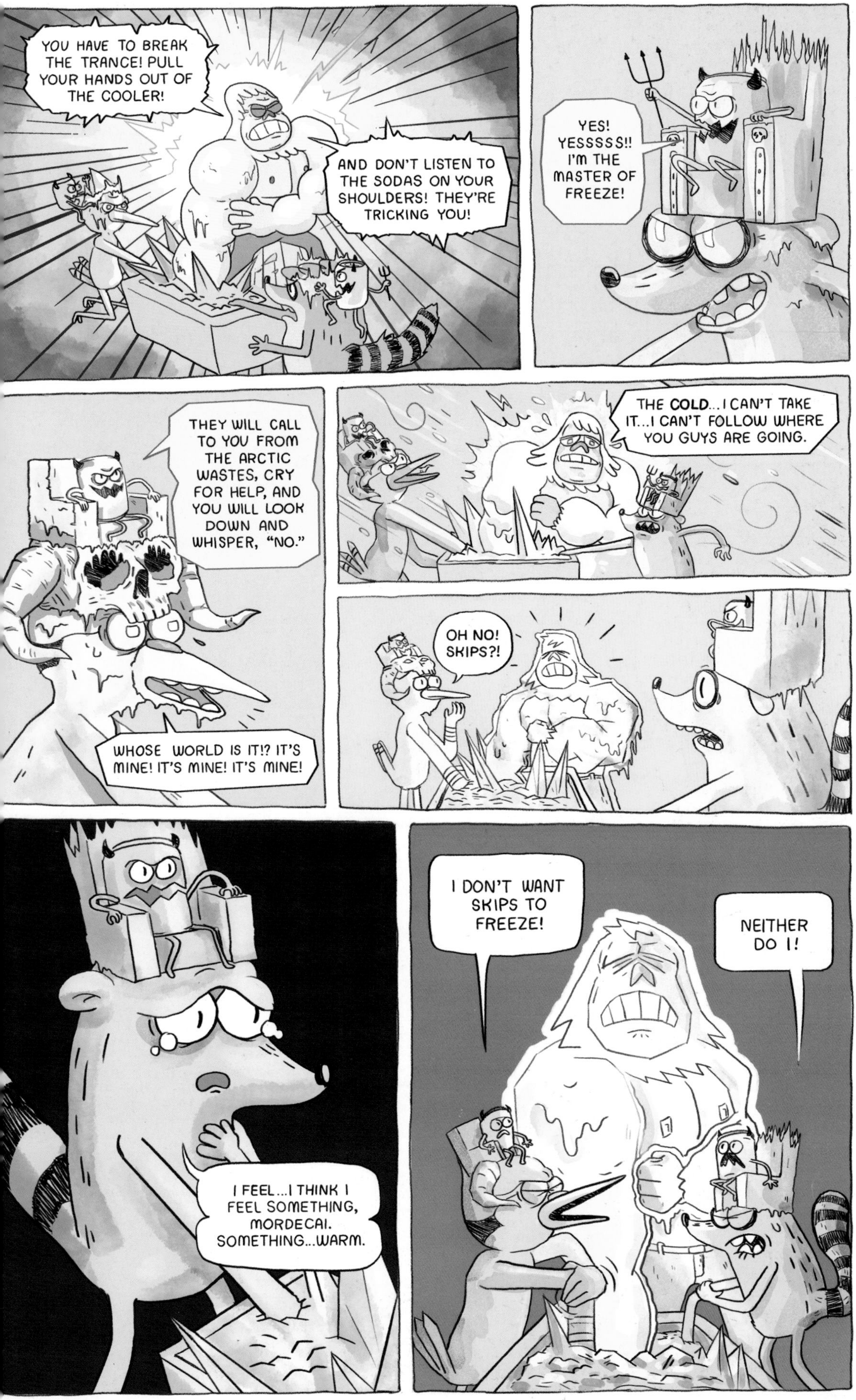
YOU HAVE TO BREAK THE TRANCE! PULL YOUR HANDS OUT OF THE COOLER!
AND DON'T LISTEN TO THE SODAS ON YOUR SHOULDERS! THEY'RE TRICKING YOU!
YES! YESSSSS!! I'M THE MASTER OF FREEZE!
THEY WILL CALL TO YOU FROM THE ARCTIC WASTES, CRY FOR HELP, AND YOU WILL LOOK DOWN AND WHISPER, "NO."
WHOSE WORLD IS IT!? IT'S MINE! IT'S MINE! IT'S MINE!
THE COLD... I CAN'T TAKE IT... I CAN'T FOLLOW WHERE YOU GUYS ARE GOING.
OH NO! SKIPS?!
I FEEL... I THINK I FEEL SOMETHING, MORDECAI. SOMETHING... WARM.
I DON'T WANT SKIPS TO FREEZE!
NEITHER DO I!

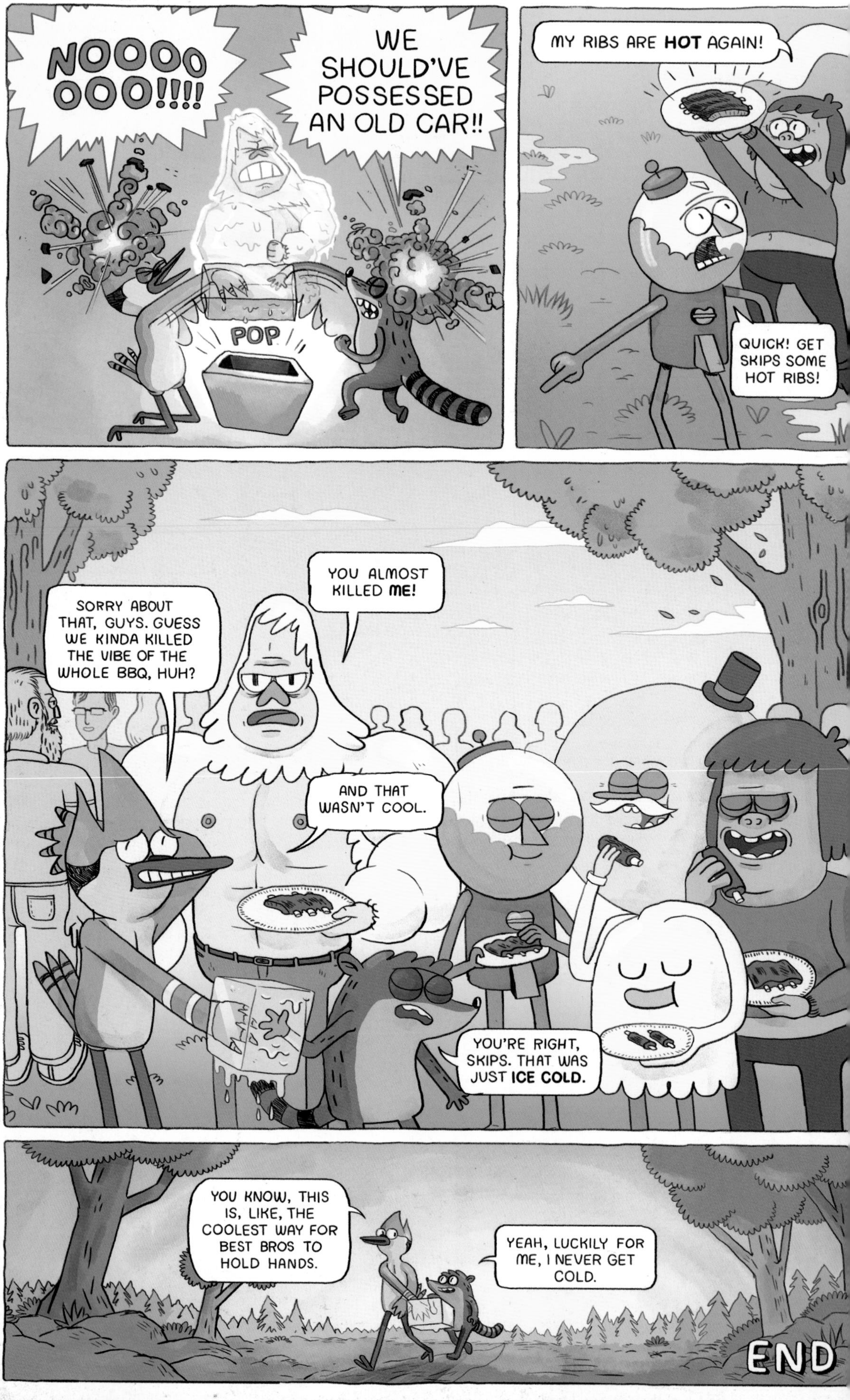
NOOOOOOO!!!!
WE SHOULD'VE POSSESSED AN OLD CAR!!
POP
MY RIBS ARE **HOT** AGAIN!
QUICK! GET SKIPS SOME HOT RIBS!
SORRY ABOUT THAT, GUYS. GUESS WE KINDA KILLED THE VIBE OF THE WHOLE BBQ, HUH?
YOU ALMOST KILLED **ME!**
AND THAT WASN'T COOL.
YOU'RE RIGHT, SKIPS. THAT WAS JUST **ICE COLD.**
YOU KNOW, THIS IS, LIKE, THE COOLEST WAY FOR BEST BROS TO HOLD HANDS.
YEAH, LUCKILY FOR ME, I NEVER GET COLD.
END

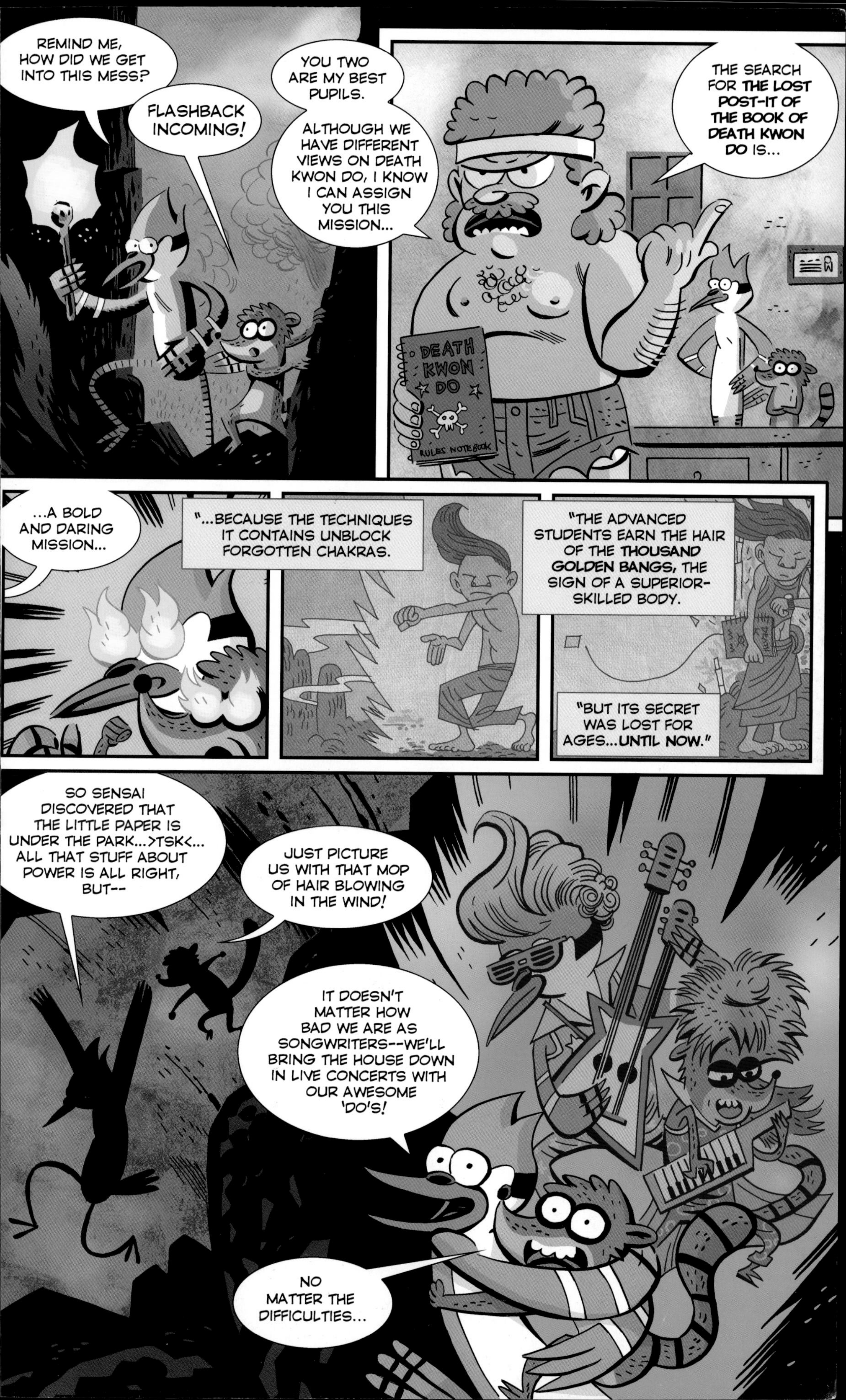
REMIND ME, HOW DID WE GET INTO THIS MESS?
FLASHBACK INCOMING!
YOU TWO ARE MY BEST PUPILS.
ALTHOUGH WE HAVE DIFFERENT VIEWS ON DEATH KWON DO, I KNOW I CAN ASSIGN YOU THIS MISSION...
THE SEARCH FOR **THE LOST POST-IT OF THE BOOK OF DEATH KWON DO** IS...
DEATH KWON DO
RULES NOTEBOOK
...A BOLD AND DARING MISSION...
"...BECAUSE THE TECHNIQUES IT CONTAINS UNBLOCK FORGOTTEN CHAKRAS.
"THE ADVANCED STUDENTS EARN THE HAIR OF THE **THOUSAND GOLDEN BANGS**, THE SIGN OF A SUPERIOR-SKILLED BODY.
"BUT ITS SECRET WAS LOST FOR AGES...**UNTIL NOW.**"
SO SENSAI DISCOVERED THAT THE LITTLE PAPER IS UNDER THE PARK...>TSK<... ALL THAT STUFF ABOUT POWER IS ALL RIGHT, BUT--
JUST PICTURE US WITH THAT MOP OF HAIR BLOWING IN THE WIND!
IT DOESN'T MATTER HOW BAD WE ARE AS SONGWRITERS--WE'LL BRING THE HOUSE DOWN IN LIVE CONCERTS WITH OUR AWESOME 'DO'S!
NO MATTER THE DIFFICULTIES...

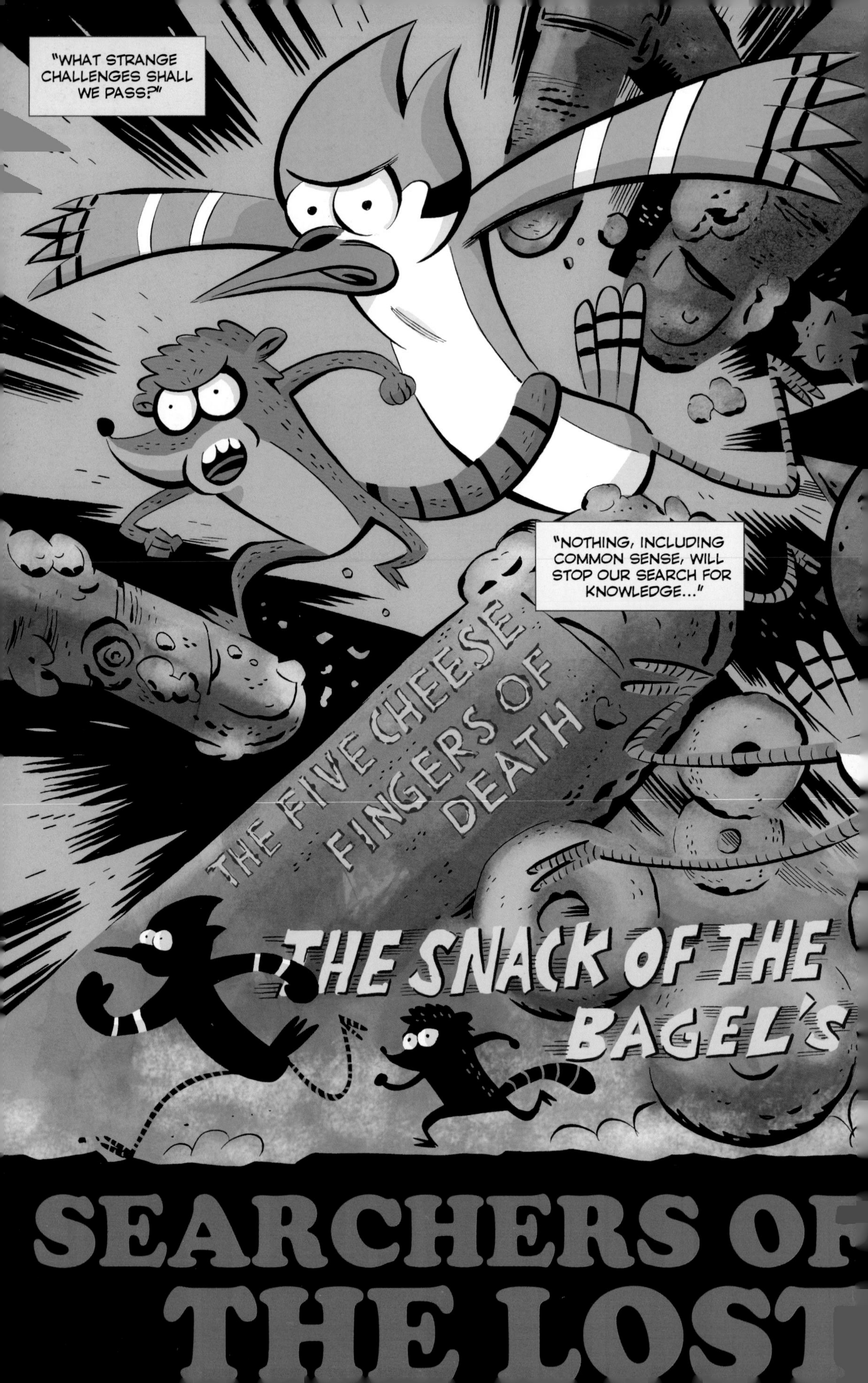
"WHAT STRANGE CHALLENGES SHALL WE PASS?"
"NOTHING, INCLUDING COMMON SENSE, WILL STOP OUR SEARCH FOR KNOWLEDGE..."
THE FIVE CHEESE FINGERS OF DEATH
THE SNACK OF THE BAGEL'S
SEARCHERS OF THE LOST

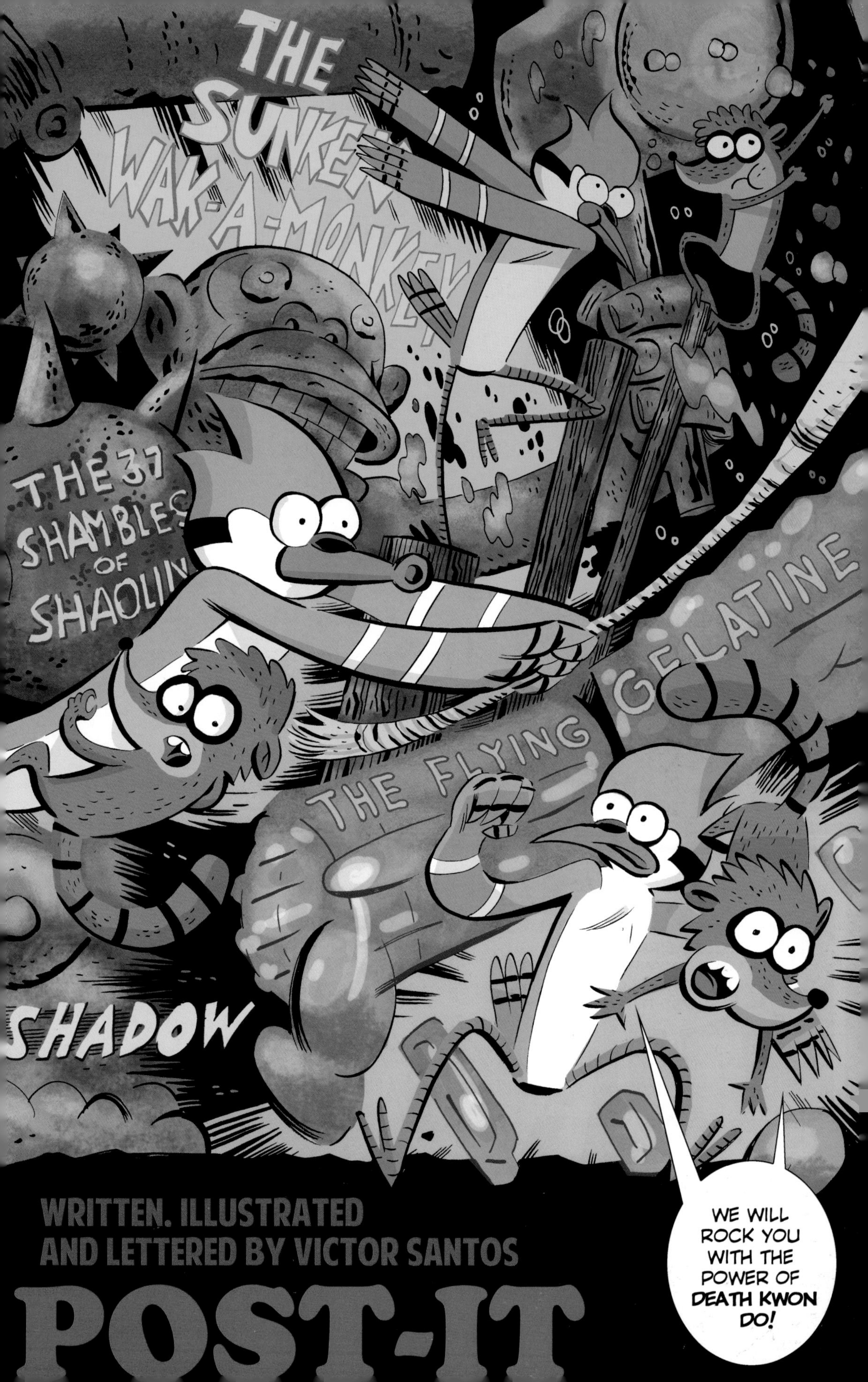
THE SUNKEN WAK-A-MONKEY
THE 37 SHAMBLES OF SHAOLIN
THE FLYING GELATINE
SHADOW
WRITTEN. ILLUSTRATED AND LETTERED BY VICTOR SANTOS
POST-IT
WE WILL ROCK YOU WITH THE POWER OF DEATH KWON DO!

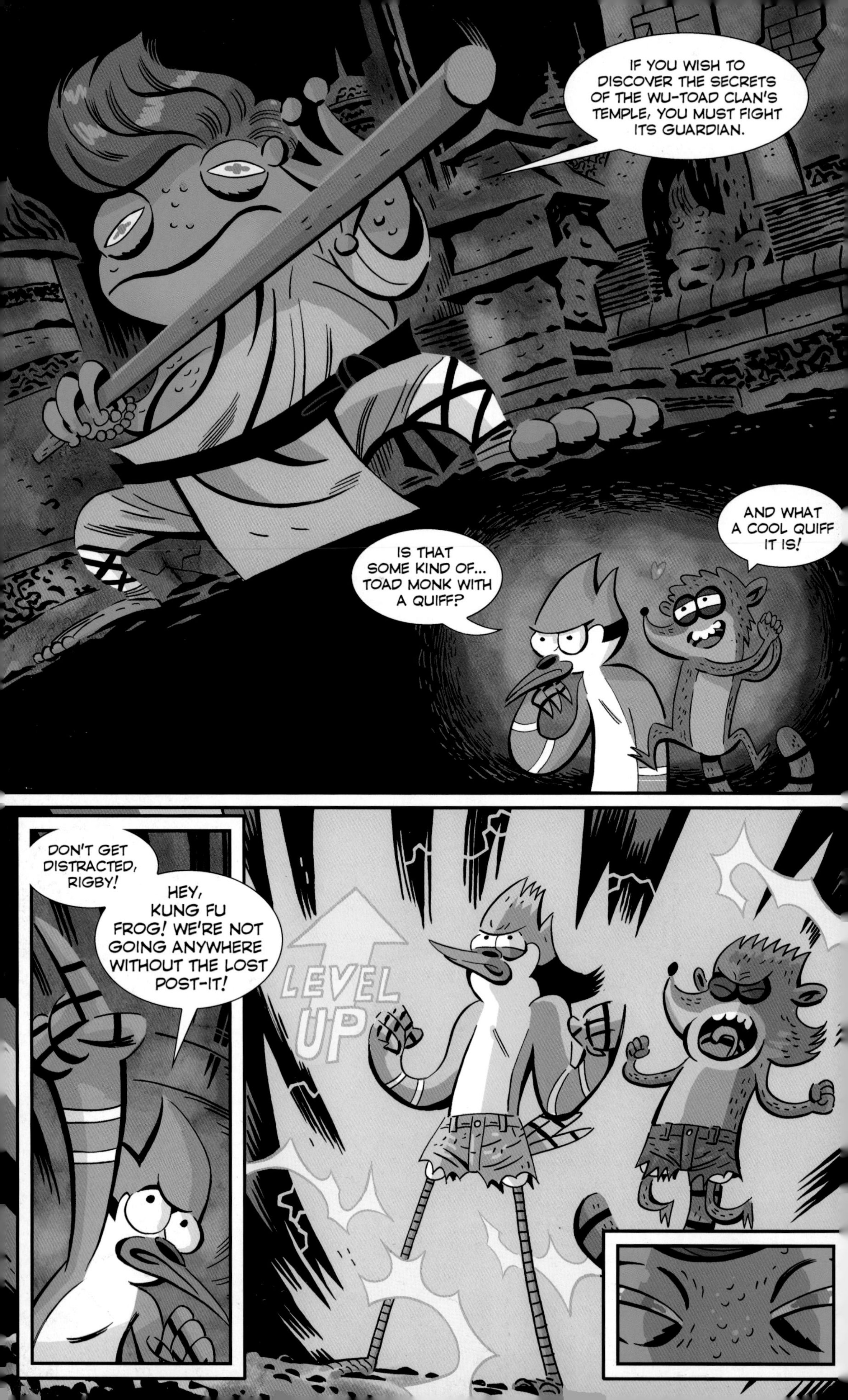
IF YOU WISH TO DISCOVER THE SECRETS OF THE WU-TOAD CLAN'S TEMPLE, YOU MUST FIGHT ITS GUARDIAN.
IS THAT SOME KIND OF... TOAD MONK WITH A QUIFF?
AND WHAT A COOL QUIFF IT IS!
DON'T GET DISTRACTED, RIGBY!
HEY, KUNG FU FROG! WE'RE NOT GOING ANYWHERE WITHOUT THE LOST POST-IT!
LEVEL UP

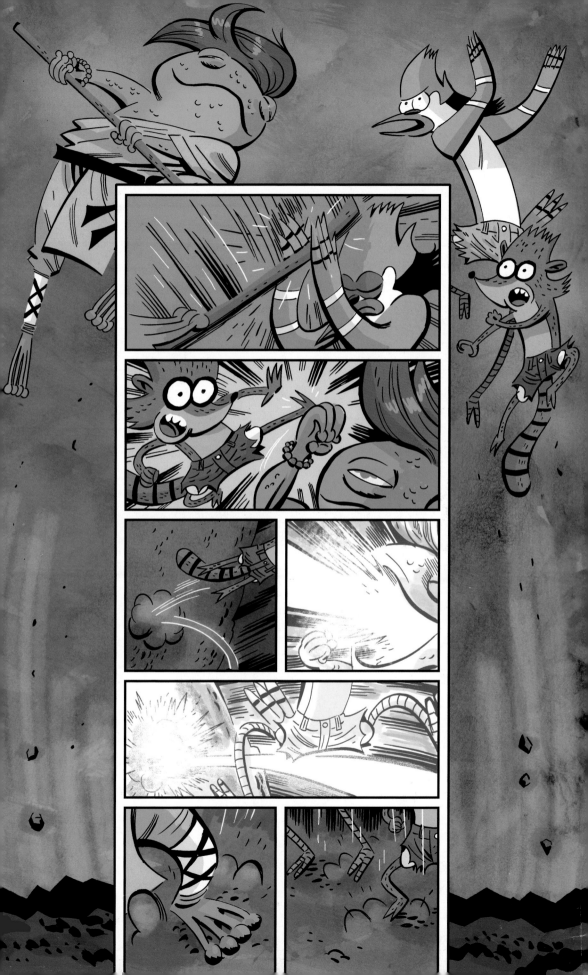

I KNOW ALL YOUR MOVEMENTS... YOU'RE USING DEATH KWON DO.

SENSAI HAS SENT YOU...

YOU'RE NOBLE WARRIORS. DO NOT LET HIM MANIPULATE YOU. WHO KNOWS WHAT THAT POWER-THIRSTY SCOUNDREL PLANS TO DO WITH THE LOST POST-IT--HIS INTENTIONS ARE EVIL.

THE DUDE IS RIGHT, MAN.

THAT SENSAI HAS TRICKED US MORE THAN ONCE.

YEAH! WE DON'T NEED HIM! WE'RE MASTERS NOW, IN OUR STYLE.

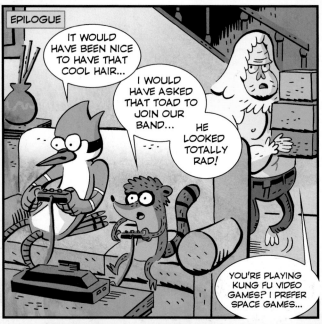

EPILOGUE

IT WOULD HAVE BEEN NICE TO HAVE THAT COOL HAIR...

I WOULD HAVE ASKED THAT TOAD TO JOIN OUR BAND...

HE LOOKED TOTALLY RAD!

YOU'RE PLAYING KUNG FU VIDEO GAMES? I PREFER SPACE GAMES...

END

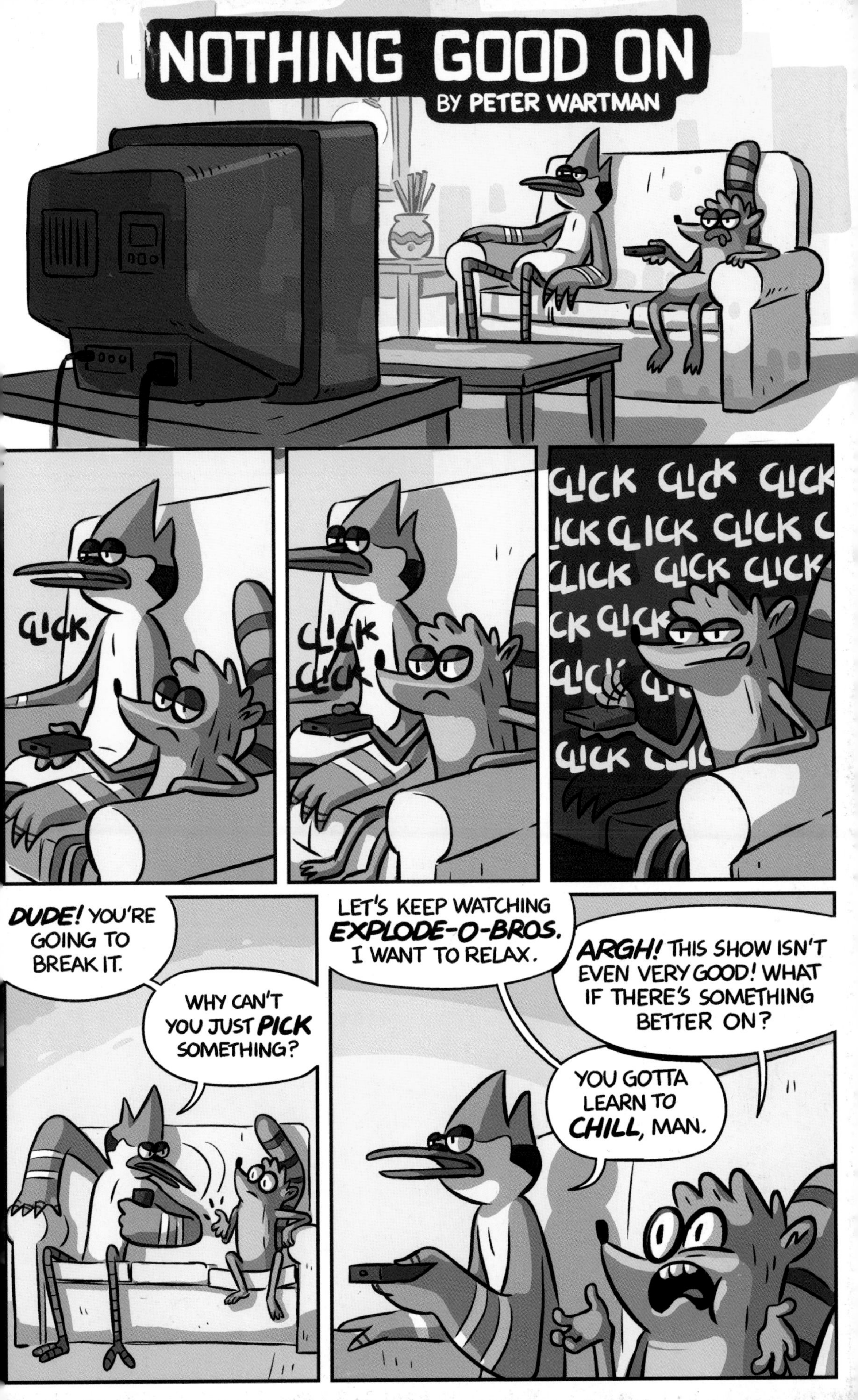
NOTHING GOOD ON
BY PETER WARTMAN
CLICK
CLICK
CLICK
CLICK CLICK CLICK
CLICK CLICK CLICK
CLICK CLICK CLICK
CLICK
CLICK
DUDE! YOU'RE GOING TO BREAK IT.
WHY CAN'T YOU JUST PICK SOMETHING?
LET'S KEEP WATCHING EXPLODE-O-BROS. I WANT TO RELAX.
ARGH! THIS SHOW ISN'T EVEN VERY GOOD! WHAT IF THERE'S SOMETHING BETTER ON?
YOU GOTTA LEARN TO CHILL, MAN.

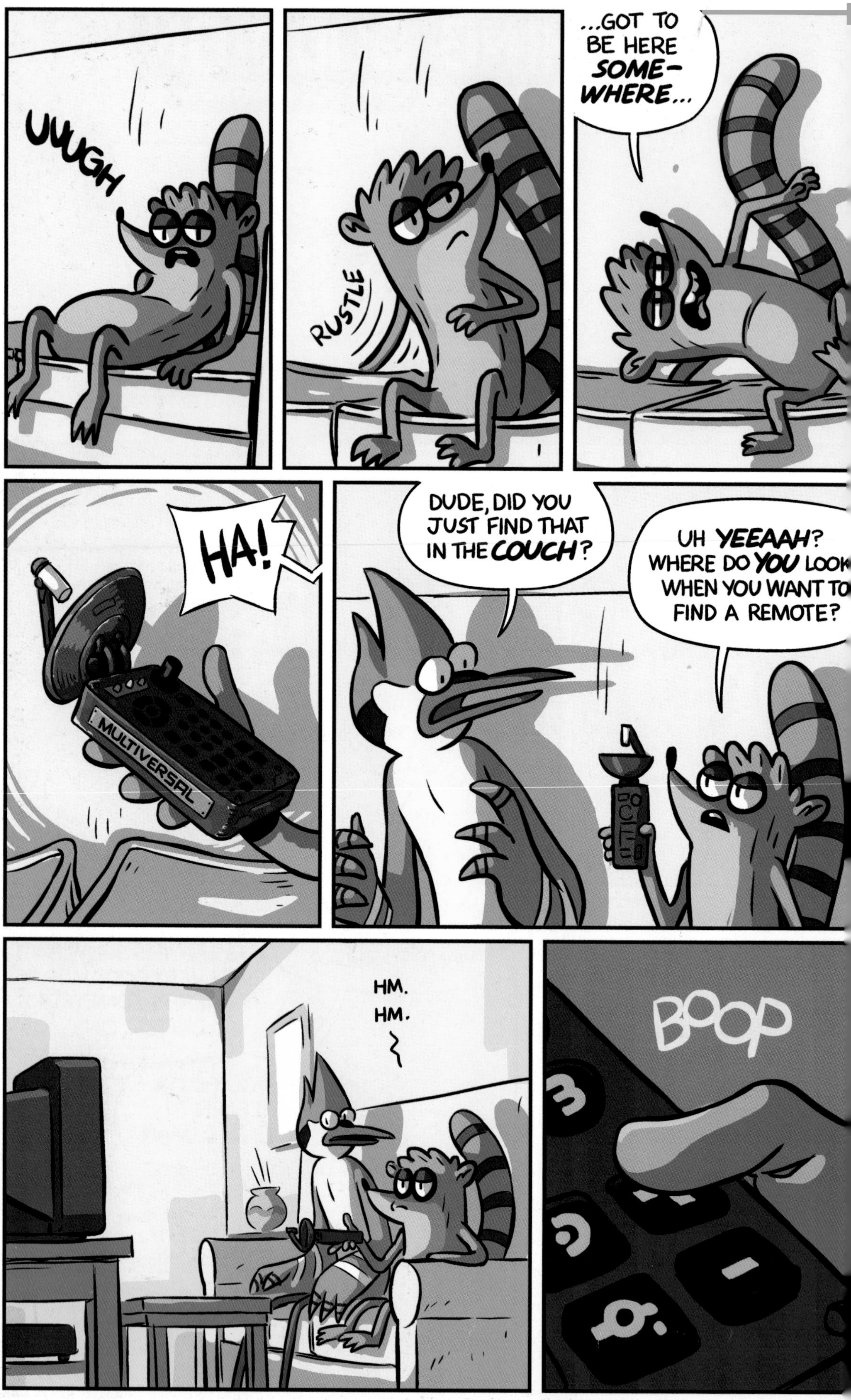
UUUGH
RUSTLE
...GOT TO BE HERE SOME-WHERE...
HA!
MULTIVERSAL
DUDE, DID YOU JUST FIND THAT IN THE COUCH?
UH YEEAAH? WHERE DO YOU LOOK WHEN YOU WANT TO FIND A REMOTE?
HM. HM.
BOOP

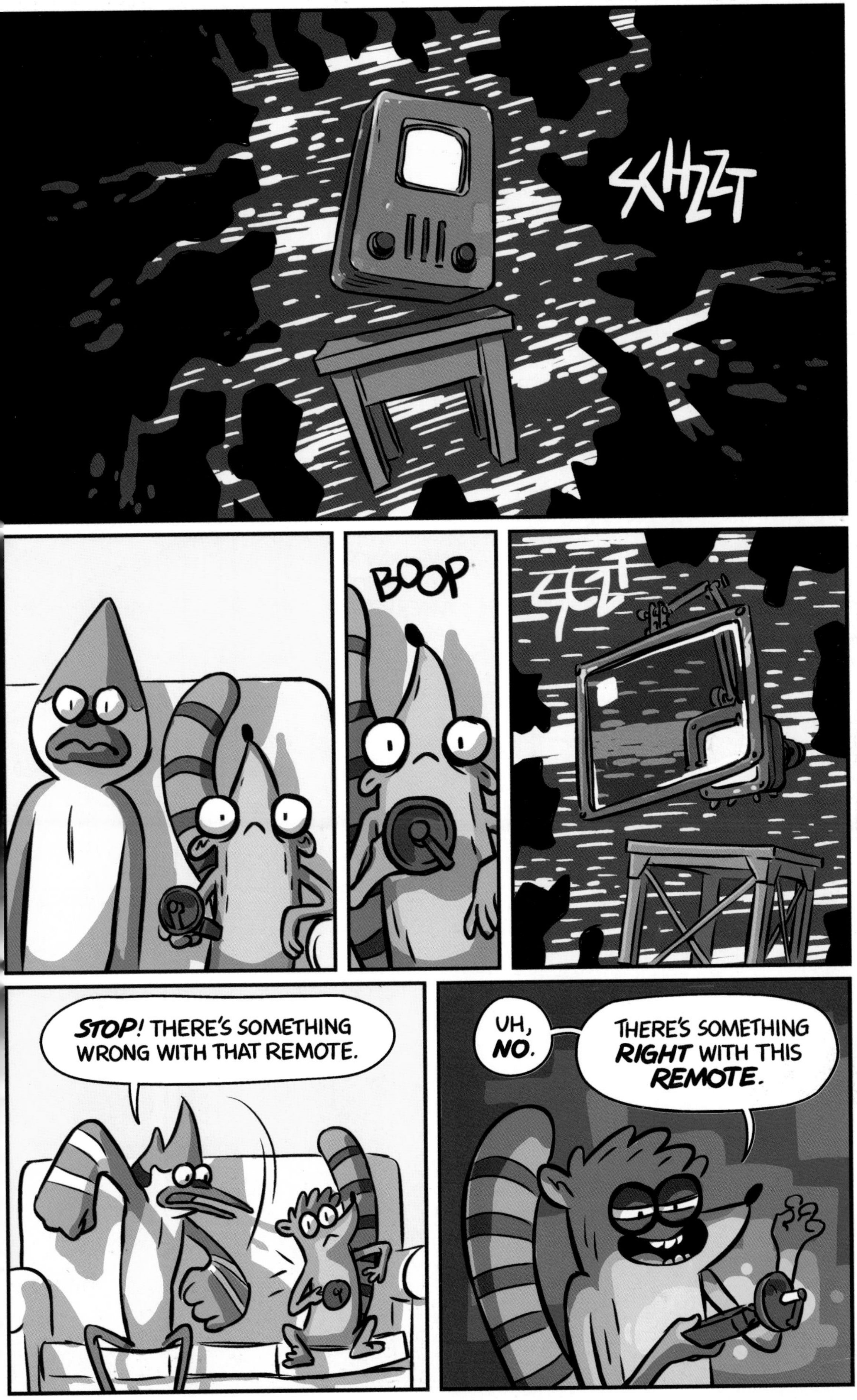
SCHZZT
BOOP
STOP! THERE'S SOMETHING WRONG WITH THAT REMOTE.
UH, NO.
THERE'S SOMETHING RIGHT WITH THIS REMOTE.

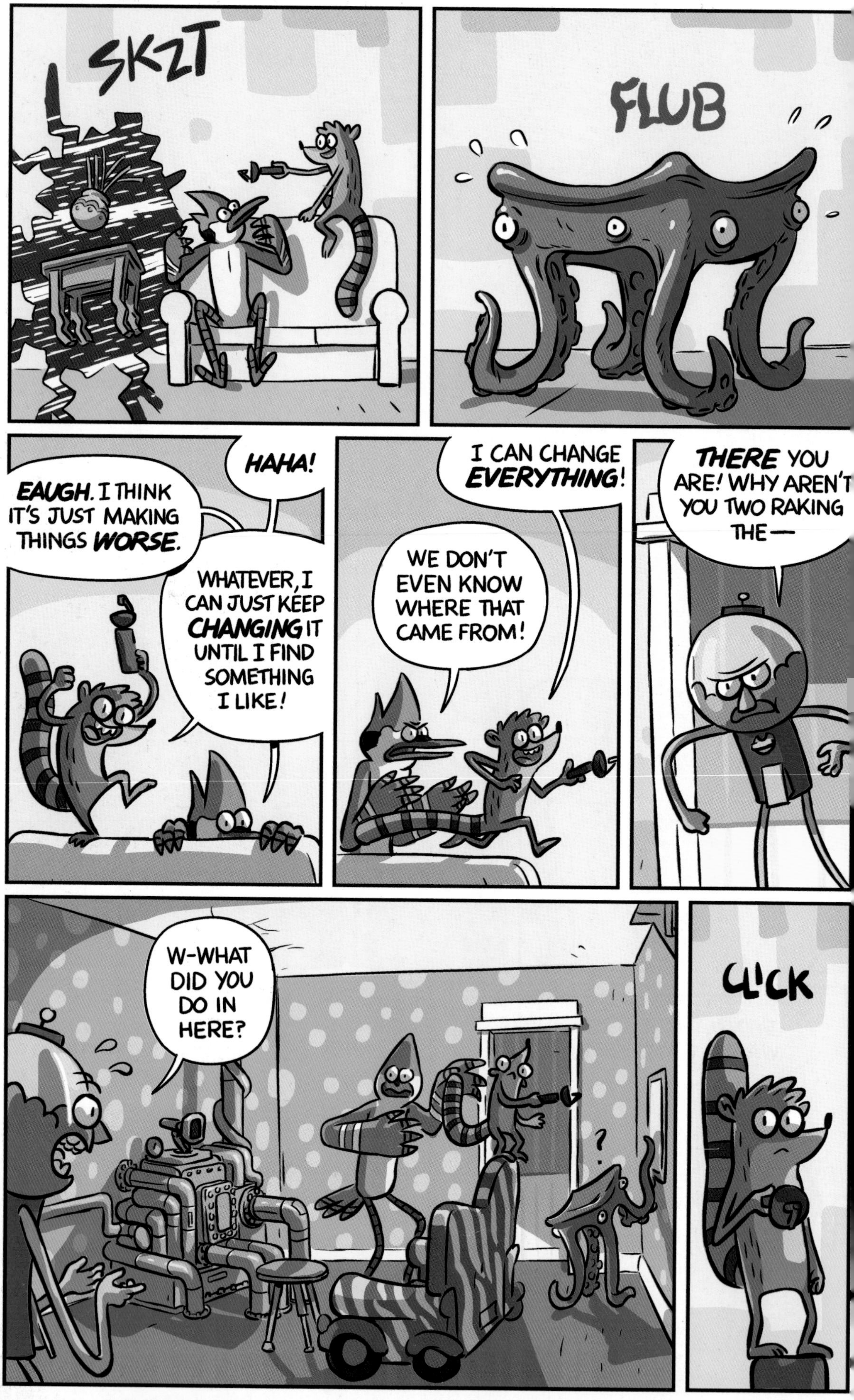
SKZT
FLUB
EAUGH. I THINK IT'S JUST MAKING THINGS WORSE.
HAHA!
WHATEVER, I CAN JUST KEEP CHANGING IT UNTIL I FIND SOMETHING I LIKE!
I CAN CHANGE EVERYTHING!
WE DON'T EVEN KNOW WHERE THAT CAME FROM!
THERE YOU ARE! WHY AREN'T YOU TWO RAKING THE—
W-WHAT DID YOU DO IN HERE?
?
CLICK

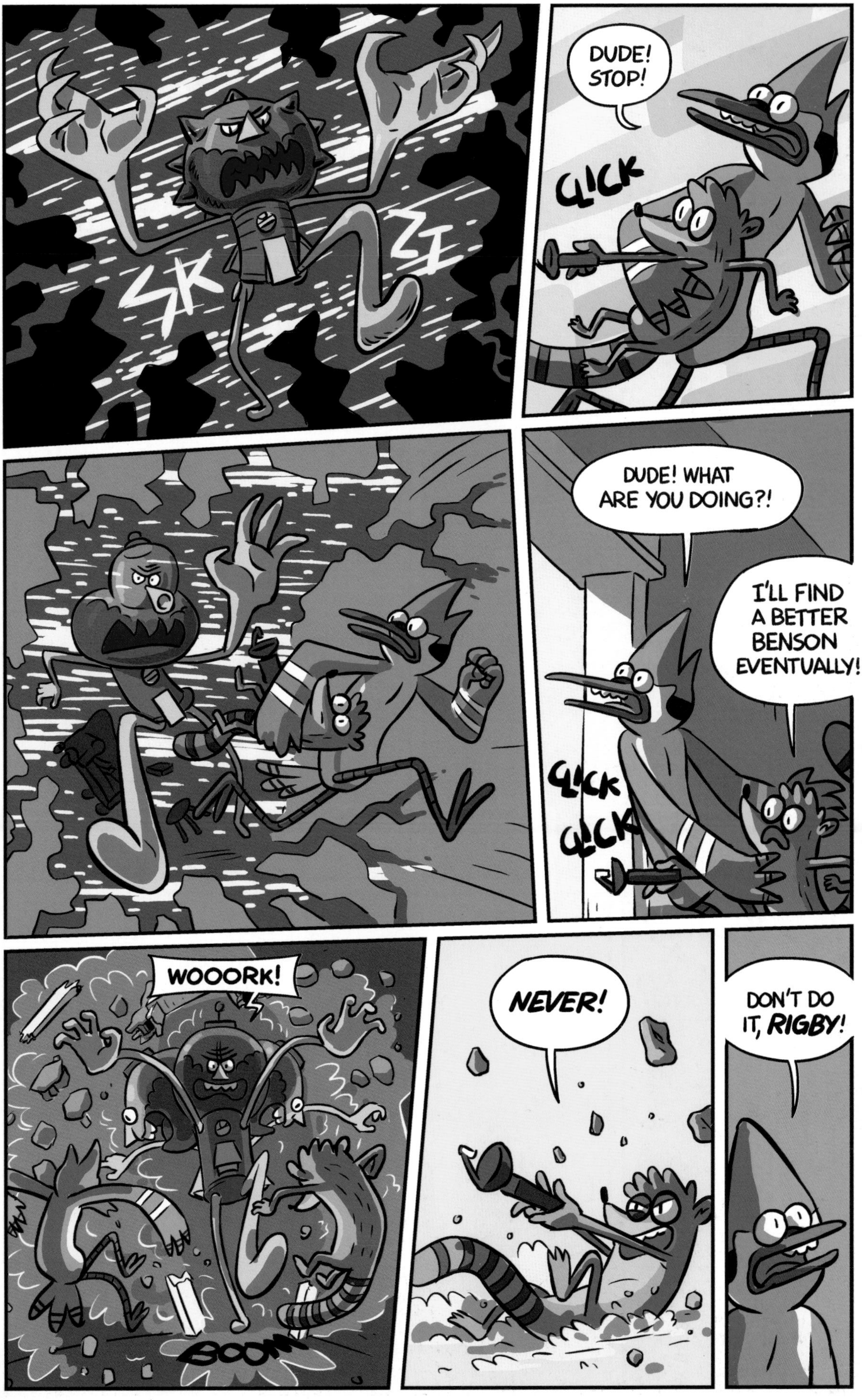
SKZZT
DUDE! STOP!
CLICK
DUDE! WHAT ARE YOU DOING?!
I'LL FIND A BETTER BENSON EVENTUALLY!
CLICK
CLICK
WOOORK!
BOOM
NEVER!
DON'T DO IT, RIGBY!

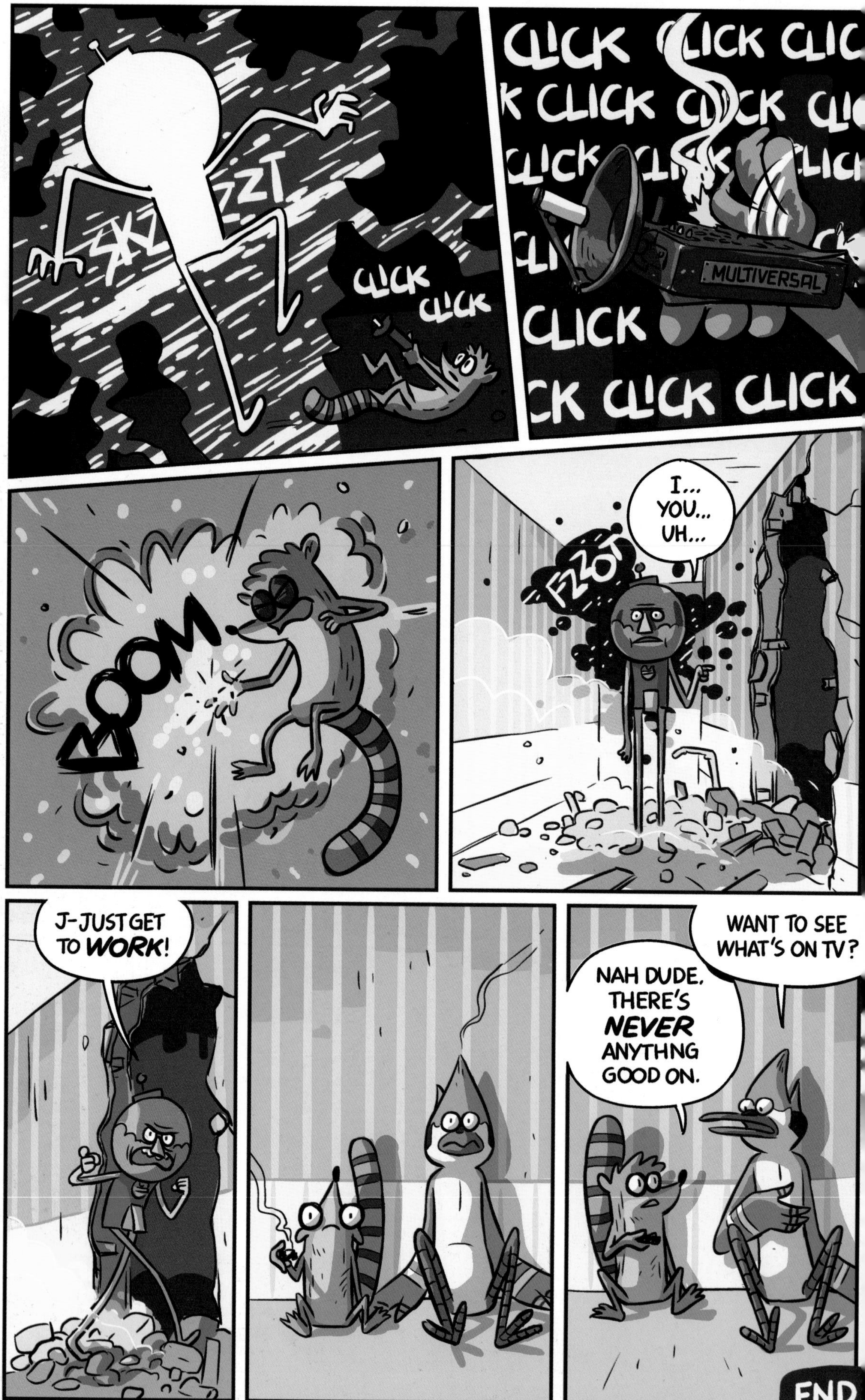
SKZZZZT
CLICK
CLICK
CLICK CLICK CLICK
K CLICK CLICK CLI
CLICK CLICK CLICK
CLI
MULTIVERSAL
CLICK
CK CLICK CLICK
BOOM
FZZOT
I... YOU... UH...
J-JUST GET TO WORK!
WANT TO SEE WHAT'S ON TV?
NAH DUDE. THERE'S NEVER ANYTHNG GOOD ON.
END

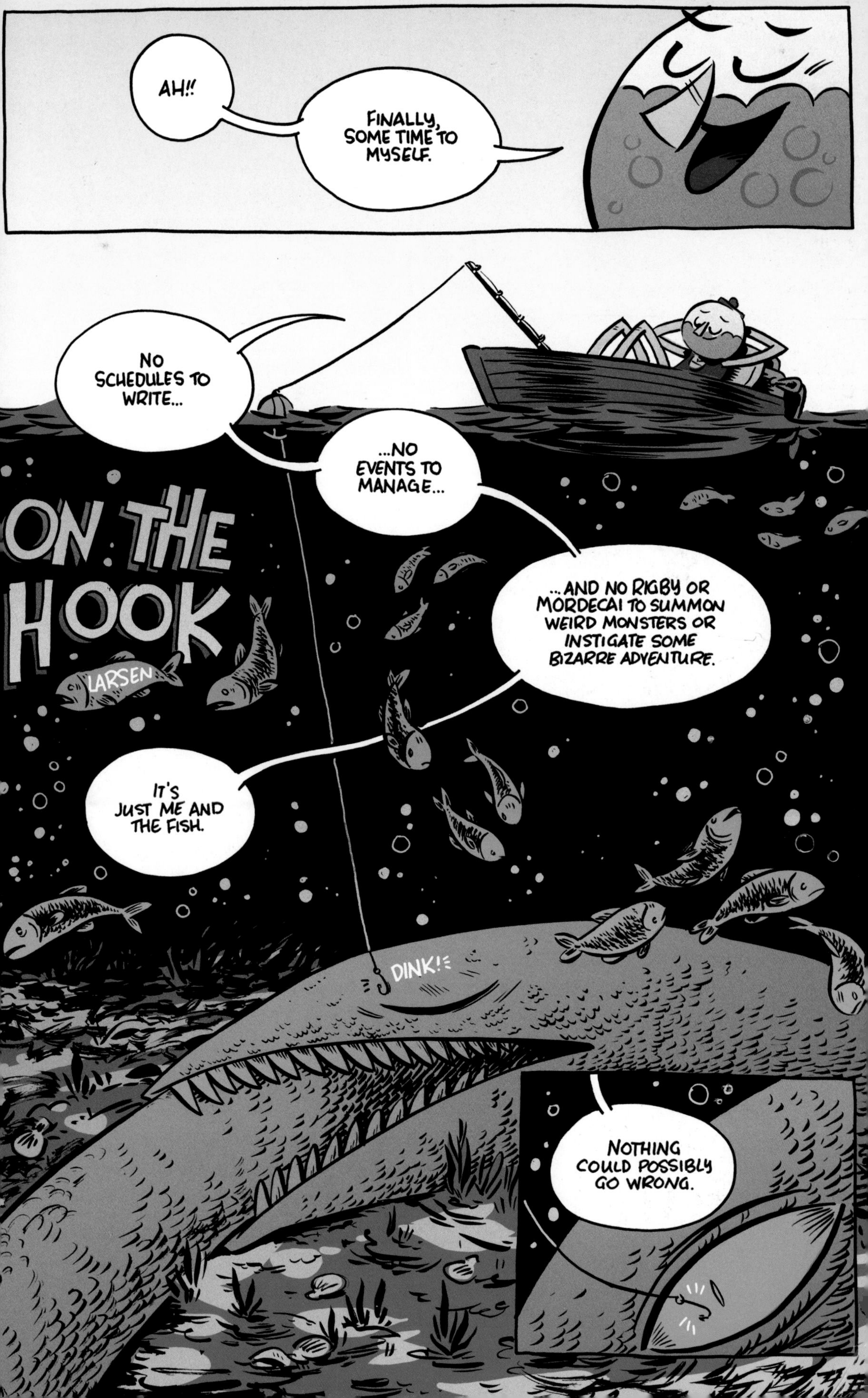
AH!!
FINALLY, SOME TIME TO MYSELF.
NO SCHEDULES TO WRITE...
...NO EVENTS TO MANAGE...
...AND NO RIGBY OR MORDECAI TO SUMMON WEIRD MONSTERS OR INSTIGATE SOME BIZARRE ADVENTURE.
ON THE HOOK
LARSEN
IT'S JUST ME AND THE FISH.
DINK!
NOTHING COULD POSSIBLY GO WRONG.

GURGLE GURGLE
OH NO.
ROAR!!
YOU'VE GOT TO BE KIDDING ME!
BLUB! BLUB!
I FEEL LIKE I HAD THIS COMING SOMEHOW...
WHAT THE GOOD GRAVY IS THAT?!
YO! HO! ROW, ROW! YO! HO!

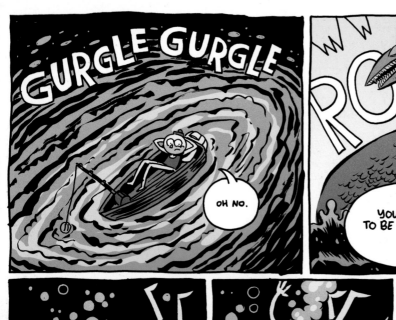

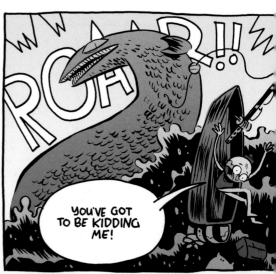

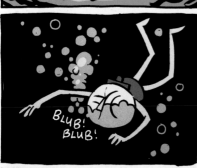

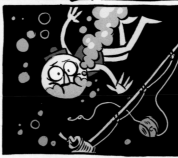

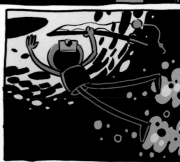

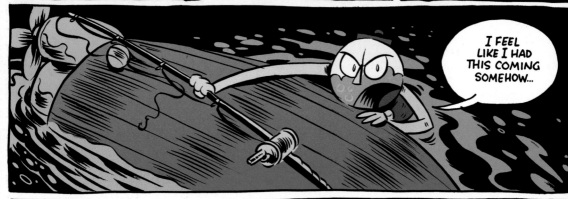

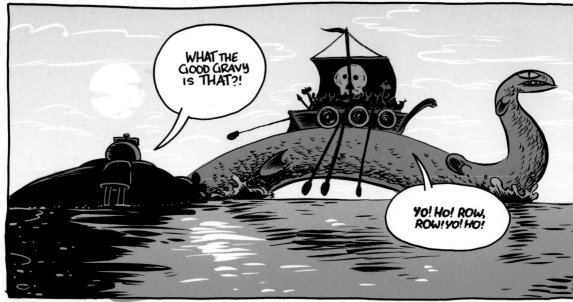

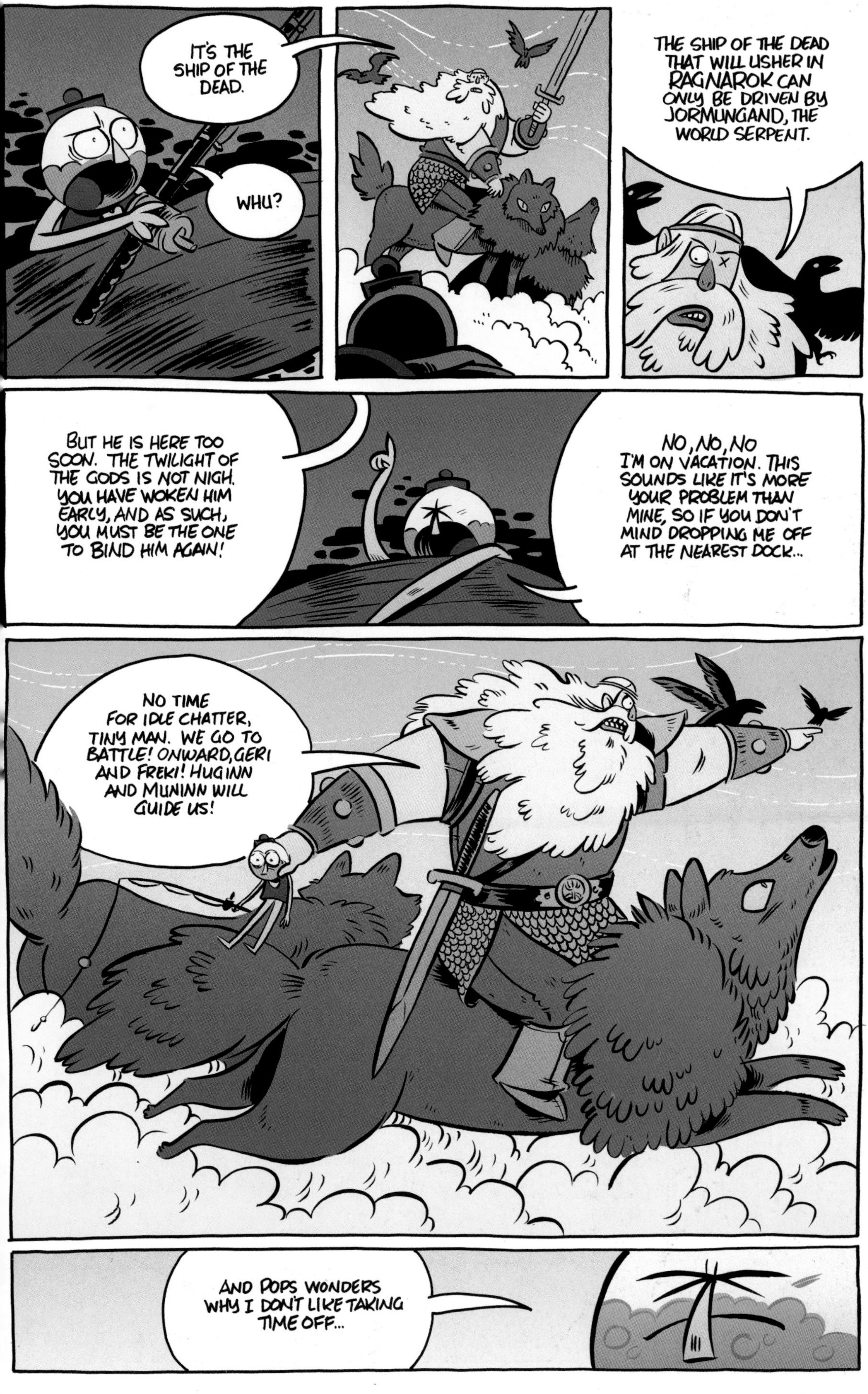
IT'S THE SHIP OF THE DEAD.
WHU?
THE SHIP OF THE DEAD THAT WILL USHER IN RAGNAROK CAN ONLY BE DRIVEN BY JORMUNGAND, THE WORLD SERPENT.
BUT HE IS HERE TOO SOON. THE TWILIGHT OF THE GODS IS NOT NIGH. YOU HAVE WOKEN HIM EARLY, AND AS SUCH, YOU MUST BE THE ONE TO BIND HIM AGAIN!
NO, NO, NO I'M ON VACATION. THIS SOUNDS LIKE IT'S MORE YOUR PROBLEM THAN MINE, SO IF YOU DON'T MIND DROPPING ME OFF AT THE NEAREST DOCK...
NO TIME FOR IDLE CHATTER, TINY MAN. WE GO TO BATTLE! ONWARD, GERI AND FREKI! HUGINN AND MUNINN WILL GUIDE US!
AND POPS WONDERS WHY I DON'T LIKE TAKING TIME OFF...

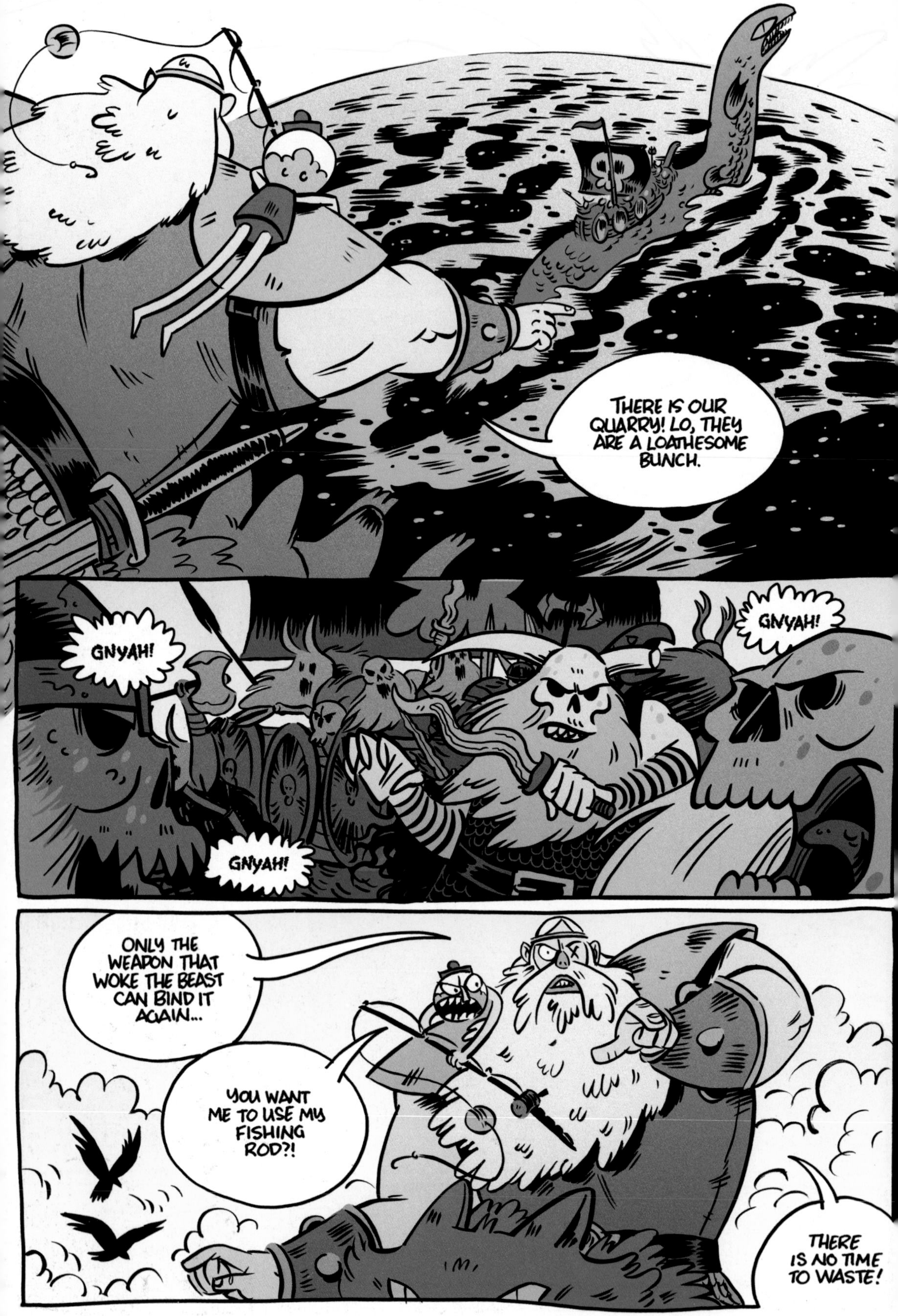
THERE IS OUR QUARRY! LO, THEY ARE A LOATHESOME BUNCH.
GNYAH!
GNYAH!
GNYAH!
ONLY THE WEAPON THAT WOKE THE BEAST CAN BIND IT AGAIN...
YOU WANT ME TO USE MY FISHING ROD?!
THERE IS NO TIME TO WASTE!

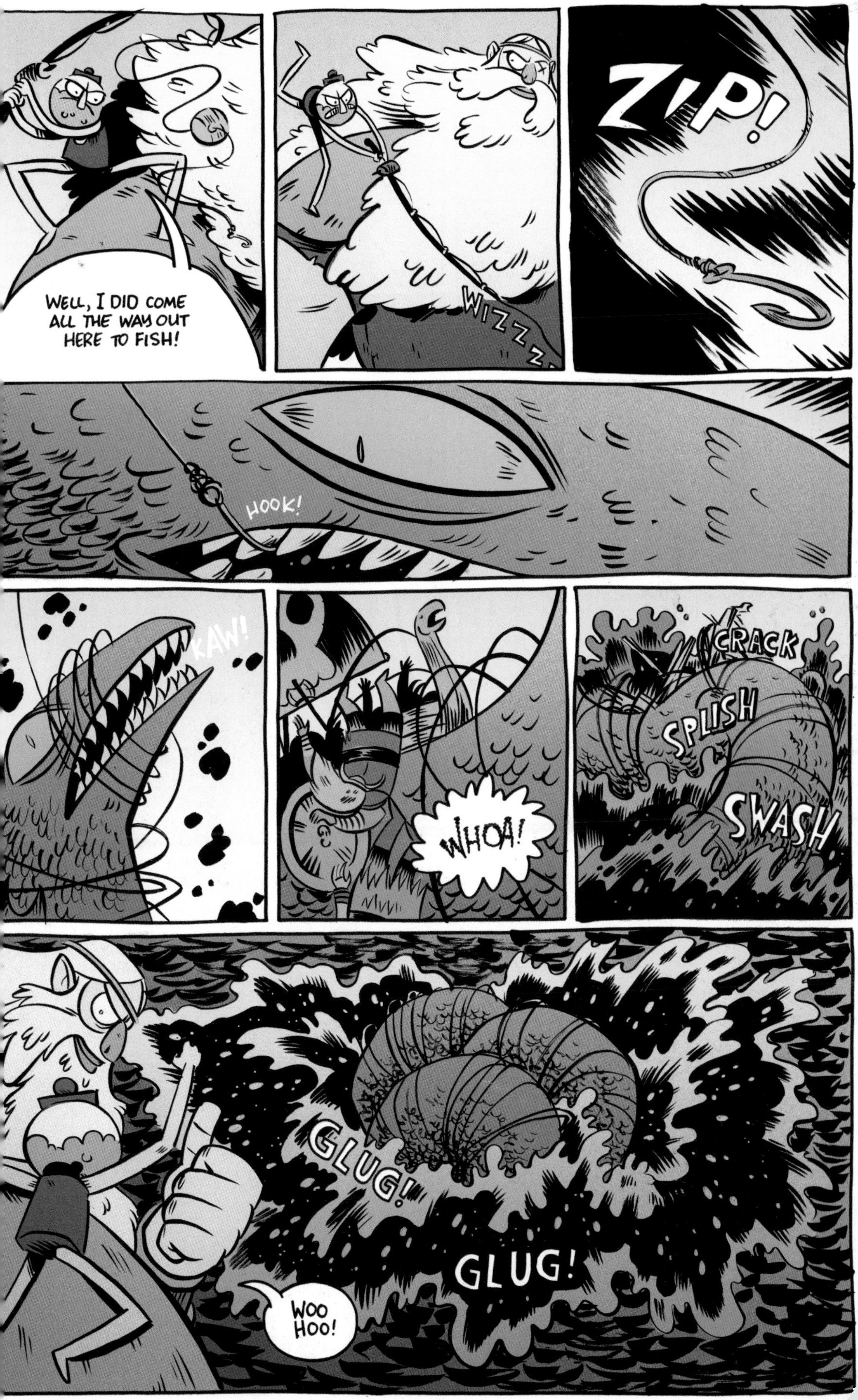

WELL, I DID COME ALL THE WAY OUT HERE TO FISH!
WIZZZZ
ZIP!
HOOK!
KAW!
WHOA!
CRACK
SPLISH
SWASH
GLUG!
GLUG!
WOO HOO!

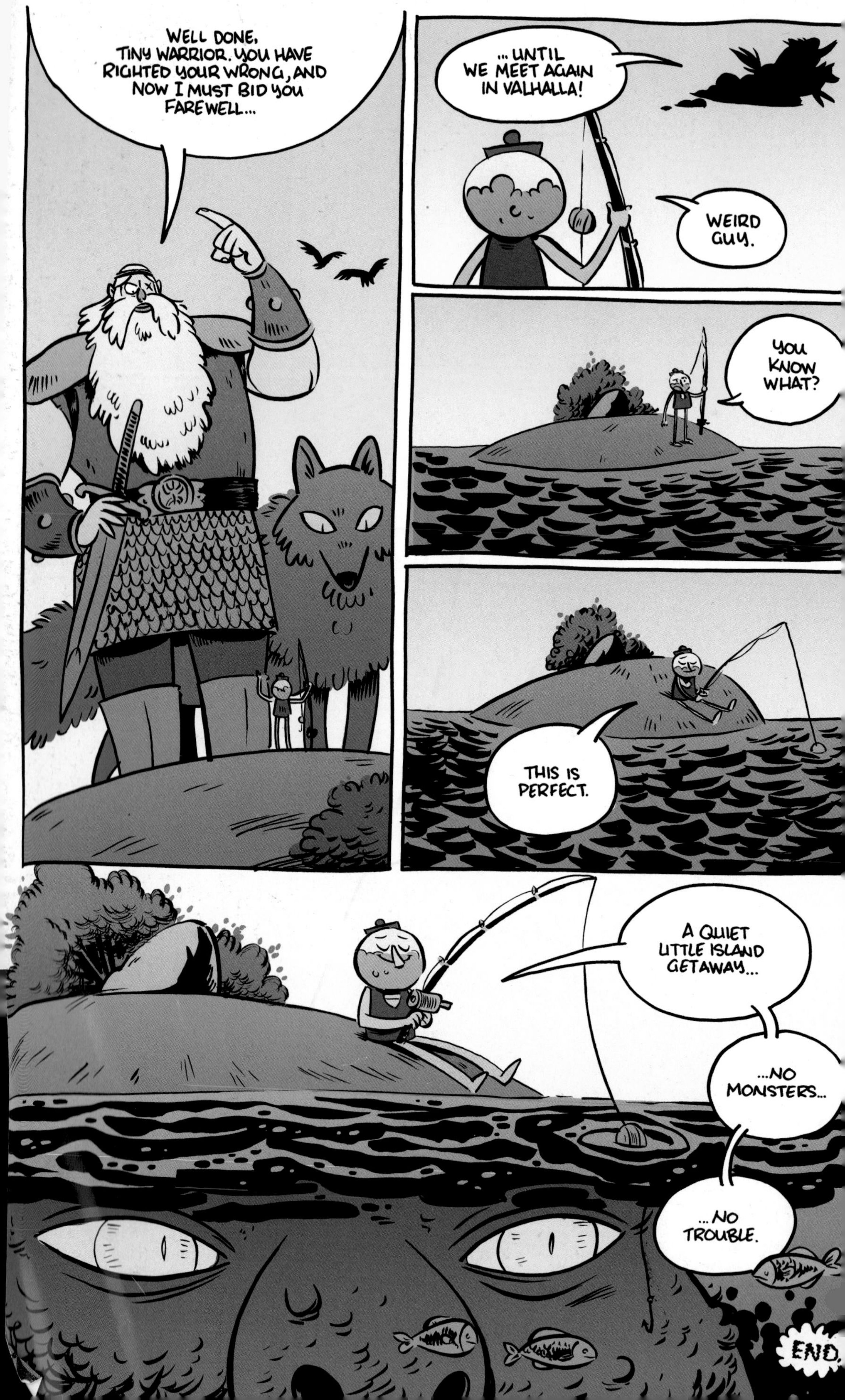
WELL DONE, TINY WARRIOR. YOU HAVE RIGHTED YOUR WRONG, AND NOW I MUST BID YOU FAREWELL...
... UNTIL WE MEET AGAIN IN VALHALLA!
WEIRD GUY.
YOU KNOW WHAT?
THIS IS PERFECT.
A QUIET LITTLE ISLAND GETAWAY...
...NO MONSTERS...
...NO TROUBLE.
END.

COVER GALLERY

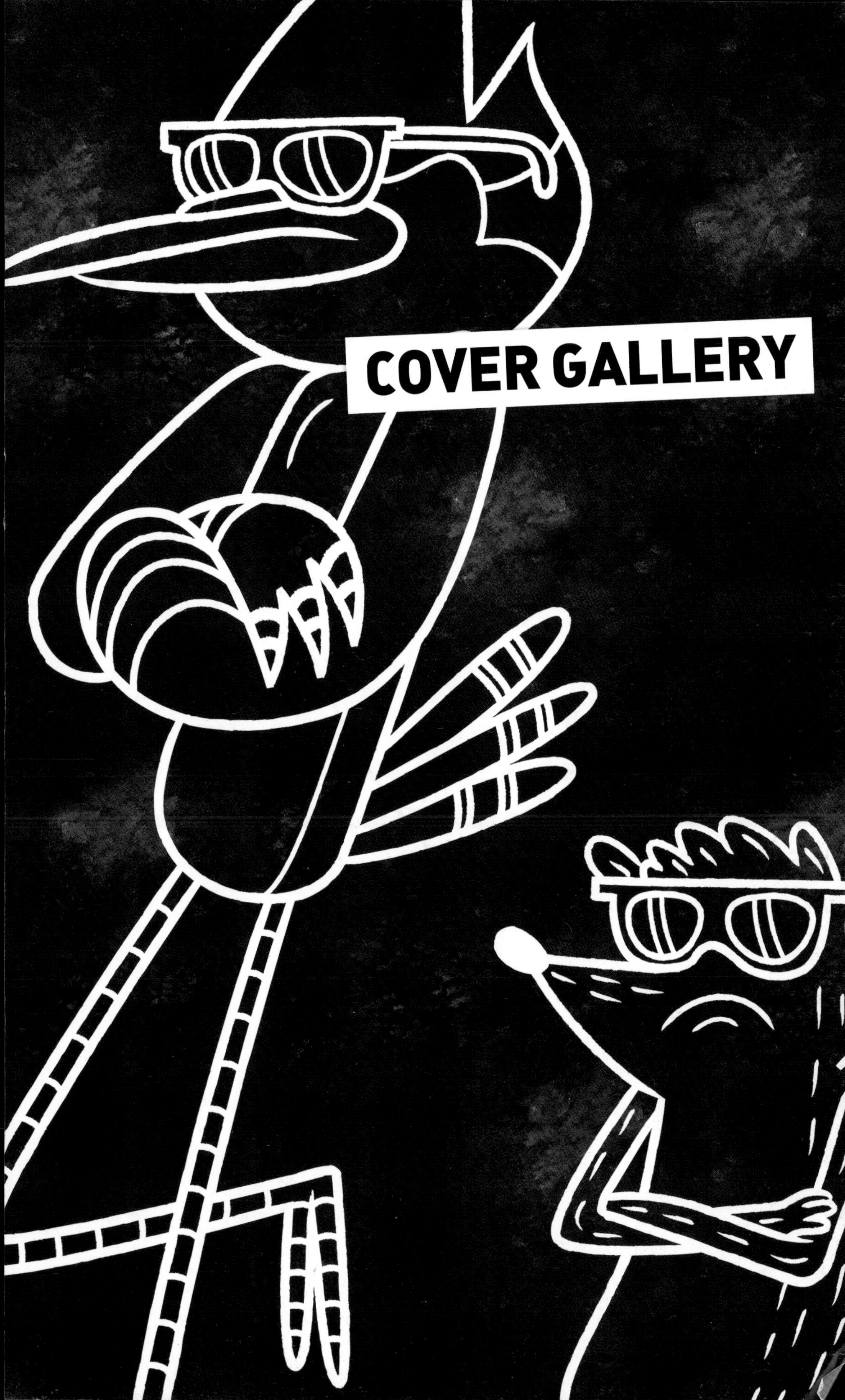

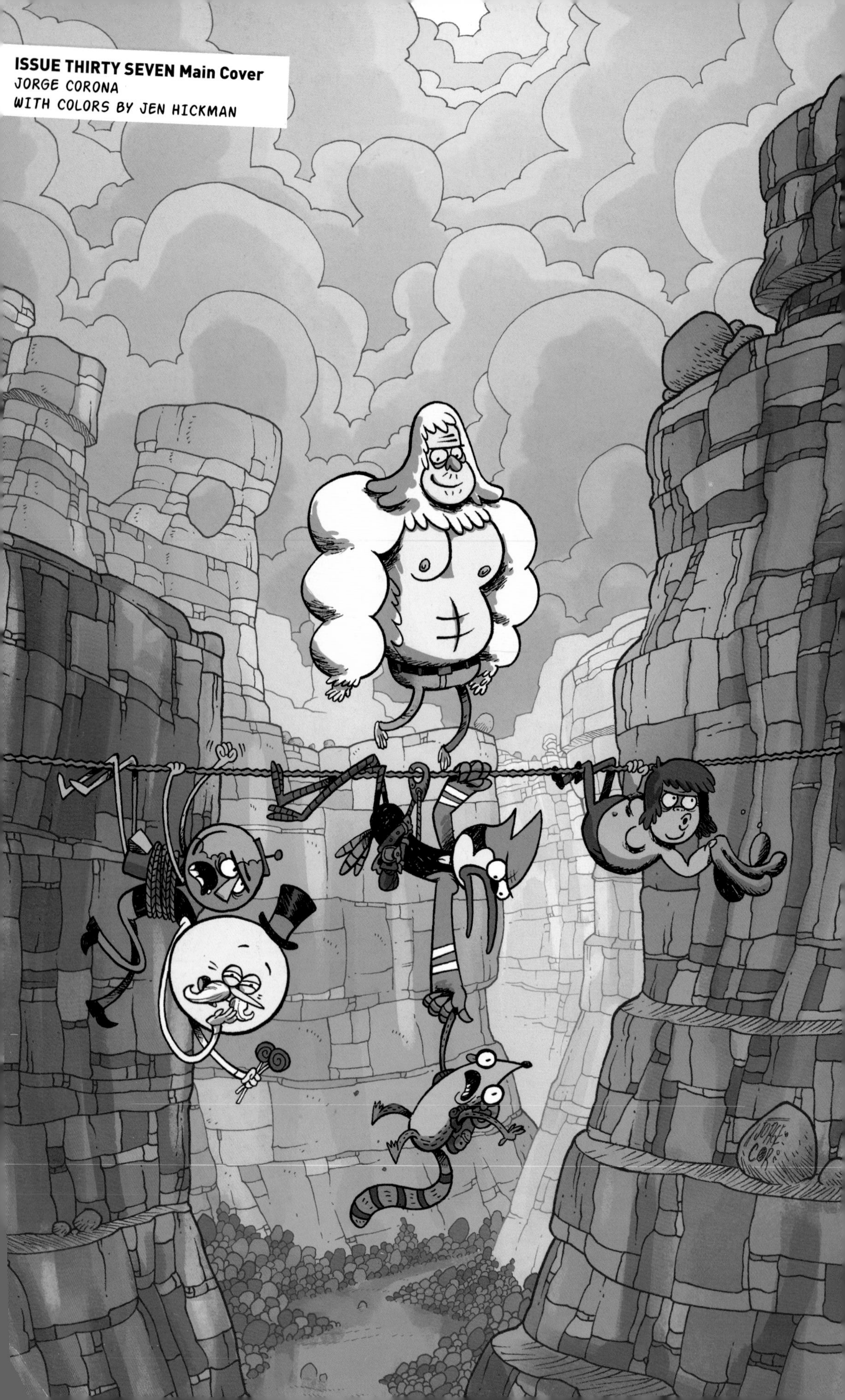

ISSUE THIRTY SEVEN Main Cover
JORGE CORONA
WITH COLORS BY JEN HICKMAN

ISSUE THIRTY SEVEN Subscription Cover
TYLER JENKINS

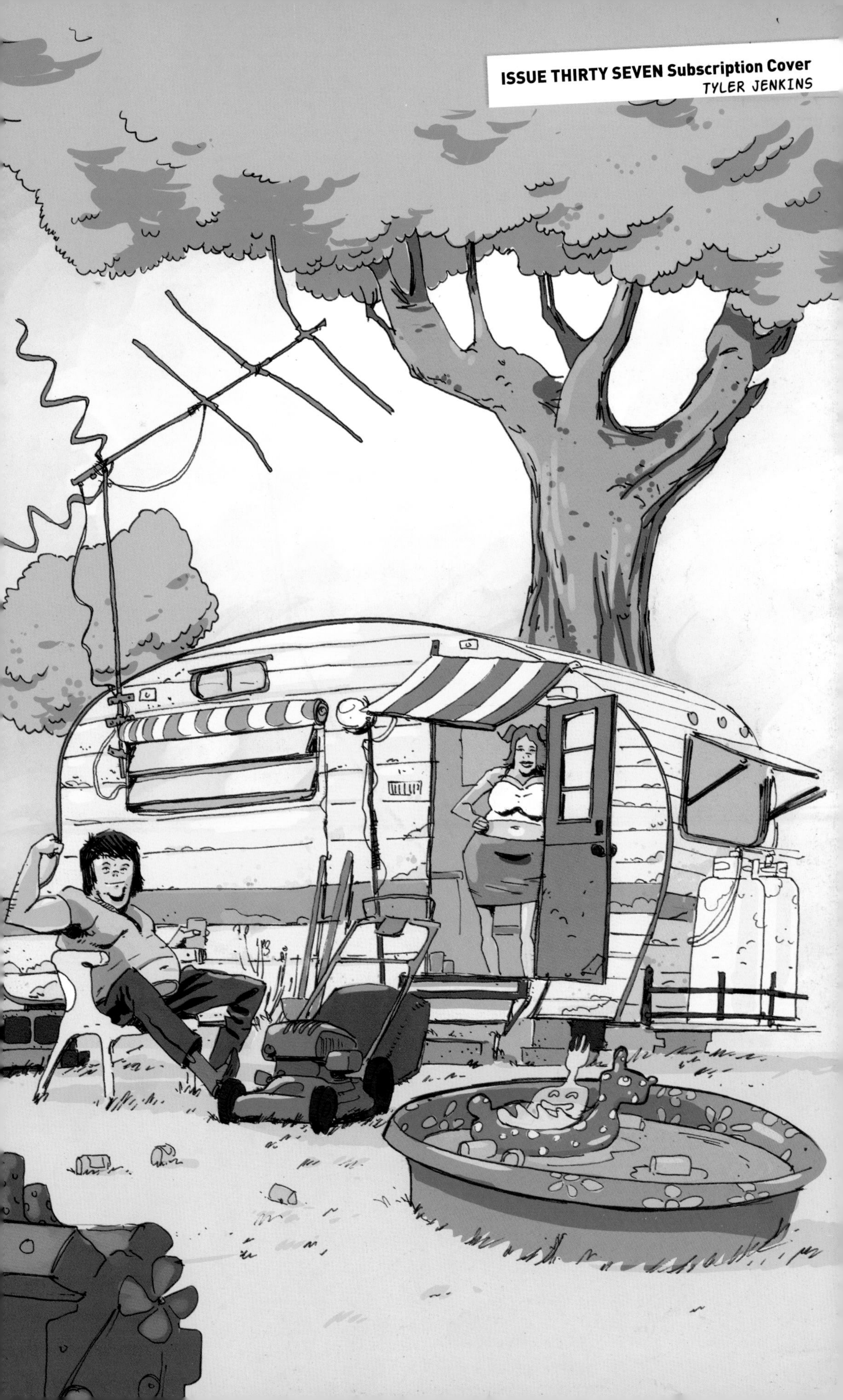

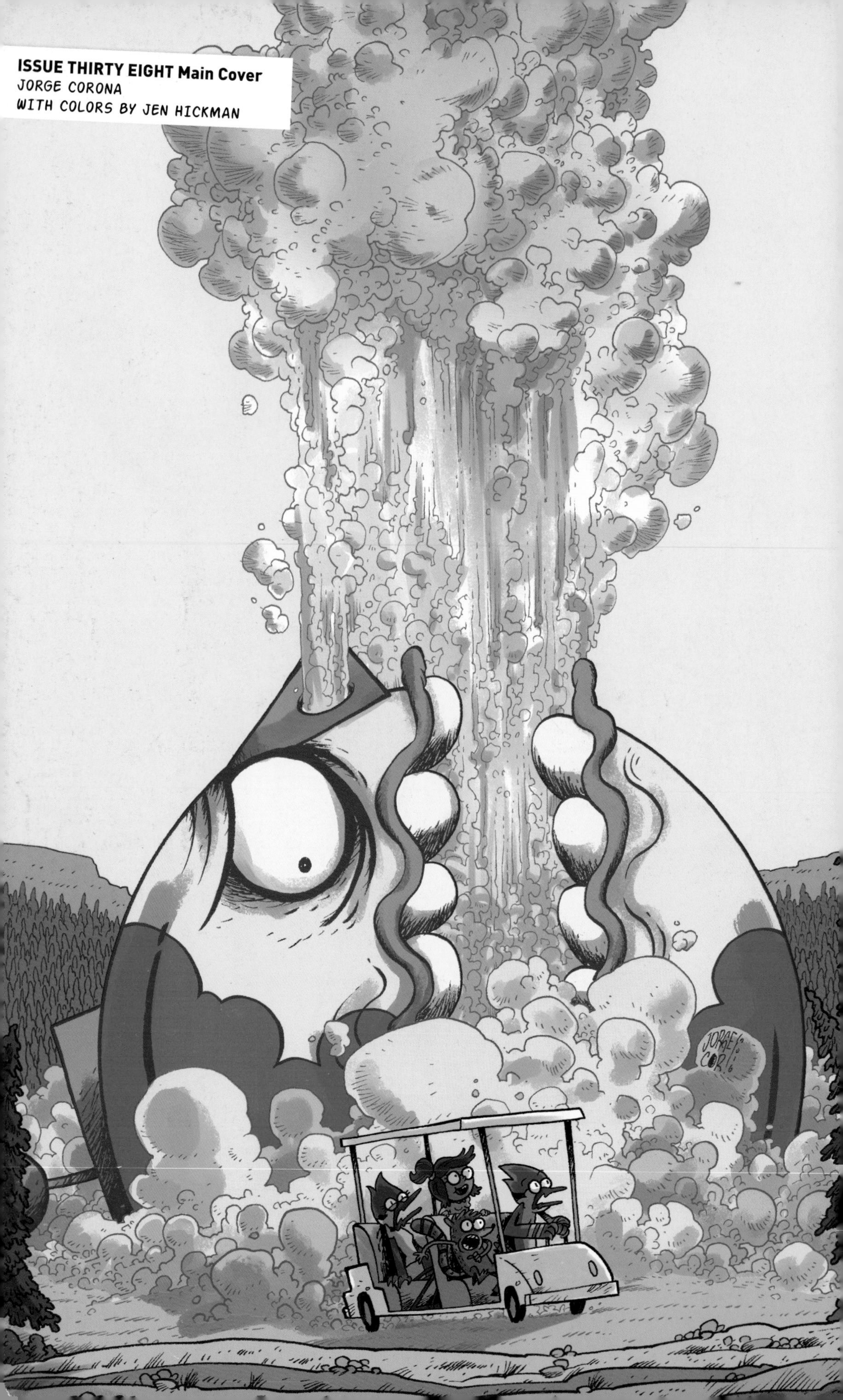

ISSUE THIRTY EIGHT Main Cover
JORGE CORONA
WITH COLORS BY JEN HICKMAN

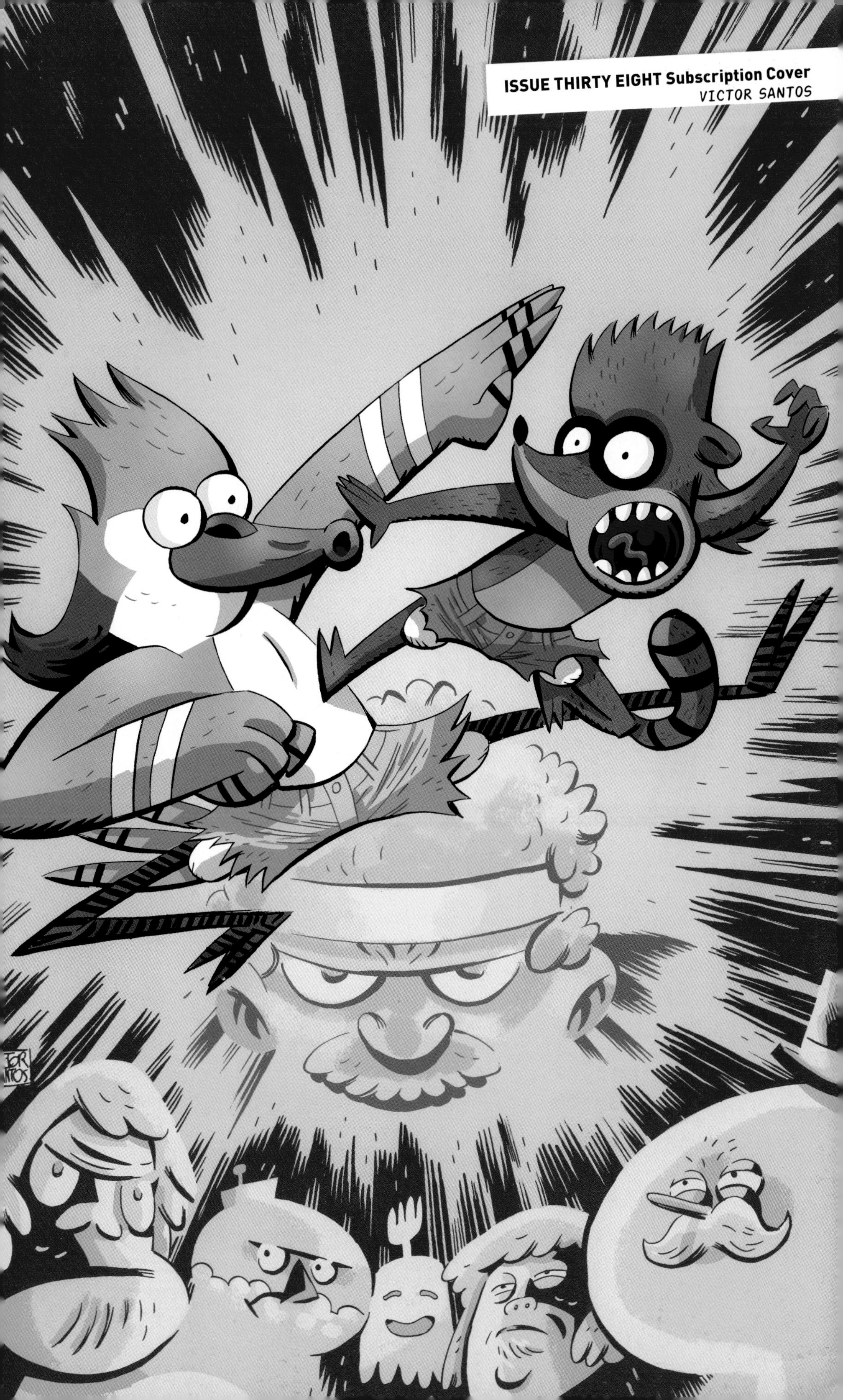

ISSUE THIRTY EIGHT Subscription Cover
VICTOR SANTOS

ISSUE THIRTY NINE Main Cover
JORGE CORONA
WITH COLORS BY JEN HICKMAN

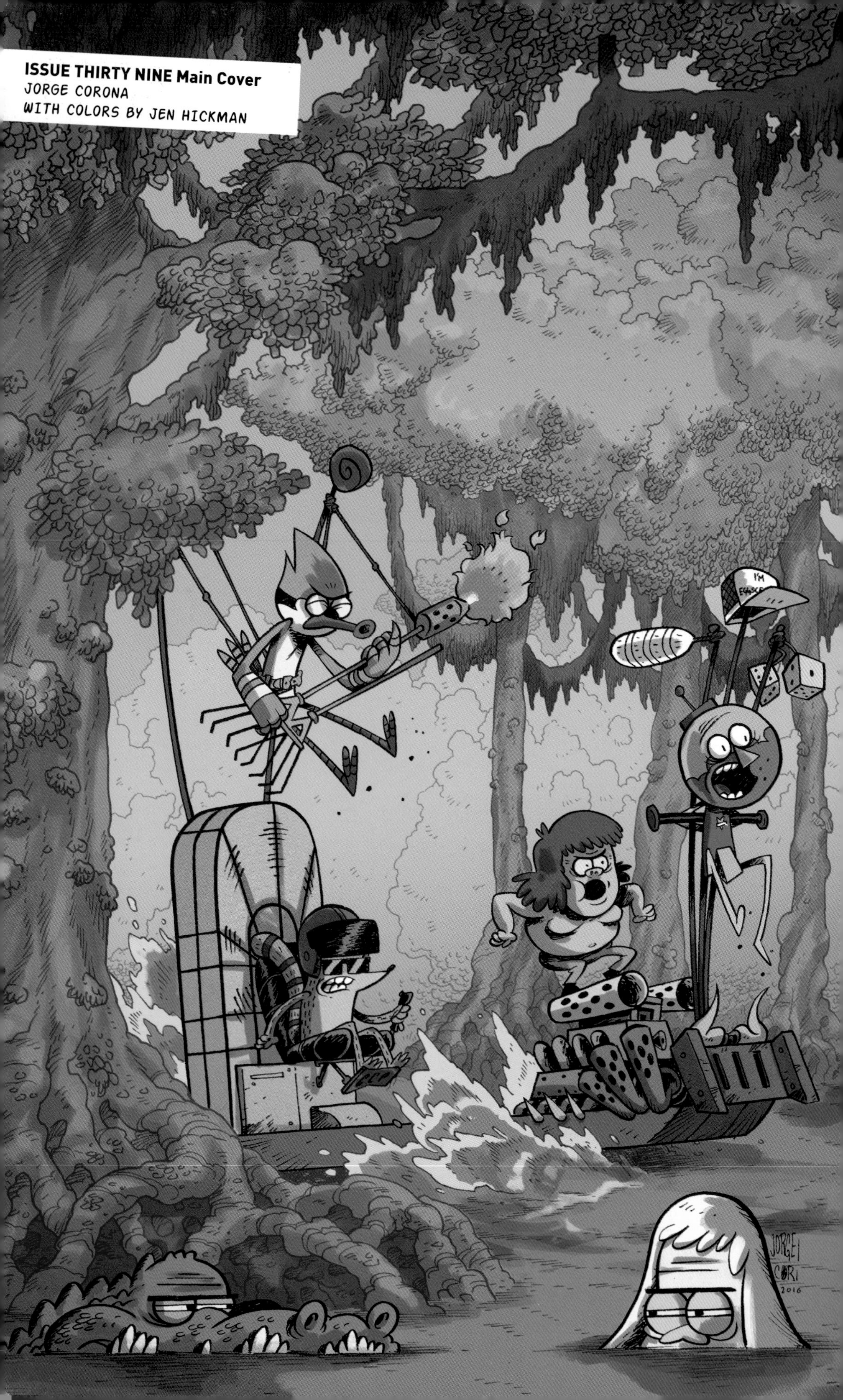

ISSUE THIRTY NINE Subscription Cover
ROGER LANGRIDGE

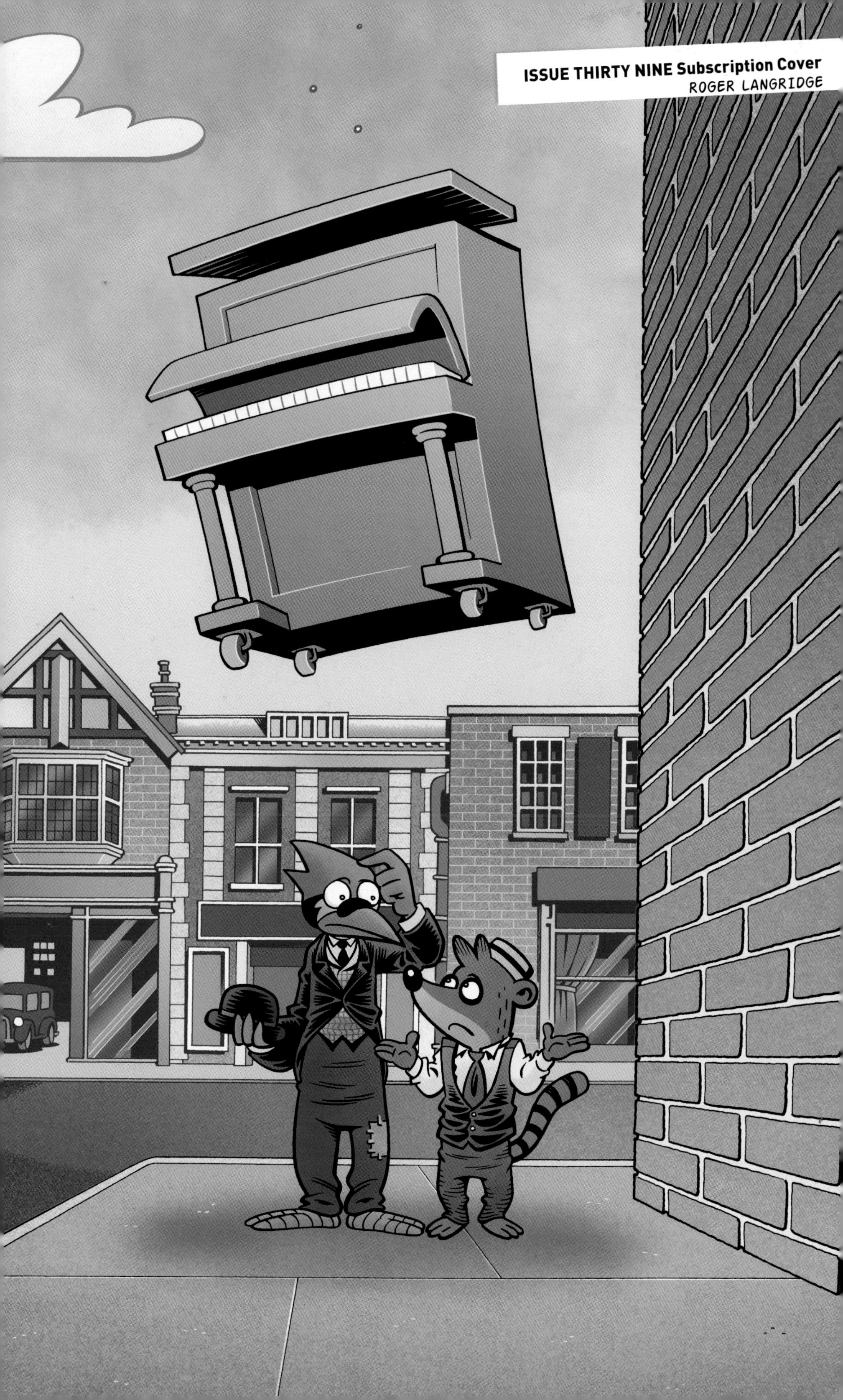

ISSUE FORTY Main Cover
JORGE CORONA
WITH COLORS BY JEN HICKMAN

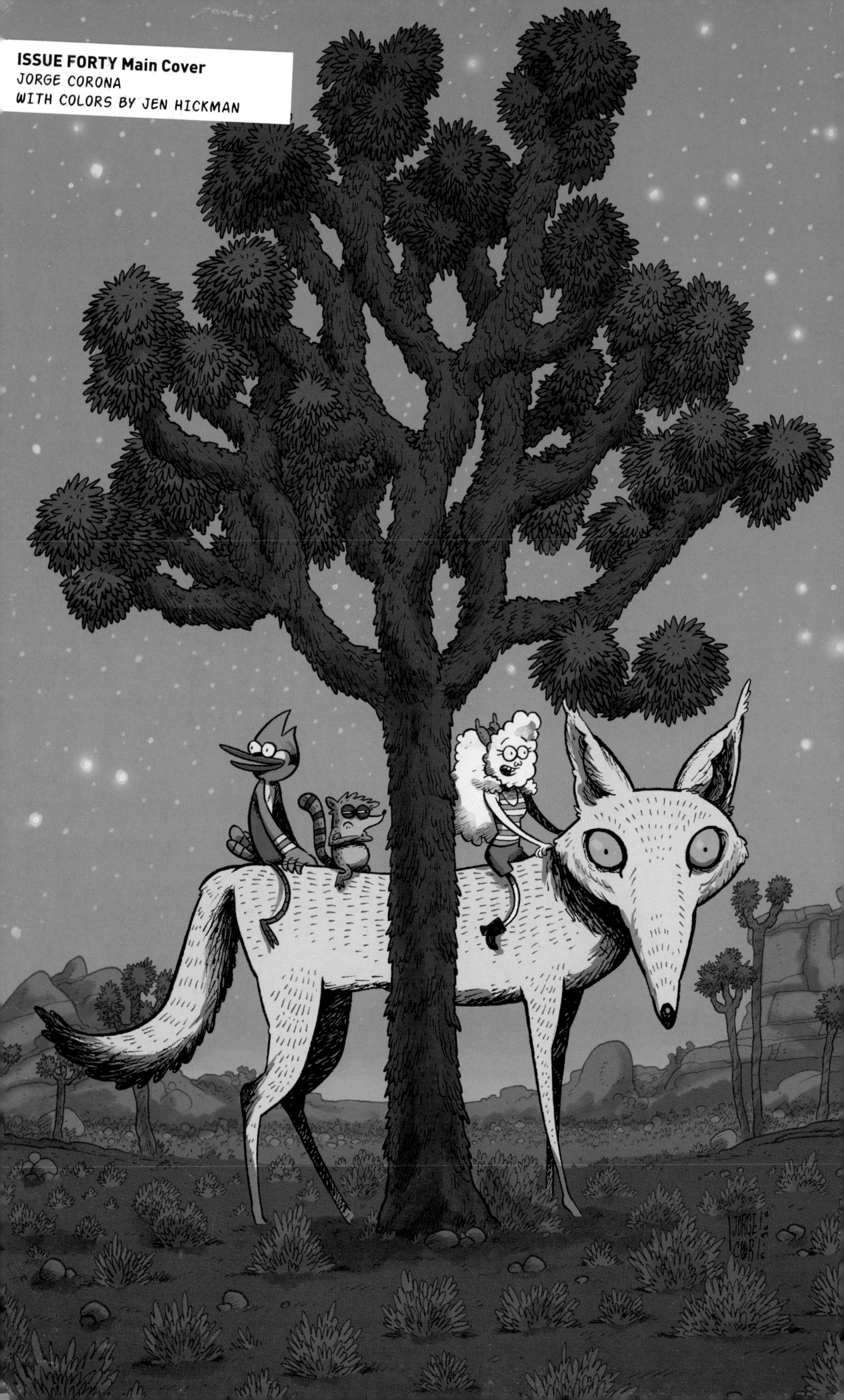

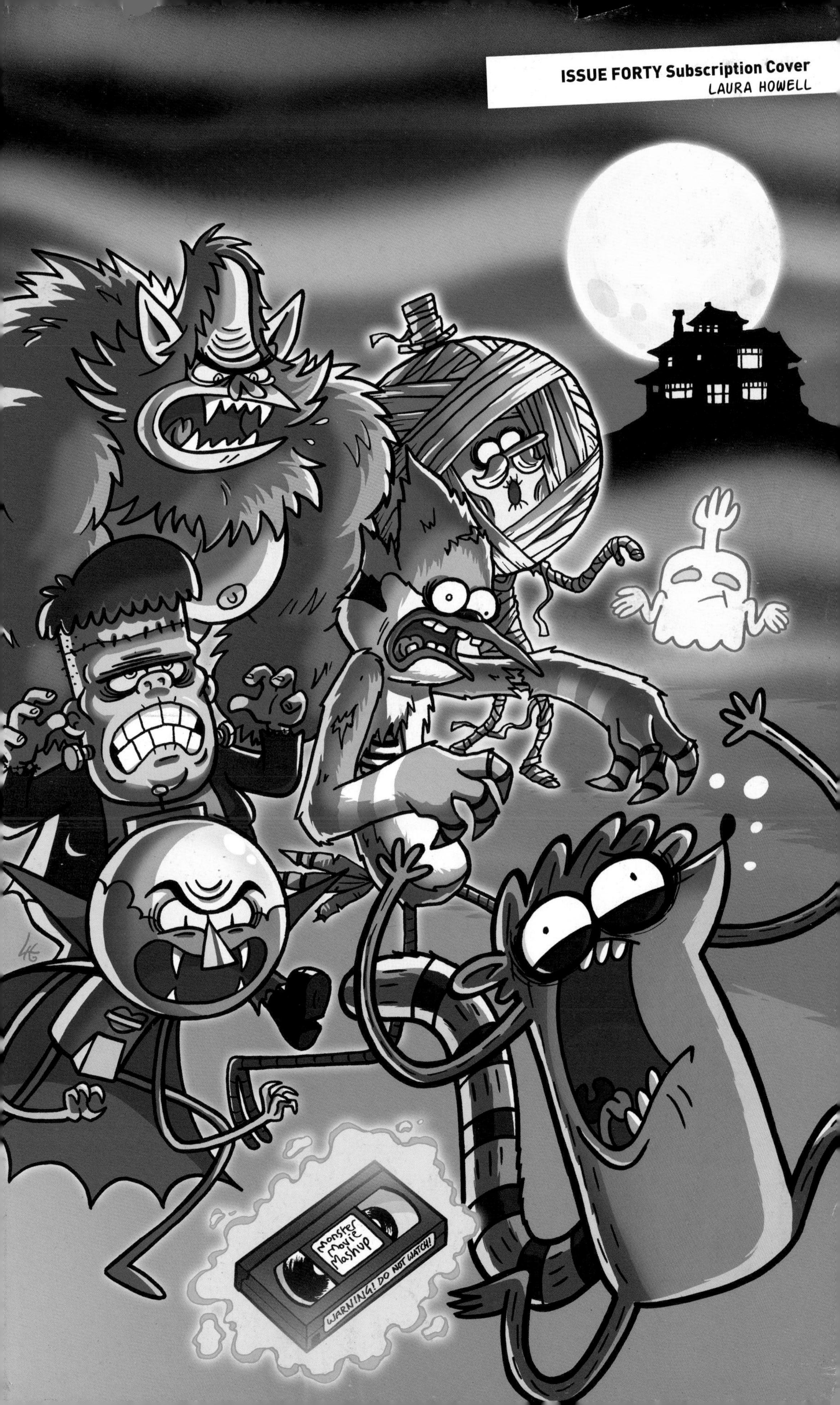
Monster Movie Mashup
WARNING! DO NOT WATCH!

ISSUE FORTY Subscription Cover
LAURA HOWELL